I0762279

PRAISE FOR CAROLYN HAINES

THE SEEKER

"Inventive...Aine's struggle with her own illusions is genuinely effective."

—PUBLISHERS WEEKLY

"This mix of thriller and ghost story is all about what is just glimpsed for an instant, whether physically or psychologically. And the suspense is intensified by the fact that readers can't be sure whether they're following the thoughts of someone sane, unhinged, or in the process of coming apart...Great for both lovers of Thoreau and suspense fans."

—BOOKLIST

THE DARKLING

"[A] spellbinding tale . . . eloquent evidence that Southern storytelling is indeed a very special art form."

—THE NEW YORK TIMES BOOK REVIEW

"#6 on the list of 10 best horror novels of the year—But it's Haines' knack for good, old-fashioned storytelling that truly sets *The Darkling* apart. The scares are parceled out sparingly, but assuredly. After the first few chapters, I found myself saving the novel for late nights, when I could pour a cup of coffee, light a lamp in a dark room, and allow the hyper-eerie visuals to seep into my bones. While Haines has found previous success with crime and romance, *The Darkling* may be proof of her true calling."

—RYAN DALEY, WWW.BLOODYDISGUSTING.COM

"Absolutely riveting as it pulses forward with mounting tension...brilliant!"

—ROCKY MOUNTAIN NEWS

SUMMER OF THE REDEEMERS

"Carolyn Haines is the last of the great Victorian novelists: a wide viewpoint, a big cast of characters, a free-form narrative that in the end is seen to be thoroughly controlled by the author. What she does so well is the sense of a peopled landscape; none of her characters are walk-on parts, each has his or her place. Rather like a Fellini film. And how subtle the nuances of character! Nobody is two-dimensional. The teenage heroine is really unforgettable in her mélange of enthusiasm, undefined insights, need for action, and soaring imagination. And I haven't even mentioned the animal characters and the perceptive depiction of the small-town Deep South reality. In all things, a highly satisfying read."

—EUGENE WALTER, LIPPINCOTT PRIZE NOVELIST, EDITORIAL ASSOCIATE OF *THE PARIS REVIEW*

"In a voice that is funny, wise and clear as a country spring Carolyn Haines has fashioned a tale that is utterly original and completely unforgettable."

—MARK CHILDRESS

"Surprising events, most of them sinister, catch the reader unaware in this coming-of-age story set in rural Mississippi in 1963. Narrator Rebekkah Rich, an independent and smart 13-year-old, is secretly thrilled to be staying at home on Kali Oka Road for her summer vacation. Busloads of religious zealots from The Blood of the Redeemer Church have set up headquarters at the end of the street, and, even more intriguing, a glamorous young woman, Nadine Andrews, has moved in nearby with her show horses and has promised to give the delighted teenager riding lessons. Kali Oka is drenched in history and haunted by tales of a murdered baby, stories never far from Bekkah's mind as she spies on the grimly repressive church members and becomes further involved with Nadine, who seems to be behaving in an increasingly bizarre and dangerous fashion. Meanwhile, the civil rights movement is reaching Kali Oka and Bekkah's parents, liberals and intellectuals, are at risk from local racists. While her parents are out of town, Bekkah digs deeper into myth and reality. Why are there so many new graves on Redeemer property? Who is the woman, naked underneath a bloody dress, who seems to be following her? Harrowing, richly atmospheric and sharp-edged, this hardcover debut maintains suspense until its final pages."

—PUBLISHERS WEEKLY

"A coming-of-age novel set in rural Mississippi during the 1960s offers up such potentially juicy elements as racial strife, religious fanaticism, child abuse, and grown-up duplicity...."

—KIRKUS REVIEW

"The security and comfort of life on Kali Oka Road in rural Mississippi is altered forever with the arrival of the Blood of the Redeemers Church and the mysterious Nadine Andrews. Bekkah Rich, a headstrong and impulsive 13-year-old with a passion for horses, unwittingly initiates a disturbing chain of events. In defiance of her mother, Bekkah begins to work at Nadine's horse farm. But even the attractions of horses cannot divert her curiosity about the fanatical religious group. Bekkah is convinced they have hurt a young woman and may be a danger to Nadine, but her interference only helps to fuel community tensions and contributes to a tragic killing. Part murder mystery, part coming-of-age novel, Bekkah's story evokes the emotions and rhythms of a Southern summer. This hardcover debut should appeal to a wide readership."

—LIBRARY JOURNAL

TOUCHED

“Like the heat of a Deep South summer, Ms. Haines's novel has undeniable intensity; it's impossible to shake its brooding atmosphere.”

—*THE NEW YORK TIMES BOOK REVIEW*

“So vivid, so energetic, so poignant that it seems to move on reels rather than pages.”

—*CHICAGO TRIBUNE*

“Haines's fresh and suspenseful second novel (after *Summer of the Redeemers*) is set in 1926, in the "bleakly ugly" Bible-belt town of Jexville, Miss., where dancing is looked upon as a sin and women are expected to be docile and religious. Written with a languid sensuality, this rich and complex work features quirky, fully developed characters involved in an unpredictable story, with Mattie's long-awaited revenge providing a bittersweet but satisfying coda.”

—*PUBLISHERS WEEKLY*

“Absolutely riveting as it pulses forward with mounting tension...brilliant!”

—*ROCKY MOUNTAIN NEWS*

"Action overload as Mattie and friends more than prove their credentials as cool, modern, and independent women able to cope with everything."

—*KIRKUS REVIEW*

"The Deep South never gets any deeper than 1920s Jexville, Mississippi. Dirt poor Mattie is the arranged bride of the town's barber Elikah, who is prone to deliver vicious beatings to his young wife. When a little girl is struck by lightning at a party and not only survives, but seems to have attained the ability to predict the future, Jexville is turned on its ear."

—AMAZON.COM

JUDAS BURNING

"My favorite fiction drenches you with the sights, smells, and emotions swirling around the characters so that I am transported into their story; Carolyn Haines takes a step further, putting me right inside their hearts. She also makes me laugh–not bad for a suspense story in which some people, like newspaperwoman Dixon Sinclair, rebuilding her life in Jexville, Mississippi, disinter secrets. And some people die."

—BARBARA PETERS, THE POISONED PEN BOOKSTORE

"If Robert B. Parker and Flannery O'Connor were locked in a room with a single typewriter between them, this is the novel that could have resulted. By turns a compelling murder mystery, a dead-on evocation of the deep, twisted South, and a penetrating character study of a tortured newswoman whose struggle to bring a killer to justice just might earn her a ticket back to life. Miss this one, and you have missed something."

—LES STANDIFORD

"With vivid imagery and subtle character development, Haines crafts a story as rich as a thick slice of Mississippi mud pie. But there's nothing sweet about what's happening in Jexville."

—*BOOKLIST*

"This suspenseful mystery twists and turns like the Big Muddy. With an assured voice, Carolyn Haines masterfully ratchets up the tension, pitting her colorful and unique characters against public murder, personal demons, and a small town's darkest side."

—JULIA SPENCER-FLEMING,
EDGAR AWARD FINALIST

"Haines builds suspense with images of violent crime and the thrill of breaking news, then undermines it by chasing too many leads, stopping only for mind-numbing recaps of suspects and clues. Her uneven storytelling is mitigated, though, by a resilient, likable heroine."

—*PUBLISHERS WEEKLY*

"Religion, passion, lust, politics, betrayal...Haines mixes them into a hot and steamy tale that'll clutch your heart and steal your breath. Wrap the covers tight and hang on."

—JACK KERLEY

"Jexville, Miss., is a quintessential sleepy southern town whose beauty, a newspaper publisher learns, covers a lot of ugly secrets. Sympathetic characters and an unblinking look at the banality and breathtaking evil below Jexville's surface make this latest from Haines a must-read."

—*KIRKUS REVIEWS*

THE BOOK OF BELOVED

"A tour de force from an accomplished writer who has a gift for delivering vivid sensory impressions to deepen the impact of her story...A powerful book you will not soon forget."

—*HISTORICAL NOVEL SOCIETY*

"Carolyn Haines is a master wordsmith who has succeeded where so many in the horror/supernatural genre fall short. She has created a story that will haunt its readers..."

—AMAZON REVIEWER

"This work is a slice of history, changing attitudes and a really good mystery all wrapped up in a well written story."

—AMAZON REVIEWER

THE HOUSE OF MEMORY

"What a page-turner! This book has it all. Ghosts of murdered young women, a haunted insane asylum, an antebellum house where evil lurks, and a still-living young woman threatened by human and superhuman forces. This is a classic and beautifully-crafted ghost story in the tradition of *Ammie Come Home* or *The Turn of the Screw*."

—AMAZON REVIEWER

"This is a more than a mystery about spirits. The story is intriguing and cleverly plotted; it truly kept me engaged. Haines never disappoints!...Excellent series!"

—AMAZON REVIEWER

"Haines once again spins a Southern Gothic ghost story so wonderfully complex that when the human villains are finally exposed on the last pages, it's a total surprise, yet nonetheless makes perfect sense...a perfectly satisfying ending to a gripping book."

—AMAZON REVIEWER

"A gifted storyteller, Haines writes with a direct, crisp style that is at once lyrical and often sensual. As the menace and dangers build, the pacing and tension increase exponentially. And, when the suspense and characters are so compelling, as in *Specter of Seduction,* one might lose track of the fine quality of the writing itself. But this is a book that shines with refined, sharp prose. Haines has a poet's ear for language and knows how to utilize words to set a tone, evoke a feeling, and capture a moment."

—AMAZON REVIEWER

"This is a great read--one you will not be able to put down once you start."

—SOUTHERN LITERARY REVIEW

SKIN DANCER

SKIN DANCER

Carolyn Haines

KaliOka Press

First published (digital edition) in 2011 by KaliOka Press.

2nd edition (hardcover) published in 2023 by Good Fortune Farm Refuge.
2486 Ellen Dr.
Semmes, AL 36575

Cover Design by Cissy Hartley
Interior Design by Priya Bhakta

Hardcover edition ISBN: 978-1-7330169-9-5

For Ron O'Gorman

CONTENTS

PROLOGUE

The sharp tang of burning spruce scented the cool night. Hank Welford squatted beside the campfire, patiently waiting for the coffeepot to finish percolating. He did his best to ignore his companion, who sat leaning against a rock, his expensive boots angled toward the fire.

"My flight out is at six tomorrow. You sure we'll bag my moose by then?"

Hank glanced at Ashton Trussell, a Boston plastic surgeon who'd come to Criss County, South Dakota, to snap up a trophy. The man had plenty of money and no ethics about how he got his moose. He was the perfect client for Hank, who had a great need for money and no ethics about how he staged the kill.

"I'm sure." He used an old shirt to grab the hot handle of the coffeepot as he removed it from the flames. "Want a cup?"

"I brought something to help pass the night." The doctor leaned over to his fancy bag and pulled out a bottle of Courvoisier. "Hand me my coffee, and I'll spice it up."

Hank passed him a tin cup filled with the strong brew. The doctor poured a good measure of the liquor into his cup, recapped the bottle, and leaned back.

"How long have you been leading these hunting parties into the Black Hills?" Trussell asked.

"A long time."

"You ever been caught hunting out of season?"

"Nope." Hank had been lucky. All it would take to put him out of business was getting busted by the game warden--once. Jake Ortiz didn't mess around with illegal hunters. He pressed for the heaviest fine, including taking the hunter's weapons, vehicles, and equipment. It hadn't always been that way in Criss County.

"I got enough trouble right now. I've got a patient—a little bitch—making accusations that could ruin me. I don't need a hunting citation."

Hank glanced at the man's diamond Rolex, his five hundred dollar hunting clothes, and his expensive Remington. So what if he was caught? He'd pay the fine and buy more equipment. Trussell was a plastic surgeon in Bean Town. He made more in a day than Hank made in a month.

"You got some pull with the local law?" Trussell asked.

"Don't worry about it. We'll get up in the morning; you can shoot your moose and make your flight. Once the head is mounted, Zell's will ship it to you." He sipped his unlaced coffee and sat back on a felled tree. "You can hang it on your wall and tell whatever story you like about how you shot it."

They were still two miles from Dixon Point where the moose was hobbled and waiting. The whole camp-out and hunt was an exercise in vanity for the doctor, who wanted to pretend that he was actually tracking an animal. Hell, he couldn't find his ass with both hands. As hatred brushed over Hank like a dark cloud, he was glad for the darkness. It wouldn't do a lick of good for Ashton Trussell to see what contempt he felt for him.

"Well, I'm going to turn in." Trussell dropped his empty

cup in the dirt. "I'm eager to try out my new sleeping bag. It was designed for the astronauts."

"Don't let the bedbugs bite." Hank laughed at his own wit.

He stood up to kick out the fire when a stick snapped in the woods. He paused, foot raised.

"What was that?" Trussell asked. His hand had gone to his rifle.

"Calm down. It was probably a deer or something. This is a wilderness area. The reason it's called that is because there are wild animals roaming around." It amused Hank to see Trussell so on edge.

"It's black as pitch. I can't see anything."

Hank rolled his eyes. "Get out that fancy sleepin' bag and use it. I'll stay up a bit and play guard."

"Good. I've got to get my rest."

"Yeah, you do that." Hank had a regular job on a road crew, but the money he made on his hunting expeditions far outweighed what he could make running a dozer.

The fire crackled brightly and he leaned back against the tree. Overhead, the stars were brilliant. He'd never been out of South Dakota. Never seen a reason to go elsewhere, even for a visit. He had everything he needed right where he was.

The sound of something moving through the underbrush outside the illumination of the campfire made him sit up.

"What's that?" Trussell asked.

The doctor was certainly a nervous Nellie. Hank couldn't suppress a grin. "I don't think it's anything, but there have been several reports of strange goings on."

"What kind of 'goings on'?" Trussell asked, an edge to his voice.

"The local Indians believe there's a spirit that lives out here, a brave who killed animals for their skins and wasted their meat. Sort of a Injun trophy taker, if you get my drift."

Trussell didn't say a word. Hank bided his time, waiting for the next snap of a limb. "The story goes that he got a curse laid on him. His skin fell off, and he had to go around borrowing skin from other people." He found it difficult to control his laughter. He hadn't thought of the story in twenty years. Now, though, he could tell it was working on Trussell's nerves. Served the rich bastard right.

"That's ridiculous. Borrowing skin."

"I guess borrowing isn't exactly the right word, since the Injun never returns it. He uses it for a time, then it sloughs off and he has to hunt for another...donor."

"No wonder the Sioux were defeated if they believe that kind of drivel."

"Hey, I'm just passin' on some local lore. Some folks enjoy a few campfire stories." He shifted around the fire, kicking dirt onto the embers. It was close on to midnight, and if he intended to get the good doctor up and moving by dawn, he needed some shut eye.

"Sounds more like you're trying to make me nervous." Trussell rolled over in his sleeping bag. "It won't work, but the story is interesting. Where'd you hear it?"

"My grandpa, I suppose. All the kids in Criss County know it." The flames fought against the dirt he kicked over them, finally suffocating. In the sudden blackness, he sensed movement to his right. He turned slowly, trying unsuccessfully to pierce the darkness with his gaze. Something moved. Something big.

He thought of bear and felt a whisper of fear. Most of the wild animals stayed away from humans. The truth was he and other hunters had done their best to eradicate the bear and mountain lion population. They'd worked on the gray wolves, too, when no one was looking. Still, it could be that one of the predators had smelled them and come for a closer look.

"What is that?" Trussell asked for the third time.

"Hush." He wanted the doctor to shut up. He couldn't tell anything as long as the man kept flapping his gums.

"Hand me my rifle." The doctor issued an order, not a request.

Hank eased next to both weapons but hesitated. Trussell was liable to shoot him in the back. The man had no concept of how to use a rifle. "Shut-up a minute and let me listen."

Whatever moved in the treeline had no fear of them. It made no effort to be quiet.

The wind gusted and Hank heard a sound that made every hair on his body stand at attention. The gentle chatter of a bone rattle rode the wind. "Fuck," he whispered.

"That's not an animal." Trussell unzipped his sleeping bag.

"Someone's trying to scare us." Hank tried to remember which of his buddies he might have told about Trussell and the moose hunt. He only had a couple of confidants, and he seldom told them about his hunting expeditions until they were over, when he could brag about the ten grand he'd taken from a rich man for a drugged kill.

Beneath the rhythmic rattle of the bones was another sound, the soft chanting of a Native American. Hank had gone to a few of the reservation powwows on grammar school trips, and he'd always been amused by the Sioux link to the other world, the belief in spirit journeys and the dancing and chanting ceremonies. About like praying--not much good except for wearing blisters on knees. No, Hank believed in a god that helped men who helped themselves.

"I don't care for this!" Trussell was starting to stand up. "Tell whoever it is to stop this bullshit now. I paid for a hunt, not some Mickey Mouse stage production."

"Hey! Cut it out!" Hank yelled. So far, he and Trussell had done nothing illegal. They were carrying high-powered hunting rifles, but there was no law against that. They hadn't killed anything, so if it was the game warden having a joke at their expense, now was the time to get him to show his face.

The low chanting and the clatter of the bones in the hollowed gourd continued unabated. With the wind blowing, Hank couldn't tell how far away the sound might be coming from. He dug the flashlight out of his pack and swung the high beam into the treeline. Shadows leapt in all directions, and his finger tightened on the trigger of his gun. There was nothing to shoot. No one stood in the trees. As far as he could tell, the night was empty of everything except them.

"This isn't amusing, Welford. Tell your friends to fuck the hell off."

Hank cleared his throat. "That isn't anyone I know. I swear. I didn't tell anyone about this hunt, and if I had told my friends, they'd know better than to screw around in the wilderness at night with two men with loaded weapons."

He kicked the dead fire, hoping for a burning ember, but the dirt had completely snuffed it out. "I've got to get some dry wood. We need some light."

"You're just going to leave me here with that—"

"Get your ass up and come with me if you want." Hank had lost the last of his patience.

"I'm not going to put up with you speaking to me like that. I've paid you a lot of money for this hunt. You're my employee, in case you've forgotten."

Hank ignored him. The sound of the chanting and the rattle had stopped. He listened intently, but the only noise was the wind whispering among the fir fronds, a soft sigh of nature.

"Are we going for firewood or not?" Trussell was standing, his rifle in his hand.

"It stopped." Hank had an almost irresistible urge to take the butt of his rifle and slam it into the doctor's jaw. The thought of the satisfying crunch of bone made Hank grit his teeth to control his fury.

"When you get back to town tomorrow, tell your friends they couldn't scare a four-year-old. And understand I won't be using your services for my next hunt."

"You've paid for this hunt, and you'll get your moose, Dr. Trussell. After tomorrow, forget you ever met me."

"Sounds like you spooked yourself."

Trussell's arrogance was like salt in an open wound, but Hank unclenched his grip on his rifle and sat back down. Guys with lots of money were always dicks. Trussell was just a bigger dick than most. In less than twenty-four hours, he'd be on a plane headed back to Boston and his tit-plumping, fat-sucking practice. And Hank would have the ten grand he needed to pay off the overdue bills on his four-wheel drive and his manufactured home.

CHAPTER ONE

A blast of wind swept up the steep slope and through the fir trees, rattling limbs and sending grit flying into Rachel Redmond's face. She used the back of her hand to wipe her mouth and then licked her dry lips. She was the only woman in a group of four men, and she forced her gaze back to the hellish scene where two naked, headless bodies hung from a tree limb like dead game. With each gust of wind, the rope that ran through the dead men's Achilles tendons sang a quiet complaint. It was an eerie, keening sound like a badly tuned funeral fiddle.

The men had been decapitated and mutilated, one more severely than the other. Long strips of skin and muscle had been removed from their backs, stomachs, buttocks and thighs, as if someone had been harvesting the skin or inflicting the most intense pain possible. The idea made her want to look away, but she caught a glimpse of Jake Ortiz watching her. This wasn't the time to show squeamishness.

The scene appeared staged. This was a killer with a very personal motive. Aside from some type of silver ornament jabbed into the chest of one body, there was a bamboo pole decorated with one feather. Footsteps around the body indicated that the killer, or killers, had moved in a repetitive circle, a dance perhaps.

Beside the men was the carcass of a moose. She walked over to it, examining the gunshot to the chest that had brought it down. The animal had been shot at close range, the exit wound cavernous. It looked as if the men, poachers hunting out of season, had been removing the head for a trophy when someone had taken them by surprise and killed them.

"Should I cut them down?" Marston French, one of the Criss County Search and Rescue volunteers, asked her.

"Leave them be for now. The forensic team should arrive any minute." Until the techs processed the evidence, nothing could be moved or touched. The procedure was carefully outlined in the manual she'd memorized while training as a deputy. Even when she'd been studying at the police academy, beginning a career where she could make a difference, she'd never truly anticipated investigating a crime like this. The level of cruelty was beyond her comprehension.

Jake started to step forward but she maneuvered herself in front of him. He was a state game warden and as such held authority over state forests and parks. But this was Criss County, South Dakota, not state land and not federal land or the Sioux Indian reservation. For better or worse, this was her case, and Jake wasn't going to upstage her.

"As soon as Gus gets here with the camera, make sure he gets a close-up of that silver thing pinned to the heavy one's chest." She spoke to Wilt Baker, another volunteer. She had to take charge and issue some orders or the men would view her as ineffective. It was bad enough that she was a head shorter than all of them—and almost a decade younger. And Jake's protectiveness wasn't helping.

She stepped closer to the bodies, avoiding the blood that had pooled beneath them. The bamboo pole and feather spoke of some kind of Native ritual. The ornamental silver had been skewered into the man's chest with what looked to be a porcupine quill. She couldn't tell the purpose of the silver—if it was jewelry or what. Obviously hand-crafted, it glinted in the bright June sun and drew the attention of a big crow that watched from one of the trees.

She bent to examine the footprints that surrounded the victims. Her first impression of a dance seemed right. The ground looked as if a troop of school kids had played Ring-Around-the-Rosie. And where the hell were the heads? If the bodies had been skinned, was it possible someone had lopped off the heads like trophies? Rachel tried not to imagine it.

"Deputy Redmond, can I send the moose down to the retirement home?" Wilt asked.

"No." She started to walk the perimeter of the scene.

Jake came up beside her. "It's tradition, Rachel. We always send the meat from any poached game we get to the retirement home. Give the old folks some protein."

"Whoever killed that moose was pretty damn close, Jake. That's just one more element in this crime scene that doesn't make sense." She was behind the bodies now, looking at the musculature of the man on her left. Whoever he was, he'd been a strong son-of-a-gun. The other body was lean, with more of a gym-sculpted look. Younger, too. Someone with money and time to devote to fitness training.

There was no way to tell the identity of the men. She'd have to rely on fingerprints or the tattoo of a pit viper on the fat man's chest. The killer had left that particular piece of skin, as if he were trying to be helpful in the identification of the bodies. The idea made her antsy, and she started to walk away, almost bumping into Jake, who'd stepped too close behind her yet again.

He slipped a hand under her elbow for support. "I sure hope they were dead before they were skinned."

She glanced at him to see if he was testing her. "Mercy doesn't appear to be a priority for this killer." His gray eyes met hers squarely, and with a hint of humor.

"Helluva first murder case for a rookie." His fingers tightened slightly on her flesh, just a hint of pressure. "What made Gordon drop this one on you?"

"I have to start somewhere." She tempered the tone of her reply. "You know Scott's wife is expecting any day now. He didn't want to be stuck up here in the woods working a double homicide. And I asked for it."

"You always liked a challenge." Jake gave her arm one final squeeze.

"Yeah. That's me." Since she was sixteen-years-old, Jake had been a part of her life. He'd influenced her to go into law enforcement. Long ago, he'd saved her life.

"Ms. Redmond...I mean Deputy Redmond, the forensic boys are just coming over the ridge." Wilt pointed down the trail where two techs from Rapid City were headed their way. The men carried big suitcases, and a camera hung from around one's neck.

"Thanks." She walked forward to meet the team and to put some distance between herself and the crime scene. The blood pooled beneath the bodies had enticed a host of flies. The droning noise and the metallic smell were beginning to wear on her.

"This sure ain't no job for a lady." Wilt's words, meant to be a whisper, carried to her. What she couldn't hear was Jake's response.

A short way down the, Rachel faced a vista that stole her breath. A mile away, granite rock formations pushed high into a pale blue sky. Evergreens covered the steep slopes, some of the trunks enormous. There were waterfalls and caves and mysteries beyond the ken of mortal men. The Sioux believed that some of the caves were a portal to the underworld. The red men had come from that portal in the Black Hills, and it was here that the Great Spirit gave them the buffalo as a source of meat and shelter and clothes. The Native Americans' bond with the land was meshed with history and pride and knowledge that man and the wilderness were irrevocably linked.

For Rachel, the Black Hills were savagely wild and untamed, a place where humans seldom encroached, and she'd grown to love this land. As a kid, she'd been all about cars and malls and drugs and the party life. She'd changed, though. Now she could hardly remember the frightened young girl who'd been so alone and so angry at the world.

"Looks like some poachers got caught with an illegal moose and someone else took justice into his own hands." Jake's voice came from behind her. He was talking to the advancing techs.

"Could be that," she told the techs. "Just document everything. The feather on the pole appears to be owl. I want that checked out as soon as possible."

"Will do." The two men moved to the crime scene and got busy.

In the distance an eagle caught a high draft and moved in a slow circle. The county and state lands were protected by stringent hunting laws. Many hunters, though, had no respect for borders, laws, or even the rudiments of sportsmanship. It was all about trophy.

And that, perhaps, was the motive behind these murders. The moose was illegal. Hunting season didn't start until the fall. It looked like the men were poachers, and it was possible that someone finally got tired of it.

But she didn't think so.

"Deputy." The tech nodded at her but looked to Jake for direction.

She walked back and gave a rundown of the photographs she wanted. She'd worked with Gus once before on a suicide. He knew his business, but it was her job to be sure. "Nothing has been touched, unless it was by the hiker who found the bodies. He called it in and we got here as fast as we could. Wilt and Marston came along to help us get the bodies down to the road for transport back to town."

"Good lord almighty." The other tech stopped and simply stared at the scene. "I've never seen anything quite like this. Either someone has a burn on for illegal hunters or these two guys really pissed the hell out of someone."

Rachel didn't say anything. Someone had brutally and methodically killed two men. The mutilation of the corpses was a message, but one she didn't fully understand. Maybe the science guys could give her a few hints as to what direction to pursue.

Frances "Frankie" Jackson swung up into the cab of the dozer and backed it away from the majestic virgin pine tree. She glared at the burly man whose job it was to push the four-lane through the Black Hills. No one on the crew was particularly glad to see her as boss, and the truth was, she didn't care. If a road had to go through this place of wonder and beauty, she'd make sure it did the least amount of damage possible. That was the job Belker Construction had hired her to do—to build the highway while preserving the wilderness.

She parked the dozer and jumped to the ground. "Ben, this is a historic tree. See the marker." She pointed to the woodcut emblem. "We don't need protesters out here halting our progress. You're twenty yards off course. If you can't follow the engineer's outline, you'd better tell me now."

Several men stopped working to glance at her long legs encased in skin-tight jeans and the knee-high cowboy boots she favored. She was lean as a whippet, and she kept her body honed with kick-boxing and Pilates. Once she'd been a chubby pre-teen, drowning her stuttering sorrows and inadequacies in boats of gravy and bowls of ice cream. Lida Jane's finishing school had skimmed off the pounds and given her a whole new view of herself and a new menu of options for achieving her goals. Of course, if Lida Jane or any of the Montgomery ladies she'd grown up around knew her ambitions, they'd be horrified. Ladies didn't run road crews, and that was just the tip of the iceberg in her lack of conformity.

"Look, I don't care how much it pisses you off, we can't take down that tree."

"It's a tree. There are a billion more right over there." Ben swung his hand toward the forest. "The original route went right through there. It's the easiest and fastest—"

"And the road was changed to preserve that specific tree. Accept it or leave now." Frankie caught a glimpse of movement in the dark protection of the firs. The Black Hills were so-called because, from a distance, the thick perfection of the trees made the hills look ebony. She saw the vague outline of a tall man at the edge of the woods. Before she could say or do anything, he was gone. She turned her attention back to the crew.

"This tree isn't going anywhere. I'm headed into town, and when I come back, if there's so much as a scratch on it, I'll see that every one of you is fired. When I find out who damaged the tree, and I will find out, he'll serve time in a federal prison." She looked around the circle of men who'd fallen silent. At times they hated her, but that was just part of her job.

She walked off, feeling the daggers of resentment digging

into her spine. She hadn't come home to South Dakota to make friends.

The project foreman fell into step beside her, talking as they walked. "Hank Welford never showed up for work today. That's the third time in two weeks. I'm going to cut him loose."

She nodded.

"If he comes in tomorrow, I'll tell him he's fired."

"Yep. He's not reliable. Probably holed up drunk somewhere."

"Or else on one of his illegal hunting trips. That bastard has every game warden in the state looking for him. Makes it hard on the rest of us who are real sportsmen." He shook his head in disgust.

The dry taste of dust from the road work made Frankie wish for a Diet Coke. "Hank's been living his life to his own tune for at least thirty years. I doubt he's going to change. When you fire him, he'll be furious. Watch out because he has a gun in his truck—I caught him shooting at crows last week during a break. He may try something stupid. Then he'll get over it and hire on some place else until he gets fired again." She looked back at the men who were still standing around, talking among themselves. "Put them back to work. I'm going into town to pick up the specs the engineers faxed over."

She climbed into her pickup truck and drove close to the forest. Whoever had been watching was gone. If she were the kind of woman to be scared, the idea of someone hiding in the woods and watching might creep her out. But there was always a logical explanation.

The local Sioux resented the intrusion of the road through their sacred land, and it was likely that someone had come to make sure the huge fir tree—a magnificent creation with a circumference of over 100 feet--was left undisturbed. The tree had once provided shade for the council meetings of the Sioux leaders. Now the knot-heads on the road project had the idea that if they ignored certain things, they wouldn't be challenged. They were wrong.

She gunned the motor and spun out, bringing a smile to the men's faces. It took so little to redirect a guy's focus. Put a woman in a truck spinning a bit of gravel and every thought in a man's head dropped right down to his crotch. Amazing.

Aiming the truck toward the county seat of Bisonville, she notched the needle over eighty and let her thoughts drift. The road project was moving forward, slowly. Things were on track. She had a dinner party planned to honor some of the state politicians and civic leaders. Although trained as a civil engineer, Frankie knew that it was her ability to build bridges between diverse groups that had gotten her the high six-figure salary she earned. She made all sides on the gnarly issue of the new road feel that they'd won some points. And she did it with style. Lida Jane's training, while irksome at the time, had proven invaluable.

She was just outside Bisonville when she decided to check the radio. A male DJ's voice came over the airwaves.

"...mutilated bodies were found high in the Black Hills this morning by a hiker. Criss County Sheriff's deputies and state game wardens responded and the bodies have been recovered, but no identification has been made.

"Deputy Rachel Redmond refused to comment on the condition of the bodies or the possible motive behind the brutal slaying, but eyewitnesses at the bizarre scene report that the decapitated and skinned bodies, believed to be two hunters, were found beside a dead moose.

"We'll update the story at the top of the hour. Right now, we're back to Toby Keith and 'It's a Little Too Late.'"

Frankie turned the radio off and slowed the pickup. She

pulled her cell phone from her pocket and punched in Jake Ortiz's number. "Hey, Jake, it's Frankie. When you get a minute, give me a call. I'm a little worried about my crew out there. I just want to get some details on that double homicide so I can decide whether to send them home or keep them working. Thanks."

She held the phone a moment before pressing down hard on the accelerator and sending the eight-cylinder truck up to eighty. She had work to do.

CHAPTER TWO

The clack of a cue ball breaking drowned the soft play of the radio in Bud's Bar. Rachel looked over her shoulder to the heavy-set man. A cigarette dangled from his mouth, and his beer dripped condensation on the edge of the table.

"You got stripes," he told the man he played with as he bent, took aim, and shot the cue stick forward. The report was solid and confident. The yellow one-ball zipped into the back corner pocket. He walked around the table and took his next successful shot.

Rachel wasn't as interested in the game as she was in the man. He was nearly six feet, in his forties or fifties, strong but gone to pot.

Physically, he was much like one of the dead men. How had someone with that physique been taken down without obvious signs of a struggle? Of course, if the killer had a gun, it was possible both men had been forced into co-operation or shot in the head. She had no way to tell, since the heads were still missing and the preliminary forensics had revealed only that the two men had lost vast quantities of blood. Whether from the skinning or decapitation, the state pathologist wasn't ready to say. One body had been mutilated worse than the other.

She sipped her Diet Coke and drummed her fingers softly on the varnished wood bar. Bud's was a historical locale, dating back to the Indian wars and the cattle drives that brought the colorful characters of the Old West through the small town. In all likelihood, the bar hadn't had a good cleaning since Custer took his last stand. But it was quiet, for a bar, and not nearly as smoke-filled in the early evening as it would be later that night.

Someone cranked the jukebox up, and she smiled at the first strains of "Okie from Muskogee." Merle Haggard was still a star in Bisonville, but few of his fans would recognize that the beat of this classic country song was a cha-cha. Rachel remembered a full, royal blue skirt twirling as her mom's bare toe nails painted bright red, moved forward and back in a cha-cha across the faded linoleum of their kitchen. Junie Redmond had loved to dance, even through chores.

The door of the bar swung open and the last golden slant of daylight fell across the wooden floor. Blinded, Rachel could only see the tall silhouette of a slender man. His boots echoed on the boards, and she felt a sudden measure of disquiet. She hadn't expected to see Jake in Bud's. He did his drinking in the more upscale bars of Rapid City.

"Rachel, what are you doing in here this time of day?"

Jake was forever the big brother. It was an act that was beginning to make her angry. "It's six o'clock. Work day's over. And I wanted a Diet Coke."

He surveyed the bar, making it clear he found nothing there that should interest Rachel. There were Diet Cokes available at Lulu's Café or the U-Tote 'em or any of the dozen gas stations. "I just read an article that said carbonated drinks can make a woman's bones porous." He sat down beside her.

"Jesus, Jake. Breathing might pollute my lungs." She

turned back to the bar so he couldn't see the aggravation on her face. "You act like I'm addicted to a diet drink. My mother had the drug problem, not me." The minute she spoke, she knew it was true. Jake was always vigilant for the first sign of addiction in her. Even to a cola. Heat flushed her face and she had to struggle to control the angry retort that sprang to her mind.

"Sorry, Rachel. I guess I need to back off." He signaled the bartender for a beer.

"That would be a relief."

Instead of getting angry, he laughed. "Old habits die hard." He slipped onto the bar stool beside her. "Remember John Henry James?"

Rachel couldn't help but smile. "Yeah, I had the worst crush on him when I was fourteen. Good thing he never knew I existed." In a drunken rage John Henry had hit his wife and accidentally snapped her neck. His remorse had been great, but remorse didn't bring life back to the woman he'd killed.

"Oh, he knew you existed. He used to ride by your mama's place in that black Camaro. He was like a shark swimming by, just hoping you'd walk out the door."

Rachel sat taller on her bench. "How do you know this, Jake?"

"Because after school I'd drive by your place. I put down some shingles with roofing tacks in them, and when he had three flat tires, I pulled him out of the car and told him if I saw him hanging around you again, I'd bury him under the asphalt."

Jake was smiling, but Rachel felt the throb of a vein in her temple. "You had no right to do such a thing."

"Maybe not, but he was a predator and a creep." The bartender put a Bud in front of him and Jake popped the top. "Your father was gone and your mom sure wasn't paying attention. Somebody had to look out for you, Rachel. You were headed down a long, hard road."

She sipped her drink and swallowed her angry responses. Jake was right. "Is John Henry still in the state pen?"

"Got out about four weeks ago. Folks say he's living out in the wilderness in some kind of survivalist mode."

So this was the reason Jake had brought up the past. Not to devil her but to toss her a possible suspect. "John Henry never struck me as a killer."

"Tell his dead wife that."

"Point made and taken. I'll run a check on him at the office and see if I can dig up anything on the time he spent in prison. He was always a big hunter, as I recall."

"A big poacher, as I recall." Jake drew the distinction with a nod of his head. "Prison can take a messed up person and push him right over the edge, Rachel."

"I thought you viewed the crime scene today as the work of some anti-hunters."

"That's my best theory right now, but I'm open to all possibilities. John Henry is just that, a possibility."

She hesitated. "Jake, I want you to let me handle this on my own. I have to step forward and be a deputy if I'm going to wear this badge."

"It's your case. I'm only trying to help."

She saw hurt touch his features, gone as quickly as it had come. "I know. And I appreciate it. But I have to be able to solve crimes or else I should change jobs."

He put his hand on her shoulder. "Rachel, this is a case that would put even the most seasoned detective to the test. Just take what help I can give you." He stood up. "I tracked you down to ask a favor."

Jake Ortiz didn't ask favors of anyone, much less the kid he viewed as little sister-slash-permanent responsibility. "This'll be a first. What is it?"

"There's a woman, name of Frances Jackson, a friend of Dad's. She's the liaison between environmental groups and the new four-lane that's going through the Black Hills. Anyway, she's having a party tomorrow night and I need a date."

"A what?" Rachel almost knocked her cola over.

"Like a social date. Calm down, I'm not asking you to kiss me." Jake swallowed the last of his beer. "This Frances Jackson is real interested in the killings, which is why I'm invited and why I'm inviting you. She wants to be certain her crews are safe up in the hills. So, I'll pick you up tomorrow about eight. From what I hear tell, she knows how to throw a party. Cocktail attire is what Dad told me."

Before she could answer, he stood up. "Thanks for the beer." He stepped out into the dusk.

Rachel sighed. Even if Jake had given her a chance, she couldn't refuse. Jake had invoked the name of his father, Mel Ortiz. There was nothing Mr. Ortiz could ask that Rachel would ever say no to. Her debt load to the man was way too high.

She put five dollars on the bar to cover their tab and headed home. Along with everything else she had to do tomorrow, she'd have to find time to buy a dress.

Rachel drove through the quiet streets of Bisonville watching the distant vista of sky and the Black Hills change constantly, a panorama of nature's most impressive abilities. The winter snows would start just after Thanksgiving, but for now, the June weather was perfection. South of town in the plains, farmers would be harvesting. Maybe if she didn't find time for a workout at the dojang today, she'd at least take half an hour for a drive. She needed to do something to release the tension that had kept her awake all night.

Two men were dead, and she had no idea how to go about catching their killer. She didn't have a college degree, not yet, but she'd learned a lot about the psychology of criminals during her law enforcement studies. What terrible motivation had made one human being skin another? And she had a bad feeling that at least one of the men was alive when he'd been tortured. Blood had covered his arms and torso, which meant to her novice eye that his heart had still been beating when the skin was removed.

The grotesque horror of it was one of the problems. The act was so depraved that it numbed her mind. She couldn't begin to figure out why someone would do such a thing. Yet that was exactly what she had to do. If she didn't, she knew she'd never be given a case more significant than a traffic accident. Bisonville was a small town. She was a young woman with a checkered past working in a man's world. No one was going to cut her the first inch of slack.

When she entered the office at 7 a.m., Gordon Gray, the sheriff, was already at his desk. He looked up.

"Deputy Redmond."

Rachel put her things on her desk and walked to the private office where he waited for her. "Sir."

"I got a call from the crime lab boys in Rapid City. They told me some preliminary stuff, but I want you to talk to them as soon as they get to work. I also got a call from Frances Jackson who's running the road crews. She's concerned for the safety of her men."

Rachel nodded. What else could she do? The sheriff generally left the deputies alone to handle their cases, but Gordon was taking a personal interest in this one. It was high profile with the potential for serious trouble—if the residents of Criss

County began to believe the wrong thing—but Rachel needed Gordon and Jake to step aside and let her work it. "I'm on it, Sheriff."

"There's a lot at stake here, Rachel. Millions, if not billions, of dollars."

"I know." The development of Paradise, a high-tech city planned to rival Silicone Valley, depended on the road. Richard Jones, a techno wizard had unveiled his plans for what amounted to a bright and shiny community, an Emerald City of urban planning and modern marvels. Such a development would change the face of South Dakota into a destination for growth and prosperity.

"We have to contain this and catch the killer." Gordon held her gaze a long moment. "We could hand this off to Game and Fish. Jake would take it."

She cleared her throat. "No. I can solve this case. I can, Sheriff. You have to give me a chance." For most of her life, she'd viewed herself as a victim. The job had given her self-confidence and a sense of self-worth. She couldn't let the sheriff take that from her.

"The county is stirred up. There're a lot of high emotions about Paradise, both for and agin' it. A killer on the loose is the last thing we need."

"I know." The different factions of the county—hunters, Natives, the scattering of green individuals who'd moved into the hills to escape development, ranchers, loggers—had worked out a tenuous peace. These murders could easily disrupt it and send the county into all out war. With the added tension of the four-lane that was going through land sacred to the Sioux, the place was a powder keg. Maybe that was why Jake was so staunchly promoting the poacher-on-poacher theory of the murders. If it was just lowlifes killing each other, none of the political factions were involved. It made sense.

"You know what's at stake here?" Gordon asked her.

"I do."

"Deputy Amos could take over the case. His wife may not deliver for--"

"If I need his help, I'll be sure and ask."

Gordon rubbed his clean-shaven cheek and smoothed one side of his mustache. He always looked immaculate. A rancher who'd spent most of his life working from sun-up to sunset, he was lean, sharp featured and nobody's fool. If he took this case from her, she'd never recover in the department. He'd gone out on a limb to hire her, and now he was standing with the saw in his hand.

"I can do this. I have to do it." She spoke quietly.

"Ortiz talked to me yesterday. He said the same thing."

For once Jake's interference was an asset. She'd have to remember to thank him—after she beat him with the high heels she'd have to wear to the cocktail party.

"Then call the crime lab. Gus Langstrom said he'd be in early to talk to you."

"Thanks, sheriff." She started to say more but decided that the best way to show her gratitude was to solve the case, and in record time.

At her desk she felt Scott Amos watching her. She gave him a smile and mouthed "How's Betty Lou?"

"Glad you caught this case instead of me." He shook his head. "She'd have a conniption if I got stranded in those hills and couldn't get home."

Rachel shrugged, dialed the lab, and waited for Langstrom to answer and identify himself.

"What do you have for me, Gus?"

"I've e-mailed the photos to you, and I'll send a hard set by courier. The smaller man was dead before his skin was removed. The silver ornament was attached to the victim's chest with a porcupine quill, as you thought. The feather, which was wrapped and attached with standard fishing line, came from a great horned owl, illegal to own because of the endangered species law. Only Natives can own them, but as you know, there are always illegal sources. Also, and this was the most interesting of all, we did manage to get some prints from around the bodies. There was a pattern, all clockwise. And whoever made the prints wore the victims' boots."

Rachel felt a chill. The killer, or killers, was clever. Very clever. "What about prints from the bodies?"

"Nothing. The killer had to be wearing gloves. Whoever it was made sure not to leave any forensic evidence. The tool used to skin the men had a serrated blade, exactly like what a hunter might use. Jesus, that could have taken a while."

"Thanks, Gus. You guys make a tough job a little easier."

"Put that in writing and send it to my boss. Documentation never hurts at raise time."

She was smiling as she hung up.

She spent the rest of the morning checking with law enforcement agencies around the country for similar crimes. It was a long, grueling exercise that yielded nothing useful, so she also ran background on John Henry James. His cabin was so far back in the wilderness that it would be faster to trailer in a four-wheeler than walk it, so she decided to wait until the next day to talk with him.

She'd just started an Internet search on militant anti-hunting groups when Jake walked in. He put a folder on her desk. "This is a list of the most wanted poachers in the area."

He waited for her to open it. At the top of the list was Hank Welford, followed by about thirty other names.

"I think Hank is one of the dead men." Jake sat on the corner of her desk. "We could never catch him with the goods, but every game warden in the state and along the Montana border has been after him."

"I know who he is." Rachel had seen him drinking in Bud's, bragging about his prowess as a hunter and guide for rich doctors and lawyers from the East who came to bag trophy game. As far as Rachel was concerned, the world would be a better place without Hank Welford. Even so, she meant to find the person or persons who'd killed him. "What makes you think one of the dead men is Hank?" She waved the list. "Could be any of them."

"Several of his buddies remember the snake tattoo on his left pec. I'm pretty sure it's him. We can get one of them to ID the body. He doesn't have any next of kin, as far as I can tell."

"Thanks, Jake." She stood.

"Want to grab some lunch?"

"I've got something to do." She picked up her purse, knowing that the tiny air of mystery would get under his skin.

"Need some help?" He stepped back to allow her to walk in front of him. Jake always had excellent manners.

"No, I can handle this on my own." She flashed a big smile at the doorway and walked to the parking lot. Hell would freeze over before she admitted she had to go shopping.

RACHEL HELD the sales slip in her hand, hesitating. At last she wadded it up and threw it in the trash in the kitchen of her small cottage. She held out the cocktail dress, examining it once more before she pulled it from the hanger and stepped into it. Her mother had always adored shopping, and a new dress was an occasion for a party. Rachel had never developed such fondness for clothes. In fact, she seldom thought about what she was wearing, which made the uniform a real pleasure.

She was going to this party because the debts incurred

during her teen years demanded a certain type of payment. This act wouldn't even dent the karmic IOUs she owed Mel Ortiz. An eight-foot brick wall had separated the trailer park from the nice subdivision where the Ortiz family lived. Mel—and Jake—scaled that class barrier again and again to look out for her.

She licked her lips, the taste of lipstick unfamiliar. The saleswoman at the only cosmetic shop in Criss County had taken pity on her and done her make-up and even helped with her hair. Rachel was ready for Jake to pick her up.

The rumble of her stomach reminded her that breakfast had come and gone hours before. She'd been so involved in finding a suitable dress that she hadn't had time to even grab a burger. In the kitchen, she glanced at the clock, an old frying pan that her mom had "made" during one of several therapeutic craft marathons at church-supported homes for addicts. In her various attempts to kick her addictions, Junie had made clay vases, painted the praying hands of Jesus and glued colored macaroni montages. But the clock had been Junie's favorite, because it had a purpose.

Rachel stared at it. The minute hand jumped forward on a whir, paused, then lurched forward again. Junie had been so proud of the damn clock, proud of herself for staying clean for two weeks. But she'd gone back to using, back to working the streets.

Rachel tried to shake free of the past. It was time to get a move on. Jake would be there to get her. The clock showed seven straight on the dot.

The clearest image of her mother came back to Rachel with visceral force. This time Rachel was older, and Junie stood in the kitchen of the trailer they rented. She wore a red dress that emphasized her figure, three-inch heels, and the makeup she artfully applied to look like a movie star from the 50s. Behind her the frying pan clock showed seven on a Friday night in July, ten years before.

"You stay inside, Rachel," Junie said. "Lock the door as soon as I leave."

"Where are you going?" The anger in the teenager's voice echoed back to her through the years. "I'm hungry. There's nothing to eat in the house. You can't go out and leave me with nothing to eat and no money to get groceries."

"We'll go shopping tomorrow. I have a date. So you lock the door and do your homework."

"Mama, don't go." Even at sixteen, Rachel had recognized the widened pupils, the fluttering hands, the constant swallowing. "Mama, there are people who can help you."

The slap had been so hard that Rachel had spun onto the sofa. When she turned back, her mother was gone. There was only the lingering trail of cheap perfume.

And that had been the last time Junie Redmond had been seen alive. Her body was found the next morning in a dumpster on the edge of Rapid City. She'd died of an overdose.

The ring of her cell phone nudged Rachel out of the memory. She answered it mechanically.

"Deputy Redmond, you might want to come and take a look at this autopsy report." Charlie Newman, the coroner, was chewing into the telephone as he talked.

"I'm...certainly." She fumbled through the correct response. "Right now?"

"There're some really interesting things here, but I don't want to talk about them on the phone."

"Thanks, Charlie. I'm on my way."

"Good. Things are quiet at the courthouse, so this may be the best time for us to talk."

Rachel caught a glimpse of her shadowy image in the front

window. For one brief instant, she thought she saw her mother standing behind her. They were both dressed for a party.

"Rachel, did you hear me? I'll meet you at the sheriff's office."

She cleared her throat. "I'm on the way."

Snapping the phone shut, she picked up her purse. She'd get a certain amount of teasing from the night shift who happened to see her, but she didn't have time to change and then come home and change back. She dialed Jake. When she got his voice mail, she left a message.

"Pick me up at the sheriff's office in the courthouse instead of home. Thanks." She walked to the kitchen, and her hand reached for the clock's plug as it had done a hundred times before. She should toss it, buy something new that didn't have so many memories attached. But she stopped, mesmerized by her reflection in the toaster. No one had ever said it to her, but made-up and with her hair pinned in a French twist, she looked just like her mother.

THE SEVEN PEOPLE gathered in the room were tense with excitement. Dressed in dark clothing and jittery with nerves, they sat around the darkened room and waited.

Derek Baxter stood by the open window and looked out upon the perfect blackness of a South Dakota night. The stars were incredible, untainted by any other light. The breeze that blew to him from the Black Hills contained the scents of pine and juniper. He thought of the gin and tonics his mother drank and felt a charge of empowerment. He'd decided to use his life for something worthwhile, not to fritter it away.

He turned to address the four women and three men. "The note claiming responsibility for the murders of the two poachers has already been sent to the newspaper. By tomorrow morning, WAR will be on the lips of every South Dakotan."

A smattering of applause went around the room, but it did nothing to relieve the tension.

One of the men raised his hand. "Derek, they're going to look at us like murderers now." His voice rose. "I mean, I think this is a great because it gets publicity for our cause, but each one of us should be aware that law officers are going to shoot first and ask questions later."

"Good point." Derek felt his own stomach flutter. The brutal murders of the poachers had the potential to give Workers for Animal Rights the biggest boost in public awareness since he'd come to the southwest corner of South Dakota to organize a cell of the activist group. "When we agreed to send the note claiming responsibility, we all knew what we were risking." He paused for effect. "They will shoot you if they catch you."

"Just like the hunters shoot the wild creatures. Just another thrill for the Neanderthals." The girl who spoke was pretty. No more than twenty-two, she sat a slight distance from everyone else. Derek noticed because he noticed everything about Justine Morgan.

"Okay, let's focus on tonight. We'll take the black van almost to the road site. We'll park it in the woods and make the rest of the way on foot. When we get to the heavy equipment, everyone knows what to do, right?"

A murmur of assent spread through the room.

"Get the blow torches." He moved toward the door.

"Won't they have a guard up there?" Justine asked.

He shook his head. "Not tonight. That's the beauty of it. Not one of those big, macho construction guys wanted to stay up there to guard the equipment while a psycho killer is on the loose."

"They're the psycho killers." Justine rose slowly as she spoke. "They're the people who slaughter animals for sport. They're the sportsmen with high-powered scopes, radios, automatic weapons and four-wheelers because they're so fat and out of shape they can't even haul their kill out." Contempt rested in the way she held her lips. "I say let's kill more of them."

"Yes!" The affirmation spread among the young men and women as they hurried after Derek, out the door and into the night.

CHAPTER THREE

"Whi-irt-whirl." The wolf whistle cut through the nearly empty sheriff's department. Marston French stood up and put his hand over his heart as Rachel walked in.

"Cut it out, Marston." She felt naked, though her dress was conservative by anyone's standards. It was merely the fact that it was a dress that made her so uncomfortable. And a party dress at that. If he didn't quit ogling her she'd be tempted to kick him in the throat with the side of her foot, a very effective Tang Soo Do maneuver. She'd become blindingly fast at the kicks.

"Who's the lucky guy?" Marston asked. His gaze lingered on her bare shoulders. "You sure do clean up nice, Deputy."

It was the "deputy" that saved his ass. "None of your beeswax." She looked around for the coroner. "Where's Charlie? He said to meet him here."

"He ducked out to get something to eat. I don't know how he can eat after spending the last few hours over at the hospital with those corpses."

"Thanks." Rachel headed back into the hallway but stopped at the door. She heard footsteps in the empty corridor and recognized the tired gait of the coroner. He rounded the corner and signaled her down to his office in the basement.

Rachel had never seen an autopsy, except on television. She could hold her own with wrecks, hunting accidents, drug overdoses. An autopsy was another matter. Lucky for her, such procedures were performed at the hospital or else in Rapid City at the state lab.

"Come on, deputy. The bodies are over at the hospital. You won't have to look at them." Charlie threw the words over his shoulder as if he could read her mind. He kept his forward momentum going, a burger from the Copper Kettle swinging at his side in a paper bag.

Rachel jogged to catch up, no mean feat in her high heels. She wasn't a sissy, but after the brutality that had been heaped upon the dead men, it seemed a sacrilege to cut them up further. Still, she was eager for the facts.

Every time she walked into Charlie's office, she was surprised at the bare essentials. A desk and lamp, a chair and metal filing cabinets. That was it. Coroner was a part-time job in Criss County, and while Charlie sometimes assisted at procedure, he always had the reports.

She took a chair without being asked. "What was the cause of death?"

He eased back in his chair, his gaze on the bag of burgers. A grease spot was widening on the brown paper. "You already know one was alive when he started cutting."

"What a way to die."

"The heads were severed last. Oh, yeah, we got an ID on one of them."

Rachel leaned forward, excited despite her best intention of showing no emotion. She'd been accurate in her assumption about the cause of death. "Who is it?"

"The big one is Hank Welford. Professional poacher,

drunk and general bully. The other guy...so far nothing on him. You gotta figure he's not a local."

"Jake Ortiz thought it was Welford. The tattoo." She crossed her legs, then realized it wasn't the most refined gesture in the dress and put her feet solidly on the floor. "Were the men drugged by any chance?"

"Nada. They'd been drinking, but not excessively. Looked like they were hunting and took down that moose, which will take a few days to get a tox screen on. The state lab guys were hollering that we asked them to work a moose."

"Tough for them." Rachel picked up the report. "So someone surprised them." She visualized the scene in her mind. With Hank and the other man so intent on taking the trophy head before they were caught hunting illegally, they hadn't heard the person, or persons, who slipped up behind them. "How did the doctor figure the men were subdued?"

"He found ligature marks on the stump of the neck on Hank. Looked like he'd been garroted from behind, maybe suffocated a little and brought into submission. He could have been shot in the head, a non-fatal wound. Can't tell without the heads. But if that's the case, whoever did the shooting would have to have some basic medical training."

"There had to be more than one killer," Rachel speculated aloud. "I mean those were two strong men. Even if one of them was garroted, the other would have run or tried to fight back unless he was outnumbered. Unless he was shot first."

The coroner shrugged. "I just pronounce them dead. You're the one who has to figure out all the intricacies of the sicko's mind." He leaned forward abruptly, grabbed the bag, and opened the waxed paper. The aroma of hamburger filled the room, and her mouth began to water.

Rachel was a little appalled to hear her stomach grumble.

She was toughening up. The discussion of two awful murders hadn't even taken the edge off her appetite.

THE SOFT STRAINS of a cello rose above and then sank beneath the murmur of conversation. Rachel kept step with Jake as he led her through the entrance hall and into the large room that served as parlor and banquet hall. It was a huge house, elegant with an old world style.

Jake had been silent on the ride to Frankie Jackson's. He was pissed that the coroner had called her and not him. She'd wisely decided not to press the topic, but she did tell him what she'd learned and saw the satisfied curl of his mouth when he found out he was right about Welford. Jake was competitive to a fault, but she had no intention of cutting him out of any information that might help to catch the killer or killers.

Rachel barely had time to look around the entrance hall when Jake propelled her toward a slender woman who bore a striking resemblance to the manifestation of Aphrodite. Dark hair framed her face in a cloud of curls. A neck as delicate and slender as a gazelle's rose from prominent collar bones. Her bright red lips drew into a crooked smile as Jake led her forward.

"Frankie, this is Deputy Rachel Redmond. Rachel, this is Frances Jackson, soother of troubled waters and spin doctor for those with political ambitions. She's heading the road crew for Belker in an attempt to keep down protests from the granola segment."

Rachel held out her hand and was surprised that Frankie's hand, so obviously designed for piano or something equally elegant, had the grip of a rancher.

"I've heard about your first big case," Frankie said, going

right to the heart of the reason Rachel knew she was invited. "Are you excited or appalled?"

Rachel couldn't help but admire that. Frankie wasn't going to pretend to a social interest in a lowly deputy. If Rachel served any purpose at all at this party, it was to provide details about the two murders.

"Criss County doesn't have a lot of homicides, Ms. Jackson," Rachel responded, avoiding the question. "Jake told me you were worried about your crew." She glanced around. The room was too crowded for her to reveal that Hank Welford, one of Frankie's employees, was a victim. "Could we talk privately?"

Frankie took Rachel's arm. "Excuse us, Jake." She drew Rachel across the room and into the library, closing the thick mahogany doors with determination. All sounds of the party ceased.

Frankie went to a decanter and poured liberal measures of bourbon over ice cubes in crystal highball glasses. She held one out to Rachel. "What a pleasure to see a young woman in a tough job." She sipped her drink. "Our mothers fought hard so the two of us could stand here, and our generation is going to kick ass in the man's world." She held up her drink. "To strong women and supine men." She drank the bourbon in one swallow.

Rachel sipped her drink and felt a smile tug at her lips. Supine men. It was a strange and evocative image. She hadn't expected this side of Frances Jackson—hadn't expected to like her. "Jake told me you want assurances that your road crew won't be targeted by our killer." She put her glass on the table. "I can't give you those assurances in light of the fact that one of the two dead men worked for you. Hank Welford."

Frankie lowered her drink slowly. "He missed the last few days of work. I figured he was either drunk or poaching."

"Both."

"Jesus. I heard the victims were skinned."

"In a manner of speaking." She debated how much to tell Frankie. "The killer meant for Hank to suffer."

Frankie walked quickly to a credenza and picked up the telephone. "I'm going to pull my crews. I don't want them in danger."

Rachel held up a hand. "Hold on. While the road is controversial, I don't think the person who killed those two hunters is worried about the four-lane."

"What makes you so sure? What do you think was the reason?"

She didn't want to reveal additional details. The solution to the murders might rest on specific details, such as the silver ornament jabbed into Hank's chest, that only the killer would know. "I believe Hank was specifically targeted. The killer knew him, or knew what he was. It wasn't about the road. I'd be willing to bet the motive was revenge." She'd just overloaded her ass with her mouth.

Frankie nodded. "What I can tell the men is that the sheriff's department is reasonably certain the road crews won't be targeted. Is that a fair statement?"

"Yes."

Frankie's eyebrows rose. "Jake said it was poacher-on-poacher crime."

"Jake would say that. It's his theory. And if you know Jake, he's pretty damn good at promoting his own theories."

"And his own reputation." Frankie laughed at the expression Rachel knew she hadn't hidden well. "Look, I've known Jake a while. His old man knew my parents. Jake knows the wilderness like nobody else, but he's an ambitious man. I see politics in his future."

"Jake?" Rachel almost laughed. "Why would you think that?"

Frankie shrugged and poured them both another drink. "Woman's intuition. I also sense something between the two of you."

Rachel felt the blush she hated touch her face. In high school she'd been teased mercilessly about sleeping with her "brother."

Jake was no blood kin, but after her mother's death, she'd moved a few hundred yards and up several socio-economic levels into the Ortiz house. Despite the fact that Jake had never shown the least romantic interest in her, the idea still caused the blood to rush to her cheeks.

"Jake is like my big brother. My big overbearing brother. Nothing more." She walked to the door and opened it. "We should rejoin the party. I'm sure your guests are wondering where you got off to."

"I didn't mean to upset you." Frankie joined her. "Have you ever thought about the FBI? With your looks and intelligence, you'd rise through the ranks quickly."

"I've thought a few things about them." Rachel grinned. "Nothing exceptionally positive."

Frankie laughed out loud, drawing the attention of several guests. "I like you, Rachel. You're way too smart to stay in Criss County, but while you're here I think we should be friends. Hey, I'm looking for a workout partner. What's your routine?"

"Tang Soo Do. There's a small dance studio-slash-dojang on the west end of town. It's called—don't gag now—Prima Donna's. I work out there late in the evenings. They actually have some pretty good equipment."

"I've done some kickboxing, but that's sissy stuff compared to Korean martial arts."

Rachel's eyebrows rose. "Hardly anyone here knows what

Tang Soo Do is. I took a few classes when I was at Quantico for some training and got hooked."

Frankie struck a pose, her face hardening into a mask that lost every shred of humanity. Rachel was caught unprepared, but felt slightly foolish when Frankie lowered her arms. "I've watched a lot of martial arts movies."

Rachel felt a bit stupid. Frankie had unsettled her. "You've got the facial expression down pat. You should give it a try. I'll mention it to the owner. I'm sure he'd be glad to give you a key. It's impossible to work out when the dance classes are going."

"You sure I wouldn't be imposing? I don't want to crowd your space."

Rachel looked around the room. There was more money in Frankie Jackson's parlor than she'd make in five years as a deputy. "We're not exactly birds of a feather."

"Maybe not externally but here—" Frankie touched her heart--"I think we may be a lot alike. I'll give you a call and see if we can coordinate our schedules. Now, I'd better work this room. I'm not paid to enjoy myself."

She moved away, greeting a man that it took Rachel several moments to recognize as U.S. Senator Harvey Dilson. Dilson was one of the most powerful men in the Senate. His gaze followed Frankie, appreciating the toga-cut of her dress that left one shoulder bare and revealed perfect cleavage.

Feeling out of her league, Rachel walked through the crowded room looking for Jake. She'd answered the summons of Frankie Jackson and passed inspection. Now she was ready to get back to Bisonville and work on her case.

CHAPTER FOUR

When he opened the door to the house, Derek Baxter knew he was outgunned. Though he'd sought this meeting—had worked for months to achieve it—he realized he was unprepared. Not in the literal sense of the word, but in presence. The four men, though they bore no physical resemblance to America's white heroes on Mt. Rushmore, perfectly imitated the stone countenances. They sat in straight-back chairs around the dining table in the small cottage. No one smiled or acknowledged him, except for the four pair of dark eyes that pinned him in the doorway."You said you wanted to see me?" Derek took long strides toward the men. He'd had maybe two hours of sleep since his foray on the road equipment, and he wasn't in the mood to be treated like an impertinent child.

One of the men picked up a newspaper and pushed it across the table so Derek could read the headline.

ANIMAL RIGHTS FACTION CLAIMS KILLINGS

Derek smiled. The two-inch headline spanned the page. He hadn't had a chance to see a newspaper yet, but the article was top of the fold and perfect. "I was afraid they'd bury it."

The youngest of the Native Americans stood up. "My

name is Adam Standing Bear. You've jeopardized years of effort, Mr. Baxter. We have legislation working through the court system. We can't afford to have public sentiment turned against us."

Derek bristled. The raid the night before on the road equipment had been successful. They'd managed to pretty much destroy two huge earth movers and fuck up the wiring on some other equipment, which would grind the roadwork to a halt, at least for a few days.

"I don't know why you think I've jeopardized anything." He tapped the paper. "Before this, I couldn't get the name of Workers for Animal Rights in the classified section if I bought an ad. Every person in this county hunts or benefits from hunting in one way or another. WAR is dedicated to stopping the use of animals for human entertainment and sport, and we're willing to do whatever it takes to get there."

"Even kill people?" Adam asked.

The men were watching him, completely expressionless. Derek had only one ace, and he intended to use it. He'd drawn a line, clearly separating those who killed animals for pleasure from the rest of mankind. "Those two men weren't humans. They happened to walk upright, and they looked like men, but they weren't. They were culls, rejects of humanity, men who deserved to be pulled from the human race. Let's just hope we got them before they bred."

"Your rhetoric is strident, Mr. Baxter." Adam took a deep breath. "Your claim to the killings will bring law enforcement agents all over this area, and us, as they search for you. The things we've been working on for the last four years are at risk because of you."

Derek felt a bubble of interest. Native American support could be huge. "What things?"

Adam shook his head. "Things no white man can truly understand."

"Bullshit. You just don't trust me."

Adam's smile was slight. "You speak the truth, white man."

Derek's insulted pride was tempered by his admiration for Adam. "Tell me and maybe we could throw in together. WAR has a tough bunch of dedicated members." He punched the paper. "And we're not afraid to take action."

The four men stared at him. He felt anger flush his skin. They acted like they were the judge and jury of how to stop the destruction of the earth. Just because they were Native Americans, they didn't have any god-given solutions to anything, yet they were going to disapprove of him and his tactics. At least he and WAR were doing something.

"Have you ever heard of a creature that roams the wilderness?" Adam asked.

Derek rolled his eyes. "What? Big Foot? Are you telling me you think Big Foot killed those guys?"

Not a single eye blinked.

"Sasquatch is a legend based on fact. As most legends are." Adam's voice was controlled. "But that isn't whom I speak of. There is something in the Black Hills. Something unsettled by the road cutting through the mountains. Something unhappy with the human race."

Despite knowing he was being manipulated, Derek felt a shiver. "Cut the crap. Tell me your plan and I'll try to help or I'm outta here."

"Our plan is to hold a ceremony to try and placate the angry spirit."

Derek studied Adam. He had the classic good looks, the physique, the long braids that marked him as a Sioux warrior, and he played his part to perfection. "Man, you're so full of shit." He shook his head. "I'm not interested in stories used to scare kids around the campfire."

"The Skin Dancer isn't a legend, Mr. Baxter. It's very real, and if you doubt it, you can ask Deputy Redmond to let you see the autopsy photographs of the two dead men."

"The men were killed, but I happen to know that it wasn't some "Skin Dancer" who did it. Because WAR has claimed responsibility. We skinned those hunters."

The four men stared at him in silence. He could read nothing on their faces and thought again of the Indian Mt. Rushmore.

He walked to the door. "If you want our help, call me. Otherwise, lose my number. I've got a press release to write. The national media is finally interested in hearing what WAR is all about."

The two huge bulldozers smoldered, black smoke rising in a straight column on the windless day. The destruction was complete. They'd been professionally burned, and several other pieces of equipment had been crippled by butane torch attacks on their electrical systems. Rachel began the work of looking for evidence that was scarce at best and most likely non-existent. This on top of the newspaper headline where a faction of terrorist animal rights people claimed the brutal killings of Hank Welford and the second man who'd just been identified as Ashton Trussell, a plastic surgeon from Boston.

The only good thing that had come of the day was that Jake wasn't trying to hog her investigation. Heavy equipment didn't fall under his purview. But insurance investigators would be there before the morning was over, and they'd expect a preliminary report and some progress toward catching the vandals who'd trashed a half million dollars worth of machinery.

Frankie Jackson wheeled onto the scene, gravel spraying, and Rachel had to resist the impulse to avoid her. Instead, she walked to the big three-quarter ton pickup and waited for Frankie to get off her cell phone and step out.

"The one night I leave the equipment unguarded." Frankie glared at the ruined machines. "Damn it all to hell."

"At least no one was hurt." Rachel expected to be ridiculed for such pabulum.

Frankie blew out a large breath as she stared at the wreckage. "You think this is connected to those murders?"

Rachel had spent the drive to the site thinking about the answer to that question. "I know you've seen the paper and WAR has claimed responsibility for the murders. But this vandalism looks more like the work of that group. I wouldn't put them down for the murders, but this, hell yes."

"I don't really get it." Frankie waved a hand at the damage. "We're not hurting animals."

Rachel glanced off into the distance where the trees were so thick they looked impenetrable. "When you destroy forest land, you affect the animals."

"They're vandals at best and murderers at worst." Frankie started walking toward her crew. "This will set us back a week or more. Not to mention that half my crew is threatening to quit."

"Scott's working to locate members of WAR. They've been around here for the past year, but so far they've just protested hunting season, scared a few hunters in the woods, stolen a few vehicles and dumped them in a ditch." She shrugged. "It's a big step from harassment to murder."

"I want them arrested."

"That makes two of us." She didn't say that WAR had also

been effective in hiding the identity of its members. Then again, the Criss County Sheriff's Department hadn't really pursued them. So a few hunters had been scared and had to walk out of the woods. It wasn't a high priority. Even in Cress County there were better ways to spend departmental time.

"Can you identify the membership of the group?" Frankie asked.

"It's going to take awhile. The truth is, it could be any number of young people in the area. There's a lot of wilderness with hunting camps and cabins where they could be meeting. We suspect the members are from respectable families. We'll get a lead on them." If WAR fit the description of most radical groups, they were young, disaffected kids from upper-income families who wanted to change the world—immediately and without regard for the rights of others.

"This isn't petty vandalism," Frankie said. She fitted a hard hat over her shining hair. "This is arson and property damage at nearly half a million dollars."

Rachel nodded. "We're doing everything we can, Frankie. We only have Scott, the sheriff, and some volunteers who are sometimes more trouble than help. I won't lie to you. The murders have to be our primary focus, but we'll do everything we can to catch the people who did this. You should post a guard in the future."

"That I'll do, if I have to sit out here with a shotgun myself."

Rachel hesitated. "There are always a few out-of-work guys at Bud's Bar. You might pick up a nightshift guard there."

"Thanks. Now I'd better get these guys motivated before they decide to hightail it out of here."

Rachel watched her walk away, a slim woman in jeans so tight every guy on the crew couldn't resist looking. Rachel thought of something and jogged to catch up with Frankie.

"Hey, I know you're talking with the Sioux. Any chance this is their handiwork?"

When Frankie turned around, Rachel was surprised to see the worry on her face. "God, I hope not. I'm paid the big bucks to mediate issues between the Sioux nation and Belker. If the Natives are sneaking around destroying equipment rather than addressing their concerns at our meetings, I'm a pretty big failure."

A dump truck roared past them, halting all attempts at conversation. When it was gone, Rachel gave a half-shrug. "There's no evidence to show it was the Natives." She thought about the pole with the dangling owl feather. It looked Native, but anyone could imitate such a thing to create the illusion. "I just have to cover all possibilities."

"Whoever it is, I want them caught and prosecuted." Frankie wiped her forehead under the hardhat. "Four or five days of delay are going to put us over budget. We were tight anyway, but this is bad. As you know, the development of Paradise depends on the road. A lot of locals have money invested, and they're going to be squawking. My head will roll."

The cell phone on Rachel's hip buzzed and she slipped it into her hand. "I'll be in touch," she promised as she stepped back from the construction sounds to take her call.

FRANKIE WAITED ten minutes after Rachel left before she dialed Jake Ortiz. She'd deliberately cultivated his friendship, trading on past history between their families. Not that she didn't enjoy his company and his lean good looks in and of themselves. He was the kind of man she enjoyed bedding, but she'd held off. Sometimes her job required her to use people she liked. This was one of those times, and a sexual relationship could get messy. She'd flirted with Jake but had been careful not to go any further.

"What can I do for you?" Jake asked, and Frankie had to smile. He was a willing partner in this game. Ambitious men understood the rules of advancement, just as she did.

"Rachel was up here a little while ago, and I'm worried."

"Afraid she won't be able to catch the arsonists?"

Frankie noticed clouds were building to the west. Big clouds. As if she needed another problem. "No, I think Rachel is ultimately competent. She was asking about the Sioux, though. I don't need her stirring the pot with them. This whole project brings up the issue of the violation of the Treaty of Fort Laramie. They claim the Black Hills, and I'm not certain they don't own the land. This roadway is not something they want, Jake. I've got a tenuous trust going, and if Rachel runs out there and accuses them of burning my equipment or, worse yet, killing those two poachers, it could unravel everything I've built here. I don't have to tell you how important Paradise is."

There was a long pause, and she knew Jake was considering what to do.

"Look, Rachel is diplomatic. She wouldn't accuse anyone of anything unless she had evidence."

"It would still be best..."

"I can't interfere with her investigation, Frankie. Not even subtly. Besides, you and I both know there's a militant faction of the Sioux nation that might have done this. It wouldn't be the first time."

Frankie sighed. "I know. I'm just trying to keep a lot of things in balance here. The four-lane is going through. At least with me on the project, the damage will be as minimal as possible. If Belker views me as ineffective, they'll fire me in a heartbeat."

Jake's voice was wry. "Then that group of environmental rapists will have their way and take down every tree that gets in their way."

Frankie bit back an angry reply. "This isn't a joke to me. I care about the Black Hills and the heritage here."

Jake cleared his throat. "Sorry, I didn't mean to sound flippant. We all care, Frankie. Rachel cares, too."

"Could you at least explain the delicacy to her?"

"Okay, but it'll only make her mad at me. She's tired of me interfering. Twisting her arm to go to your little soiree didn't help matters, either. Rachel is growing up, and she doesn't like to be pushed around."

"Good for her." Frankie noticed a cluster of men who weren't working. They were talking vehemently and pointing to the tree line. She walked toward them. "Jake, I'll call you back later." She closed the phone and addressed the men. "Is there a problem here?"

"There's someone in there watching us, Ms. Jackson," a local named Layton said.

Frankie swung her gaze to the trees, instantly alert. "Did you get a look at him?"

Layton shook his head. "No, but I saw him, movin' through the trees. I mean he moved, like he was drifting through the trees." He spit a stream of tobacco on the ground. "Like some kinda fuckin' spook out there watchin' everything we do."

"I'll hire some guards." Frankie searched the thick trees. There was nothing there, at least not now. But she didn't doubt what Layton had seen. After all, she'd been aware that someone was watching them for several weeks.

CHAPTER FIVE

The damn county was on a crime spree. There was no other explanation for it. As Rachel sped back toward Bisonville, her shoulders knotted with tension. Two men dead, a half million dollars in heavy equipment ruined—it was all more than she could account for. In her eight months as a deputy, Rachel's experiences included the robbery of an all-night convenience store, some cattle rustling, vandalism of a church, and a couple of lost hikers.

She was past Piker Road before she slowed down. Around her the wilderness was serene. Bitter juniper spiced the wind, and through the distance she could see the unique rock formations that gave the area such a distinctive profile.

Rachel realized she was in the vicinity of John Henry James's cabin. If she let this opportunity pass, she'd waste half a day tomorrow getting back up here. She backed up and eased onto the dirt trail known as Piker Road. Once upon a time it had led to a gold mine, but judging from recent usage, only a few deer had been down it. She pulled out a detailed map of the maze of dirt paths that led through the wilderness. She'd marked the location of John Henry's cabin—or at least the location he'd listed as his address.

Since she was so close, she'd drive as far as she could. If it looked like she'd need an ATV, she'd leave. The most she could lose was an hour, and the time alone in the woods would give her a chance to think. There were things about the case that, in her opinion, didn't make a lot of sense.

After checking her weapon and making sure pepper spray was in her belt, she started south on Piker Road, headed into a black cloud that was rolling its way over the badlands. She had time, but none to waste. She pressed the accelerator, leaving a trail of dust behind her as she rose and then fell along the ridges of wilderness.

The trees were dense, cutting the sun and causing the temperature to drop at least ten degrees. With the crisp smell of the conifers, the shade and the approaching storm, Rachel felt as if she might have bitten off more than she could chew when the road ended abruptly at a steep drop-off.

The footpath continued down a sixty degree decline, easy enough to descend, but coming back up, especially in the rain, might prove challenging. She debated going back to the sheriff's office but started down the trail. She'd give herself twenty minutes. If she hadn't found John Henry's cabin by then, she'd come back with the proper equipment.

She hit level trail quickly and lengthened her stride. On the off-chance that it might work, she pulled out her cell phone. No signal. Typical of the region where the spectacular hills and towering rock formations played havoc with radio frequency waves.

"Stop or I'll shoot!"

The call came from the trees to her right and she halted and held up her hands.

"John Henry James, it's Deputy Rachel Redmond. Put down your weapon." She slowly lowered her hands as she spoke.

A man with a long beard stepped out from behind a rock. He held a hunting rifle in his hand, and though it wasn't pointed at her any longer, it was at the ready.

"I'm Rachel Redmond," she said again, walking toward him. "I'm here to ask a few questions about something that happened some five miles from here, up at Dixon Point."

John Henry eyed her as if she were speaking a foreign language. She wasn't certain he understood, and she felt a tingle of concern. The way he looked at her was more than a little creepy.

"John Henry, do you remember me?" she asked.

He nodded, breaking the spell. "I do. Used to live in a trailer park. Your mama liked the blow."

He did remember, probably far better than she liked. He'd once been a boy with dark wavy hair and dreamy brown eyes that held a spark of danger. Now he was a middle-aged hermit, a man old before his time. He looked fifty instead of late twenties.

"Rachel Redmond," he said. "Your mom died of an overdose, and you became a pig." His tone was conversational.

Silence, filled with the sound of the wind in the trees, dropped over them. It grew awkward before she figured how to break it. "It's nice up here. I guess it must be a relief to be where it's so quiet and isolated."

"I did my time in prison. Not a moment of peace in six years. Once you get out of that, you don't ever want to be in a place that never goes silent."

She noticed his use of the second person, a way of distancing himself from the experience. "That's a tough place to come back from, John Henry."

His gaze went to the thunderhead gaining in size and darkness. "You ought to get on home. That road gets slick with rain."

"I have to ask some questions first."

"Ask 'em and go." He didn't look at her.

"Where were you two nights ago?" Frustration gnawed at her. She'd gain nothing from this except to let John Henry know that whenever a crime was committed, he'd come up on the suspect list.

"I was back in my cabin, alone. No alibi. If you're goin' to arrest me, just do it. What is it I supposedly done?"

"I'm not accusing you of anything. But you do have a criminal record. A violent criminal record. You're just out of prison and two men were killed out here in the wilderness." She slid behind the professional demeanor she'd worked so hard to generate. Show no emotion. Just the facts, ma'am.

"Somebody got tired of the poachers? Well, good for them."

"How'd you know it was poachers?" She was instantly alert. He didn't strike her as a man who followed the news. Not for a second had she believed it was John Henry, but his last statement made her wary.

"Educated guess, Rachel. Got to be either hikers or poachers. I don't particularly care for the hikers, showing up in the brush like jack rabbits poppin' out of a hole, but mostly they're just annoyin'. Those fuckin' poachers, though, liable to shoot your head off. Except most of the game they go for is drugged or crippled so it can't get away from them. I saw these two guys take a moose. Big fearless hunters. That animal could barely stagger. Guy walked up to it and shot it from about two feet. That bastard Hank Welford set it up. Somebody ought to shoot him."

The blood beneath her skin heated. "You saw two men kill a moose? When?"

"A couple of days..." He finally looked into her eyes, fear showing in his. "Those the dead men?"

"Yes." She lifted a hand to touch his arm but didn't. "It's okay." She could see he felt trapped, and that wasn't a good place for John Henry. "I don't think you're involved in this John Henry, except as a witness. But you may have helped me out a whole lot."

His arm was jittering, as if he'd lost control of it to some electric pulse. "I just want to be left alone." He backed up from her. "Just leave me alone!" He was shouting. "I done my time. I paid." His gaze ricocheted around the area, searching for something Rachel knew she'd never be able to see.

"When did you see the hunters, John Henry? Time is really important." She put a hand on his forearm. "Please, I need you to slow down and think."

"I don't remember!" He edged away from her touch. He was coming apart at the seams.

She held out a hand, palm up. "There's a killer loose out here. Think about it. Two men were brutally killed not far away. You're in danger, too."

It took a few seconds for her words to sink in, but he finally looked at her. "You don't think I killed 'em?"

"No, I don't. But I'm worried about you. What time did you see Hank and the other hunter?"

"About nine o'clock. Near Dixon Point. I was up on Dragon Tooth Ridge. I saw 'em, and I figured they wouldn't be too happy about a witness to what they done. After they killed the moose, I kept goin'. I'd meant to ask 'em to trade for some supplies, but once I saw what they did, I left 'em behind."

John Henry was a nervous man, and a smart one. Walking up on a poacher could be a dangerous practice. When he saw what was happening, he'd eased back into the forest. "I can bring you some canned goods and things." She pointed up to the top of the trail. "I have to come this way tomorrow, so I'll leave some stuff at the top there."

"I won't be caught in no trap."

"No trap, John Henry. You've helped me more than you know. Think of it as a trade for the information you gave me."

"Trade is good. I don't have money to pay."

"Did you see anyone else up around the area that afternoon?"

He considered. "I can't say I seen anyone for sure. There was someone in the woods though." He rubbed his jittery arm with his other hand. "Creepy like. Someone slidin' through the trees. Couldn't see 'em clear cause they was always in shadow."

"Could it have been a hiker?"

"Could have." He hesitated. "Didn't move like a hiker, though. Fact is, it didn't move like a human, either."

The thick edge of the thundercloud shifted over the sun, casting the small valley into deep shadow as if night had suddenly fallen. Rachel looked to the sky, the clouds roiling like angry water.

"You'd best get goin'. Watch that third curve. The gravel's washed off and there's no purchase for your tires."

She nodded. "I'll be back tomorrow with some supplies."

She was almost at the top of the incline when he called out to her. Taking a careful grip in the steep trail with her boot toes, she turned back to see that he had almost faded into the darkness.

"Don't go in the woods alone, Rachel. There is somethin' in there that ain't right. I felt it before. Something in the trees is mighty pissed off."

DEREK TRAILED the man shifting between the big spruce trees. He was bird-dogging one of the Natives, the spokesman from his meeting in the house with the stone faces, but he couldn't remember what the man had said his name was. Bear something or other. Odd how the Native names, which were unusual, actually began to run together in his head. When the man in front of him slowed, Derek also slowed, careful to keep a good distance behind. If the Indians were up to something, he intended to find out what it was.

It had been Justine who suggested that Derek follow the Indian. And she was right--there was no better way to know what they were up to than to spy on them and see with his own eyes. So far, though, it had only been a tough hike through rugged wilderness. Bear Whoever just seemed like he was out for a stroll, without any real purpose. If so, Derek had wasted a whole afternoon.

In the distance he heard the rumble of what could have been heavy equipment or thunder. The storm that was blowing in was making it more and more difficult to stay back from the Indian yet not lose him. The darker shadows of the forest had begun to blur, and now Derek had to pay strict attention to the figure in front of him or risk giving up his vigil.

Lightning zigged across the sky, popping close enough that he could smell the sizzle of sulphur. When his eyes had recovered from the flash, the Indian was gone. Vanished. As if the thunderbolt had zapped him to the Happy Hunting Ground or wherever the fuck dead Indians went.

Fuck this shit. He turned back, ready to retrace his steps to the ATV he'd left parked three miles behind. As it was, he was going to have a freezing, wet ride back to the hideout—and he had nothing to show for all his time and effort. He hunched his shoulders and ducked his head as the first rain began to fall.

He felt a gentle shove and turned to see who'd pushed him. Suddenly, something grabbed his right foot. Before he could recover, he was snatched upside down. Dangling by one leg and bobbing as if he was on the end of a bungee cord, he couldn't get his eyes to focus. He saw someone standing in the trees, but the motion of his body suspended in air and the upside down view disoriented him.

"Hey!" He kicked out with his left leg, but it only made him bounce harder. "Hey, lemme go."

He spun, dangling by his right leg. Reality touched him like a hand from the grave. The dead hunters had been hung upside down. Before they'd been skinned and decapitated.

"Hey!" He lashed out with his free leg again. "Shit! Let me down. Shit!" Panic set in and he felt the gorge rise in his throat. "Let me down!"

The whack of the wood on his skull was so sudden that he felt nothing before he was lost to the blackness that surrounded him.

CHAPTER SIX

The storm cloud writhed in the Southern sky, moving in fast, another aggravation in a day fraught with obstacles. Reginald "Mullet" Bellows cursed god, the mountains and the weather. On his way up the mountain, he'd been pulled over for an expired tag by that son-of-a-whore Deputy Scott Amos, then he'd had to sit another ten minutes for the lecture on danger in the woods that the deputy delivered with such enjoyment, and then he'd finally gotten up to the campsite only to discover that Burl Mascotti hadn't left the supplies where they were supposed to be. He'd found them stuck in the hollow trunk of a pine tree, not a spruce, after a thirty-minute search in the failing light. Burl was a fucking moron. He couldn't recognize one tree from another. His only redeeming quality was that he'd do whatever it took to make money. And he could bullshit with the best of them. He had a great act going—a philanthropist who took in unwanted zoo animals to give them a retirement home. Right. What he gave them was a shot of drugs so strong they couldn't even stagger away from the stupid fuckers who paid upwards of ten grand to shoot a panther or a tiger.

Mullet went to the cage where the black panther waited.

She was older, but she wasn't too old to hurt him if she got the chance. She'd been docile when they'd first gotten her, but now she'd caught a whiff of her future, and she meant to go down fighting. He'd have to use the dart gun on her, but not until tomorrow. There was no way the two lawyers from Albany, New York, would make it to the campsite in a flood, so the kill would have to be postponed. Damn it all to hell. He'd hoped to move the lawyers in, set up the cat, let them shoot it, and get them back on a plane tomorrow with their trophy left down at Zell's Taxidermy to be stuffed.

Now, the weather had thrown a monkey wrench in his plans. The cat would just have to sit in the cage another day. Hell, it was going to be killed anyway, so another twelve hours of discomfort wouldn't matter.

He reached into his inside jacket pocket and pulled out a pouch. He rolled the joint with dexterity. He thought about giving the cat some water, but after the first two tokes, he didn't feel like doing anything until Burl showed up. Burl said this cat came from some small zoo in Mississippi. They'd given it to Burl, thinking it was going to a loving home. He chuckled aloud at the irony.

The sound of an ATV roaring through the thick trees told him Burl was on the way. He saw the headlight bobbing along the dim trail.

He lost sight of the headlight when it went into a small hollow. When it came back up it was only five yards from his extended feet. He waited for his friend to turn off the engine.

"Burl, you bring any beer?"

Burl kicked his foot, hard. "Those fucking lawyers didn't want to spend the night in the rain. I tried to get them to come on up and finish this, but they wouldn't think of getting their expensive guns wet."

"I figured as much. Pansy asses." He re-lit the joint, took a hit and offered it to Burl. "This'll make it all seem better." He frowned. "Hey, fancy footwear. Where'd you get the money for boots like that?"

Burl took the joint, a grin splitting his face. "I bought 'em this morning at Abe's Outfitters. Some hiker ordered 'em special but never picked 'em up. I got 'em half price." He inhaled, holding the smoke until he expelled it on a cough. "Man, that's some good shit."

"Once we get the money from those lawyers, I'm gonna make a little investment in this. Buy five pounds and cut myself in for a nice profit by selling it." He could see Burl's eyes light up at the thought of a profit.

"Got a line on a wolverine. That oughta draw some big bucks next week." Burl glanced around the woods. "You think those two murders are gonna hurt our business?"

Mullet ran his fingers through the long hair that hung down the back of his neck. The front and top were close-cropped, a style he'd adopted when he was in his prime some twenty years earlier. The haircut, and a certain way with the ladies, was his signature and had earned him his nickname.

"Naw, our out-of-town clients don't know about it 'til they get into town, and by then it's too late. We've got their money, so they can't back out." He yawned. Damn but smoking dope made him lazy. "I think putting ole Hank in the ground is only gonna help our business. Less competition."

Burl cocked his head as if he heard something.

"What's wrong?"

"I smell gasoline." Burl walked off two steps, then turned to the ATV. He knelt down beside it. "Well, I'll be a son of a bitch. There's a damn hole in the gas tank."

Mullet closed his eyes to hold on to his temper. Burl was such a major fuck-up. "You could tear up a steel ball, Burl."

"I didn't tear nothin' up. Look at it. Someone punched something in it. Like a screwdriver or something."

Mullet stood and pulled the flashlight from the pack of supplies beside the panther's cage. Once he looked at the hole, he had to back off Burl a little. It did look as if someone had punctured the gas tank deliberately. The idea of it made him turn slowly in all directions.

"You see anyone around when you got the four-wheeler out of the woods?"

Burl shook his head. "It was right there, covered up with limbs like we left it."

"Someone found it, though." Mullet remembered a paragraph from the newspaper story he'd read about Hank Welford's death. The state game warden, Jake Ortiz, had speculated that it was likely some poachers killing other poachers. Mullet tried to think if he'd pissed off any of the competition lately.

"Hank was skinned alive," Burl said, as if he could read Mullet's mind. "He bled to death from where the person peeled the hide off him. They took his head and nobody's found it yet."

"Shut up." He and Hank had had a bitter falling out, but he didn't like to think of him being tortured.

The snap of a stick made both men turn to the south. The edge of the storm cloud was right on top of them, a black thunderhead that looked as if divine justice was about to come down from the sky. "Let's get back to town. We can double on my four-wheeler." He staggered a bit, ruing the effects of the joint. Now his imagination was on overdrive and his reflexes were dull.

"What about the cat?" Burl asked.

"It ain't going anywhere. Now move." He had the creepiest sense that someone was watching them from the trees. "Get your fat ass humpin', Burl. I want to get back to town."

"Let me get some water—"

"Fuck the cat!" He roared the words, taking some courage from the sound of his own agitated voice. He was still in command. "Pick up this shit here, and I'm going to grab the drugs up on the top of the ridge where I left 'em."

He straddled his four-wheeler and roared off, leaving Burl to pick up the beer and sandwiches they'd planned to eat while waiting for the lawyers to "find" the panther. He was halfway up the ridge when he heard a high-pitched sound that was neither human nor animal. He cut the engine to listen and was about to turn the machine back on when he heard it again, this time a distinct scream. Burl's scream.

He hesitated, his fear blooming, as alive and powerful as the forces barely contained in the overhead cloud.

Burl's cries tore through the gloom. He spun the ATV toward the site where he'd left his partner.

Mullet re-entered the camp area as the first drops of rain began to fall. Hard and cold, containing small crystals of hail, the rain sang as it struck his nylon jacket. He shone his headlight on the area.

The door of the panther's cage swung open. The lock that he'd taken such precautions to buy so that some happenstance hiker wouldn't free the animal had been sprung.

A blood trail disappeared into the woods.

Terrified, he wanted to flee. He could always claim he thought he should get help rather than search for Burl on his own. He could claim...

The headlight caught the boot.

He left the ATV running as he got off and walked slowly toward the hiking boot that stood all alone on the forest floor. The blood trail ended at the boot, Burl's brand new boot.

The rain came down harder, washing away all traces of Burl and what might have happened in the small clearing.

Rachel shuffled the papers she'd been studying and glanced out the window of the sheriff's office. Night had fallen early with the help of the storm. She was alone, except for the dispatcher, Gladys, who was reading a novel. Judging from the expression on Gladys's face, she wouldn't have paid attention if a bomb exploded in their building.

Rachel rubbed her eyes, aware that she was tired and hungry. She'd done a comprehensive ten-year search for murders where the victims were mutilated. There were plenty of cases, but none that resembled what was happening in Criss County. While statistically she'd bottomed out, she had come across some interesting information about Dr. Ashton Trussell, the dead plastic surgeon. Trussell's background complicated an already complex case.

A shadow fell over her desk, and she looked up to see Jake reading the report over her shoulder. She hid her annoyance with a hello.

"You got something on that doctor?" Jake motioned to the papers in her hand. "What's the story?"

"He was being sued by one of his patients."

Jake's eyes showed immediate interest. "What kind of suit?"

"The kind that can get a man killed." She handed the papers to him. He'd get them anyway, and it was better to show the spirit of cooperation that was vital to Criss County law enforcement if she intended to solve this case.

Jake studied the report for a moment before he lowered it. "He molested a sixteen-year-old girl?"

"Not just any girl, but a patient who claims she was raped

while sedated. The girl's family was asking for half a million to settle."

Jake put the pages on her desk. "Want to grab a burger at Lulu's?"

"Sure." She slipped the report into her desk drawer and locked it.

"A little paranoid, aren't you?"

She didn't look at him as she got her purse. "Force of habit. That way nothing goes missing and there's no time lost hunting for things that someone picked up and forgot to return."

Jake held her jacket for her. "I've got to admit, I prefer working alone. If something gets lost in my office, I have no one to blame but myself."

The rain had begun to slack off when they opened the door of the courthouse. Rachel hunched into her coat. Though it was summer, the storm had brought with it cooler temperatures. "Jake, do you think it's possible someone from Boston followed this guy here and decided to take justice into his own hands?"

Jake didn't immediately answer, and she didn't press as they walked to his Land Rover. He opened the door for her and handed her in. As he walked around, she suppressed a smile. Jake's father, Mel, insisted that no matter what happened in life, good manners could soothe most troubled waters.

"It's possible." He started the vehicle and pulled out onto Main Street. "But why kill someone who might pay you half a mill?"

"Maybe to spare your daughter having to testify in a courtroom. They can still sue the estate."

Jake glanced at her. "Some fathers would do that."

"Yeah, some would." She fixed her gaze out the passenger

window. "And some wouldn't. Like mine." She wanted to take the last two words back as soon as she spoke them. This was one of the reasons she found it difficult to be around Jake. He knew too much of her history. And sometimes, when she was tired and her guard was down, she slipped too close to being the teenager who'd viewed her own life as worthless.

"You know it wasn't you that your father abandoned, Rachel. Your mom made it impossible for anyone to stay around."

"Except for me." Jesus, why not just send out invitations to the pity party? "Look, I don't want to talk about this." She sat up taller, determined to shed the memories as she lost the slumping posture she'd assumed as soon as she thought about the past.

"I've never told you about the day your dad left, have I?"

Rachel felt the skin on her face tighten. "You saw him leave?" It was one of Jake's habits, to reveal things by layer and degree. Sometimes she wondered if he made things up based on the situation.

"Wasn't much to see. I'd ridden my bike to the Little League game and stopped to say hi to your mom. Your dad threw a pillowcase full of clothes into the front seat of his truck and reversed out of the driveway. I figured he and your mom had had another fight and that he'd be back in a day or so. They fought pretty regular toward the end, and it was nothing to see him pack his things and light out for a bit."

There was nothing Rachel could add. They were talking about a ghost, a man she'd never met. Her only image of him came from an old photograph she'd found in her mother's things.

The windshield wipers swished back and forth as they drove slowly down Main Street. On the edge of town they passed Prima Donna's, a modern glass and steel structure that looked out of place among buildings that bore the distinctive stamp of the old West. The studio/dojang was closed. The little tappers and ballerinas were cute, but Rachel liked to work out in the wee hours of the morning when sleep wouldn't come.

"I've grown to love this town," Jake said, his thoughts paralleling hers.

"I know. It's a special place. Do you think Paradise will change it a lot?"

He sighed. "Change is inevitable."

She grasped what he meant instantly. Bisonville and Criss County would change greatly. She took in the empty streets that had seen a bloody history and now a deep peace.

Neon lit Bud's Bar and Lulu's, as well as the local pharmacy. Almost everything else was closed. Bisonville rolled up every day about five o'clock when the work day was over. Growing up in Rapid City, she would've been appalled at the idea that she'd ever find this solitude and isolation comforting. "What would my life be like now if your parents hadn't taken me in and moved here, away from all the drugs and bad influences?"

"I figured your dad never knew about you," Jake said as he parked the Land Rover right in front of the café. Red neon advertised barbecue, and green promised short orders.

She opened the car door and started to get out, but his hand gently stopped her. "If he'd known about you, he would have come back. Nobody had a clue until months later when Junie started showing. By then there was no denying it, and though Dad tried to find your father, he never could get a trace on him."

"You ever think I might not belong to Edward Redmond?" It was a question that she'd asked herself a million times, but she'd never asked her mother. "I mean, Mama wasn't all that particular who shared her bed."

Jake's thumb rubbed the top of her hand. "She wasn't like that always, Rachel. You know that. I think she got desperate. She loved you. For all of her flaws, she did love you. I think she felt trapped by her life."

"She was the most imprisoned person I've ever known." Rachel was impatient to get out of the vehicle and the conversation. Jake wasn't usually so sentimental, and she was wary of falling too far down the black hole of the past.

He nodded. "She constructed a perfect hell for herself, but I remember her when you were first born. I was just a kid myself, but she'd sit on the steps of the trailer and bounce you on her knees. You laughed a lot as a baby. And drooled."

"Thanks for the image and the walk down memory lane." She slipped free of him and stepped into the cold air. "Let's grab that burger. I'm starving. I want to get a workout in later tonight." If she didn't burn off some of the anxiety she felt, she'd never get to sleep.

CHAPTER SEVEN

The burger was delicious. Lulu's husband, Jimmy, charcoal-grilled the meat out back, creating a juicy, tender sandwich replete with organic tomatoes and lettuce. In their sixties, Lulu and Jimmy still wore jeans with peace symbol appliqués, beads and headbands to contain their long gray hair. Had Rachel been one to think in certain directions, she might have thought that between the rows of carefully tended vegetables a weed or two of marijuana might have strayed. But Rachel didn't think that way, and neither did the sheriff. Lulu and Jimmy were valued local residents.

She bit into the burger again, relishing the taste.

Jake put his sandwich down. "Jesus, Rachel, you act like you're starving."

Rachel grinned around a mouthful of meat and bun and wiped her mouth. "I am. I'd forgotten anything could taste this good."

"Cheap date. How about another glass of tea?"

She shook her head. "Coffee and some chocolate pie."

Jake signaled Lulu, who personally came over to take the order. "One chocolate pie and two coffees." He winked at Lulu. "Rachel's trying to empty my wallet."

"Get him his own pie because I'm not sharing." Rachel nodded at Lulu. "Bring him a piece or he'll eat most of mine."

"I'll be sure I make those generous pieces," Lulu said as she patted Rachel's shoulder. "You look good in that uniform. Although you turned a few heads when you wore one of my paisley aprons."

"I like the way you lie." Rachel smiled up at the older woman. She'd moved with the Ortiz family to Bisonville, and Lulu had given her a job. Waiting tables had taught Rachel a work ethic and a lot about human nature. She'd learned to smile when a customer was being unreasonable and to take a twenty-five cent tip with grace.

Lulu went to get the pie and Rachel found Jake was staring at her. She sopped up the last bit of catsup with her bun and gave him her attention. "What are you thinking?"

"I take it from your interest in Ashton Trussell that you don't believe WAR had anything to do with the murders."

Rachel gave a sound of disgust. "Those are kids. I think they destroyed that heavy equipment, but I never put any credence into them killing Welford and Trussell."

"It's just that they were...skinned and their heads taken. Exactly like a hunter does an animal." Jake tapped the table with his forefinger. "WAR is against use of animals for sport. It fits."

"I agree. What a boost for WAR to take none of the risk and all of the credit, but what I don't get is why the real killer didn't strip the skin that contained Hank's tattoo. We'd still be trying to identify the body if not for that."

Jake nodded, conceding her point. "Have you talked to the editor at the newspaper?"

She shook her head. "Gordon talked to the publisher. He's cooperating with us. I talked to the reporter who got the note. It was slipped under the door of the office during the night, not mailed. We dusted it for fingerprints. None. The writing is block print on copy paper with a black ballpoint ink pen. Every store in the nation sells the stuff."

"The editor should have called before he printed that story."

Rachel wondered why Jake had such a burn on for journalists. As far as she knew, Jake's dad had been a media darling. The local newspapers and TV stations had made him a celebrity when he stayed out in a snow storm and rescued two lost children.

"Jake, give it up. The editor did us a favor by printing the confession. If the killer is local, maybe he'll think we aren't hunting him anymore."

Jake looked around the café to be sure no one was interested in their conversation. "That plastic surgeon troubles me. If someone flew out here just to kill him in a gruesome way and took Welford down because he was in the wrong place at the wrong time, we may never catch the murderer."

"That's a possibility, but I think Hank was the target. That silver pinned to his chest must have a special meaning."

"Everything at the scene means something. We just don't know what."

She picked up a fry and dragged it through a puddle of catsup on Jake's plate. "You can mark John Henry James off the list of suspects." She gave Jake a brief summary of her meeting with the ex-con.

"You're sure he wasn't lying."

She nodded. "I'm positive. He didn't kill anyone." The certainty she felt was even more satisfying than her burger had been.

"So what's the next step?"

"We got some prints off the heavy equipment. No match was found in the FBI's IAFIS system, which isn't surprising if my theory is correct that WAR is behind it. Most of those kids come from good families. They won't have criminal records."

"Any luck getting a membership roster of the group?" Jake pushed his plate aside to make room on the table for the slab of pie Lulu put in front of him.

"I don't think they pay dues. I found an Internet site for them but so far haven't been able to trace it to a webmaster. It's mostly an information page, and I'm pretty sure I'll be able to get at least one name—the person who maintains and pays for the website—but I don't see that lead panning out. These people are dedicated to the cause and won't rat on each other. The web page is informational only—no call to action." She looked up at Lulu as her pie slid in front of her. "Tell Marge that the meringue is a work of art."

"Will do." Lulu patted Rachel's dark curls. "Be careful. I hear what you're talking about and it worries me."

"I will." She blew Lulu a kiss and waited until she went back behind the counter. "I think it's a dead end."

"A charge of accomplice to murder might rattle some information loose." Jake's blue eyes were hard.

She nodded. It wasn't that she hadn't thought of that approach. She just didn't think it was worth the effort. WAR hadn't killed Welford and Trussell.

"I need to talk to Adam Standing Bear. I gather he's the official spokesman for the faction of Sioux who are vocal about the four-lane going through." She cut a bite of her pie and lifted it to her mouth. "Mmmmmm. That is if I can still fit into my pants. I'm definitely going to have to work out tonight."

"Want me to go with you to talk to Ad—"

The ring of her cell phone cut through his question. It was a good excuse not to answer him. Jake had worked hard to develop a rapport with several of the local factions of Sioux, including the more militant ones. But she wanted to talk to

Adam without Jake. If she was going to work Criss County, Adam was someone she needed to develop her own relationship with.

"Deputy Redmond. Can I help you?"

The woman on the other end sounded breathless. "This is Hannah Bellows. My husband should've been home today before dark, but I haven't heard from him."

Rachel checked her watch. "The bad weather may have delayed him. Where does he work?" She'd have to talk to Gladys about giving out her cell phone number to anyone who called in, especially anyone with a straying husband.

"He and Burl Mascotti went up to plant some...I mean to check out some camping sites. They spent the night up in the woods last night, but he said he'd be home this evening by five. With the storm and all, he should've been home by now."

Rachel's gaze met Jake's as she answered. She tried to keep a cool expression but her heart had begun to race. "He's only an hour late, Mrs. Bellows. I'm sure he'll be home before long."

"Mullet never misses the NASCAR races. Never."

"Mullet Bellows?" She knew him. He hung out in Bud's most evenings, strutting like a rooster with his outdated hair cut and an abundant supply of what he thought was charm but she viewed as obnoxiousness.

"Mullet never misses the NASCAR. I'm telling you, something bad has happened."

Outside the café another burst of wind blew rain slashing against the plate glass window. "Do you know where the campsite was located?" Rachel pushed her half-eaten pie back as she focused on the conversation and ignored Jake. She had a bad feeling.

"Mullet didn't talk about it much. He said women didn't belong in a hunting party, so I never took much notice of what he and Burl carried on about."

The woman at least sounded calmer. "Does he have a cell phone?" Rachel asked.

"He does." She gave the number. "There's no reception up there, though."

"I'll notify the deputies on the roads tonight and let them know to call you if they see him."

"You're going to look for him, aren't you?"

Rachel watched the rain lash the window on another gust of wind. The helicopter out of Rapid City couldn't fly in these winds. Searching on foot would be a waste of manpower until daylight. Between the darkness and the storm, a rescuer could walk right by a victim.

Victim.

She focused on gaining control of her own anxiety and the conversation. "We'll do what we can, Mrs. Bellows. Someone isn't considered missing until he's gone for twenty-four hours. Although it's raining, the temperature is mild. He isn't in any danger of freezing."

"What if he's hurt up there? What if that killer has him?" Hysteria made her voice shrill.

"I know Mullet, and he's a competent guy. Chances are he's just hunkered down for the night." She stared into Jake's eyes and saw his concern grow. "If he isn't home by morning, we'll launch a full-scale search. There's just not much we can do in this storm. If you had some idea where he was camping, we could check that."

"Well that's a stupid damn answer. My husband is missing up in the woods where two people were murdered, and you can't look for him because you might get wet."

Rachel slowly inhaled. There wasn't any point in explaining to Mrs. Bellows that if she and Scott and Jake and all the volunteers went up to search right now, without a specific location to begin, it would be futile.

"I'm calling the sheriff. He'll put make you do your job."

"We'll do what we can, Mrs. Bellows. I'll let you know if I find him. And you call the S.O. if he shows up, okay?"

Mrs. Bellows slammed the phone down and disconnected.

Rachel put her cell phone on the table. People didn't understand that deputies and volunteers for search and rescue didn't automatically get special powers with the job title. They couldn't see in the dark or fly in gale-force winds.

"Mullet gone astray?" Jake asked, deliberately keeping it light.

"Yeah. Maybe Burl Mascotti, too. Mrs. Bellows said they went up into the wilderness to check out campsites last night and haven't come back." She bit her lip, then stopped herself. It was an old habit she'd worked hard to break. She knew it made her look about fourteen.

"Those two are probably up to a little illegal hunting." Jake nodded toward the window. "Nothing you can do about it tonight."

"Not with the storm. The winds are too high to call out the rescue helicopter. I'll stop by the office and give Gordon a heads-up on this. Call the state troopers just in case he's on the road to Rapid City instead of up in the woods."

Jake nodded. "Mullet isn't known for his fidelity. He and Burl will probably show up home when they run out of beer."

It was the logical assessment of the situation, but Rachel couldn't shake the disquiet that had settled at the table with them. "I saw the storm coming this afternoon about three. What would make an idiot stay out until it hit?"

"You've answered your own question." Jake placed a twenty on the table. "They're idiots. Mullet and Burl are two-thirds of the three stooges and neither of them are half as smart as Moe."

. . .

THE CANDLES LIT the table with a glowing luminescence. Outside, thunder rumbled and rain pounded the windows, but at Frankie's dinner table, conversation softened the sounds of the storm. It was a select gathering, one more step on the yellow brick road to the Emerald City of Paradise. She rolled one shoulder, then the other. She'd had a busy few days with lots of physical exertion.

"Frankie, are you going to be able to keep the four-lane on track?" Harvey Dilson's question cracked like a whip amidst the genteel murmur of her guests.

She met his gaze. Her family had known him since his first election to the state house. Power had coarsened his features and sharpened his tongue. Harvey was used to getting what he wanted when he wanted it.

She gave him a cool smile. "Let's save that for later, Harvey, and talk about more pleasant things." Several of the multi-million dollar investors in the Paradise project—and in Dilson's political future--were at the table, yet Harvey didn't have sense enough to keep his mouth shut. "How is your re-election campaign shaping up?" she asked.

His blue eyes were flinty, but he nodded his head, the candlelight catching in his silver mane. "I never underestimate an opponent, but I don't see any serious problems ahead."

"You have the advantage of incumbency," Frankie noted. "The people of this region have come to rely on you to look out for their best interests."

"Senator Dilson, is it true the new highway is your idea?"

Everyone at the table paused, caught by the sharp tone of the young woman who'd asked the question.

"Miss Morgan, are you an investor in Paradise?" Harvey leveled his gaze at her.

Frankie arched an eyebrow. "Harvey, Justine's parents are the cardiac specialists in the valley. She graduated early and returned to the area after finishing her master's at Yale. Business, wasn't it, Justine?"

"Accounting." Her gaze never left the senator. "My parents supported your campaign last election, and we have some concerns about this four-lane. So I ask you again, was the new roadway your idea?"

Conversation at the table stalled. Frankie considered taking action to put the dinner party back on foot, but she rather enjoyed the discomfort that now marred Harvey's features. He wasn't used to being confronted, especially by someone young, passionate, idealistic and female, which was exactly why she'd invited Justine. A successful dinner party depended on the proper mix of guests. Justine's youth and brains balanced Harvey's political power. If Harvey couldn't handle her, it would at least provide for a bit of entertainment.

"Young lady, the road is necessary for future development in our area. Paradise is a dream, a pollution free industry that will grow our economy in ways you can't begin to comprehend. Folks won't live in a place where access is difficult."

Justine speared a tender asparagus tip and daintily ate it. "You make several points, Senator, which are completely inaccurate. First of all, any development that requires miles and miles of asphalt to prepare for thousands of polluting automobiles is not what I'd call pollution free. Secondly, we already live in paradise; we don't need a high-tech city. Why change perfection? Tell me, why do politicians equate growth and development with progress?"

Frankie watched the reactions of her guests with casual alertness. Richard Jones, the man with the Midas touch when it came to computer technology, had stopped eating completely. Paradise was his dream, his concept, his existence. And he was riveted by Justine. He was a shy man to begin with, and Justine's passion had unsettled him even further.

The sheriff, another big investor in Paradise, put down his fork. His wife was flushed, whether from embarrassment or too much wine, Frankie couldn't say for certain. The only one who seemed to enjoy the moment was Douglas Sparks, an investor from Omaha. The party was designed to introduce him to some of the people backing the Paradise project.

"The dinner table isn't the place to debate politics." Harvey picked up his knife and cut the prime rib. "Not when this delicious repast is growing cold while we talk."

"I'd like to hear your answer," Douglas said quietly. "Since I'm thinking of investing, I'm interested in hearing how the... locals view Richard's project. I mean 'the Emerald City of technology' will affect everyone in the area. Is this what the population wants? Do the residents want Oz in their backyard?"

Harvey's cheeks, already pink from the wine, colored more deeply. He'd been caught off-guard at a dinner where he expected only praise and the closing of a deal that would feather his nest for the rest of his life. Frankie knew for a fact that he'd invested close to a million dollars of his own money in Paradise.

"Senator Dilson, we're all very interested in this question," Justine said. "As our elected representative, I'm sure you're well versed in the public's desires."

"You know damn good and well--" He looked at the shocked faces at the table. "We haven't consulted the locals, as you so quaintly put it. But we will. Once we have the architectural renderings for Paradise and figures on the potential employment and payroll this technology center will generate, you can bet we'll let the constituency know. We'll put it on the ballot for a vote. We certainly don't intend to ram anything down the throats of the community and I resent--."

"So far you've managed to ram the four-lane down our throats." Justine folded her napkin. Frankie noticed she'd eaten the vegetables on her plate but the meat was untouched. Frankie studied the beautiful young woman. Had she come home from Yale to join up with WAR?

"This great country was built on the ability of the population to move westward, and this highway is no exception. We need access to Bisonville and Criss County if Paradise is to become a reality. This development will bring thousands of high-paying jobs to an area that's been economically depressed since the 1800s. It's a good thing, young woman, so don't try to paint it as something bad."

"Do the Native Americans feel this way?" Justine was completely unruffled by Harvey's bravado.

Frankie signaled the servant to refill the wineglasses. Justine was a ballsy little thing to sit at her table with such cool aplomb. She had no doubts now. Justine was a member of WAR. Frankie sipped the crisp shiraz. Life was about passion. Even misplaced passion was better than none. Justine was enchanting, as long as she didn't become too much of a thorn.

Harvey was almost spitting. "The Indians have no say whatsoever in this matter."

"Except that the Black Hills were deeded to them in the Fort Laramie Treaty of 1867. I believe the wording reads that the lands are granted 'in perpetuity' to the Sioux." Justine licked her lips.

Silence filled the room, and Frankie saw that now Douglas, as well as Richard, was enraptured with Justine. Not exactly what she'd planned. She rose. "Let's have an after-dinner drink in the parlor."

She left the room, wanting only to corner Justine somewhere private. If WAR was planning another raid on the road project, she needed to be one step ahead of them.

. . .

THE DANCE STUDIO/DOJANG looked abandoned, except for Rachel's truck in front. Frankie cruised to a stop in the parking lot and considered her next move. Her body hummed with tension. Justine had given very little away, but enough for Frankie to believe she was involved with WAR. The question was what to do with the information. She thought she knew, but she'd have to be careful how she went about it.

During her years at Lida Jane's Preparatory School for Young Women, Frankie had played field hockey, soccer and danced. It was the discipline, both mental and physical, of ballet that had won her heart. Lithe and quick, she'd been a natural. In fact, she enjoyed any intense workout that demanded all she had to give. Living in that moment of total concentration and focus on a goal was one of her biggest thrills. She smiled to herself at the thought of such pleasures and rolled the tension out of her shoulders. Right now she needed a workout as much as she wanted to talk to Rachel.

The front door of the building opened easily with the key Rachel had helped arrange for her, and she stepped into an anteroom where a reception desk filled one corner. The smell of sawdust and sweat brought back a memory from high school. She'd danced the lead in Swan Lake, and been told repeatedly of her "potential." She hadn't been interested in pursuing a career on stage. Dance wasn't her destiny, and though she loved it, it was an aside.

Beyond the reception area she could hear the sounds of someone breathing heavily. Rachel. She walked in that direction, her slippers soundless on the polished oak of the floor. When she entered the large room, she was struck by the serene emptiness of the room, and the lone figure executing a series of side kicks that showed practice, skill, determination and speed.

Frankie watched silently. Rachel was good. Very good. The black belt that tied her dobok held four white stripes that represented long years of hard work. While the movements Rachel executed were as precise and beautiful as ballet, they could also be deadly.

She continued to watch as Rachel leapt into the air and kicked with such force that her body shifted horizontal to the floor. She landed on the balls of her feet with a soft thud.

Frankie applauded, causing Rachel to whirl. "Sorry, I didn't mean to startle you."

"I didn't hear you come in."

"You were absorbed in the movement. I think that's the point."

Rachel wiped her sweaty forehead with her sleeve. "I figured I'd be the only Criss County resident working out at two in the morning."

Frankie heard the message beneath Rachel's words. "I saw your truck here and presumed too much. I'll see you later." She turned to leave.

"Wait up!" Rachel walked toward her. "It's okay. I don't mean to act like I own the space. The manager gave me a key because I like to come in when I can't sleep. The exercise..."

Frankie nodded. "I know exactly what you mean. When I can't sleep...I just thought..." she shrugged and rolled her eyes. "Obviously I didn't think at all."

"Stay."

Frankie considered. "Are you sure?"

"I'm positive. I'm almost finished anyway. If I don't get home and get at least a few hours sleep I won't be able to work tomorrow."

Frankie saw the doubt in her face. "Has something else happened?"

"Probably not. A couple of local hunters are missing."

"Who?"

"Mullet Bellows and Burl Mascotti."

Frankie nodded. “Mullet works on the road crew. When he feels like it. But you sure can’t start a search party tonight. It’s pouring and the winds are hitting gale force at times.”

As if to emphasize her words, a gust of wind howled against the front door causing it to knock against the jamb.

“I alerted the troopers who’ll pass the info on to the road and power crews. If they find Mullet and Burl, someone will call in.”

“If you need some help looking for them in the morning, I’d be glad to lend a hand. I’m a pretty fair tracker.” She felt Rachel’s assessing gaze. The deputy was young, but at times she could be a little disconcerting. Frankie enjoyed that. Most people were so easily manipulated. Rachel was difficult to manage.

“What brings you back to Criss County, Frankie? Jake told me you grew up down South. Alabama, I think.”

Frankie had wondered how much Rachel knew about her past. She’d made it her business to know about Rachel, but she wasn’t certain how much the deputy had pried into her history.

“I spent most of my life in Montgomery, but I was born here.” Frankie hesitated. “Because of a head injury, I don’t have many memories of those early years. I can’t remember birthday parties or playing with friends. But I never forgot how to do certain things. Like tracking or riding a horse. Setting up a camp or building a fire. I remember the skills, but not the emotional aspects.”

“What kind of injury?” Rachel motioned to a wall where several folding chairs had been stored. “Let’s sit for a minute.”

Frankie followed more slowly. When they were seated and facing each other, she answered. “I was shot in the head when I was twelve.”

Rachel’s face registered concern, and Frankie felt her gaze

searching for the bullet wound. Everyone did it. "Was it a hunting accident?"

"Sort of." Frankie shrugged. "I don't really remember what happened exactly, but my mother said my father went up in the hills looking for some cattle that had strayed. He told me to stay home, but I waited until he had a lead and then I saddled Dolly and went after him. He had a pretty good head start, I was a good tracker." She let her voice grow husky with emotion. "I don't remember anything else. I was shot. No one really knows what happened."

She could almost see Rachel's thoughts. "If you're thinking illegal hunters shot me, you may be right. My personal theory is that my dad caught some poachers and they panicked and killed him. I rode up on them and they shot me and left me for dead."

"Your father was shot, too?"

"I can't answer that. His body was never found. Some folks think he abandoned the family because he was losing our ranch. Cattle prices had bottomed out and things were bad economically. It was a tough time, or at least that's what Mother always told me. So the gossip was that he couldn't face it and left."

"But you were shot. He wouldn't have left you."

"They found horse tracks that led to the main road and then some tracks from a horse trailer pulled by a dually."

"That could indicate foul play to me." Rachel took a deep breath trying to contain her frustration. "Did they question any witnesses or find any evidence? Your father wouldn't have left you wounded in the wilderness."

Frankie tried not to show the strange elation she felt. Rachel understood. She was smart, and she saw the obvious.

"Gordon was a deputy then, and he and Mel Ortiz, who was the head of the state parks, figured Dad was too far ahead of me to know what had happened. He said Dad had probably loaded up his horse and was down the highway before I was even shot. Had he known, he wouldn't have left."

"That makes a certain kind of sense, I guess." Rachel rubbed at the deep furrow between her eyebrows. "But—"

Frankie wanted to hug her. She was a stranger, but she saw the stupidity of thinking Dub would abandon his family.

"They did put out a missing person's report and they got a couple of calls. Someone saw Dad working the rodeo circuit in Amarillo and Houston. Then there was an airline ticket purchased in his name in Missoula. I was really sick then and my mother didn't pursue any of it. She said if Dad would abandon us, she wasn't going to track him down and force him to take care of his family."

"But you never believed that?" Rachel asked.

Frankie shook her head. "I think the same people who shot me shot him."

"But a body just doesn't disappear."

Frankie nodded. "I was shot on state land, but Gordon was a family friend, so he worked it with Mel. They found where I'd been shot, and what looked like a practice target deeper in a clearing in the woods. There was no trace of my father or any sign of a struggle." She met Rachel's gaze squarely. "The official version was that I was shot accidentally and that Dad left. I think Dad was killed and they took his horse and his body. I don't believe the shooters even knew they'd hit me."

Outside a gust of wind whipped a branch into the building. Both women looked toward the front door.

"How long ago was this?"

"Sixteen years."

"You never saw who shot you?"

"The bullet went in here." Frankie pulled her hair back to show her scalp just above her forehead. "It came out over here."

She knew the scar was faint and it was unlikely Rachel could see it. "Small caliber, the same that matched the holes in the target."

"So Mel and Gordon figured that someone was practice shooting and a stray round got you?"

"That's right. The damage from the bullet and resulting swelling damaged the part of my brain that controlled motor skills and memory. I don't remember anything. When I came to, I didn't know my own mother. I lost my father in more ways than death."

"How did you get home?" Rachel stared at the towel in her hands.

"I can't say. All I know is that Mother told me everyone was looking for Dad and me. Gordon and the search and rescue were out. Mel had mobilized all the volunteers to comb the state lands. She said she looked out the kitchen window and saw Dolly, my horse, slowly walking toward the house. I'd somehow managed to get up in the saddle and hang on to the horn. Dolly brought me home. Dad's horse was never found. Never a trace of him anywhere, except for those tracks leading to a horse trailer."

"Jesus, Frankie." Rachel wiped her forehead with her palm.

"Hey, it's not as bad as it could be. I don't remember any of it. Everything I told you is only what my mother told me. My childhood, except for an occasional flash or a splinter of memory or emotion, is simply gone." She tapped her head. "I started life at twelve with a clean slate."

"And your dad? Nothing ever turned up?"

Frankie inhaled slowly. "I have this one picture of him. I don't even know if it's real or if it's something I saw on TV and incorporated as my own." She swallowed. "It's hard not to have memories like other kids. But in this image, I see my dad. His name was Dub. I see him lifting me into a saddle on a horse.

His eyes are blue like the South Dakota sky, and he's laughing and telling me I'm going to be the best cowgirl ever born. Mother said I was really good. Dad preferred working the cattle with me over the ranch hands because I was so adept at cutting."

Rachel pushed her hair back. "I feel like I'm playing forty questions with your life, but why did your mom move down to Alabama?"

"It's okay. I want you to know this, because in some ways we share a lot. We've both lost our parents. We've both grown up and made something of ourselves. We both had to learn to be tough. And I'd rather you hear it from me. That way I know you got the straight story—or at least as straight as my mother's version can be. When they got me down off Dolly, I couldn't walk or talk. The local doctor wanted to send me to a brain center in Omaha, but Mother had family in Montgomery. We went there so her sister and cousins could help. The therapy was intensive and it took a lot of physical work. I had to learn to sit up, to crawl, to stand. I was like a baby." Frankie realized her tone had gotten harsher. "I hate to think of those years. It's humiliating not being able to go to the toilet without help. I was deaf at first. I couldn't speak. I couldn't even ask for water. It took months of intensive therapy. My mother and aunt devoted their lives to helping me heal, and in the end I think the stress of it all took both of them. Heart attacks."

Rachel put a hand on her arm. "To look at you, no one would ever think you'd been through anything worse than a bad hair day. Frankie, I'm amazed at you."

"Survival is the strongest primal instinct, Rachel. I didn't do anything spectacular. I merely did what we're all biologically programmed to do. I survived."

"A lot of biologically programmed humans would've given

up. I mean, look at you. You're a superb athlete. You didn't just learn to walk again, you're an advertisement for fitness."

Frankie stood abruptly, fueled by a surge of impatient energy. Whenever she inched too close to emotion, her body demanded action. She paced the area. "I made a promise to myself that I'd never feel helpless again. I won't." She faced Rachel. "I won't."

Rachel rose also. "I don't know what I could do, Frankie, but if you want me to look at the old case files on your dad's disappearance, I will."

Frankie stopped. "No one has ever offered to do that. After the initial investigation and the fake leads that never panned out, folks assumed that Dad had abandoned the family and I was hit by a stray bullet. It was hard times. Like a lot of other ranchers, Dad was overextended, and the bank was going to foreclose. We moved south, and folks let it slide into the past."

"It's hard to let go of something until you know the truth. Once we find Welford's killer, I'll look into your dad's disappearance." Rachel picked up her towel. "It's late. I need to get some sleep. I have a feeling I'm going to be out in the wilderness this morning looking for Mullet and Burl."

"If he shows at the job site, I'll give you a holler, but Mullet doesn't work regular. In fact, he prefers not to work at all, except for setting up canned hunts. He's another poacher Jake has been after."

Frankie followed Rachel to the front door. "If it's okay, I'm going to stay another half hour and do some stretches. I'll lock up."

"Enjoy yourself." Rachel opened the door and was almost pulled into the street by a gust of wind.

She ran to her truck and was backing out of the lot when Frankie waved her to a halt and ran to the driver's window. "Rachel, I had another dinner party tonight. Investors for

Paradise. Justine Morgan, the cardiologists' daughter, I could be wrong, but she might be a place to start with WAR."

"Justine Morgan? She graduated from Yale or some Ivy League school and came back home, right?"

Frankie nodded. "I'm not trying to interfere—"

"It's okay. Why would Justine be messing with WAR?"

Frankie shrugged one shoulder. "Because she's always had everything handed to her and never had to work for a damn thing. I think her heart's in the right place. Look, I understand the objections to the road. I do. It's hard to imagine what this area will be like in fifty years with growth and development. But it's coming, and I'm trying to make sure there's at least some wilderness left to preserve."

"I'll check her out." Rachel put the truck in reverse. "Thanks for the tip."

"I could be wrong about Justine. She's a beautiful young woman with passionate political views." She shrugged. "Since when is that a crime?"

"That's not a crime. Burning two bulldozers is."

Frankie stepped back as the truck reversed and then slowly pulled onto the empty, windswept road. She'd come back to Criss County to do a job. She had to keep her mind focused on that singular goal.

CHAPTER EIGHT

Derek awoke to rain pelting his face. When he tried to sit up, a wave of nausea forced him back onto the cold, sodden ground. He couldn't remember where he was or how he got into the woods. He only knew that he was hurt, perhaps seriously.

The rain was freezing and he shifted in the mud. He could move his legs and arms, even though he felt as if he'd been savagely beaten by someone.

Or some thing.

The images of a creature, furry and malformed, tumbled in his head, bringing with them a full jolt of terror. He'd seen something. Something evil.

He eased up on one elbow, scrambled to his knees and finally gained his feet. Unsteady, he leaned against a tree trunk. When he started to walk, he found a rope around his right ankle.

As he slowly bent to remove the rope, he remembered.

Someone had trapped him. The snare had been set using a bent tree as leverage. Once he was in the trap, the tree had been released. As it straightened, it had yanked him off his feet. He'd been caught like a wild animal, hung upside down and knocked in the head while he dangled helplessly.

Yet he was still alive.

Why?

Why wasn't he dead like the two poachers?

His thoughts were still jumbled, but he had the presence of mind to look around the rain-drenched woods. Was the thing that had hurt him still around? To escape the area, he had to remember the way he'd come.

He'd followed the Indian into the woods. That's why he was in unfamiliar territory. The Indian had led him into areas that were new to him where the lay of the land was unknown. Some motherfucker had set a man trap. And then the Indian had vanished, like a mirage.

Derek shook violently and not just from the cold. He had to remember the way he'd come in, but all of the landmarks were gone, diffused by the rain and the black night. Trying to calm himself, he rationalized that the person who'd caught him meant for him to escape. Hell, someone had cut him down. Otherwise, why hadn't he been killed when he was helpless?

He stumbled from one large tree trunk to another, headed vaguely in a downhill direction. Without the moon and stars, he was navigating blind. But he couldn't stand still. He couldn't wait for the trapper to return and finish what he'd begun.

Wet tree limbs slapped him in the face, and each step made his head throb painfully, but he stayed on his feet and kept moving.

When he stumbled on a path, he almost couldn't believe his luck. He didn't remember it from his trip into the woods, yet here it was, wide enough for a four-wheeler or Jeep. It would take him to civilization, sooner or later. As long as he kept moving, kept his body temperature up with exertion, he'd make it. He couldn't think about brain damage or concussions or anything negative. He was on the trail home. That's what he had to tell himself, until he made it come true.

Somewhere in another lifetime, he'd asked Justine to meet him for dinner and to plan another assault on the road equipment. She'd looked at him with more respect, because the first raid had gone without a single hitch. He'd finally begun to make some headway with her. But then she'd said she had dinner plans. And she hadn't elaborated.

He trudged on, picturing Justine, with her dark auburn hair and moon-touched complexion. She came from money, which made her secure. And she was smart, which made her difficult. But those things didn't bother him, because she was beautiful, and if he could ever get her to see him as a dynamic leader, then maybe she'd see him as a date, too. Or even as a boyfriend.

He pictured her standing down the trail, waiting for him. All he had to do was walk to her. Using Justine as the reward, he bribed himself to move forward.

He'd just rounded a corner when he saw her twenty yards ahead, this time in a pale gown, something almost flesh colored. She'd be cold in the rain, and he fantasized gathering her into his arms and sheltering her from the elements.

He stumbled along, and when he looked up again, Justine was much closer. Except she was dangling in the air three feet above the ground.

His heart registered that something was wrong long before his brain accepted it. But the object suspended from the tree limb wasn't Justine. It was a pale, nude body hanging upside down. It took a moment to register that the corpse was decapitated.

His shriek echoed against the rain-soaked ridges of the wilderness. Unable to stop himself, he screamed again.

He turned to run, but he'd barely scrambled five yards before he realized that to go back into the woods would mean his own death.

He had to go past the headless cadaver to get to civilization. He stood for a long moment, the rain sluicing off his face and running cold into the collar of his shirt. He was numb, but he managed to force his legs forward. He had to get by the body. The rain dripped into his eyes, and he lowered his head.

"Who-who-whoooooo!"

The owl's question drove a spike of fear into him, firming his resolve to get out of the wilderness. He ricocheted off a tree and ran. He tripped, but he kept going, picking up speed as his limbs thawed.

When he saw his ATV sitting in the middle of the road, he stopped. It was possible it was a trap. He glanced all around, aware that an army could be hidden in the dense forest, and he'd never be able to figure it out.

He decided to run for it. When he made it to the ATV, he couldn't believe his luck. His keys were still in his pocket.

He didn't question it, didn't wait at all. He straddled the machine as quickly as he could, started it and roared in a tight circle, headed toward the main road and help.

STRANGE that it was the absence of wind and rain that woke Rachel. She'd been asleep for less than two hours, and her eyes felt like sand had been rubbed in them.

She pulled back her bedroom curtains and looked out on a dawn tinted with the purest pink and gold. Summer mornings in Bisonville, with the Black Hills warming under the sun, could match the beauty of any place in the world.

The only reminders of last night's violent storm were wet

asphalt and the crystal drops that accumulated on the shrubs outside her window.

She'd begun to brush her teeth when her cell phone rang. She scrambled to the bedside table and captured it, answering quickly.

"It's Gordon. We've got a situation. I need you at the S.O."

"Give me ten minutes." She showered, twisted her wet hair into a knot, threw on her uniform and headed to the sheriff's office.

When she pulled up, she knew trouble was brewing. The news van from WKKT in Rapid City was there, as well as camera crews from Sioux Falls and Pierre. A couple of reporter types she didn't recognize were milling around, too. The story had just gone from local to regional, and national crews were probably heading their way. It had to be another murder. Mullet Bellows and Burl Mascotti. Had the two missing men been found skinned and decapitated?

Her mouth was dry, and she paused for water from the fountain when she got inside the courthouse. She walked into the S.O., feeling like a deer caught in the headlight glare of the sheriff, Jake, Scott and Marston.

She stopped and waited.

The sheriff dropped the local paper on her desk. Moving forward, she picked it up and scanned the front page. KILLER STRIKES AGAIN, the headline blared. Skimming through the article, she felt the knot in her stomach tighten. The anonymous leader of WAR, in an exclusive interview, claimed responsibility for another murder. He said he would call the sheriff's office at seven to give directions to the body.

"Until the campaign to destroy the wilderness ceases," he was quoted as saying, "WAR will continue to strike at poachers, the road crew and anyone else who endangers the last vestiges of a natural environment for wild creatures."

"Dad and Wilt are organizing volunteers to search for Mullet and Burl," Jake said. "You did everything you could have done last night, Rachel. We're on top of this, but it's going to look bad in the media."

She put the paper on the top of her desk and looked at the telephone. As if obeying her command, it rang.

Before she could answer, the sheriff snatched it up. Jake and Scott ran to get on extensions and start the process of trying to trace the call. Rachel stood, watching the sheriff's face as he jotted down a few directions.

Gordon cleared his throat. "We'd like a chance to talk to you. Maybe we can negotiate—" He removed the receiver from his ear and replaced it in the cradle. "He hung up."

"No time for a trace," Scott said. "He was calling from a cell phone, though."

The sheriff handed her the paper with directions. "I want you to locate the body. Take Marston with you and work the crime scene, then get back here as soon as you hand off the body to forensics. You, Scott, get your ass in gear. I want the members of this animal rights group arrested. All of them."

He turned to face Jake. "In the meantime, you and Mel take the volunteers up around Lost Creek. As of this minute, Mullet is only missing. Some of his buddies said he talked about camping up there. Take the reporters with you. It'll get them out of my hair and give them a taste of what it feels like to conduct a search."

Rachel started to say that she didn't think WAR was responsible for the murders. The group was taking advantage of someone else's twisted impulses. One look at Gordon's face, though, and she realized that now wasn't the time. He didn't want to hear her theories. He didn't want to hear anything except results.

Gladys, the dispatcher, walked over to the desk. "You're not gonna like this, Sheriff, but a reporter from Time magazine wants to talk to you. She said she was booking a flight. And there are three more reporters on hold. They've got all the lines tied up. They want to know what the killer said. They want—"

"Tell them to kiss my ass," Gordon said.

Jake stepped forward. "Wait, I'll talk to them if you want me to. The one thing we don't need now is for the media to crawl up our backs questioning every decision we make. If that happens, there'll be a major panic."

Gordon nodded. "You're right. Talk to them, Jake. Tell them we'll release a statement as soon as we have something to say." He looked at Rachel. "Why are you still standing here? Oh, yeah, Frankie Jackson has volunteered to track for you. She'll meet you outside."

Rachel executed an about face and left the office, Marston at her side.

"The sheriff is really pissed," Marston said. "This doesn't look good for him, folks being murdered and hung in the woods. Especially not with him all involved in that new high-tech community. I heard he's one of the investors. That whole deal could go sour if folks are afraid to live around here."

Rachel handed the directions to Marston. "I'll drive, you navigate. Let's get this done."

CHAPTER NINE

Frankie tapped on the driver's window and realized she'd startled Rachel. She offered an apologetic grin and held up a camera.

When Rachel rolled down the glass, Frankie leaned forward. "Gordon said I might be helpful as a tracker."

Marston gave her a grin that told her he appreciated the faded jeans that molded to her body and the thermal shirt that clung to her back and breasts. Though her wardrobe was casual, it was selected with thought.

"Hop in." Rachel signaled to the back seat. "We're headed up toward Granite Gulch."

Frankie slipped into the vehicle, nodding at Marston as she closed the door. The set of Rachel's head and the rigidity of her shoulders spoke volumes about the pressure she was under. "I hope I can help," Frankie said.

"We can use all the help we can get," Marston said. "If it's anything like the last one, though, it ain't gonna be pretty."

"Gordon said there was a decapitated body?" She left the question open. This third murder had caught her completely off-guard. She had to get to the crime scene—to see it for herself—before the law officials dismantled it. There were things to be learned from the scene.

"That's what the spokesman for WAR is saying." Rachel kept her eyes on the road as she pressed the Land Rover to top speed on the wet asphalt. The storm had blown debris around the town, and Rachel dodged trash cans and torn awnings.

"You really think those kids are killing people?" Frankie asked.

"I don't know. We'll be able to tell more when we get there."

Frankie nodded. "True. I know these woods. I studied all the geographic maps when Belker was planning the construction. I even know some shortcuts that aren't on the forestry maps." She checked the small, expensive camera she held. "And Gordon asked me to document the crime scene for him until the Rapid City crew gets there."

"That's a good idea." Marston grinned at Frankie. "You're gonna be a big help."

When Rachel didn't say anything, Frankie put a hand on the back of her seat. "I'm not some voyeur or curiosity seeker, Rachel. My career is riding on this project. My crew is losing its nerve. If I can't keep them working, the roadway is history. If this crew shuts down, I'm screwed. I want to go along to help. And I am a good tracker."

Marston cleared his throat. "Frankie's dad, Dub Jackson, was one of the best trackers in these parts. When she was just a kid, he'd take her along on search-and-rescue rides."

"I can be a help," Frankie said softly.

"And I thank you, but right now I have to focus." Rachel swerved to miss a tree that was partially in the road. "Marston, radio back to the office and see if Scott found out anything about Bellows."

Marston keyed the radio. "Gladys, what's the word on Mullet and Burl?" he asked.

There was a burst of static, then the voice of the dispatcher. "Not good, K-4. The wife is hysterical. No sign of her husband or Burl."

"Keep us posted," Marston said before he signed out.

Frankie watched the familiar scenery flash by the window. Rachel drove too fast, but with great competence. She studied the back of the deputy's head. Her dark hair was still wet, clamped into place.

They climbed higher into the hills, the sunshine almost too bright, creating thick shadows in the trees and casting the hills in black relief.

After the Civil War, this land had been given to the various Sioux tribes in the Treaty of Fort Laramie. The land had been considered too savage for the white settlers who were spreading west from the Missouri River. She could easily imagine how daunting the Rocky Mountains had seemed to travelers wanting only to get to the other side, to press onward to California and the streets made of gold. The Badlands with its blistering heat and arid conditions had seemed worthless, the Black Hills an obstacle that could be avoided by a more southern passage. So the land had been deeded to the Indians.

Until the Gold Rush. That had changed everything.

Frankie cleared her throat. "Rachel, there are old mines everywhere in these hills. A murderer could hide anywhere."

"Let's hope that we can put your tracking skills to use today."

"So far, this guy's been pretty careful," Marston added. "Nothing at the other crime scene except two decapitated bodies. And we still haven't found the heads. But we might get lucky today."

Rachel slowed. Something was in the road ahead. "Damn."

A huge spruce had fallen. "I guess we're going to have to hike in. When we get radio contact, we need to call for a road crew."

"Fine by me." Frankie climbed out. "I could use a walk."

"According to the map, we still have about two miles to go up that timber trail," Rachel said as she got out and stretched. She caught the gaze of both of her companions. "Thank you both for being here. I'm glad for your help. Now let's do this."

Half an hour later, Rachel wiped the sweat from her forehead. The climb had been mostly uphill and made more difficult in places by loosened shale. The storm had rutted the minimal road the wildlife crews maintained, and now the uneven terrain and loose rocks made even walking difficult. She was beginning to wonder if WAR had played the sheriff's office and everyone else for a fool. There was no sign of the body where the WAR spokesman had claimed it would be.

Frankie touched her arm. "There are tire tracks there. You might want to mark the place to make a cast."

Rachel stared closely at the ground. The marks were almost indiscernible. "Thanks. I missed them."

"Most of the tracks have been washed away by the rain. See how that limb lodged up above this one. Must have diverted the rainwater."

Rachel put down three red flag markers around the print. She'd come back later and make the molds. The tire imprint could be a valuable piece of evidence. Frankie had already carried her weight.

She started walking again, listening to the murmur of conversation between Marston and Frankie. The volunteer was obviously smitten with her. Mullet and his reputed skills with women was their topic, and she tuned it out, focusing on the trail ahead. She didn't want to miss any other pieces of evidence.

"What's that?" Frankie stopped in the road and pointed up ahead where the trees created a thick canopy of shadows. Something pale flashed in a ray of sunlight.

Rachel's stomach dropped. She'd almost convinced herself that this was a wild goose chase, that no one else had been murdered, that Mullet and Burl were holed up drunk in some abandoned cabin.

"Let's go, but remember we need to preserve the integrity of the crime scene." She glanced at Frankie. "You might want to wait here until we check it out."

Frankie shook her head. "I'm not the squeamish type. Don't worry, I'll be okay." She held up her camera. "I have a job to do."

Rachel nodded. "Thank you." She continued up the trail, Marston and Frankie following behind.

The shadows of the pines and spruce were so deep that she couldn't be certain what was hanging, but there was something there, something large enough to be a human and pale enough to consist of flesh. When she could clearly make out the dangling arms, and the place where a head should have been connected, she accepted the inevitable. The killer had struck again.

She was about to key her radio and see if she could transmit when she stopped. Something wasn't exactly right. Even in the dim light, there was something wrong with the body.

"What the hell?" Marston saw it, too.

She stepped forward, her pace increasing. In the dimness of the woods, she didn't believe her eyes. There was a human form hanging upside down from a tree limb, swaying gently in the breeze, arms pointed toward the ground, the head missing.

It wasn't right, though. The body was rigid. It didn't move like a human body. It moved like--

"It's a mannequin," Rachel said, hardly daring to believe it. "Somebody hauled a mannequin up here."

"Who would do such a sick thing?" Marston asked. "Look at that." He started forward.

"Don't touch it." Rachel caught his sleeve, halting him in his tracks.

"It's one of those store window dummies," Marston said. "I—"

"It's still a crime scene." Rachel got out her pad and began to diagram. "There may be footprints or fingerprints or something we can use. We still have to work it."

"The crazy fucker who killed Welford and that plastic surgeon is laughing at us." Marston's tone was angry. "He's up here in the woods playing jokes while we're running all over trying to catch him. He's got so much free time, he can plan pranks."

"He's a clever son of a bitch," Frankie said as she brought out the camera. "I would never have thought of such a thing. This is truly creepy."

Rachel tried the radio but she got only static. "Marston, would you walk back to the Rover and drive to a telephone? Call the sheriff right away. Cancel the forensic guys from Rapid City, and tell Gordon to call a press conference. Either the spokesman for WAR is playing with us or he's dumber than a post."

Frankie held up her camera. "Shall I do the honors, Rachel?"

"Sure thing." As they walked toward the dummy, Rachel felt a chill touch her neck. She swung around to see if someone was behind her.

"Something wrong?" Frankie asked.

She shook her head. "Just the sense that someone is watching us."

Frankie lifted the camera and began to snap photos. "Funny you should say that. I felt it coming up the trail. I didn't want to say anything because I didn't want you to think I was a sissy and send me back to the Rover."

Rachel couldn't help the gooseflesh that ran over her lower back. "You felt it, too?"

"Like someone's gaze boring into my spine. Yeah, I felt it. Several of the guys on my crew have said the same thing. They think there's an evil spirit in the woods." She laughed, but it was half-hearted. "I guess all the environmental damage is coming back to haunt them. They think it's the Skin Dancer."

"The what?"

"It's an old Sioux legend. You mean someone hasn't mentioned this to you?"

"No. What's the story?"

Frankie lowered the camera. "I don't think I'm the one to tell it, but I can arrange for you to hear it from someone who knows it intimately. Maybe this afternoon."

"And who would that be?"

"Adam Standing Bear. He knows a great deal about Sioux folklore."

"I've been wanting to talk to Mr. Standing Bear."

"I can arrange it for you." Frankie moved carefully around the mannequin, photographing it from all directions. She stopped when she was on the west side. Bending over, she examined something on the ground.

"What is it?" Rachel asked.

Frankie squatted. "You'd better take a look at this."

Rachel knelt beside Frankie. Half-buried in the mud was a hair clamp. She used a stick to slowly pry it loose from the mud. The clamp was beautiful, a twist of gold with what looked to be real pearls along the rim.

"It looks expensive," Rachel said.

"It is. And I'm almost positive I know who it belongs to."

"Who?" Rachel felt a rush of excitement.

"Justine Morgan. In fact, she was wearing one exactly like it at my dinner party last night."

Rachel absorbed the information and what it might mean. "I think I'm going to have to bring Miss Morgan into the sheriff's office for questioning."

Frankie nodded. "Sounds like the thing to do."

Rachel pulled an evidence bag from her pocket and captured the hair clamp. It was the first solid piece of evidence against a living, breathing suspect they had.

CHAPTER TEN

"Could you quit yelling long enough to get me a glass of water?" Derek's tongue had stuck to his teeth his mouth was so dry. He'd shown up at Justine Morgan's apartment expecting her to praise him for his latest endeavor. Instead, she'd been furious.

"Derek, you act without thinking." Justine stomped into the kitchen.

He heard the tap running and then her returning footsteps. His head was pounding and his leg throbbed. All he really wanted to do was curl up on the sofa and sleep. Whenever he closed his eyes, he saw that body dangling in the night, a whisper of pale skin illuminated by lightning. He'd managed to get the ATV down to his vehicle and drive into town, and somewhere along the way he'd concocted the brilliant plan of calling the newspaper and claiming another murder for WAR. Only Justine didn't seem to think his plan was so smart. He tried to swallow and couldn't.

"Here." Justine put the water in his hand. "You've made it dangerous for all of us. They're hunting for us, Derek, and they aren't as stupid as you think. Mom said someone had called her office, asking about my 'affiliations.'"

Derek didn't think he could feel worse, but the spurt of anxiety her words generated made his heart pound, which in turn increased the pain in his head and leg. "Why did they talk to your mom?"

"From what Mom understood, they're checking all the upper-class young people. They have sort of a profile of the type of person who would belong to WAR. White," she ticked the items off, finger by finger--"wealthy, educated, unemployed." She pointed at him. "All because you had to say we'd killed those two men. And now you did it again!"

"The benefits outweigh the negatives." He felt the glass nearly slip from his hand, but he tightened his fingers in time. "I don't feel well, Justine. Would you please stop yelling at me?"

She paced the floor. Twice she started to say something but he saw with relief that she stopped herself. At last she sat down in front of him on a footstool that looked to be hand-embroidered. Her apartment held decorating touches he'd never expected. A Louis XIV sofa, a heavy mahogany secretary—the kind of antiques he associated with his mother and her bridge club. He was beginning to understand that he didn't know Justine at all. The weariness was too much. He let his eyelids close and his head fall back against the sofa.

"So I went to that dinner party last night."

Her tone of voice made him open his eyes. "And?"

"I met Senator Dilson and several of the men who want to invest in Paradise." Her voice mocked the meaning of the word.

Derek was suddenly interested. "Did you talk to them?"

Justine laughed, and it wasn't pretty or musical. "I'm not an idiot. If I'd tried to talk to them about how this new city will destroy thousands of acres of wilderness, they would have walked away and ignored me." She took the glass from his hand and put it on the table beside him. "I have a better plan."

He didn't like the sound of that.

"While you're stirring up trouble for all of us with your big mouth, I'm going to get on the inside."

"How?"

"I'm having dinner with Richard Jones." When he was looking at her, she finished. "He likes me." She smiled, and Derek thought suddenly of a fox, lovely and cunning.

"Jones is the brain behind all of it," he said. "Without him, it won't happen. If you could convince him--"

"I know. But first I have to get to know him. Frankie Jackson gave me the key to the city, and soon she's going to be out of a job."

Derek could only stare at her. Justine was smart, smarter than anyone he knew. She was dedicated to stopping the road and the destruction of the wilderness. But what young woman could resist the power offered by a business man with millions of dollars at his disposal.

"How are you going to make Jones change his mind?"

"My parents are investors in the concept, too, and I've learned one thing from listening to my father's boring dissertations on wealth and investments."

"What?" Derek hadn't even bothered to listen to his mother's attempts to involve him in business strategies.

"Timing is everything, Derek. I may not be able to stop the development forever, but if I can distract Jones long enough, I may be able to change the entire time table and therefore everything."

"I don't think this is a good plan."

"It's perfect."

"It sounds like you're willing to prostitute yourself to distract this guy."

Justine's laughter was rich and amused. "People should be willing to sacrifice for a cause. I can work them from the inside.

I'll know what they're planning before they know themselves, and we can throw a few monkey wrenches into the works."

He had a sudden picture of her dressed to kill and on the arm of Richard Jones at some D.C. function. Spying only sounded glamorous when it was him playing James Bond. "Whatever their plans, Justine, they'll have to announce them publicly. Knowing them a few days in advance won't be of any real use."

The look she gave him made him shut up. "How did you hurt your leg?" she asked.

It was another of her unnerving tactics. She switched topics suddenly, but never without a purpose. He reached for the water and took another swallow. He wasn't about to admit that he'd been caught in a man snare. She already thought he was inept. "I fell into a ravine last night. In the woods, when I was coming back down."

"You never told me why you were in the woods," she said. "What were you doing up there by yourself?"

"I'd followed Adam Standing Bear. Remember? It was your idea that I follow him and see what he was up to."

"And?"

Derek shrugged. "It's possible the Indians are behind the killings."

Justine's answer was another enigmatic smile. "Do you really think the Native Americans are finally killing the men who've slaughtered their animals since the 1800s?" she asked.

"If we could join forces..." He didn't finish. Justine was distracted by the ringing of her cell phone.

"Shit, it's my mother. If I don't answer, she'll send the posse over here to check on me." She flipped open the phone with a curt hello. She listened for a moment, and Derek could see the impatience in her face.

"I have plans—" She broke off and sighed. "I'll be there in

half an hour."

After she put the phone down, she gave it the finger. "Fuck her. I have to go to her office and work. The receptionist isn't coming in, and the regular floater is on vacation. The patients are complaining."

Derek had to admit that he took a tiny bit of pleasure in seeing someone pull Justine's strings. "Hey, it's only for a day. My mother's trying to get me to take a full-time job. She said if I don't find gainful employment pronto, she'll quit sending money."

Justine picked up her car keys. "I have to go. I have no idea why Hannah stays married to that moron Mullet. She's okay, but he's always doing something stupid and making her miss work. He's AWOL again and she's crying and whining. I told Mom the last time this happened that she should fire her."

"Can I stay here a while? Until my head stops hurting?"

She walked to him and turned his head so she could see the knot. "Okay. There's some bread and cheese in the kitchen."

"Thanks."

"If the phone rings, don't answer it. I'm expecting Richard to call, and I don't need the complication."

She was gone before he could even frame a reply.

THE ENTIRE MANNEQUIN had been dusted for prints. Nothing. Marston had gone down to Zimlich's Dry Goods to see if any of his mannequins were missing and had learned that Louis Zimlich had disposed of three unwanted mannequins—two female and one male—only two nights before. He'd put them out in the back of the store for garbage pickup. All three dummies had gone missing before the trash truck could arrive. Louis hadn't given it another thought, assuming kids had taken the dummies for a practical joke.

Rachel shuffled the stack of papers in front of her. The tracks at the crime scene, if the hanging of a dummy could be considered a crime, had been muddled by the rain. Except for the one Frankie had pointed out. Rachel had made an impression on her way down the mountain. Now the lab guys were trying to match the tread with a brand.

The photos Frankie had taken were in a stack to Rachel's left, and she picked them up to study them again. True to her word, Frankie had e-mailed them as soon as she got to her computer. The Criss County Sheriff's Department wasn't loaded with technology, but Rachel had been able to make prints to better examine them. In the morning light, the crime scene looked laughable, and Rachel had to wonder if WAR had set the whole thing up as a publicity stunt.

The phone on her desk rang, and she picked it up. "Deputy Redmond."

"It's Hannah Bellows. My husband is still missing. Why aren't you looking for him? Why are you sitting on your ass doing nothing? I've been up all night worried sick while you sat on your hands. I want--"

Rachel pulled a pad toward her. "Didn't Deputy Amos stop by and talk with you?" Scott had said he was going to the Bellows home to tell Hannah the reported body was only a mannequin.

"He came and told me that the dead body was a hoax. That may be well and good for you, but my husband is still missing. If you'd quit playing with dummies and look for my husband, you might earn your paycheck."

Rachel held the phone away from her ear and shot Gladys a black look. The dispatcher lifted a hand in denial.

"We have two search parties up in the woods." Rachel had been chapped that the sheriff had ordered her to stay in the office while he went out with Jake to search for Mullet and

Burl. "And the helicopter from Rapid City is en route. Once they arrive, they can cover more ground at a quicker pace. If you could give us some idea where your husband and Burl might have been camping..."

"If I knew where they were, I'd drive up there myself and see what happened to them. Do you understand plain English? Mullet didn't discuss his hunting trips with me."

Another line rang, and Scott picked it up. He looked up at her, signaling with his hand that she needed to take the call.

Mrs. Bellows kept talking. "They generally went up around Dixon Point, but I can't be sure this time. Mullet likes to keep his camping spots to himself so he won't be bothered."

"Thank you, Mrs. Bellows. We'll be in touch." Rachel disconnected. Scott was waving at her like he was on fire. "What?"

"It's for you. The guy is pretty upset, and he said he wouldn't talk to anyone but you."

She punched the second line. "Deputy Redmond."

"Rachel, it's John Henry." His voice was shaking. "I walked down to one of the summer cabins, and the folks let me use the phone. You need to get up here."

"What's going on?" Rachel asked. John Henry sounded drunk, or worse.

"I found something," he whispered.

He sounded frightened, and Rachel spoke calmly. "What did you find, John Henry? Just tell me."

"It's best if you come right away."

"Look, I've got a couple of missing men and the sheriff left me here in the office. Tell me what you found." She hadn't meant to encourage John Henry to call her every time the wind blew.

"Maybe I found one of them missing men. Or at least a part of one of them. I found a foot."

CHAPTER ELEVEN

Pure white light streamed into Mullet's eyes. For a minute he thought he was in heaven, the illumination was so intense, so...holy. Then he realized he was on the bare floor of a cabin and he was cold. His clothes were wet, and he'd been dragged through a fetid bog. In places the mud had begun to dry and cake. It wasn't until he tried to move that he realized he was seriously injured. His right arm functioned, but his left didn't respond to his commands.

And his neck was throbbing. His throat and tongue were swollen to the point he could only make grunting noises. He traced the fingers of his right hand under his chin and felt something sticky and wet. When he held his hand up, it was covered in blood. He remembered then. And with the return of memory came terror.

He'd discovered the empty cage and had been flying down the mountain on the four-wheeler when he'd found Burl's boot with a foot and leg bone still in it, gnawed off at the shin. Gnawed! Someone had opened the panther's cage. He'd thought the old cat was beyond any real violence. He'd considered giving her a sedative, but he was afraid as old as she was that she'd keel over before the hunters got a chance to shoot her, so he hadn't given it to her.

Someone had let the hungry, unsedated cat loose on Burl.

As his body woke to full consciousness, Mullet could hardly contain his fear. The events of the night before were almost unbearable to recall.

He'd put the four-wheeler in high gear and headed back to his truck at full speed. That's when he'd hit the trip wire or vine or whatever some maniac had strung across the path.

He felt his throat again and wondered if the intention had been to decapitate him. It had almost worked. The wire had been put at the perfect level. He'd been pulled off the four-wheeler by his neck, and that was the last thing he remembered, until now.

He turned his head to take in the rough wood of the floor. He was in a cabin, most likely one of the old hunting camps. He saw a table and chair legs. Close to a dead fireplace, a cheerful rag rug covered the cold floor. When he looked in the other direction, he could see curtains pulled over dark windows. A couple of rocking chairs were set side-by-side, an oil lamp on a table between them. The cabin spoke of intimacy shared between two adults.

Though he racked his brain, Mullet couldn't think of a single cabin that fit this description, and he'd certainly broken into plenty of the lodges that were scattered across this wilderness. He tried not to panic, fought to console himself with facts that led to something other than abject fear. Someone had found him. Someone had brought him here. Surely if they'd meant to kill him they would have done so in the woods. Surely...

His chest tightened, and he had to do something. Using his right foot to push, he maneuvered across the floor until he came to one of the chairs. Grasping the seat and edge of the table, he pulled himself into a sitting position. He got a better look at the cabin, noticing that it was fairly clean. If he could get to his feet, he'd feel better, safer. Sprawled on the floor, he felt like a helpless baby.

He used the chair as a brace and managed to sit taller, but he couldn't stand. His left arm was useless, and his left leg wasn't behaving either. When he pulled up into the chair, he felt the first full force of the pain--a knife cutting through his body. Because of the damage to his throat, he couldn't even scream properly.

Gripping the table edge, he held himself upright. If he fell back to the floor, he'd never get up again. It took a moment for his vision to clear, and then he saw the tape recorder sitting in the center of the table. It looked harmless enough, but he knew better.

For the first time he considered that he'd been specifically targeted for the events that had unfolded. He wasn't a random victim.

He dragged the machine toward him and looked at it. It was older, a cassette player instead of a new digital model. When his finger reached out to hit the play button he realized he was shivering.

He didn't want to listen, but he knew he had to. If there was a way out of this alive, he'd have to figure it out himself. Listening to the tape was the first step. The button was cool to his touch, and he punched it hard.

At first he heard only the static of an old tape, then a voice came through that turned his stomach upside down. It was inhuman, electronically altered, a voice filled with anger.

"You're a bad man, Mullet. I've been watching you. I know what you're doing out in the woods. How does it feel to be the prey, to be trapped by a hunter? In the hours you have left, you have much to atone for. There's paper and a pen on the table. Write down your confession of sin. Perhaps I'll be lenient."

The tape whirred on, empty of the voice.

Mullet found he couldn't press the stop button. He couldn't make his fingers work at all anymore. Urine dribbled off the edge of his chair.

He put his head on the table and sobbed.

THE BACKDROP of the small cabin with the worried elderly couple, arms about each other's waists, was in stark contrast to the gruesome body part that Jake held by a shoe string. John Henry glanced at it, then looked away. Rachel didn't have the heart to tell John Henry that he shouldn't have touched the foot. He'd helpfully picked it up and brought it all the way down from Dixon Point. She read Jake's expression and realized he had no such compunction about sparing John Henry's feelings.

Scott walked over and whistled. "Looks like something big got real hungry." He nodded toward the couple on the porch. "They're shook up, but they're okay. They're packing up today to leave. Say they're going to be at their daughter's in Sioux Falls if we need to contact them."

"Good. I'd feel better if we could clear out the whole area." Rachel looked around at the beauty. This was normally a quiet, serene summer paradise. But not with a killer on the loose. Even a four-legged killer. What kind of animal could bite through a human leg bone? A bear was most likely. A wolf, possibly. Or a panther.

Jake gingerly bagged the hiking boot with the tibia protruding from the top. "Where'd you find this, John Henry?" he asked.

John Henry stepped back from the force of Jake's question.

Rachel maneuvered so that she stood by John Henry's side. The man had done the right thing, and she didn't like the way Jake was pushing him. "It's okay. No one here thinks you were involved in anything except reporting what you found." She glared at Jake to make her point.

John Henry looked from Rachel to Jake and back to Rachel, directing his answer to her. "I found it up the trail. I heard something yesterday right before dark. Sounded like someone screaming. The rain come on about then and I let it go, but this morning I got up and went to check. That's when I found it. Right in the middle of the trail, like someone put it there deliberately."

"What time did you find it?" Jake asked.

Rachel wanted to slap him. Hard. Instead she took a deep breath. "What Jake wants to know is a time frame so we can begin to reconstruct what happened. You heard the scream about eight last night, and then you found the foot about what time?"

"First light. About five o'clock."

"It's eleven o'clock. That's five hours that passed since you found the foot. What have you been doing?" Jake either couldn't or didn't want to manage the aggressiveness in his voice.

Rachel walked over to him so she could speak softly. "If you don't stop intimidating John Henry, I'm going to ask you to leave. He had a freaking ten-mile walk to a telephone, Jake. He doesn't have wings, so he couldn't fly." She looked him in the eye as she spoke. If Jake didn't quit being such a bully, she'd never get another word out of John Henry.

"Rachel, you're overstepping your bounds." Jake turned his anger on her. "Who the hell do you think—"

"I think I'm the investigating officer. I called you because I needed your help, but you aren't helping, Jake. You're making it harder, in fact. So either help or leave."

"He knows something."

Jake's eyes were chipped ice and Rachel knew it would take him some time to forgive her for this, if he ever did. Jake had always taken charge of her and her life. Now she had stopped him, and in the one place he would tolerate it the least —the job.

She schooled her voice to be soft, reasonable. "I know John Henry knows something, and he's going to tell it to me. Not because I scare it out of him, but because he wants to help me. Jake, he called to tell me about the foot. He could have walked past it and never said a word. But he didn't. Instead, he walked ten miles to call me. So you back off and let me interview this witness without interference, or you leave. It's as simple as that."

Jake's cheeks were red and his blue eyes pale with fury. "You got too big for your britches mighty fast, Rachel."

"My britches are my concern." She walked the few steps back to John Henry. "I just want to thank you. You went out of your way to help, and I appreciate it."

John Henry glanced quickly at Jake and then away. "He's going to make it hard for me, ain't he?"

Rachel put her hand on his arm and felt the slight tremor that racked his thin body. She moved him several yards away from Jake. "No, he isn't. He's angry with me right now."

"He used to do things all the time to people he didn't want you to hang around with."

Rachel thought of the flat tires. "I know. I didn't know it then, but I know it now."

"Maybe if he'd left me alone, my life would be a lot different. He made me feel like trash." John Henry looked into the distance. "I wanted to be a pharmacist. Did you know that?"

A pang of loss pierced Rachel, and she had to clear her throat. She couldn't go around feeling sorry for everyone who made bad choices. "It's not too late to do something worthwhile with your life."

"Convicted felon can't get a pharmacy license." John Henry's jaw had set into rigid lines.

"Maybe not, but there are other things, John. Worthwhile things that could make a difference for you as well as others."

"Like what?"

She didn't have time for a counseling session now. "How about I come up to your place and we'll talk about some options? As soon as I clear this case and find out who's killing people up in the hills and catch whatever animal did that." She jerked a thumb to the bag with the foot that Jake was still holding. She noticed that Scott and Jake were examining the hiking boot as if they might know something. Mullet Bellows. Burl Mascotti. Did the foot belong to one of them?

"When will you come see me, Rachel?" John Henry asked.

"As soon as I can. I won't make a promise that I have to break, but as soon as I can. Listen, Deputy Amos is going to give you a ride on the back of his ATV so you can show us where you found the boot."

John Henry nodded.

"After that, he'll take you home."

"I'll be waiting for your visit."

She forced a smile. "We'll work something out."

She signaled Scott and walked over. She didn't have to turn around to realize Jake was behind her. She could feel his gaze penetrating her spine.

"I can't believe you've still got a sweet spot for John Henry James. The man killed his wife." Jake grasped her shoulder and attempted to spin her to face him.

It took all of her restraint to keep from chopping Jake in

the throat with a blow that would incapacitate him for several days at least. He's always been slightly contemptuous of her martial arts practice, and now she was ready to show him how tough she could be.

She faced him slowly and deliberately. "Fuck off, Jake."

The corners of his mouth tightened. "I'm trying to protect you."

"I don't want, nor do I need, your protection. I'm twenty-six, Jake. I've been through training at the academy. I've taken extra courses at Quantico. I've got an associate degree in criminal justice, and as soon as I can save up enough money, I'll get my last two years. And I'm proficient in tang soo do. I'm not the sixteen-year-old kid who was on the verge of making some really bad choices with her life. You saved me, it's true. I owe you for that, but I won't have you treating me like I'm feeble-minded. Especially not in front of a witness." She had to stop because she was out of breath.

The anger in Jake's eyes faded, and the corners of his mouth crooked up into a smile. "You're a little hellcat when you get riled up, aren't you?"

"Fuck off!" She walked away from him. He'd only succeeded in arousing her anger even more.

"Rachel." He called her name as he jogged to catch up with her. "I'm sorry. You're right. I have to get used to the idea that you're capable of taking care of yourself."

"And I'm capable of doing my job."

"I'm sorry. You are. It's just that I..." He blew out a breath. "It doesn't matter. I overstepped myself. It won't happen again."

Rachel almost didn't believe what she was hearing. Jake never apologized, and he never admitted he was wrong. The Ortiz men, even Mel, as much as she loved him, were testosterone-driven creatures who'd fail even the most rudimentary of sensitivity tests. Yet Jake had apologized.

"I know you're trying to help." She waved the olive branch reluctantly. "Trust me, Jake. If you keep doubting me, I'm afraid I'll start to doubt myself."

He nodded. "Listen, Mom and Dad are going to the presentation Richard Jones is giving on his concept for the new 'techno city.' Dad asked me to invite you along. Since he retired, he's always looking for that grand investment opportunity, and he's high on this one."

"Mel wants this?" Rachel was surprised. Mel had always played the stock market a little, and he'd charted a middle course between using wilderness land for recreation and timbering. It was logical that he'd view a high-dollar development as positive, but it still surprised her.

"He's not certain how he feels about it. That's why he wants to hear the presentation. He says it's up to him to ensure his pension can support him and Mom during the next twenty years."

Rachel didn't want to hear a presentation, but she could hardly refuse Mel anything. All she had to think about was when he'd shown up at her trailer after the power had been shut off for non-payment. She'd eaten everything consumable, and she was hungry and cold and afraid. Mel Ortiz had sat beside her and told her that she was going to live with his family. He'd gathered a few of her clothes, helped her into his vehicle and driven her to a new life in a suburban home with his family. She'd never gone back to the trailer, but he had. He'd gotten her clothes and books and the few photographs that depicted her family life. When the Ortizes moved to Bisonville, Rachel had gone with them.

"Rachel? Will you go?"

"Sure." She forced herself to smile.

"Great. Dad will be relieved. He worries about both of us. You know, he told me the other day we should get married." Jake slapped her shoulder lightly. "If he starts that crap, don't let him get under your skin. He's just planning our futures because he cares about us. If we were together, he could focus his worry better."

"Right." The very idea of it was so unnerving that she was relieved to see the elderly couple on the porch waving frantically for her to come over. "Let me see what they want, and we'll head up into the woods."

"Deputy Redmond, there's a phone call for you," the woman said. "It must be important. It's the coroner, and he sounded out of breath. He said to get you to the phone right away."

CHAPTER TWELVE

"Got the autopsy back on the moose," Charlie Newman said. He was eating something and the words were a little muffled by the food in his mouth.

"It was drugged, wasn't it?" Charlie wouldn't have bothered to call her if something hadn't been fishy.

"Had enough Rompum in it that it couldn't walk. Probably was barely able to stand. It was shot at close range. Two to five feet."

"Hank Welford got that animal somewhere, drugged it, then set up the kill so the plastic surgeon could get his trophy head without having to actually hunt. He just walked up to a drugged, helpless animal and shot it point blank." She couldn't stop the disgust that seeped through her and leaked into her voice.

"Not much sport in that kind of kill." Charlie took another bite of whatever he was eating. She wondered if anything could dampen the coroner's legendary appetite.

"There's not much sport in any kind of hunting today. Most game animals' only defense is flight. That isn't much of a defense against scopes, ATVs, a catered food supply—"

"And don't forget the catered poontang." Charlie continued, "You know those rich guys hire whores to stay up at the hunting camps to show them a good time. That's why they don't want to walk the woods and hunt. Got to save the energy for humpin'."

Charlie was sometimes crass, but he was well-informed, and Rachel had grown to like the fact that he talked to her like she was one of the boys.

"I'm surprised at the number of wives who have no problem with their husbands staying a week at the old cabin." Everyone knew how the "hunters," many of them wealthy, indulged their tastes for kink and everything else money could buy. Prostitutes from Rapid City made enough money during hunting season to tide them over the winter months.

The women would stay at the camps for weeks, supplied with food, liquor, drugs, whatever it took to keep them content while they provided pleasures for men who liked to be in control. Junie Redmond had worked the hunting camp circuit the fall before she was killed. Rachel had no doubt the men had clamored for her mother's movie star looks and her breathless, little-girl voice.

"Rachel, I'm not spoiling your virgin ears with this, am I?"

She pulled her thoughts back from the past. "No, Charlie. Heard it all before. But the news on the moose helps."

"Look, if this killer is taking out a few of these poachers who set up canned hunts, maybe you should just leave him alone for a few weeks. Let him reduce the population of miscreants."

Rachel smiled. "I was thinking exactly the same thing."

"But find the idiot who hung a mannequin. Got us all stirred up for nothing."

"You're right. That's the one who needs to go to prison."

Charlie was laughing when she put the phone back in the

cradle. She thanked the couple and hurried outside before they could ask questions.

Scott and John Henry were astride one ATV, and Jake was waiting for her on the other. She chafed at the idea that she had to be his passenger, but Criss County made do with loans and whatever equipment individuals and other agencies offered. Scott had the S.O.'s ATV. She'd have to share a ride with Jake or walk.

She climbed up behind him and put her hands lightly at his waist.

"Hold on tight," he said as he gave it gas and spurted forward, forcing her to hold him more firmly.

Hold on tight, baby.

She tried not to think about her mother and the things she'd done to put bread on the table. And cocaine up her nose. Junie Redmond had never been an angel, but Rachel's love for her had never faltered.

Sitting in Justine's apartment, Derek figured he'd sunk as low as he could get. All around him were Justine's things, and on the television was his demise. Reporters from the major networks and several big newspapers who'd come to cover the story of the wilderness serial killer were now mocking and making fun of WAR.

The body he'd seen hanging in the woods wasn't human. In fact, it wasn't even a living thing. It was a freaking mannequin, taken from the old Zimlich's Dry Goods store and placed in the woods.

He still couldn't conceive of who would go to that much trouble just to frighten him.

He got up and hobbled into the kitchen for another slug of wine. He'd found an open bottle of a good merlot, and by God he needed something to drink as he watched all his hard work slip from his grasp.

WAR was a laughingstock now. His statement to the press that WAR had taken another victim—a stupid dummy--showed him to be a liar and a fool.

And the person who'd set him up was that damn Indian. Somehow, Adam Bear Fucker had known that Derek was tailing him. The Indian had led him straight into the perfect man trap.

He finished his wine and poured the last of the bottle into his glass before he limped back to the living room where the television continued with coverage of the "woodland prank" as it was being called. The newscasters' tried hard to keep a straight face as they talked about the "person who'd executed a prank that put egg on the face of both WAR and the Criss County Sheriff's Department, and unnerved a large segment of the population."

Screw them! He swallowed a gulp of wine. The alcohol would probably give him a worse headache in the long run, but right now, he needed it.

The phone rang and he checked the caller ID. It was Justine calling from her mother's office. He picked up, dreading the things she'd say to him.

"Yeah," he answered.

"Your luck has finally turned, fuck-up."

One thing about Justine, she didn't mince words. Now she was merely deviling him because he was still laid up at her place. "Right."

"They have another body. Or at least part of one."

He carefully placed her wineglass on a coaster. "What are you talking about?"

"That female deputy and some others are up around Dixon Point. Some old recluse found a severed foot in a hiking boot."

"Shit." He saw a glimmer of hope that it could all be turned around. He didn't know how, but there actually was a body. Maybe...

"And guess who's missing? All of the women in my mother's office are gossiping about it."

"Who?"

"That creep Mullet Bellows. And Burl Mascotti." She laughed softly. "Can you believe it? Someone is finally taking out those fucking poachers." Her voice grew playful. "I wonder who that someone is?" She laughed again and hung up before he could respond.

Derek had the sense that he'd lost touch with his body. He held the telephone, but he couldn't really feel it. The worst thought had crossed his mind. The very worst. It was so stunningly awful that it numbed him.

Justine knew a lot about the killings. Was it possible... He couldn't finish the thought. Justine, with her milky white complexion and auburn hair that caught the sunlight. She was so delicate. But he knew that was only the physical shell. Mentally, Justine was the toughest person he knew. Of all of the WAR activists, she was the most dedicated, the most passionate. The smartest.

He pushed his body off the sofa and limped to the door. He had to find out details. If Justine had done this thing, it would fall on him to protect her. She might come to value him at last.

RACHEL STOOD in front of the empty cage. She wasn't a professional trapper, but she could read what had happened at this scene. She saw the footsteps leading from the cage and then the bloody area where the animal had brought down its prey and begun to devour him. It didn't take a whole lot of skill or imagination to put together the sequence of events. What she didn't know was what kind of animal had been in the cage in the first place, and who had opened the lock on the door. She had a pretty good idea that the victim was one of the two missing men, but which one? And where was the other one?

"Rachel, take a look at this." Jake pointed to a bit of fluff on the side of the cage. Black fur.

She held out an evidence bag and he dropped it in. As she lifted it to the sun, she saw that it was sleek. A cat and not a bear.

"Are black panthers indigenous here?" she asked.

"Maybe a hundred years ago." Jake looked at the tuft of fur. "Sure looks like a panther, though."

"Fucking hunters." She swore softly. "They shoot them in the cage or drug them, Jake."

"If we catch them, we prosecute them, Rachel."

She sighed. "I wasn't implying that you didn't do your job." She was already wearing latex gloves, and she bent to retrieve the busted lock and chain that had been used to secure the cage door. She put them in another evidence bag for fingerprinting.

"Who would deliberately let a wild cat free?" Jake asked. He walked around the cage, examining it from all angles.

She stood up. "They had to bring this cage in here on some kind of four-wheel drive truck. I got some plaster casts of the tracks. You really think this is what happened to Burl or Mullet?"

"I do." Jake motioned her over to the ATV. "The ground is soaked with blood. I think once we get the tracking dogs up here we're going to find what's left of whoever this was."

The walkie-talkie on Rachel's hip vibrated and she pulled it out. "Go ahead, over."

"Rachel," Wilt's voice crackled through the static. "We

found an ATV down the trail about a mile. Looks like the driver wrecked it. And there're signs of someone being dragged off."

The mental pictures forming in Rachel's mind weren't pretty. Her reading of the scene, so far, was that either Burl or Mullet had been attacked by the panther. The other man had attempted to flee on an ATV. "I'll be there in a few minutes."

She found Jake marking what looked like a blood trail. "Wilt and Marston found an ATV down the trail. I'm going to check it out."

"Take my ATV. I'm going to be busy here for a while."

"Thanks." Rachel accepted the key he offered. She straddled the machine and roared down the trail trying to keep her mind blank. The biggest drawback for any criminal investigation was an officer who'd already begun to narrow her suspicions. An open, curious mind was the most effective tool. She tried to recall passages from the textbooks she'd studied. Anything to hold at bay the images of claws and teeth savagely ripping into muscle.

The two search and rescue volunteers were beside a mud-covered ATV that had coasted into a big pine. The trail was clear. What had caused the driver of the machine to wreck it or abandon it?

"You're not going to like this," Wilt said as he walked to a young spruce. She went over to see what he was pointing at. The slender coil of wire was all but covered by the fallen needles and fronds of the trees. Using her toe to kick the debris off the wire, she followed it to the other side of the trail. Boot prints could clearly be seen at the base of a huge fir.

"Someone stood right there and waited for that four-wheeler to come down the trail. Then he pulled that wire tight and clothes-lined the driver." Marston blew out his breath.

"Who would do such a thing? Look here. There's blood, and it looks like someone was dragged into the trees."

Rachel read the scene exactly as Marston had. Once the driver of the ATV had been knocked off, he'd been pulled through the underbrush.

"Let's see where the trail leads us."

Marston shook his head gloomily. "I followed it. It goes back to the main trail at a small gully. Looks like someone had a truck parked there. They loaded up whoever they were dragging and took off. The rain washed most everything useful away."

"Well, shit." Rachel wanted to punch something. "Whoever is doing this planned it carefully. He's always one step ahead of us."

"If that foot belongs to Burl, what happened to Mullet? Or vice versa?" Marston asked. His long face twitched. "I don't like to think what might be happening. Could be the Skin Dancer is at work on 'em right now."

Rachel tried, unsuccessfully, to block out the image. "The question is why? Why Hank Welford? Why Mullet Bellows? Why Burl Mascotti? They're low-life poachers, but this goes beyond a dislike or a disgust for someone. This is personal."

"Very personal." Marston pulled a plug of tobacco out of his pocket. "What are we going to do?"

"Get some molds of those boot prints by the tree. Bag the wire. I'll send Scott down here as soon as he's finished. We might be able to use some tracking dogs to pick up a scent."

Wilt nodded, but his expression said most plainly that he had no faith in the efforts Rachel was making. "Almost makes you want to believe that whatever is doing this ain't human."

The skin along Rachel's neck prickled. "Don't start talking supernatural. We've got to keep our heads here."

"There's lots of old legends and stories about spirits that live in the Black Hills."

"I'm going to talk to the Sioux this afternoon. I'll be curious to hear the legend of the Skin Dancer, but I tell you, whoever is doing this is flesh and blood. They might be clever enough to mimic some ghostly story, but this killer is human. And a very smart human at that."

Marston nodded again. "I'll get with Scott and see about them dogs."

"Thanks." She headed back up the trail, unable to stop herself from searching out the pockets of dark shadows among the trees.

CHAPTER THIRTEEN

Sitting in the passenger seat of the big dually, Rachel admired the way Frankie handled her truck over the rutted road. They'd left behind a large herd of bison grazing in grassy prairie before twisting and turning into the empty moonscape of the Badlands. Rachel watched the scenery pass by. She'd visited the Badlands numerous times, but the stark beauty of the undulating hills and canyons never failed to awe her. The shades of umber, coral, peach, and mauve, shifting constantly as the sunlight changed, disguised the deadliness of a sharp land eroded and worn by centuries of wind and rain. Beautiful, yes, but inhospitable to mammals.

"Where are we meeting Mr. Standing Bear?" Rachel asked.

"At Table Butte. I know Gordon didn't think this was a valuable use of your time, but I'm confident you'll get a lot out of talking to Adam. He knows more about the history and folklore of this area than anyone alive."

"I'm not really interested in stories about skin dancers." Rachel shifted in her seat. She hoped she wasn't wasting precious time on a wild goose chase, but Frankie had convinced the sheriff, and her, that if the killer was using the legend as the spine for his modus operandi then they needed to familiarize themselves with it.

The butte was located on the Pine Ridge Indian Reservation of the Oglala Sioux. Though the tribe had once owned the plains, Badlands and Black Hills, they'd eventually been confined on the reservation. Looking at the land it was impossible not to think of the long, bloody history of the Sioux and the European settlers who'd taken their land.

"What do you make of the foot and Burl and Mullet's disappearance?" Frankie asked.

Rachel was transfixed by the landscape, but she'd also been observing Frankie. Her chiseled face showed no ill effects from a nearly sleepless night.

"To be honest, I think they're both dead. What has Gordon told you?" Both Jake and Gordon had taken Frankie into their confidence, so Rachel saw no reason to withhold information. Besides, Frankie had proven herself helpful more than once.

"He hasn't told me much, only what the media knows. The foot belongs to which one?" Frankie asked.

"Burl. We identified the boot. He'd just bought a pair at Zimlich's Dry Goods that a hiker had ordered and failed to pick up. He was so proud of those high-tech hiking boots he showed them to everyone he knew."

"Then there's no doubt Burl is dead. So where is Mullet?"

Rachel had no answer. Volunteers had combed the area for several hours. "We found a place where it looks like he was clothes-lined off his ATV and dragged for a distance. Then the trail disappears. Jake and the sheriff took dogs up there, but nothing. No sign of the remainder of Burl's body or Mullet or the black panther that escaped. Whoever is doing this has planned this out to the last detail."

Frankie down-shifted for a steep incline. They were

moving deeper and deeper into the raw beauty of the Badlands. In the afternoon light, Frankie reminded Rachel of a big cat, relaxed and powerful. It was part of Frankie's allure, Rachel realized. She presented the soft finish of Alabama, but beneath it was Badland granite.

"Jake told me some facts, and of course, gossip is flying, but I got enough to figure out that Burl and Mullet had a big cat in a cage for one of their canned hunts," Frankie said. "How'd the cat get loose?"

"Another question without an answer. The lock was smashed. Someone deliberately opened the cage." Rachel leaned against the passenger door so she could talk more easily. "Frankie, do you think it's possible the Sioux are behind this? I know I asked you before, but please give it some consideration."

"Anything is possible, Rachel, but why? Why now?"

"The road?" The long hours and sleepless nights were beginning to take a toll on Rachel. She felt bruised, like a peach that had rolled around in a basket. She fought the weariness back. "Maybe the Sioux are trying to stop the four-lane. I mean each step toward development is one step away from the sacredness of the land and the animals."

Frankie slowed the truck and eventually stopped on a small rise. "That's true. But everyone has to survive here, Rachel. Tourism, the casinos, the Sioux are dependent on access, too. I'm not saying there isn't a faction of traditionalists who are fighting the road. That's my job, to make sure their objections are heard and considered. But you can't look at the Sioux as only one thing. They're complex."

Rachel nodded. "I'm at a disadvantage out here sometimes. Growing up in the city..." She waved a hand at the window. "I love this as much as anyone can, but I don't have a claim to it. I didn't know it twenty years ago, or even ten. Even so, I understand how someone could want to protect it and keep it pristine."

Frankie let the truck idle as she stared out the front window. "Once you meet Adam, you'll understand some things better."

"Thanks for taking the time to do this. I'm concerned that you're neglecting your job."

Frankie moved forward. "Adam's dad and mine were good friends, and Tom Standing Bear helped me a lot after I was shot. He never gave up looking for my dad."

Rachel sat up, interested. "Did he ever find anything? Any evidence of foul play?"

Frankie shook her head. "Nothing. But that's the past. Listen to Adam. I think the goals of some of the Sioux are misunderstood. They want to protect their rights, but Adam knows violence isn't the route to take." She flashed a grin. "But remember, it's in my best interest if you don't view Adam as a suspect in any of this, because if the finger of blame points at the Sioux, then it's only going to complicate the road project in ways that'll make my head spin around in circles."

As Rachel relaxed into the comfortable leather seat, she felt the need for sleep closing down on her again. She let her eyelids drift shut. Frankie was so easy to be around. She was smart and upfront in a way that many women weren't. It made Rachel realize that she'd missed the companionship of a girlfriend. Someone to confide in. To laugh with.

"You need to get some rest, Rachel. You look tired. We're not far now."

Rachel nodded. It had been a hard week. Not the hardest she'd ever endured, but difficult enough. Right now, though, the sunshine was warm, and the movement of the struck, the heat—it was all so lulling. That and she felt comfortable in Frankie's company. She admired Frankie. She'd overcome obstacles that would have stopped most people. She was smart and generous. And best of all, competent.

Frankie spoke, her voice soft and lilting with the inflections of the South. "I knew Hank and Mullet. The world is probably a better place without them. But why them?"

"That's the million dollar question, isn't it? Because they were poachers? Now that's an interesting motive, but why not just shoot them and make it look like a hunting accident? Someone went to a lot of trouble to kill Hank Welford. Mullet is still missing, but I feel certain he's dead. I think Dr. Trussell and Burl Mascotti are collateral damage."

"That's an interesting way to phrase it."

"It's my gut instinct. Jake disagrees on some level." As soon as she said his name she remembered her agreement to go with Jake and Mel to the Paradise meeting. She blew out her breath.

"Something wrong?" Frankie asked.

"I just remembered a commitment for tonight. Jake and his dad want me to go to the Paradise meeting. Mel thinks it might be a good investment opportunity, and since he retired, he's all about investments." She sat up. "Are you going?"

Frankie nodded. "I'm in charge of the media. And Mel is right. It's a great investment opportunity. Boring, but then dealing with money often is. It's nice that Mel Ortiz cares about you, Rachel. And Jake. You're lucky in that way."

"Maybe so." She had to be careful how she handled this. Frankie and Jake were friends. Pretty good ones as far as she could tell. "Jake has always been sort of a pain in the ass. And Mel...well, he's always been Mel. Mrs. Ortiz is nice, too, but she doesn't stand a chance with all the testosterone in that household."

Frankie's laughter was rich and light. "We share the same opinion of the male species, I see. Another thing we have in common. But Jake does care about you. A lot more than I think you want to see."

Rachel looked out the window. "We're like brother and sister."

"Okay, I'm not pressing Jake's case. He's going to have to do that for himself."

They turned off onto a dirt trail that rose swiftly on sharp switchbacks. "We're not far now. Listen, Rachel, Jake told me a bit about your past. I know your dad was absent and your mom died when you were sixteen. It's hard to clear that feeling of loss and abandonment. We're almost like sisters in that regard. Grieving and worry killed my mom. I survived, but from what I've been told, I'm not the Frances Jackson that she raised for eleven years."

"How are you different?"

Frankie shrugged. "I became driven. It's what I had to do to overcome the damage to my body. I focused on accomplishment. First it was speaking, then walking, then—" She jerked the wheel to avoid a washout. "I didn't have time for anything except the next step in recovery, and from there, the next step toward a life. Since I've been back here in Criss County, I've been trying hard to live a little instead of adding notches to my belt. Hang on, we're there."

The truck moved up the last incline and leveled out at the top of the butte. Frankie drove another half mile and stopped. Some twenty yards ahead, a tall, muscular man rose to his feet from the ground where he'd been sitting. Framed with the sun behind him, he looked like an ancient god.

MULLET SAT at the table and watched the light change from the zenith of high noon to mid-afternoon. Time was creeping by. Soon it would be dark again, and he knew that wouldn't be a good thing. He'd managed to hop to the kitchen area and tear the tinfoil from the windows, which had been hammered shut from the outside. Cast iron security bars prevented escape.

The door, too, was locked from the outside and the front windows, though unboarded, were secured with bars. If he had the use of both legs and arms, he might have been able to claw his way out, but his left side was dead weight. Well, not exactly dead. His knee hurt like an abscessed tooth, shooting white hot flames into the backs of his eyes. And his left wrist was broken in at least one place. He'd managed to stabilize the pain a little by tearing his shirt into strips and binding it as tightly as he could with his right hand and his teeth.

His gaze drifted around the room for the millionth time. There had to be some clue that he was missing. Who had done this to him? And why? He looked at the tape recorder. There was no need to play the tape again. He remembered it, word for word. He'd been ordered to confess his sins. Jesus, he had no idea where to begin.

Each person had a different definition of sin. He'd gotten Wanda Pyle pregnant and then denied it. Was that a sin? His buddies thought it was self-preservation. He stole tools and equipment from every worksite. He sold drugs. Those weren't sins in his book. They were economic necessities. Take for instance the way he killed animals. Some folks thought that was sinful, while others figured it was the natural order. Man was put on Earth to wield dominion over animals. They were there to be used. Some folks had told him he should take into account what it might feel like to be trapped or kept in a cage or... His gaze moved back to the barred windows and lingered.

A chill of precognition brushed sweat across his forehead. The person who'd captured him meant to make a point about the animals. He couldn't deny that he'd been trapped like a wild animal and caged. And Burl. Shit. Burl had been eaten!

His gut twisted with a sharp pain. Mullet knew there would be no mercy for him if he didn't escape.

Fear gave him strength, and he hopped to the door. Using everything he had, he yanked at the knob. Nothing. Swallowing a curse, he hopped to the cabinets. He flung them open to reveal bare shelves. The drawers he pulled out and threw to the floor were empty. He opened the refrigerator door on a sour smell, but the interior was bare. The refrigerator was running, though.

Why?

He paused with his hand on the door to the top freezer compartment. Maybe there was something there he could use as a tool. Still, he hesitated. He swallowed twice and pulled the door open.

The frosted eyes of Hank Welford stared into his. Welford's moustache bristled white, and what looked to be one crystalline tear was frozen to his cheek. The pool of blood beneath the head was frozen black.

"Shit! Oh, shit, oh shit, oh shit!" Mullet stumbled away from the refrigerator. The door remained open, as if Hank were waiting for an invitation to enter the room.

"No!" Mullet yelled at the head. "No! Leave me alone!"

He wept without shame, standing on one leg and balancing against the kitchen cabinets. He pointed a finger at Hank's head. "You stay away from me, you hear!"

Hopping forward he slammed the freezer door and hobbled back to the table, gasping for breath and control. He had to get a grip on himself. He had to keep his shit together. Burl was dead. Hannah had no idea where he'd planned to camp. He never told her anything because she couldn't keep her mouth shut. She blabbed all over that doctor's office, telling his business, her business, her drunken step-father's business. She never stopped talking. He beat the butt of his hand against his forehead trying to knock out the image of her mouth, opening and shutting, ugly words spilling out in a tirade.

"Shut up!" he roared, almost falling out of the chair.

He arm swept over the table, knocking the recorder and the pen and paper to the floor. He wasn't confessing to anything. Whatever he might have done in the past was done. He'd gotten away with it. He'd lived in fear the first couple of years afterward, but now it seemed like it was another person who'd done it. He shouldn't have to pay now, years later, when he'd moved on with his life and made something of himself. And he damn sure wasn't going to apologize for killing some old animals.

"I'm not writing a fucking thing!" He shook his fist at the empty room. "You aren't gonna break me!"

But even as he shouted the words, he looked on the floor for the pen. It had rolled under the table, out of his reach. He tried to get it with his good foot, but he couldn't manage to touch it.

Cursing and weeping, he slowly slid under the table and crawled toward the pen.

CHAPTER FOURTEEN

A yellow dog came out from behind a rock and barked at the truck as Frankie pulled up. Rachel opened her door but stopped as the dog bared his teeth at her.

"Finder." Adam Standing Bear spoke the word softly, but the dog hurried back to his side where it stood at the ready.

Rachel got out of the truck, her gaze on Adam. He was tall, handsome in a weathered way. He wore jeans, cowboy boots that had seen a few miles, and a plaid shirt. Though his clothes were ordinary, his eyes were striking. He took her measure slowly, not caring that she knew exactly what he was doing.

"Adam!" Frankie jumped to the ground and threw her arms around him. "It's good to see you." She hugged him tightly again. "And Finder, too." The dog sat at her feet, waiting for another word. Frankie didn't disappoint. She knelt and ruffled the dog's ears, whispering something that sent Finder into a barking, jumping frenzy.

Frankie signaled Rachel over. "Adam, this is Deputy Rachel Redmond. And this is Adam Standing Bear."

Rachel took his hand in a firm grip. She could feel the calluses on his palm, and she noticed his fingers were long, artistic, the nails worn but clean. A wound cut across his entire palm, as if a rope or wire had been pulled through the flesh. The image of the wire in the woods where Mullet Bellows had disappeared flitted through her mind.

"This is a beautiful place," she said, walking to the edge of the butte. Below her five horses wheeled and ran. So many of the mustangs had been killed, were still being killed by those who viewed their existence as a threat.

"I wouldn't use the word beautiful," Adam said. "Savage describes it better."

Frankie put her arm around his waist and walked him toward Rachel. "Savage can also be beautiful, can't it?"

Adam looked at Rachel, then into the distance, following the horses. "Only if you don't intend to tame it. Like those horses. They're magnificent in the wild, running and living free. They could be tamed, but in the process, that savage thing is lost."

Talk of losing the wilderness was a perfect opening, and Rachel took it. "That's what I came to talk to you about, Mr. Standing Bear. We have two bodies, a foot and a missing man."

"I know." Adam signaled them to the place he'd been sitting. Rachel approached and saw a notebook filled with writing. Before she could read anything, he closed it. "I take notes on the natural life here. I'm documenting it before it all changes."

"And the road will change all of this?"

Adam looked her dead in the eye. "Yes, it will. Asphalt always brings big changes to the wilderness. Erosion, pollution, tourists, commerce, all of the things that make capitalism the form of government for the profiteer."

"Are you a socialist, Mr. Standing Bear?"

Rachel was unprepared for the power of his smile. "No, Deputy Redmond, I'm not a socialist. I think anarchist might be more apt. A non-practicing anarchist, in the mode of Thoreau or Emerson."

Rachel was at a loss. She'd heard of both writers, but her high school days hadn't been focused on American literature. At the time, she'd been specializing in partying.

"Adam, you're baiting Rachel, and she doesn't like it, nor do I." Frankie took his arm. "We came to hear about the Skin Dancer. If you keep acting like a jerk, Rachel and I will leave."

Adam's dark gaze held Rachel's. "My apologies. I thought I was answering your question. But have a seat. Frankie has this idea that I'm the tribal shaman and historian. It isn't true, but I do enjoy the old stories."

Rachel settled into the lotus position in a small circle with Frankie and Adam. The sun heated her shoulders through the fabric of her uniform. In a bit, it would be uncomfortable, but at the moment it felt good.

"The Sioux believe that the buffalo are a gift to us. During a time of starvation, the Great Spirit sent them to feed us. Because of that, we honor the buffalo. In Sioux tradition, we honor all living things that die to provide for us. When an animal is sacrificed, we dance and sing to honor its spirit, and to assist it in passing into the next life."

Rachel nodded. She'd learned the very basics of Sioux belief when she first came to Criss County, but that was about the extent of her knowledge.

Adam gazed past her into the distance before he spoke. "There was a warrior named Running Elk, a talented young Oglala with the gift of speed and accuracy with his bow and arrows. He never went hunting without bringing food back to his people. It was said that the Great Spirit led him to the game and then gave him magic to affect the kill."

In the warm afternoon sun that colored the world around them in reddish earth tones, Rachel found that she was leaning forward, listening intently as Adam spoke. His voice had a mesmerizing quality. He was an excellent story teller, as Frankie had promised.

"As sometimes happens with the young when they're very talented, Running Elk became vain and arrogant about his abilities. He refused to participate in the ceremonies honoring the sacrificed game. He told the other members of his tribe that he honored only his own skill. No animal could escape him once he decided to kill it."

Frankie touched Adam's knee. "You should explain that in the Sioux tradition, such prideful conduct is generally punished by the gods."

Adam nodded. "The Sioux believe in the order of the earth, Deputy Redmond. In balance. When the balance is unsettled, it must be put back right."

Rachel nodded. "Our justice system is about balance. The scales of justice. The guilty are punished."

Adam looked at Frankie before he spoke. "Except that man is the judge in your system. With the Sioux, it is the Great Spirit, the cycle of life."

Frankie leaned back. "I'm sorry I interrupted, Adam. Please tell the rest."

Rachel had already begun to draw interesting parallels between the part of the legend she'd heard and what was happening in Criss County.

"Running Elk became so arrogant and prideful that he refused to sit at council with the elders. Each day he proved his skill by killing something new, until the bodies of the dead animals began to rot, the hides unused, the meat uneaten. Running Elk's father, the chief, ordered him to stop killing. He told his son that the waste was shameful, and that his actions would bring sorrow down upon the Sioux. But Running Elk cared only for the adoration of the young warriors who lived to hear the adventures of his last kill."

Hank, Mullet, Burl and the plastic surgeon were all men who had no regard for the animals they killed. Rachel could almost taste the connection she sought. Adam Standing Bear held her riveted.

"Running Elk's last great hunt involved the most scared of all animals to the Sioux. He'd bragged that he could kill twelve buffalo on foot, without the help of a horse or another warrior."

Adam's gaze had shifted toward the distant mountains, which had changed to a golden dun in the afternoon light. Rachel thought it was almost as if he watched the story play out against the sky.

"When Running Elk's father, Spotted Eagle, rode to the grasslands and saw the dead buffalo there with the buzzards feasting on the meat that no one had harvested, he knew what his son had done. He knew the Great Spirit could no longer avoid punishing Running Elk, no matter how much Spotted Eagle prayed.

"He turned his horse back to the camp and rode home singing a song of mourning for the young warrior, because he knew his son was as good as dead."

"Did Running Elk die?" Rachel asked the question before she could stop herself. She hadn't meant to interrupt.

"His punishment was more severe. As he stood among the dead buffalo, taking stock of the death he'd delivered and his prowess as a hunter, he felt a terrible burning sensation all over his body. To his horror, the skin on his arms began to fall away. The rays of the sun were horribly painful, and he ran in circles screaming as the skin from his legs and back and stomach sloughed off, revealing raw muscle and nerve."

Adam brushed a strand of dark hair from his face. "Running Elk hurriedly skinned one of the buffalo and used the hide to shelter from the sun, which was cooking him alive. He waited for night, until he could slip away from the plains and into the forests of the Black Hills where the dark shade of the trees protected him. To this day, he lingers there, waiting to find another skin, a human skin to replace the one the Great Spirit took from him."

In the stillness left by the absence of Adam's voice, Rachel tried to ignore the chill bumps that had formed on her arms despite the sun's heat.

"Remember this morning when we found the mannequin?" Frankie asked. "I had the creepiest sense that someone was watching us."

Adam picked up his notebook. "My grandfather would say that the road going through the hills has stirred up the ancient and angry spirits of the dead."

"And what would you say?" Rachel asked. It was a mighty convenient answer.

"I wouldn't say anything." Adam rose to his feet in one fluid motion. "I enjoy the old legends. I collect them and tell them to keep them alive. Most of our history is oral, Deputy."

"Do you believe in the Skin Dancer?" She rose and stepped to face him.

"What does it matter what I believe?"

She ignored his question as he'd ignored hers. "How many people know that story?"

Frankie answered. "Just about every kid who ever went to school in Criss or Custer or Pennington Counties. I was surprised you hadn't heard of it before, Rachel. It used to be a tradition in public schools for an older member of the Sioux to come and tell stories." She glanced at Adam. "Is that still done?"

He shook his head. "No one is really interested anymore.

Not the public school children or even those on the reservation."

"The thing that troubles me is the whole matter of the decapitation." Frankie put a hand to her mouth. "I'm sorry, Rachel. I hope I'm not talking out of turn."

"It's public record." Rachel nodded at Adam. "Both Welford and Trussell were decapitated. The heads were removed from the scene and so far, we haven't recovered them. With Burl, we just don't know. We've only found his foot. And there's no trace of Mullet Bellows. He's vanished."

Adam wrote something in his notebook, and Rachel wondered if perhaps he'd lied to her about what he was recording. When he looked up at her, his eyes were narrowed in thought. "I've gone over the many versions of the legend of the Skin Dancer that I know. None of them involve taking the head of the victim."

Rachel knew she was going out on a limb, but she spoke anyway. "I have the sense that the heads are trophies. Like hunters take the animal heads. That's what's so confusing here. The murders are a little of this and a little of that, a blend of different things. As if the killer were creating his own vision of reality."

"You think we're going to see those guys mounted in someone's living room?" Frankie asked.

It was the perfect question to break the tension. Rachel felt the smile spread across her face, and suddenly, Frankie and Adam were laughing with her.

"God, I hope not," Rachel said. "Hank isn't exactly what I'd call a prime specimen."

Frankie rolled her eyes. "I know what you mean. But the file photograph of the surgeon that the newspaper ran, now he was hot. I might have let him operate on me."

Rachel started to agree but was aware that Adam was

watching her. She wasn't as comfortable expressing herself as Frankie. "Mr. Standing Bear, do you think someone took the legend of the Skin Dancer and tried to use it to stage Hank Welford's murder?"

"Call me Adam, please, and the answer to your question is, I don't know."

"There was a bamboo pole left at the site. A single owl feather had been used to decorate it. Sound familiar?"

Adam shook his head. "The owl is an important animal to the Sioux, but it plays no part in the story of the Skin Dancer. I'll ask some of the elder members of the tribe if it has meaning to them."

"At the crime scene, it looked as if a ceremonial ritual had been performed, a dance around the bodies." Rachel could clearly see the pattern of the dance steps. "The dancer or dancers used the boots belonging to the victims. Whoever is doing this knows a lot about physical evidence."

"For the Sioux, the dance can have many meanings. Perhaps in this case, the killer is celebrating victory. He has conquered his enemy, rendered him dead in a most brutal way. The feathers could be a symbol of victory or a warning." Adam shrugged.

"Maybe it was just someone who had a score to settle with these particular men," Frankie said as she stood up. "I hate to end this, but I've got things to do before dark."

"If you keep lying down with dogs, Frankie, you're going to end up with fleas." Adam spoke quietly, but his eyes held another message.

"Thanks for the tip." She stood on her toes and kissed Adam's cheek lightly. "Come to one of my dinners. This road is going to happen, whether you want it to or not. You might as well get the best bargain you can while there are still points to be negotiated."

He nodded but turned away. He walked to the edge of the butte, the yellow dog instantly at his side.

Rachel followed him. He was one of the most compelling men she'd ever met. "Adam, there was a silver ornament pinned to Hank Welford's chest with a porcupine quill. Does that mean anything to you?"

He pointed into the distance. A cloud of dust began to settle and reveal the horses she'd seen earlier. They'd covered a good bit of ground and were still moving.

"This weekend I need to move the herd to the south. Would you like to join me?"

Rachel hesitated. She had the sense that Adam Standing Bear had told her only what he wished her to know. "I'd love to see it, but I need answers. Men are dying, and I have no idea what to do to stop it."

"Meet me at the base of the butte Saturday at two. I'll have a horse for you."

"I never learned to ride." Rachel cast a look at Frankie, who stood at the truck, watching them with interest.

"My horse will teach you. Be here at two."

When Rachel joined Frankie at the truck, she saw that the other woman was wearing a wide grin.

"And don't even try to tell me this is business," Frankie whispered as she opened the truck door and got in. "I just wonder what Jake Ortiz is going to say. He's not going to like competition."

CHAPTER FIFTEEN

Derek punched in the number to his mother's cell phone, pacing the confines of his apartment as he waited for her to answer. He'd spent the whole day moping around, flipping on the television and turning it off. He hadn't claimed the death of Burl Mascotti for WAR. That moron Mullet was still missing, and Derek understood that if Mullet was alive and able to hold a gun, he'd kill Derek or any member of WAR. It had gone from a publicity strategy to a dangerous situation.

The phone continued to ring and he checked his watch. It was five o'clock in Bisonville, which meant she'd had a couple of hours to put herself into a martini frame of mind. It was always easier to deal with her when she'd had a drink or four.

"Hello, Mom?"

"Derek, darling, you must need money because you never call unless you do."

He hated that she always made him feel small and powerless. "Yes, Mom. I need some money."

"Let's see, what am I funding now? Organic gardening, no, that was the last ten thousand I sent. But it didn't work out. Too many bugs, too little water." She sighed. "Rammed earth houses? No, I think that was 2005, wasn't it? Seems your partner cheated you out of the start-up funds."

"Stop it, Mom." She listed each of his failures like jewels on her fingers. "I need some clothes. And a nice car."

"Oh, don't tell me you're interested in the 'capitalistic trappings of success.'"

She could mock him if she wanted. All he had to do was put up with her long enough to get her to agree to send the money. "There's a new development going in here in Criss County. It's computer related. Clean, non-polluting. I thought I might apply for a job in the marketing department."

The silence that stretched over the phone line made him smile. At last he'd stunned the old bat into shutting her mouth.

"Are you serious?"

He made it a point never to lie to her, even when it would have been so much easier. "I am. I need a sharp suit, some shoes, a fancy car—second-hand is fine, but it has to look corporate and successful."

"How much?"

"Twenty grand?" It wasn't like she was taking it from her own accounts. He had a trust fund, thanks to his father who'd died when he was eight. The old man had left him piles of money, but he couldn't get to it without his mother's permission until he'd "achieved a level of success that proved his ability to manage money." And his mother was the judge of that level.

"I'll send the money, but under one condition. I want you home for the Fourth of July."

He started to complain.

"Stop it, Derek. You will come home. The newspaper carried a story about some awful killings out there in South Dakota. Some maniac is on the loose and one of those crazy animal rights groups is involved." There was a hesitation.

"You aren't—"

"I know all about it, Mom. If I'm working in corporate Oz, I'll be perfectly safe. That's what they're calling this development. Paradise, the Emerald City of technology." He knew how too manipulate her, and by giving her that nugget to focus on, he could avoid questions he didn't want to answer. "Can you wire the money to my account here?"

"Yes, tomorrow."

"Thanks, Mom. We'll talk later." He hung up before she could say any more. He tapped the phone against his palm and grinned. If Justine was going to get cozy with the movers and shakers of corporate rape and pillage, he intended to join her.

He went to the closet and brought out the plastic covered suit he'd purchased. On the floor was a shoebox with a new pair of shoes. Leather. The micro-fiber boots he preferred wouldn't work where he was going. Now that he knew his mother would send the money to cover the bad checks he'd written to make his purchases, he could attend the Paradise development meeting without financial worries. Justine would be there, with Richard Jones. He had to be there, too.

THE BEIGE TELEPHONE on Rachel's desk rang and she reached for it. She was trying to clear the paperwork, but since she'd come back from talking with Adam Standing Bear, she'd found herself distracted, trying to match the elements of the legend he'd told her with what had happened in the hills. And trying to stop thinking about the way he somehow symbolized the land around him. Romantic foolishness, she knew, but it held a strange power. Adam was what most would consider a prime suspect. He had motive, means, and opportunity. If she had good sense, she'd steer clear of him. But he had the potential to help her solve this case—if he wasn't involved. She had to take the risk.

She picked up the receiver and started to answer when the sheriff stepped out of his office and signaled her in. Hannah Bellows' sharp voice came through the receiver before she could get it to her ear.

"You sat on your hands and did nothing. Now Mullet is gone. Everyone in town is saying the murderer got him or else he got eaten by a panther. My husband is dead because you're an incompetent bitch."

Rachel took a deep breath. "Mrs. Bellows, I don't have any new information. I'll be in touch if I do."

"Bunch of Barney Fifes. Why don't you get back to nippin' crime in the bud? Just nip it! I hope they don't give you real bullets--"

Rachel put the phone gently back in the cradle. When she looked up, Jake was standing at her desk. "Gordon's got the CSI report from Rapid City. Gus is on the speaker phone."

She followed Jake into the office and closed the door. It was unnecessary. There was no one else in the department. Every available member of the sheriff's posse, the Search and Rescue, the mounted police, and volunteer fire departments were all in the Black Hills searching for Mullet and the remains of Burl. The S.O. was like a funeral home.

Gus was speaking when she walked to the desk and took the chair Gordon indicated.

"I wanted to give you a heads-up on something at the first murder site," Gus said. "Is Rachel there?"

"I'm here. What did you find?" Something was missing from the puzzle pieces she had, and she hoped the forensic guys could do some television magic and tell her what it was.

"That silver ornament in Welford's chest is some kind of toe guard for a boot. Handmade, ornate, it's a series of what looks like malformed alphabet letters. I've tried every boot manufacturer in the states, and no one has ever seen it. That's what took so long."

Rachel tapped her fingers on the arms of the chair. "Thanks, Gus. I don't have a clue what that means, but then I'm not sure of much in this case."

"Is Ortiz in the room?" Gus asked.

"Right here." Jake stepped forward.

"The owl feather came from a mature bird. Illegal to own, except for the Natives, who have some exemptions to the federal law for ceremonial purposes. We're checking illegal sources, too. Sad to say, but there are plenty of those. The pole wasn't anything special. Normal bamboo can be found all over the United States, used for fishing poles. The feather was tied with fishing line. Also too common to trace. We just couldn't come up with anything that was unique or unusual except the toe guard."

There was the sound of pages turning. "At the second site, the hair that you found was from a black panther. The tooth marks on the foot that was recovered were made by a large cat. Not much doubt that Burl Mascotti was killed by the animal. And that's about all I can tell you." He cleared his throat. "Any sign of the missing man?"

"None," Gordon said. "The search teams haven't found anything."

Gus whistled softly. "Do you think these incidents are related?"

Rachel felt both men look at her. She was in charge of the case. It was something she'd considered all day. "Yes, I do. I'm not sure how, but two instances of known poachers being attacked, I'd say they have to connect."

"Then you've got a loo-loo of a killer on your hands. Check

with Charlie. I think the coroner had some new facts that went through him. Chain of command and all."

"Thanks," Rachel said. She was already headed for the door before Gordon could issue an order. Her guilty conscience made her feel that Jake was scrutinizing her every move, and that only made her angry with herself. She'd never shown a hint of interest in Jake, other than as a friend. Whether rational or not, Adam Standing Bear had turned0 her free-floating guilt into a tidal surge.

She caught the scent of barbecue before she even opened the door to the coroner's office. Charlie's desk was empty, but the remains of a pulled pork sandwich lay on his blotter.

"Be there in a minute," he called from a back room.

When he came in, he was drying his hands. "I guess they called you from Rapid City. They finally got the results back from the wounds on Hank's neck. Looks like his head was chopped off with some kind of machete-like weapon."

Rachel tried not to imagine that scene. "Anything else?"

"The blows, at least three of them, were delivered with a good amount of strength at an upward angle, which indicates the body was hanging when the head was removed. Oh, yeah, and he was dead by then."

"Thank god for small favors." She didn't bother to suppress the shudder. "What a gruesome way to die, Charlie."

"What the hell did the killer do with the heads?" Charlie mused. "Have you checked at Zell's Taxidermy? He does all the illegal mounting and stuffing for those boys. Maybe he's got Hank's and that doctor's head."

Rachel knew she shouldn't encourage Charlie with a grin, but she'd had the same thought earlier. "Zell Havers is a moron, but even he isn't stupid enough to mount a human head."

Charlie's eyebrows rose. "I'll betcha a slice of Lulu's apple pie that he'd consider it if someone offered enough money."

Rachel held out her hand for the copy of the official report. Gordon and Jake would want to read it for themselves. "I'll give you the pie, Charlie, and I'll keep that in mind next time I drive past Zell's. It might not hurt to check his freezers out."

RACHEL PUSHED the last thumbtack into the Peg-Board she'd set up in her living room. Maybe it was insecurity, but she'd felt foolish trying to create one in the sheriff's office. Neither Gordon nor Scott had gone through the police academy where such techniques were taught, and she didn't want to flaunt her training.

After Scott had brought the last of the search-and-rescue volunteers back from the hills with no results, she'd gone home to set up a time line of the murders, Mullet's disappearance and Burl's death. The clues were there—she just had to look at the evidence differently.

Four men, all involved in poaching, were dead or missing. Two had been skinned, one eaten, and one had simply vanished. And then there was the hanging of the mannequin. Beneath all the facts she'd neatly organized was Adam Standing Bear's voice telling the story of the Skin Dancer.

The first murder scene had an element of ritual. The second scene, not exactly criminal, but certainly worthy of inclusion, involved a decapitated mannequin. Had the dummy been a mere distraction, or was there a message that she'd overlooked, pushed aside by the discovery of Burl's foot? Whoever had set up the mannequin had been familiar with the Welford/Trussell crime scene. Did that familiarity come from first-hand experience or from newspaper accounts?

She moved down the board. The third event was John

Henry's discovery of the foot, which led to the realization that Burl Mascotti was dead and Mullet Bellows was missing and likely dead.

In all, the entire sequence of events had taken under seventy-two hours. It was as if one small pebble had fallen and started a gruesome rockslide.

But what was the initial pebble? The road? That was a possibility, but poachers weren't really linked with the road project, despite the glory-grabbing confession made by WAR's spokesperson.

Speaking of which, she found the notes she'd made and clipped them to the board. Frankie had mentioned that Justine Morgan was a good place to start with WAR, especially in light of the hair clip found at the mannequin scene. It was something Rachel needed to check.

She glanced at the old frying pan clock with a flash of panic. She had only twenty minutes to get ready for the Paradise development meeting. She pushed the board against the wall and hurried to her bedroom to get ready.

When she flipped on the light, she realized for the first time how austere her bedroom was. The only surface with any clutter was the bedside table where a stack of books towered precariously. Not a single feminine item was in evidence. Her mother's bedroom had been so different, with lamp shades fringed with silk, porcelain figurines of shepherdesses and belles. Perfume bottles and cheap jewelry had been scattered across the surface of Junie's dresser, and the room had always smelled of Taboo.

Rachel forced herself to hurry into the bathroom and turn on the shower. What were these sudden trips down memory lane? Every time she was home long enough to draw a breath, she found herself slipping back into the past. It wasn't healthy, and she'd be damned if she was going to let the quagmire of memory creep around her feet, grab her knees and bring her down.

Junie Redmond was dead. Rachel had no room in her stark apartment for ghosts or memories. She was an officer of the law, a deputy who dealt in facts and evidence. She was logical, not emotional.

She stepped beneath the stinging spray. Her body was slightly sore from her workout the evening before, but it was a good kind of sore. One that normally would lead to a blissful night's sleep.

She turned off the water, dried herself, and slipped into a conservative slacks suit she'd bought at a close-out sale at a department store in Rapid City. It was a nice suit, but age had put a bit of sheen on the knees. Other than the dress she'd bought for the dinner party, she hadn't worried about clothes for a long time. Perhaps her wardrobe could use a little updating—if time ever allowed for such luxuries. Hanging around with Frankie made her aware of the shortcomings of her closet.

She was applying lipstick when she noticed something in the mirror. The tube slipped from her fingers, falling to the top of her dresser with a clatter. She turned and walked to the bedside table. On top of the stack of books was a small Dresden Shepherdess, her mother's favorite figurine. Transfixed, she picked it up. The detail was exquisite. The china blue eyes met her gaze with a hint of mockery. Rachel swallowed. She'd left the delicate statuette and all of her mother's belongings in the trailer. She'd simply abandoned them, unable to carry the weight of her memories on top of the physical reality of her mother's harsh death.

Mel had packed up the trailers when he'd rescued her, and the boxes of her past life were still in his garage, as far as she knew.

But how had the collectible gotten on her bedside table? She looked around the room, reacting too late to the possibility that someone had been in her cottage. Someone had entered her bedroom and left it for her. Someone had violated her home and her past. Mel never locked his garage, so anyone could have found the figurine. But not everyone would know the significance of it. But why? Why did in her past?

She pulled her gun from the holster and kicked open the bedroom closet. Nothing. Room by room, she searched the entire house. There was no sign of breaking and entering, only a few scratches at her front door lock—the mark of a professional.

Her breathing had settled and her grip on the gun was loose but ready when she saw a small gift box in the center of the dining table.

Dread made her footsteps reluctant. The package looked so innocent, pale blue with a darker bow. Expertly wrapped. A present. She picked it up. Whatever was inside was light. She shook it, thinking momentarily of a bomb, then brushed the thought aside as ridiculous. She pulled the bow and lifted the top off. For a moment, she didn't register what was inside. When she did, she almost dropped the box.

A strip of human flesh nestled in the bed of cotton like a precious jewel. She forced herself to take several deep breaths. The reality of the skin, left by someone in her home, along with a knickknack of her mother's, was so extreme that she couldn't make any of it connect.

Someone who knew her past, who had access to her past, had been in her home. And that someone had skinned a man while he was alive.

Before she could formulate an answer, she heard Jake's knock at the door. Indecision tore her. At last, she covered the box and stuck it in a kitchen drawer.

"Coming, Jake." She grabbed her purse. Right or wrong, she didn't trust him. He and his father had packed her things to move her into their home. They were the last people to touch Junie's whatnots and still had possession of them. As much as it terrified her to think it, Jake was the most likely suspect to have left the shepherdess. And the skin?

She stuck her gun inside her purse, squared her shoulders and opened the door. She was going to play it as if she'd never found either thing.

"We're late." Jake was annoyed. He tried to step around her, but she blocked him.

"I'm ready. Let's get this over with."

He didn't say anything as he stepped back and held the door for her. As she walked past him, she felt as if she'd just entered enemy territory.

CHAPTER SIXTEEN

Mullet's hand shook as he held the piece of paper in the cabin's near darkness. He'd finished writing by the light of the oil lantern, the only source of illumination he could find. His stomach was painfully empty, and his throat raw from lack of moisture. He had a taste in his mouth like something had crawled in and died, and the repeated bouts of anxiety had resulted in body odor that even he could smell.

He re-read what he'd written. Once his captor had the confession, he'd have no reason to let Mullet live. The best Mullet could hope for was a quick, clean death. Not like Burl. Dear God, not like Burl.

His lips moved in a mumbled prayer, something he hadn't tried since childhood when he begged an unresponsive God to keep him safe from his father's strap. Mullet had no real hope that God or even Satan would intervene and save him now. He thought of the panther in the cage, watching him, waiting for any chance of escape. In the long run, the cat had more courage than he, because he'd given up. He only wanted the end to be quick and clean. He didn't want to be hung upside down and skinned.

Tears leaked down his face at the thought. If he could find a fucking knife in the cabin, he'd cut his own wrists. At the thought of his ultimate helplessness, he cried harder.

"Mullet Bellows."

The voice outside the front door was mechanical, altered by some device into an eerie, futuristic sound that held not a scrap of humanity.

"Mullet Bellows, have you written your confession?"

Mullet took a ragged breath. "Yes. Yes, I have."

"Slide it under the door."

Mullet stumbled from the table, the paper shaking in his hand. Balancing as best he could, he leaned down and pushed the page under the crack at the bottom of the door.

An eternity passed before he heard the voice again.

"Move back from the door."

"Are you going to let me go?" He sounded weak and foolish, but he didn't care. He only wanted the door to open and for him to have a shot at freedom.

"Move away from the door."

"I did everything you said. I wrote it all down." He'd thought he'd given up the hope to live, but he hadn't. He only wanted a chance. Just one.

"You think confessing is punishment enough?"

The word punishment was like a jolt of electricity. Mullet backed away from the door. He'd been a moron to write anything down. Now his captor was going to kill him and still have the confession. Had he not been in such a hurry to write down his list of sins, he might have had something left to bargain with. He slammed his head against the wall where he braced himself.

The door opened very slowly, letting the night into the cabin. A darker shape separated itself from the dense blackness and stepped inside the living room. Mullet couldn't make out any of the person's features. His captor was dressed in what looked like garbage bags, the shiny black kind that was strong enough to hold leaves. The implication of that hit him and he cried out.

"I wrote it down, like you asked. I did just what you said."

"Are you sorry for your sins, Mullet?"

He could see that the person held a voice distorter box to his throat to create the androgynous voice of a zombie. His face was covered with a ski mask.

Hope rocked his gut. "Yes! I'm sorry!"

"I don't think you're sorry enough."

"I am!"

"This is an interesting confession. You're a bigger piece of shit than I thought, but you forgot to write down the names of the others who were involved."

Mullet slid along the wall. The door was wide open. It was his only chance. He had to try. "You know who was with me. Welford is already dead. And Burl, too. Burl didn't have anything to do with any of it, but you turned that panther loose on him."

"Burl was a miscreant. He had no compassion for any of the animals he drugged and killed. The lesson here, Mullet, is compassion."

He pressed his hands against the wall. His only chance was to push himself forward and hope he could stay upright on one good leg. If he could get out into the darkness, maybe he could hide.

"You're going to write down the names of all the others involved. Before I'm done with you, you'll be glad to write them down."

He pushed off the wall with all he had, shrieking as loudly as he could. He made it past the table and was almost at the door when he tripped. He went down hard, crying out as he fell onto his already broken wrist. Before he could untangle himself, he felt a rope tighten around his ankles.

As he rolled and thrashed, the dark-clad figure pulled the rope taunt and walked outside. Before he could regain his feet, he heard the sound of a motor. He was jerked through the doorway, across the porch and onto the ground.

Bits of rock and sticks tore the skin of his palms as he tried to find something to hang on to. Dirt filled his mouth, and a stone smacked into his front teeth. The one place he didn't want to go was into the woods, but he couldn't stop it from happening. He couldn't hang on to anything. Finally the pain was too much and he surrendered to the darkness.

RACHEL ACCEPTED the wine Jake brought her with a forced smile. The presentation was over, and now the real meeting had begun as different groups of people talked about Paradise and what the development could do for each of them. A beautiful diorama of the city had been placed on the Civic Center stage so that everyone could walk by and look at it. The building lines were clean and beautiful, and plenty of green space had been included in the downtown area as well as the urban living zones that featured mass transit. The model showed a city built on one industry and filled with people who were educated.

Richard Jones, computer czar, was pressing the flesh, along with Senator Dilson, the sheriff, and other local dignitaries.

It was harder than she'd ever dreamed to act normally around Jake. She found herself watching him, hoping for some sign that would tell her of his guilt.

"How much are you going to invest?" Rachel asked as Jake took her elbow and steered her to the cluster of men where Mel Ortiz was talking with Jones.

"I don't know yet." Jake waved to some friends. Whatever

guilt he felt, he wasn't showing it. "I'll talk it over with Dad later. This is a great opportunity to get in on the ground floor."

"The sheriff obviously thinks so." Rachel nodded at Gordon and his wife as they sipped their wine and talked animatedly with Senator Dilson and two out-of-town investors.

"Gordon has never made a secret of the fact that he supports growth. The more populous the county, the bigger his salary." Jake squeezed her lightly. "Gordon's a good man, but he wants financial security, like everyone else."

"The influx of new voters that will come with Paradise may have other ideas about what good law enforcement entails." She hated this. With each statement, Jake shook her faith in everyone she knew. All the years she'd spent building her confidence seemed wasted. She was beginning to feel isolated and wary of everyone around her.

Watching the crowd of well-dressed men and women, Rachel realized for the first time that Paradise was a done deal. It didn't matter what the average Criss County citizen wanted. The road was going through, and Paradise would be developed. Billions of dollars were at stake.

Mel Ortiz, his gray hair shining like steel, drew Rachel into the group. "This is Rachel Redmond, the Criss County deputy in charge of the wilderness murders." He put his hand on Rachel's shoulder. "She's like a daughter to me, Mr. Jones."

"Frankie Jackson has sung your praises," Richard said, pushing his glasses up his nose. "You're also investigating the vandalism to the heavy equipment on the road project, I hope."

"Yes." Rachel had studied Jones during his presentation. He was tall and thin with bright blue eyes. Her impression was that while he might play the absent-minded professor, he was also plenty capable. Even more interesting was his date—Justine Morgan—who was currently bringing him another glass of wine. For a moment she forgot about Jake and focused on Justine.

"Any headway on the vandals?" Jones asked Rachel. He was watching her intently.

"We're steadily making progress."

Justine returned and handed him his wine with a glint of amusement in her eyes. Rachel watched the way he took the glass, his fingertips brushing hers in a deliberate way.

"Ms. Morgan," Rachel said, "we haven't been introduced, but I was wondering if I might have a word with you."

"Here?" Justine looked around the civic center where the crowd of at least two hundred potential investors had gathered.

"No, tomorrow would be fine. I can stop by your place, or you can come by the office."

"What is this in regard to?" she asked.

Rachel had to admire Justine's cool attitude. If she was involved with WAR and the destruction of the equipment, she wasn't going to be easy to crack. "It might be best if we waited until tomorrow." Rachel pointedly looked at Richard Jones.

"Of course." Justine put on a brilliant smile. "Whatever I can do to help."

"I'll give you a call." Rachel took note of Justine's auburn hair. Lush and thick, it would look beautiful in the clip Frankie had found at the mannequin site. "I appreciate your help, Ms. Morgan."

A brash voice interrupted them. "Exactly who are you helping?"

They all turned to the young man who'd pushed into their circle. Rachel noted the expensive suit, the polish. She'd never seen him before, but Justine had. She'd gained control of her expression, but not before annoyance and anger marched across her features.

"What are you doing here, Derek?" she asked.

"Looking for investment opportunities." He ignored everyone except Richard Jones. "Mr. Jones, I'm Derek Baxter. I was hoping to talk to you about the possibility of employment."

Jones looked from Derek to Justine. "Now isn't an appropriate time, Mr. Baxter." He turned to Justine. "Are you ready to go?"

When she nodded, he said his goodbyes and moved away. Mel and Jake drifted over to talk to the senator.

Rachel saw the dark cloud of anger settle on Derek Baxter's features. Justine Morgan was one point in a very interesting triangle. Rachel also noticed a cut and a large bruise on Derek's temple. Someone had been playing rough.

"Mr. Baxter," she said, "would you stop by the sheriff's office tomorrow at eight."

"Why?"

He was hostile and confrontational. Good. Justine Morgan was cool as a moon rock. "You might be able to help me with an investigation."

"What would I know about some investigation?"

"Oh, I don't know. Maybe nothing. Maybe something." She smiled. "Eight o'clock. Then you can get right on with work and your regular day."

Derek turned and walked away. Rachel watched him thread his way across the room and out the front door. Mel and Jake had gone on to talk with some of the other potential investors, and Rachel wandered back to the bar. Jones had dropped a good amount of cash setting up the presentation with refreshments for the entire crowd. The prominent citizens of Criss County were yucking it up as they sipped wine and let the daydreams of dollar signs pile up in their minds. Mel was probably right. She needed to care more about these kinds of things but she didn't. She sought out Jake, feeling again the jolt of betrayal and fear as she watched him laughing with another group of people.

She caught a glimpse of a startlingly attractive woman in a red dress, dark curls brushing her shoulders. Frankie was working the room, too. Rachel had looked for her during the evening but figured she was busy backstage. She considered going over, but she knew Frankie was doing her job. She could see her fine hand in all of the décor, the wine, the smooth way the entire operation had turned from a selling venue into a community support gathering.

Relaxing against the bar, Rachel decided to stay put and wait for Jake and Mel to finish their business. Once she made it home she needed to get the "gift" someone had left her to a crime lab. In her heart, she knew it was skin cut from Hank Welford, but only a lab could determine it beyond a shadow of a doubt.

After that, everything else was going to be much harder.

CHAPTER SEVENTEEN

In her dream, Rachel stood in the forest, aware that someone lurked at the edge of the shadows. She heard soft chanting, the low tones of what might be a prayer. She couldn't pinpoint the place where the sound came from—it swept around her on the breeze. She could smell the fresh scent of the fir trees, and it didn't matter that she was alone and in the area near Dixon Point where so much violence had been discovered. Instead of fear, she felt safe. The forest was a place of beauty and serenity.

She walked through the trees, caught up in the wonder of the wilderness. The first drop of blood that touched her arm stopped her cold. All color drained from the forest. There was only the red splotch against the white of her skin.

A second drop plopped onto her arm. And a third, fourth and fifth, falling faster and faster. When she looked up, she saw the bloody stump of Mullet Bellow's neck as he dangled above her, his body skinned so that the muscle glistened wet and open.

Rachel sat up in bed, her heart pounding. It took a moment for her to recognize the sheer curtains that softly undulated at the open window. She was at the Grand Falls, a renovated hotel in the center of Rapid City. She'd delivered the skin to the crime lab and exhausted, taken a room for the night.

Outside, two cats yowled, either in passion or anger, she couldn't tell. She lifted her hair, clammy with sweat, from the back of her neck, giving herself a moment to wake up. The dream was like quicksand; it didn't want to let her go.

The reality of what she faced was worse than the nightmare. Jake. Had he been in her home and left the skin and figurine? The idea made her stomach contract so harshly that she thought she might throw up.

She tossed back the sheets and went to the bathroom for a drink of water. The bedside clock showed four a.m. She needed more sleep, but it was useless. Instead, she turned on the lights and the small coffee pot and focused on the time line for the murders that she'd brought with her. She hadn't wanted to leave it in her cottage for Jake—or anyone—to see.

It was Friday morning. In less than a week, three men were dead and one missing. So much had transpired, and so suddenly.

Why? Why had these events happened now? If she could understand what had prompted the killings, she might be able to find the evidence that would lead to an arrest.

She'd made copies of all the interviews and crime scene reports that had come in, and she sat down and read through them. The killer was clever and well versed in police procedure.

He'd left almost no clues. No physical evidence that he hadn't wanted them to find. This was a calculated killer, or what a profiler would call organized. A smart person of above-average intelligence. Most serial killers were white males in their thirties. And, it was someone who knew the area. Jake.

That thought stopped her for a moment. She got a sheet of paper and began to make a list of the things she knew about the murderer. He knew the wilderness well. He had access to an

ATV, a four-wheel drive, some type of winch to hoist the bodies up to hang them, a knowledge of skinning, and enough strength to sever a human head with three blows of a machete.

Jake.

She stood up abruptly and walked to the open window. She was on the eighth floor with a view of a city park and the rapids that had given the city its name. So much beauty in such close proximity to evil. She'd known that most of her life, though. After all, her mother's body had been found in a dumpster near the park she could see from the window. Junie had died an ugly death in the midst of this beauty.

Pushing Jake out of her mind, she went back to her notes. The picture of the killer that was beginning to form was of another outdoorsman. Maybe a poacher—a competitor who wanted to eliminate his rivals. Poacher-on-poacher crime, as Jake had insisted all along. Or perhaps it was a game warden, someone who knew the wilderness intimately.

But what was Jake's motive? Sure, the poachers had been a pain in his ass for years, but not enough to kill them.

She held on to the fact that Jake received no benefit from the deaths. Unless there was something she didn't see.

She got a cup coffee and looked at the reports. Hank, Mullet and possibly Burl were the intended targets. Burl had been fed to a wild creature, which was a statement of his worth to the killer. He was meat—inconsequential. So Burl and Trussell were collateral damage. But where the hell was Mullet Bellows? And why did the killer mutilate his victims in such a gruesome way?

She had no answers.

Flipping through the photographs, she stopped at the totem with the owl feather. If the pole and feather weren't part of a Sioux tradition, they held special meaning for the killer. Or maybe the killer was clouding the water, trying to frame the

Sioux. That was the troubling thing to her. This went way beyond the elimination of a competitor.

She logged onto her laptop and went to the Internet, surfing through various sites on Native American lore. The only information she found was that, in general, the feather of an owl was associated with a prophecy of death. Did the feather foretell Hank's death, or was it the prophecy of Mullet's death?

She returned to the stack of photographs, studying the way the feather had been tied with fishing line so that it could be attached to the bamboo pole. She was dealing with symbolism, as Adam Standing Bear had mentioned, but the clues were vague, personal to the killer.

Continuing through the photographs, she stopped at a close up of the boot guard. It was a beautiful piece, the whorls of silver elegant. As Gus had said, letters of the alphabet were almost formed. Almost but not quite. Another clue she couldn't decipher.

She poured the last of the coffee. She'd brought the hair clamp that Frankie had found at the mannequin site to the forensic lab also, so the report would probably come back at the same time as the one on the skin. Would Justine claim the clamp as hers? Would she consent to a DNA sample?

What was going on between Derek Baxter and Justine? And how did that impact Richard Jones? Justine was too young for him, but that didn't appear to concern either of them. It was the way of the world and there was nothing criminal in a forty-year-old man dating a woman in her twenties.

She paced the room, aware of the loneliness that followed her like a shadow. She'd thought about getting a dog, but it wouldn't be fair to an animal unless she could commit to more time with it. Adam Standing Bear's dog had been so well behaved. Finder. An interesting name.

Her thoughts spun in all directions, and she knew she was

avoiding thinking about the dream that had awakened her. Because she knew Mullet was dead. The dream wasn't prophetic, but it represented the message her subconscious was sending. Dixon Point. Though they'd searched the area thoroughly, Rachel knew she'd give it another try.

She checked out of the hotel and headed back to Bisonville. It was several hours until dawn, and right now she couldn't stand her own company or the feeling of being hamstrung. She needed a shower and a clean uniform.

BISONVILLE WAS a ghost town as Rachel drove through the empty streets. Even the neon in front of Bud's Bar had been turned off. There were only darkened store fronts, and in the starlight Rachel could easily imagine the town as the gathering spot for prospectors and speculators. A bit farther north was Deadwood, which had captured the imagination of a television show, but Bisonville had a colorful past, too. A bloody past.

She pulled in at the courthouse and got out. The pre-dawn was soft, gentle, a kiss of summer. The winters were cold with deep snows. Her mother had often talked of spending the snowy months in the Southwest. Junie had loved the idea of San Antonio. She never made it there, but that Texas town, home of the Alamo, had represented heaven to Junie. Rachel, though, was happy in Bisonville. Or she had been until the murders occurred and a man she'd known most of her life had been tainted as a possible murderer.

In the office she wrote a full report on Derek Baxter and what she hoped to glean from interviewing him. She left the report on Scott's desk, along with a request for Scott to interview the young man. She had other things to do, but she wasn't about to tell anyone that she was following dream images back up into the mountains.

"Gladys, I've got to check something up at Dixon Point. Be sure Scott reads this first thing, okay? I'll be back by nine."

"You betcha." Gladys never looked up from her paperback.

Rachel picked up the keys to the ATV and the four-wheel drive pickup. Outside. She loaded the four-wheeler into the back of the truck. The streets had come alive while she was inside. Even though her stomach growled a demand for breakfast, she sped through town and headed to Dixon Point.

She made one stop and picked up some canned goods to leave at the trailhead for John Henry when she passed Piker Road. Jake wouldn't approve, but Jake had his own agenda. And she had hers.

She'd gone on this search, prompted by a bad dream. She had to do this alone, to prove something to herself. Jake often made her second-guess her gut, but now she was taking charge. She pressed harder on the accelerator. Sometimes it didn't matter what anyone else thought. She had to listen to her instincts.

Derek walked into the sheriff's office and looked around for Deputy Redmond, but he only saw a middle-aged dispatcher and a male deputy. The bitch who'd ordered him to appear was late.

The deputy stood and motioned him over. "I'm Scott Amos," he said. "If you're Derek Baxter, take a seat."

Derek started to argue, but the sooner this was over the better for him. He sat.

"Are you involved with WAR?" the deputy asked.

The question came so hard and fast that Derek was unprepared. "What makes you think I am?"

"Answer the question, Mr. Baxter."

"I don't have to say a damn thing. I came in here voluntarily to help you out and now you're accusing me of being part of an organization."

"No," Scott said, "I'm just asking if you're a member. Are you?"

"What if I am?"

Scott picked up the telephone. He pressed a button. "Sheriff, I think we've got our first member of WAR. Yes, sir, he's sitting right here."

Derek started to stand but Scott waved him back into his seat. He put a hand over the phone. "I wouldn't leave just yet, son, the sheriff wants to talk to you."

"I've got to go." Derek actually gained his feet this time. He was walking toward the door when a large hand caught his shoulder. He turned to face the sheriff.

"I've got some questions for you, Mr. Baxter."

"I have to go. I've got a job interview."

The sheriff tightened his grip. "I think you need to know your rights, Mr. Baxter. Scott, would you tell them to him?"

The deputy came to his other side. "You have the right to remain silent, the right to an attorney..."

Derek looked around the sad little office. He felt he was slipping beneath the surface of something much bigger than he was. He'd come in expecting to answer a few questions about his whereabouts. He'd alibied himself with the other members of WAR so that each one would tell the same story.

"What are you charging me with?" he demanded.

"Well, I have a list of things, Mr. Baxter. Come on into my office and I'll go over them with you."

Derek hated the good-ole-boy tone the sheriff used. He hated that he was powerless to resist his orders. He squared his shoulders and followed the sheriff into his office. When the door closed behind him, he knew he was in serious trouble.

. . .

Rachel throttled the ATV and roared up the steep incline. Loose shale rattled behind her as she increased the gas with a flip of her wrist. If she stopped now, she'd fall backward. Hunkering down over the handle bars, she gave the machine all she had and kept her gaze on the top of the ridge. When at last she reached a plateau, she stopped and surveyed the area around her. ATVs normally weren't allowed in this part of the wilderness. Only law enforcement and state game wardens could use them.

As soon as she switched the engine off, she was surrounded by silence. She took a deep breath and closed her eyes, wondering how the interview with Baxter was going. She was more than likely a fool to push that off on Scott. Not that he wouldn't do a good job, but she knew what she was looking for in Derek Baxter. And her trip into the mountains, so far, had proven fruitless.

She left Razor Ridge, where the outcropping of granite formed what looked like a sheer, slick razor blade. Dixon Point was over the next ridge. She'd come in from the east, hoping to see something new, something she'd missed before. The dream had been so damn real.

Shaking her head at her own foolishness, she gave the machine more fuel and took off. The sooner she checked Dixon Point the sooner she could get back to the office.

As she approached the area where Hank's and the doctor's bodies had been hung, she slowed. Near a small puddle, there were fresh ATV tracks. It was possible they'd been made by the volunteer searchers, but she'd understood most of the search had been conducted on foot so that the ravines and slopes could be thoroughly examined.

Her hand reached for the gas again, but she hesitated, yielding to the distinct sense that someone was watching her. She whirled, her hand going to the weapon at her waist.

Nothing moved. Tense and anxious, she searched the area around her.

When the large bird flapped out of the thick cover of a tree, she instinctively pulled her gun and took aim. She recognized the wingspan and grace of the eagle before she shot. As she reholstered her pistol, she realized her heart was thumping painfully in her chest. The old Sioux stories had gotten to her.

Skin dancers. Sure.

She headed on up the trail, but she hadn't gone more than twenty yards when she stopped in shock.

The blank eye sockets of Ashton Trussell were fixed in her direction. A small hole centered his forehead. Next to Trussell was what remained of Burl Mascotti's mauled head. Both had been carefully placed so that they greeted her as she slowly entered the place where Hank and Trussell had been found.

She saw the body hanging from the same limb. Mullet Bellows, or what remained of him, swung in the gentle wind. There was no way for her to identify him, but she knew it was Mullet. His body had been skinned and his head removed. A silver ornament was skewered to his chest with a porcupine quill, and beside the remains was a bamboo pole, this one containing two owl feathers.

Rachel had an urge to flee, to get on the ATV and ride as fast as she could toward town, but she couldn't. She had to secure the crime scene. And wait for someone from the sheriff's office to come and look for her.

CHAPTER EIGHTEEN

The body bag zipped shut over what remained of Mullet Bellows. The technician fixed the zipper tab and stood.

"We'll get some prints to positively identify the body. He hasn't been dead more than fourteen, eighteen hours," Gus Langstrom said to Rachel and Jake. Around them the crime scene techs finished working the site. "He was dragged a good distance, but based on the blood, I think he was still alive when he was skinned. We'll be able to give a more exact time of death once we get the body to the lab. No sign of Mullet's head, huh?"

"Nothing." Rachel nodded toward the place where the heads of Burl and Trussell had already been bagged and removed. "The killer brought two heads back and took Mullet's."

"This one is a real weirdo," Gus said. "Glad he's operating here and not in Rapid City."

"We searched this entire area over and over again." Jake paced back and forth, his agitated movement making Rachel want to shake him. "The killer is watching us, waiting for an opportunity to make us look like fools."

His words fueled her suspicions. "Is he?" she asked.

He whirled to face her. "I don't appreciate your sarcasm."

"I somehow don't think the killer cares about us at all," Rachel murmured. "This isn't about us, Jake." Or was it?

"We suffer the backlash when we look incompetent. The media is going to be all over this. Mullet was alive most of the time he was missing, and we couldn't find a single lead." Jake stepped beside Rachel and looked down at the ground saturated with blood.

Jake's words were like ice picks digging into her. If she'd been smarter, faster, more competent, she might have saved Mullet's life. "You're right. If Gus's time line is accurate, he was being skinned while we were at the Paradise meeting, sipping wine and listening to get-rich dreams." Jake had been at her side. He couldn't have been involved in Mullet's mutilation and death—if Gus was right about the time of death. Only the coroner could say that with scientific certainty, though.

"Are you okay?" Jake asked. "You're pale and you've been acting strange all morning."

"Lack of sleep." She wasn't about to mention the break-in and the skin, had in fact taken the precaution of asking the state crime lab technician not to mention it to anyone else. He'd been reluctant to comply, but she'd let him know that it was vital to her investigation to keep that information from the sheriff and Jake.

She'd told no one about the figurine. She'd fought so hard not to be defined by her past, yet it had come calling again. She turned away from Jake's probing gaze. "Mullet's wrist and knee were broken." Rachel had been able to determine that for herself. Bones didn't grow like that naturally.

"This isn't your fault, Rachel. We're all involved in this. None of us have been able to get ahead of this killer." Jake knelt, searching the ground. "He wants these men to suffer. I think he's as motivated by suffering as he is by killing."

"This is extremely personal, and whoever is doing it has left us plenty of clues. We just don't know how to read them." She held up the bag with the silver toe guard. Gus had pulled it from the body but allowed her to hold on to it. "This one is exactly like the other one, or as exact as a hand-crafted item can be. This is important. We just don't know what to make of it."

"I've never known Mullet or Hank to wear fancy toe guards. That's more of a gentleman rancher thing to wear, for show. But you're right. It has some meaning. Something significant to those two men."

"And to the killer." Rachel tucked the evidence bag into her pocket. "Gus said the forensic boys had tried every boot manufacturer in the region and nationally. But what if this was made by an artisan, created as a special request. That would signify an individual. If I could find the person who made the toe guards, then he or she might be able to tell me something about the men who bought them and how Mullet and Hank are tied to this piece of silver."

Jake rose so that he could gaze into Rachel's eyes. She started to walk away but his fingers caught her upper arm. His hold was gentle but authoritative.

"Rachel, I need to talk to you."

"Here?" She looked around at the evidence techs putting the last of their gear away. It was afternoon and she was tired and hungry. Something in Jake's eyes told her that he didn't want to discuss business.

"Here is as good a place as any."

"Not if you want me to be receptive. I haven't eaten since yesterday at lunch. I'm feeling overwhelmed, and I just want to get back to town."

He continued to hold her arm. "Could you ever view me as something other than an older brother?"

She felt as if she'd been punched. "What?"

"I know because you've said it often enough: you look at me like a brother. But I'm not. We aren't related, Rachel. I've tried not to show my feelings for you, but I talked with Dad last night, and he told me I should be honest with you, give you a chance to consider it."

"Consider what?" But she knew what. This was the conversation with Jake she'd dreaded for the past year.

"I want us to date. I want you to see me as a man, not a brother."

"Jake, I—" She stopped herself. There was nothing she could say that wouldn't hurt him. Her impulse was to lash out and tell him he was cornering her with family debt and obligation. It was a place she didn't want to be. But to say that would reveal to Jake her true feelings, and that seemed needlessly brutal.

"Think about it. That's all I'm asking. I know this is a shock, but just think about it. Frankie believes I might have a chance with you."

"Frankie doesn't know me or anything about me."

Jake looked surprised. "She really likes you, Rachel. She says the two of you are like kindred spirits."

Rachel knew she was acting like a churl. "Jake, I've been in her company three times. Four at the most. She doesn't know a thing about me."

"But I've known you half your life, and I do know what you want and need. You want a man to be there beside you, for the good times and the bad. You need someone who respects your intelligence and your heart. And you deserve a man who can be strong and also tender. I can be all of those things for you, Rachel. All you have to do is give me a chance."

He walked away and Rachel remained beside the crime scene. She finally tucked her hands in the pockets of her jacket and walked toward the ATV. She was going into town. Destination wouldn't solve her problem, but the journey might at least buy her some time to arrive at a solution.

FRANKIE WATCHED the bulldozers push the clay into position. The road was moving forward, inch by inch, foot by foot. They were laying the foundation, and they'd covered a mile in the past week. The dream of Paradise was one step closer—and so far she'd been able to keep the damage to a minimum.

Based on her expertise, the four-lane wasn't a necessity for the Paradise development. But it was necessary for Harvey Dilson and his fast-approaching bid for a presidential slot. Paradise would be Harvey's ticket to the White House. He could show that he was the man who brought progress and prosperity to his district—and he could do it for the rest of the nation. Not a single decision that had been made was about the good of Bisonville and the surrounding areas.

"You expecting someone today?"

Frankie almost jumped. She'd been so deep in thought that she hadn't noticed the foreman coming up to her.

"Just worried about our pace. We're making progress now, but we lost a lot of momentum with the equipment down."

"Yeah, we're behind, but now that the dozers are here, we can make up some time even if we have to stay late."

She nodded. "Sometimes I wonder if this project isn't cursed. Maybe it was never intended to go through."

"Don't start with that kind of talk. We might be able to put together a second shift. The men weren't as upset over Bellows and Welford as I feared they might be, but if the sheriff and his crew don't get on top of these murders, we're going to lose everyone." Phil dropped into step beside her as she walked.

"If I can't hold this crew together, my career is going to take a real hit. But I just have this feeling, like the other shoe is about to drop."

"Let's hope not." Phil took off his hardhat and wiped sweat onto his shirt sleeve. "When the summer truly sets in, this is going to be hot work."

"That's South Dakota for you." She pulled out her cell phone. "Phil would you excuse me, I need to check on a few things?"

"Sure. I'll be at the front if you need me."

Frankie paused in the shade cast by a bucket truck and dialed Jake's number. She had to know if they'd found Bellows yet. She'd spent a lot of time and energy working her way into Jake's and the sheriff's good graces and it had paid handsome dividends in the information department. Instead of Jake, she got his voice mail.

"How about dinner tonight? Maybe you and Rachel. Call me when you get this message. I need to firm up the plans. Maybe I can put in a good word for you with Rachel." She snapped the phone shut.

"Dammit," she whispered. She needed to know what was happening. She put a call in to the sheriff's office. The dispatcher was slow as molasses, but finally she heard Gordon's baritone.

"Sorry, Frankie, I'm headed out the door."

"What's going on?" She kept it innocent, but she could imagine Gordon's consternation. Another murder. Another skinning. Another black mark against his ability to protect the citizens of Criss County.

"I might as well tell you. You'll hear it soon enough. We found Mullet Bellow's body."

"You did? Where? How did you find it? Was the, uh, head..."

"Same place as Hank Welford. Rachel went back for a final search and came across the body hanging, like the others. The head was gone."

"What in the hell is the killer doing with those heads? I mean, really, what kind of freak would keep the heads?"

"The killer returned Burl's and the plastic surgeon's."

"Jesus! Returned? As in--?"

"Left them in the middle of the trail. Rachel found 'em. Gotta go, Frankie."

"See you, sheriff." She put the phone in her pocket. It would take a lot of willpower to stay on the job for the remaining hours of the afternoon, but the day would pass and then she'd sit down with Rachel and Jake and try to determine if Jake stood a chance. Rachel was such a strong woman, one who'd overcome so much. It would take a strong man to match her. Rachel deserved a man who would look after her, even through the tough times.

RACHEL WATCHED the dust roil from behind her truck as she drove along the dirt paths, headed to Table Butte. The sidewalk outside the sheriff's office had been a nightmare of media, clamoring and pushing for details on Mullet Bellow's murder. They'd gotten their money's worth, too, when Hannah Bellows had rushed out of the crowd and slapped Rachel. Hannah had screamed that the sheriff's office was an incompetent bunch of morons who'd deliberately left her husband in the hands of a serial killer. Once in front of the cameras, Hannah had been impossible to control. Jake had finally grabbed her elbow and dragged her inside the S.O.

Rachel rubbed her cheek where the skin still stung a little

from the slap. That clip would no doubt be all over the evening news. The thing Gordon had dreaded—a panic—was liable to happen.

After the episode with Hannah, Gordon had told Rachel to get some rest. She looked like crap—dark circles under her eyes, jittery hands, all the symptoms of sleep deprivation and stress. Instead of going home, she was keeping her appointment with Adam Standing Bear. She didn't want to go to her cottage, where Jake could seek her out.

She'd given Adam's story of the Skin Dancer a lot of thought. Frankie had told her that Native storytellers frequented local schools, or at least that had been a practice in the past.

She'd called the public schools and checked. The practice had been stopped in the late '80s. That would indicate the killer was close to thirty, or older. Of course, he could've heard the legend from anyone at any time. She sighed. Instead of too few clues, she felt as if she had too many. The murderer was obscuring his real motives behind layers of fog. From her training at the FBI academy, she'd learned that many serial killers wanted to be credited with their kills. They wanted the world to know why they were acting. Why was this one concealing his motives?

Rounding a curve, she saw a red truck and horse trailer at the foot of the road that led to Table Butte. Adam Standing Bear was a punctual man. She pulled up behind him and got out. The horses were already tacked up and waiting. Adam stepped out of the shadows.

"I'm glad you could make it, Rachel." Finder sprang from behind a rock and rushed over, alert and ready to guard his master. At a soft word from Adam, the dog settled down.

"I warned you that I don't really know much about riding

horses." She looked at the two big animals waiting patiently beside the horse trailer.

"I brought Cimarron for you to ride. She's gentle and quiet." He got both horses and held the mare as Rachel swung into the saddle. "Just relax and let her work. She'll take good care of you."

Rachel masked her qualms with a smile. Staying at the courthouse with Hannah Bellows might have been smarter. As they set off at a walk, then a trot, Rachel concentrated on relaxing. In only a matter of moments, she forgot about her lack of riding experience and yielded to the soothing motion of the horse and beauty of the badlands.

They rode for thirty minutes before they found the small herd of horses. John signaled her to the right and he approached, angling from the east. The herd bolted, headed toward her.

"Watch the red roan!" Adam called. "She's the lead mare. The others will follow her."

As the roan broke out of the herd, attempting to veer north, Cimarron lunged into a full gallop. Moving at breakneck speed over the rough terrain, the horse cut off the roan mare, sending her back into the herd, which surged west again.

"Good work!" Adam said, a smile tugging up the corners of his mouth. "You're a natural cowgirl."

"Right. The horse is trained." Rachel knew she spoke the truth, but she basked in his compliments.

They moved the herd for an hour before stopping at a watering hole. Around them the barren rocks and landscape had heated up under the afternoon sun. Rachel felt as if she'd stepped back in time. The thought that one day in the not too distant future none of this would remain touched her with a sharp pang. Development, population growth, climate changes —the wilderness couldn't hold out forever.

"You look serious," Adam said. He eased his horse closer so that they sat side by side, waiting for the herd to drink their fill of water.

"Thank you for letting me share this, Adam. Why are you moving the horses?"

"There are hunters who come to kill the wild herds. They'll be safer closer to the reservation. Besides, we need to vaccinate them and do some vet work."

"Then they aren't really wild horses." Rachel sat forward as the stallion lifted his head, sniffing the air.

"They're wild, but we also care for them. The days when they could roam the plains and survive are gone. Without man's intervention, they would perish."

Rachel pulled the silver toe guard from her pocket. "You haven't asked about the investigation today."

"What's the expression—'I don't have a dog in that fight.'" He smiled and took the packet. "What's this?"

"From the murder scene. You're the only person outside of law enforcement that's seen it. It's a toe guard for a boot. Ever seen one like it?"

Rachel couldn't be certain, but she thought that, for a fraction of a second concern touched his features. He looked into the distance.

"What is it?" she asked.

He frowned. "I can't be sure." He handed it back to her.

"So take a guess."

He shook his head. "I won't say if I'm not sure." He nudged his horse forward. "Let's get them on the move."

Rachel had no choice except to follow. Cimarron took off after Adam's buckskin. As if choreographed, the herd lifted their dripping muzzles. They turned to face the danger of approaching humans, wheeled and fled.

As they moved the horses forward, Cimarron and Adam's

horse, Mariah, kept the stragglers bunched. Rachel found that she could anticipate what the horse would do and shifted her balance to assist the little mare. When she looked over at Adam, he was watching her with another smile, this one touching his eyes.

"Where are we taking them?" Rachel yelled.

"About another mile."

It wasn't far, and Rachel knew her time with Adam was running short. If she was going to get any answers from him, she needed to work fast. She edged Cimarron closer to Mariah. The wild horses, tired from the run, were moving on their own at a sedate walk. Most had given up trying to escape.

"I think you know something," she said quietly.

"Are you accusing me?"

She looked into his eyes. "No. But you do know about the toe guard. Please tell me."

"I don't think you see danger even when it stands tall in front of you."

His words were like a cloud shifting over the sun. There was no way he could know about the skin left at her home. "I'm doing my job. I want to find the person who murdered four men." She hesitated. "I found another headless, skinned corpse. And the killer returned what was left of Burl's head and Ashton Trussell's. No one should die with a look like that on his face."

They rode quietly for a few moments before he spoke. "There's an old man near Custer. He made silver ornaments for saddles, boots and purses. Yuma Pete is his name. When he was in his prime, he knew a lot of silver artisans."

"Yuma Pete sounds like a made-up name."

Adam shrugged. "Might well be, but that's how I know him. He worked with silver. If he doesn't know, maybe he knows someone who does. Anyway, check with him."

"Thanks, Adam."

"Don't thank me yet. Rachel, I know you don't want to believe this, but there is something happening in the wilderness. Something dangerous."

She tried to hide her unease. Adam had gotten under her skin with his stories before, but she didn't have time for scary tales. "Please don't—"

"I'm not trying to convince you that a vengeful spirit is killing those men. But the planet is angry. Think of the hurricanes, the severe storms, the tsunamis, the wildfires. Man is destroying the planet with asphalt and a population exploding so fast that soon there will be no room to grow a food supply."

"That's a little beyond my jurisdiction, Adam. And by the way, we've arrested a young man, Derek Baxter, for the felony vandalism of the heavy equipment on the road job."

He nodded. "Passion is hard to unravel for the young."

"If he's responsible, he's going to be in serious trouble."

"Perhaps that's his destiny."

"In the interview with Deputy Amos, Derek claimed that he followed a Native American into the woods. He said he was set upon and trapped, hung upside down and whacked in the head. When he came to again, he'd been cut loose. Do you know anything about that?"

Adam gave her an amused look. "I have better things to do than scare young men."

"Do you know anyone who might have done such a thing?"

"If the young man was following someone, surely he can describe him."

Rachel sighed. "He didn't get a good look."

"And we all look alike, right?" Adam added.

Rachel felt a flush touch her cheeks. That was exactly what

Baxter had told Scott. "He said it was shadowy in the wilderness. He's a wealthy kid used to getting his way."

Adam reached across and put his hand on top of hers on the saddle horn. She felt again the calloused skin of his palm. "Balance is crucial," he said.

"I agree with the concept, but what are you saying?"

"That young man isn't the killer. This killer may be more than a murderer."

"More how?"

"It's possible he's a harbinger. Sometimes the door between the worlds opens, and what comes through is justice sent by the Great Spirit."

"You think this killer is bringing justice?" Rachel couldn't believe it. "That Hank and Mullet deserved this?"

Adam shook his head. "That's not what I meant. There's a bigger scheme out there, Rachel. This is one tiny part of it. But there's a larger framework. I'm only saying that it's possible that these murders are a part of something much, much bigger." He hesitated. "Is there a reason Frankie wouldn't want us to be friends?"

Rachel was surprised. "No. Why?"

"She said it might be best if I cancelled this ride."

Awareness dawned quickly on Rachel. "Maybe she's backing another candidate." She pressed her legs against Cimarron's sides and sent her into a trot. "Forget about it. I'd better head home."

CHAPTER NINETEEN

Derek slumped against the cold wall of the cell. He was hamstrung. He couldn't call his mom, and he wouldn't call Justine or any WAR members. Anyone he contacted would immediately be arrested. He knew how the pigs worked. They'd arrested him for the sole purpose of constructing a trap, hoping to draw more WAR activists into the web. He was too smart for them, though.

The best he could wish for would be a news story that alerted WAR's national headquarters. He didn't have their number and wouldn't call if he did, for obvious reasons, so he had to wait and hope that someone would see his predicament and make the necessary contact.

He thought back over his morning of interrogation. Christ. While the deputies were out stumbling over body parts all over the wilderness, they still had time to question him for several hours. He'd developed a real antagonism with Scott Amos, and couldn't believe his luck when the deputy got the call that his wife was in labor and needed him at the hospital. At last he'd been left in peace.

Now, though, the hours were growing long. He'd described being attacked and hung upside down. He'd admitted to discovering the mannequin and claiming it for WAR. Nothing else. He didn't have a lawyer, but on TV they always advised their client not to say anything. Keeping mum was a talent of his.

He jumped to his feet when the door to the jail opened. The old bat who was the dispatcher came in with a tray of coffee and some pie. It smacked of a setup to him.

"What's this?" he asked.

"Coffee and blueberry pie."

"I can see that." He was exasperated with the low IQ level of the sheriff's office employees. Deputy Amos hadn't been a rocket scientist, either. He'd kept asking the same questions again and again. "Why are you giving me pie?"

She grinned at him. "Because it's there." She shoved a tray under the cell door. "The sheriff thinks you're involved in those terrible murders. I told him that couldn't be. You look just like my nephew. He's a good boy, and I think you are, too. I think once you have a chance to work it through, you're going to help Sheriff Gray catch the person that's done those awful killings. My advice to you, son, is to help yourself by telling the truth. By the way, Deputy Redmond found your girlfriend's hair clamp at the scene where the mannequin was hung. Wonder what Miss Morgan was doing there?" She left, closing the door behind her.

"Fuck." How had Justine's clamp gotten there?

He glanced at the pie suspiciously, but his hunger got the better of him. He ate the piece in thirty seconds and chased it with the hot, strong coffee. He had to admit, the pie was some of the best he'd ever eaten.

He'd just wiped his mouth with the napkin when the door opened again. The sheriff walked toward his cell. Derek thought for the hundredth time how much like an Old West jail this one was, including Sheriff Gray with his rugged looks and silver moustache. He wore his badge on the pocket of a gray western shirt, and his boots, traditional cowboy fare, made crisp echoes as he crossed the cement floor.

Looking out the barred windows, Derek could see the back street of the town. In an old movie, his compadres would ride up, rope the bars and pull them out so he could make an escape. Unfortunately, the street was empty, so he turned to face the sheriff.

"Baxter, I want to ask you a few questions. Like where were you Friday night?"

He rolled his eyes. "At the Paradise development meeting asking Richard Jones for a job. I told the deputy that."

"What's your involvement with WAR?"

"I'm sympathetic to their stated goals, which are to preserve the wilderness and protect all living creatures against man's abuse."

Gordon walked right up to Derek's cell and put his hands on the bars. "You've got a lot of attitude, don't you?"

"You don't have any evidence to hold me on. I suggest you let me go before I have grounds for a civil suit against you and the county."

Gordon's eyebrows arched. "Since you don't have gainful employment, I've been wondering how you make ends meet. You rent the back half of the old Nyman house. Your ride is a new four-wheel-drive truck. You own an ATV, which we can't seem to find anywhere. I wonder why that is and how you pay for all your toys?"

Derek's heart began to beat faster. His mother had financed some of those things, but WAR had provided the ATV. It was a financial record that could possibly be linked back to them. "None of that is illegal, and it also isn't any of your business. I have a legitimate source of income."

"You still sucking on your mama's tit, boy?" Gordon asked.

"My source of income is none of your business." He kept a sneer in his voice, but he couldn't help the red that crept into his cheeks.

"We've found some tire tracks, a few careless fingerprints left here and there. Now we've got your prints on file. Is there anything you'd like to tell me before we put it together? Once we get the goods on you, there won't be any negotiating. Right now, if you were to help us out, I'd talk to the district attorney about cutting you some slack."

"I don't need any slack. I haven't done anything wrong."

"We know you destroyed that road equipment. And we're going to prove it." Gordon pulled some keys from his pocket and opened the cell door.

Derek's confidence soared. "You only think you're going to prove it. If you had the goods, you'd charge me now."

"Maybe." Gordon grinned wide. "Maybe not. While we were trying to find a body that didn't exist, two other men were killed. I'm not sure what the D.A. will say about that, Mr. Baxter, but if I have my way, you're going to be charged as an accessory to the murder of Burl Mascotti and Mullet Bellows."

Derek sighed. "Yeah, right. I'm worried."

"You should be, son. While we were busy with your bull-shit, those men died. A jury of twelve citizens might not have a hard time seeing how one is related to the other. Don't try to leave Criss County."

Beneath his ribs, his heart plunged. He had to get out of there. They were playing him like a cheap fiddle. Especially that old bat bringing him pie while she told him some made-up shit about Justine being around the mannequin. Justine wouldn't betray him like that.

He remembered, though, that it had been Justine's sugges-tion that he follow the Indian in the woods. Justine seemed to have a finger in all of it. Nausea rose up in his throat at the idea. Gritting his teeth, he met the sheriff's intense scrutiny.

"When you make the charges," Derek said, "I'm sure you'll be in touch. 'Til then, you have a nice day." He walked out of the cell block and was halfway through the office when the sheriff called his name.

All he wanted was to escape the building, but he couldn't show weakness. He turned around, a sneer firmly in place.

The sheriff tossed something at him, a plastic bag. He caught it deftly and looked down at it. One of Justine's gold-and-pearl hair clamps was inside. She had a pair she used to pull her hair back on the sides. He could even see a beautiful auburn hair still caught in the clamp. He couldn't trust his voice, so he tossed the bag back to the sheriff, continued across the office, down the hall, and, at last, into the twilight.

FRANKIE POURED another healthy dose of single malt into Jake's glass. The lights in her small, private den were low, casting most of the room into shadow. But the two chairs where she and Jake sat facing each other were adequately lit. She watched his features. He was hopelessly in love with Rachel, of that she had no doubt. And Rachel was riding the range with Adam Standing Bear. It wasn't a good situation.

"I shouldn't have said anything to Rachel." Jake slumped in the overstuffed leather chair. "She looked cornered. Now she'll avoid me."

"To quote my mother, 'Nothing ventured, nothing gained.' You had to say something, Jake." Frankie dropped two ice cubes in his glass and handed it to him. "So she didn't jump into your arms. Rachel isn't demonstrative. You know that. She's a woman who thinks before she leaps."

"You didn't see her eyes. I did."

"And I always assumed you didn't have a lot of imagination." Frankie sat on the arm of his chair. "Rachel values you, I know that. Maybe she has to turn her thinking around. She's viewed you as a brother for a long time." She touched his chin with her finger and lifted his face so she could look into his eyes. She'd done her research on Rachel, and now it would stand her in good stead. "She had to, Jake. That was safe for her. With her mother's life of prostitution and untimely death, Rachel hasn't fully come to terms with her sexual self. You'd know that if you thought about it. When was the last time she mentioned a date to you?"

"Pretty much never." He took a healthy swallow of the scotch and Frankie rose to refill his glass and handed it to him.

"I rest my case. She hasn't mentioned a date because she doesn't date. She works and she trains at the dojang. She's actually very accomplished in martial arts." She watched his expression and saw the annoyance. Just as she figured. Jake didn't want to view Rachel as someone who could take care of herself. And that one thing was enough to make Rachel turn tail and run in the opposite direction—right into Adam's arms.

"Now she's going to avoid me like the plague." Jake took a long swallow.

"Maybe for a day or two." Frankie wanted to shake him. If he gave up on her now, he wasn't strong enough for Rachel. "But your paths cross everyday. Time is your best ally, Jake. She'll adjust to this new way of thinking about you. Once she lets down the barriers that she's built about the whole brotherly thing, she may be startled by her own feelings."

"Startled and appalled."

Frankie laughed. "You don't know enough about life to be such a pessimist. You're a lucky man."

"I haven't had it that easy. I'm no silver spoon kid."

"No, you're just one of the lucky few who grew up with a

mother and a father who cared about you. Rachel didn't have that, and what I had I can't remember. If you want to love her, Jake, you're going to have to put yourself in a place where you can understand her. I know how she feels because I've been there."

Jake stood. "If you get a chance, will you feel Rachel out on this?"

She gave a dry chuckle. "Sure. But if she thinks I'm probing or pressing your case, she isn't going to be happy. By the way, I tried to ask her over tonight. She must be out of pocket." She knew where Rachel was, but she wondered if Jake did.

"She went home. She looked exhausted."

"I thought I saw her driving south." She shrugged. "Earlier in the week she mentioned something about riding horses with Adam Standing Bear."

Jake's face turned grim. "I could make her happy. I'm not going to be a game warden forever."

"Now this is something I could help you with. What are you looking at? Sheriff or state senate?"

He looked at her with amazement.

"Jake, I'm not psychic. You have ambition stamped on your forehead."

"Dad thinks I should announce my intention to run this fall."

"For state senate?"

He nodded.

"Following in Harvey's footsteps, eh?"

"I don't agree with everything Dilson's done, but he's been good for South Dakota as a whole." Jake finished his drink and put the glass carefully on a coaster.

"Have you talked this over with Harvey?" She almost held her breath. Fate had given her a true blessing.

"Not yet."

"Would you like me to set up a meeting? Maybe tomorrow."

Jake's eyes widened. "Would you consider doing that for me?"

"I think you'd be great for Criss County and South Dakota. And your dad is right. You should announce soon. Maybe at the press conference Harvey's holding about Paradise. That would be perfect! Let folks start talking. If Harvey will endorse you..." she lifted one shoulder "that's huge."

"Let's set up the meeting." Jake's steps had quickened as he paced.

Frankie went to him and captured his hands. "Jake, if you're serious about this and serious about Rachel, maybe you should tell her your feelings."

"Why?"

Frankie schooled her expression carefully. Men could be so dense. "Because if you two should get together, this will change her life."

He nodded. "I just assumed she'd be excited. I mean as a state senator, I can help Criss County get more funding, more jobs, more statewide attention."

"And Rachel would be expected to attend political functions and act as the supportive wife. She'll have to be as image conscious as you are."

He nodded. "I should talk this over with her."

"Absolutely. So I'll set up the meeting with Harvey. The sooner the better. We need to feel him out."

Jake gave her a squeeze. "I'm so glad we became friends, Frankie. I hope once the road project is finished you'll hang around Criss County."

"That's not likely, but we'll see what happens."

She walked him to the door. As soon as he was gone she

went to the telephone. The number she dialed rang several times before someone answered.

"This is Frankie Jackson. Would you ask the senator to give me a callback tomorrow? Early. Tell him politics are heating up in Criss County, and I need him on the ground floor."

She listened a moment, then hung up. Things were falling into place.

At the bar she made herself another drink, returned to the phone, looked up Justine Morgan's number and called. It was late evening, and she wondered if the young woman was putting the moves on Richard Jones. She'd seen a lot of ambitious young women launch a frontal attack on Richard, hoping to get married and stay that way long enough to get a hefty alimony check.

Justine didn't seem to be motivated by money. It was Jones's power she wanted. The power to change a community, to bring in development and progress. Justine hoped to thwart that.

Frankie was smiling when Justine answered.

"I wanted to warn you that the sheriff's office has evidence that you were at the crime scene. It's one of your hair clamps. They know it belongs to you."

"My hair clamp?" Justine was calm. "That's ridiculous. I haven't lost any clamps."

"Gold filled, pearls. I saw you wearing them earlier this week."

There was the sound of someone rummaging in a drawer. "Shit!"

"Take care."

CHAPTER TWENTY

The last vivid hues of sunset had fled, and a violent blue had taken over the east. Slowly it would shift across the sky, claiming it for the night. Rachel watched Adam Standing Bear drive south at the fork in the road. She headed north, back toward Bisonville. Instead of taking the two-lane into town, she took County Road 12 west. Adam had given her directions to Yuma Pete's.

She was tired and her legs and thighs were already sending up warning signals of what she could expect in the morning. Somehow, because she worked out and stayed in shape, she'd assumed she'd escape the legendary soreness that came from riding. Not so. She would barely be able to hobble in the morning. She could already hear the ribald jokes.

During the ride with Adam she'd been able to push back her worries about Jake, but now she found them sitting shotgun with her. Her feelings were conflicted. Jake had been a part of her life for as long as she could remember. He'd known her since she was a baby. When her mother had died, Jake had stepped into the void, along with his parents, and crafted an entirely new life for her.

The move to Bisonville had been instrumental in changing

her future. When Mel Ortiz had taken over the forest lands around the state parks at Custer and the Badlands, it had led Rachel to an appreciation for nature and small-town living. Jake had played a big role in that.

He'd taught her to negotiate the wilderness, to distinguish the tracks of animals, to name the trees. And he'd shared some of the Native American wisdom he'd learned from his dad. He'd also interfered in her life with the attitude of a blood relative--that he had a right.

And that troubled her.

Jake was a handsome man. Any woman would find him attractive, but Rachel had lived with the taboo of her kinship to him for so long that to try to move beyond it was uncomfortable. Extremely so.

She did care for him, and deeply. They were friends and competitors. Jake was the measuring stick she'd used to get through the police academy. She had to be as good a law officer as he was, or better, and that set the standard pretty high.

When had their relationship turned into something more for him? She tried to think of hints he might have dropped along the way. In the last week he'd arranged to take to her to two events. Dates.

"Shit." She pressed the gas harder, trying to outrun her thoughts. She should've seen it coming. He'd signaled the change in his feelings for her. She'd been so caught up with the murders she'd simply overlooked the indications. And why was Frankie pressing Jake's case? Did she secretly care for Adam? It was all so complicated. And it did absolutely no good to think about it.

The terrain she entered was isolated and rugged. She had to stop worrying about Jake and focus on the case. She made a mental list of questions to ask Yuma Pete.

According to the directions Adam gave her, she was close.

She slowed, hunting for the trail that would lead to his place. She saw the square boulder, just as Adam had described, and she turned down the lane that was barely distinguishable. Each bump made her shift in an effort to ease her sore backside, but as she drew close to a rough-hewn building, her attention focused on the flutter of feathers and the glitter of colored glass hung from the branches of a stunted tree. The headlights of her truck struck bottles of red, blue, green and yellow, a rattling rainbow collection.

Rachel pulled to a stop and got out, taking in the yard. Along with the bottles hanging from trees and bushes and sitting on rocks, there were strange figures made of copper and iron. Different types of feathers fluttered from limbs and eaves and totem poles. The place was remarkable, and also a little unnerving.

She approached one of the feathers and examined it. It had been hung with clear fishing line, exactly like the feathers at the crime scene.

The wooden door opened and an old man stepped onto the porch. Stooped with age, he was about three inches shorter than Rachel. His skin was brown leather and his hair, braided down his back, matched the silvery gray-and-white feather in his leather headband.

"Mr. Pete?" she asked.

"That's me." His dark eyes were alert, sharp.

She held out her badge and identification. "I'm Deputy Rachel Redmond, from Criss County." She wasn't sure what jurisdiction she was in.

"I've seen you on television."

His diction was clear, but it held a trace of an accent. Spanish? She couldn't be certain. He looked as if he'd been carved from the badlands themselves. "Would you mind taking a look at something for me?"

"Is this about the murders?" His gaze probed hers.

"Yes, it is." She held out the plastic evidence bag with the silver toe guard in it.

He took it and looked at it for a long time. Instead of handing it back, he signaled to two rocking chairs on the front porch. "Have a seat. I was hoping this day would never come, but I knew that day something bad was afoot."

Rachel inhaled quickly. He knew something. She'd seen it in his expression.

She took the chair he indicated, easing onto the edge so she could turn her knees and face him. He stared into the distance, watching the night come down hard and the sky come alive with shiny brilliance. The moon hung in the east, new and delicate and precise.

Out on the road, a vehicle idled as if it meant to come down the trail to Yuma Pete's. After a moment, it moved on, red taillights winking in the distance.

"There were four of them that came up here that day, asking for me to make something like this."

Rachel sat very still.

"Hank Welford brought them here. I never cared for Hank or his partner, Mullet Bellows. They wanted something made, something they could all have. They were drinking. Had been for several days, I'd guess. Hank came in, but the others stayed in the vehicle. I remember it clearly. Hank said they'd made a pact with the devil, and these toe clips would bind them all together."

In the silence that fell over them, Rachel took a breath. "Hank commissioned the boot clips?"

"Yes. I drew up a design, and he took it out to show them and they approved it. But that clip you're holding isn't one that I made. It looks a lot like my design, almost identical, in fact, but that's not my work."

For a moment Rachel tried to make sense of what he was saying. "You didn't make this clip?"

He shook his head. "Someone copied my design."

The killer. It made perfect sense. Hank, Mullet and two other men had made a pact with the devil—had done something, possibly something terrible. The clips bound them to secrecy. But the killer knew the men and knew about the boot clips. The killer had copied Yuma Pete's design—and left the clip stabbed into the chest of each victim—with the intent of terrorizing the remaining members of the foursome.

"Deputy Redmond, are you okay?"

Rachel swallowed. Her throat had gone completely dry. "Yes. I'm fine. Tell me about these men."

Yuma shifted in his chair so he could stare at her in the near darkness. "Hank and Mullet are dead. It might be best to leave this alone."

"My job is to catch the person responsible for four brutal deaths. Tell me what you remember." How reliable was a memory sixteen years gone. But Yuma was the best lead Rachel had.

"They paid in advance. Hank counted out the money in hundred dollar bills. I'd never seen such a wad of cash in my life."

"Did they all come together to get the clips?"

"Just Hank."

"You said Hank and Mullet were partners?"

"They ran hunting expeditions. They set themselves up as guides. Later, I heard they had a falling out and went their separate ways."

"Who were the other men?" This was the million dollar question.

"I recognized Mullet." His hands moved over his head.

"The hair cut. The others were in the back of the vehicle. I didn't see them clearly."

"And you never asked?"

"I didn't want to know. Hank and Mullet were bad men. They were always in the middle of things that were wrong. Hank had more money that day than I've ever seen, and I knew they'd done something very bad to get that much."

"You have no idea what they might have done?"

He shrugged. "I never asked. The truth is, I didn't want to know."

"Can you remember anything else?"

"Most of the commission work I do is for saddle ornaments, jewelry, belt buckles. I'd never been asked to make toe guards before. Only had one person ever call about them and that was a while back. Ornamentation for boots is unusual, and I couldn't help but wonder why someone like Hank would want such a thing, but he was always one to be gaudy. He wore spurs with spinning rowels. Things like that."

Yuma handed the plastic bag back to her. "This is good work, but it's copied off mine. Where did you find it?"

"Stuck in Mullet's chest with a porcupine quill."

Yuma didn't flinch. "I heard he was skinned and decapitated."

"He was. There was also a pole with two owl feathers. I noticed the feathers were wrapped with fishing line, like the ones in your yard."

Yuma continued to rock. "The Indians used strips of animal hide. Today, some people use thread. I like the fishing line. It holds up better."

"Is there a special message with the owl feathers?"

He shook his head. "It's hard to say, but if I had to take a guess, I'd think it was a prediction of death."

"Welford and Mullet are already dead." Rachel could

barely make out Yuma Pete's silhouette. Night had fallen over them, and in the distance was the sound of summer insects. At the last murder, the killer had left two feathers. "You think the other men who were in that vehicle are going to die?"

"I'm not a prophet or a detective, but I think those men got into something and now, I think someone is settling an old score."

"When did this happen?"

"The summer of 1992. I remember because I knew that summer that Bill Clinton was going to win. In fact, when the men drove up, I was listening to Peter Jennings on the campaign trail. It was the last race where the people's votes counted. You remember?"

Rachel laughed. "I was eight." And politics were the furthest thing from her mind. That was the summer her mother started doing heroin. "You remember anything else that happened that summer?"

"There was a lot of hardship in the area. We'd had a tragic winter, then drought took a lot of families off the land, sent them to work in factories. Things began to change around here, and not for the better. Lots of ranchers lost everything."

Rachel was about to get up when she stopped. "Was that the summer Dub Jackson disappeared?"

"As a matter of fact, it was."

"I have to go." The sense of urgency made her breathless.

Frankie had never believed her father abandoned her. Never. A sick little girl, brutally damaged, dreaming of a lost father. Rachel understood the power of such a dream. But what if it were true? What if Dub Jackson was murdered? What if Frankie was tracking down the men who killed her father and stole her life?

Yuma rose from the chair. In the darkness, he was barely a

silhouette. "Come back to see me, and I'll make you some earrings. Something with horses."

"I'd like that." She nearly stumbled in her haste to leave. It was after eight, and she was bone weary. Her legs and seat felt as if she'd been beaten with a lead pipe, but she had a lead, and she meant to follow it.

She was at the door when she remembered another question. "You said someone else had asked you about toe clips. Do you remember who it was?"

"Never said her name. It was at least ten years ago. Young woman just asked if I'd ever made any."

"And what did you tell her?" Rachel felt a sense of dread. If she was right, Frankie Jackson had been on the trail of Hank and Mullet for a long, long time.

"I told her I did one commission and didn't accept that kind of work anymore."

"She never said her name?"

"No." He inhaled sharply enough that Rachel heard him. "You think I talked to the killer?"

"It's a good possibility, Mr. Pete. Now you lock up behind me and take care."

SITTING in the study at his ranch, Harvey Dilson gripped the telephone more firmly, and his voice rose. "If you can't get this under control, Gordon, I can and will bring in federal assistance."

"What do you think federal agents will accomplish that we can't?" Gordon's voice came through the phone line, equally loud and angry.

"Success!" Dilson signaled to his assistant to refill his drink. Jeremy Parker took the Waterford highball glass, dropped in several cubes of ice and filled it with Maker's Mark. He put it back in the Senator's hand.

"We're doing everything we can do," Gordon said, his voice now modulated. "We don't have a lot to work with, Harvey. Federal agents can't generate evidence when it isn't there."

"What about a profiler?" Harvey sipped the drink, letting the burn of the premium bourbon slide down his throat and into his stomach. He'd worked too hard to bring Paradise to fruition to let some maniac with a hard-on for poachers stop the project.

"Rachel has some training in profiling."

"She's a twenty-six-year-old rookie from trailer trash! What were you thinking when you put her in charge of the case?" Harvey rose from his chair. At forty-eight, he was in the best shape of his life. He'd avoided the pitfalls that tripped up most politicians—a wife and kids. He was running for his third term as U.S. Senator from Criss County with an eye toward the White House, and he'd built a power base in Washington. He'd also invested three-quarters of his personal fortune in Paradise.

"Rachel is the most highly trained officer I've got," Gordon answered. "Have you seen my budget, Harvey? It isn't like I've got a Washington surplus to play around with. I have two deputies and a host of volunteers."

"I'm offering you federal agents."

"Who we'd have to babysit in that wilderness. That's no help at all."

"I talked to Frankie today." He had one wild thought that Frankie, of all the people in the world, had reason to want Hank and Mullet dead. <u>If she knew</u>. But she didn't. Medical experts from South Dakota to Alabama had assured him she had no memory of the past. Hell, he'd seen her with his own eyes. She hadn't remembered her name or her own mother. It was impossible. Besides, she was his most ardent supporter.

She'd worked behind the scenes for his political campaigns for years. She owed her job to him. The truth was, he owned her.

"What did Frankie say?" Gordon prodded.

"She said half her road crew has stopped showing up for work." The highway was what he had to focus on. Without it, Paradise would never be born. "The road is dead. Do you hear me—dead!" He roared the last word. "The men are afraid to go up there to work. Most everything I own is on the line—"

"You aren't the only one with everything riding on this development."

Harvey felt his blood pressure surge again. "Frankie said Jake Ortiz has his focus on public office instead of finding this killer. He wants me to help him set up his campaign for state senator."

"Jake? He's running for office?"

"State senate. Are you deaf as well as stupid?"

Gordon swore softly. "Who put that idea into Jake's head?"

"I'd say you might want to have a talk with his old man. Mel may have retired from his job, but he's sure determined to keep his finger in everything that happens in Criss County."

"I'll talk to him."

"And you might want to talk to Richard, too. He's running around with that red-haired bitch who thinks she knows everything. I met her at Frankie's house, and she's an opinionated little piece of ass. Richard acts like a puppy at her heels."

"Justine Morgan may be involved with WAR."

Harvey took another swallow of bourbon. "Now that's good news. If we could link that little whore into something illegal, it might break the spell she's cast on Richard." Harvey signaled Jeremy for another drink. Richard was the weak link. The one he'd always worried about. Mullet and Hank had been stupid, but survival motivated them to keep their lips shut.

And now they were dead, therefore no longer a potential problem. Richard was very much alive, and in the public eye.

"Harvey, the question I've been asking myself is why someone murdered Hank and Mullet. Why them? And why skin and decapitate them?"

"I have no idea. Call me when you have an answer." He put the phone down, but Gordon's question had triggered a series of unpleasant images. Frankie had finagled copies of the crime scene photos for him to see. Damn good photographs, in fact. He'd had to drink a lot of whiskey to get to sleep after he'd looked at the photos. Funny, but Frankie had seemed untouched by them. She was tough as nails. Too bad she wasn't a partner in Paradise.

He drained his glass and handed it to Jeremy. His assistant shook his head.

"Slow down, Senator."

Harvey drew back the glass, aiming at Jeremy. At the last moment, he smashed it against the stone fireplace that was large enough to roast an ox. Jeremy didn't flinch. He simply stood there, waiting.

"I've earned the right to drink when and however much I want." He looked around the room at the mounted heads of a moose, a grizzly and a big-horned sheep. When he'd bought the old Jackson ranch on the auction block, he'd seen the potential to turn the ranch house into a showplace. With a decorator from Sioux Falls, he'd done just that. Elegant, western, solid, it was a place where a man could relax in solitude. He frequently loaned it to people he needed to woo in his political career.

Jeremy lifted his chin only a fraction, but it showed the stubbornness that Harvey admired. "You need to keep your head. Last night you were so drunk you thought someone was in your bedroom. A couple of the ranch hands heard the commotion. You may have this election sewn up, but if you start acting like a fool and the word gets out, the public will turn on you like a rabid dog."

Harvey suffered the lecture, and he listened. Jeremy was one of the smartest Beltway advisors around. He paid him a high six-figure salary for his advice.

"You're right. I have meetings with the Paradise group all day tomorrow. I think I'll turn in now. Be sure you set the alarm system."

Jeremy looked at the shattered glass on the stones of the fireplace. "I'll do that. Try to get some sleep."

Harvey walked down the hall, past the many photos that showed him with men of power. Often the pictures gave him comfort, documenting his rise from South Dakota state house to the corridors of D.C. The world had changed greatly in the twelve years he'd served in the nation's capitol, and so had he. A moment of longing for the simpler days when he'd focused on South Dakota politics touched him. But like it or not, he'd been destined for greatness.

He entered his bedroom, a master suite with triple French doors that led out to a shadowed veranda where potted palms rustled in the night breeze. The doors were open and the sheer curtains billowed, causing him to catch his breath and step backward. He stopped himself before he let out a yell. Damn doors. He'd asked the cleaning staff to lock them after they'd tidied his room.

The navy blue carpet was thick and plush as he crossed the room to close the doors. In the near darkness, he saw something on his bed. Nearly twelve inches long and two inches wide, it lay stark against the white silk bedspread.

Puzzled, he picked it up. It was filthy and stank to high heaven. It was a piece of hide, something one of his hounds had undoubtedly found. But how had it gotten inside his house and on his bed? He didn't allow animals in the house.

Anger at his staff gripped him. He paid good money, and the maids left something like this on his bed. He started toward the doors, intending to throw the filthy thing into the yard.

A shaft of clear moonlight struck it. It was crusty with filth, but there was no hair. It wasn't animal skin. A terrible suspicion stopped him in his tracks. Turning on the light, he looked at it. He saw the skin, the layer of fat, the muscle. His stomach heaved, and a scream caught in his throat. He ordered his fingers to release the skin, but they didn't obey. Lurching and panting, he struggled back down the hall into the den still clutching the skin.

"Jeremy!" He stumbled over a chair and went down. "Jeremy!"

His assistant came out of the kitchen, a disgusted look on his face. When he saw Harvey on the floor, the skin in his hand, the color fled his face.

"What the hell? Where'd you get that?" Jeremy rushed to his side, reaching out to help Harvey, then stepping back as he caught the full view and smell of the flesh.

"Someone put it on my bed. Someone put it on my bed." Harvey repeated the sentence over and over.

"How?" Jeremy looked around the room as if he expected the killer to jump out from behind the drapes.

Harvey took several deep breaths. He had to get a grip on himself. If the killer had been hiding in the bedroom intent on killing him, he'd be dead.

"My doors were open."

"Betinna always locks them. She never forgets."

"They were open!" Harvey got to his knees and stood. He stared at his hand until the fingers obeyed and the skin dropped on the dove gray carpet.

"I'm calling the sheriff." Jeremy started for the phone.

"No!" Harvey took another breath. He'd regained some measure of control, and with it his wits had returned.

"We have to inform the authorities." Jeremy was insistent. "This is a threat against your life. This involves federal authorities. Now we can call in the FBI or the CIA or the NSA. We can get agents assigned to protect you. We can—"

"We're not calling anyone." Harvey walked around the skin. "Get me another drink."

"A drink? Now?"

"A whiskey. Right this minute. And stop questioning my orders. You work for me, remember?"

"Yes, sir." Jeremy made the drink and handed it to Harvey. "What are you going to do?"

"I need to make some phone calls. Until then, get some tongs from the kitchen. Seal the skin in a plastic bag and put it in the refrigerator."

"You're kidding, right?"

Any other time, Harvey would have found the expression on Jeremy's face priceless. "If I have to repeat myself, you're fired."

"But this is a threat." Jeremy hurried to get the bag and tongs even as he objected.

Harvey picked up his address book from a drawer in his desk. The skin was more than a threat, it was a promise.

"Put the skin in the refrigerator and then get out." Harvey's fingers closed over the portable telephone.

"But—"

"Go down to the bunk house and ask the hands if they saw anyone on the property. Tell them to stay away from the house until light. I want Frankie Jackson here at daybreak. Aside from Adam Standing Bear, she's the best tracker I know."

"Why not Adam?" Jeremy asked.

"Because in all likelihood, he or someone he knows is

behind this." It could only be Adam. Skinning a man. It was savage. "Now go. I need to make a private call." Before he heard the door slam, Harvey had already dialed Richard Jones's emergency number. He counted ten rings before he hung up.

RACHEL HEADED toward Bisonville as fast as she dared drive. Her eyes burned with fatigue, and her body felt sluggish but her brain whirled, churning with pieces of a puzzle that almost fit but not quite.

At the bottom of it all was Frankie Jackson.

Four men bought silver toe guards to seal a pact. Two of those men were dead—each stuck in the chest with a hand-crafted piece of silver after being skinned and beheaded. They'd been tortured, so that they suffered both physical pain and humiliation. Hank and Mullet had been executed by someone who meant for them to die in agony.

But who were the remaining two men and what had the four of them done to put a killer on the trail?

She thought she knew. The problem was that she had no proof.

Fumbling on the seat she picked up her cell phone and dialed the S.O.

"What can I do you for?" Gladys asked when she answered.

"Is Scott there?" Rachel couldn't ask for Gordon. She didn't know who she could trust any longer. If she was correct, the killer had something to do with Frankie and the disappearance of Frankie's father. Gordon had been involved in the investigation when Dub vanished. What was it Frankie had said—horse tracks that disappeared into a trailer. Reported sightings of Dub in Texas. All things that could easily be arranged if a law officer was involved.

"Rachel, did you hear me? I said Scott's at home with his wife and new baby." Gladys was almost yelling.

"Sorry. Is anyone else in the office?"

"Me, myself and I." Gladys cleared her throat. "Is something wrong, Rachel? You sound peculiar."

"I'm not sure." She felt her own panic growing.

"Where are you?"

"I'm headed back into town. Do I have any messages?"

"Yeah, let me get the pink slips." The phone clattered to the desk and there was the sound of Gladys pushing her creaking chair back and walking to Rachel's desk. She returned with a rustle of paper. "Frankie called and wanted you to meet her and Jake." Another shuffle of paper. "And Jake called, said it was urgent. That's it."

Rachel could feel the hammer of her heart in her chest. "What time did Frankie call?"

"About two hours ago."

"Did Frankie say where she was?"

"Nope, but she left a number."

Rachel forced the number into her memory as she drove. She hung up and blinked her dry eyes as she pressed harder on the accelerator.

She didn't have enough evidence to arrest Frankie for the murders. She wasn't sure that Jake or Gordon would help her find that evidence. It was possible that Gordon was one of the men marked for murder. The only thing Rachel knew for certain was that the series of murders that had rocked Bisonville stemmed from Dub Jackson's disappearance and Frankie's head wound. Now she had to find the facts and get the evidence that would allow her to put a serial killer behind bars.

CHAPTER TWENTY-ONE

She was a goddess carved from ivory and fire. Richard Jones leaned on his elbow and stared at the sleeping woman in his bed. He was a man who made his living with his brain, and he could tick off the benefits and drawbacks of the relationship he'd fallen into with Justine Morgan, but for the first time in his life, he didn't care about the bottom line or the risk percentage or the profit potential.

Justine had taken him to her bed, or his bed as it turned out, and shown him a taste of her feminine powers. Not that he wasn't experienced with women. A man with his money had no dearth of opportunity. He'd known women who were eager to please his smallest whim, and he'd used them without a thought.

The woman asleep in his bed, auburn hair spread over the pillows like a burst of sunset, was different. He thought about the hours just past and smiled. In the middle of lovemaking, she'd started an argument about the four-lane. Her passion only deepened his desire for her. And though they hadn't agreed on the issue, they'd found orgasm within seconds of each other. The sexual stimulation, coupled with the intellectual, was almost more than Richard could bear. It worked on him like a drug, and he was tempted to wake her up so they could debate and make love again.

He heard his cell phone ringing, his private number that only a few people knew. He considered answering it, but instead he let his hand drift to Justine's slender waist. His fingers glided over the smoothness of her hip. She was exquisite. Lying on her side, her breasts gently sloping and her face soft and tender with sleep, he knew he was falling in love. It was the most extraordinary sensation, like dropping out of an airplane without any means to stop himself.

The tone from his cell phone continued. Fearing that it might awaken Justine and she would decide to go home for the night, he slipped out of bed to answer it. Before he picked it up, another noise stopped him.

Someone was downstairs.

He heard the unmistakable sound of footsteps on the stairs and then in the hallway outside his bedroom.

Such a thing wasn't possible. He had a high-tech alarm system that was infallible. The only way to get in a door or window without setting off the alarm was with a specific code.

Yet he was certain he heard footsteps.

The cell phone had stopped ringing, and he moved to the door. His heart hammered. Mullet Bellows had been working with the alarm company when he'd had the system installed in his home. He'd never considered that Mullet might have access to his codes—or that Mullet could've been tempted to sell that information to someone.

That was all he could think about now.

Alongside the sound of his heart beat and the thrum of his blood, he heard something else. At first he wasn't certain what it was, but as the noise drew closer to the door, he recognized it.

The soft sigh of a bone rattle whispered under the door.

Richard froze. He searched his memory for the connection, and with it came real fear. He knew the legend of the Skin Dancer. Since Hank and Mullet's murders, he'd tried not to connect the dots that tied his past to the two dead men. With the nervous rattle of the bones outside his door, he could no longer ignore it. The past had come calling.

Hank and Mullet, both skinned and decapitated in a ritualistic fashion, had been useful in the past for setting up hunting expeditions for potential investors in Paradise. Harvey had always handled the details, since Harvey still enjoyed the kill. Richard had given up hunting long ago. After the Dub Jackson incident, he'd had no stomach for killing anything.

He hadn't really been involved in what happened to Dub. He hadn't. He'd been there, but he'd never been part of it.

Harvey had been laying the groundwork for his first U.S. Senate race, but his eye had been on the potential of Paradise. He'd arranged a "hunting trip" for several of the most lucrative backers. The men who'd flown into Criss County for a big game kill were influential in D.C. circles, known to make things happen. Harvey was a man with vision, even then. He'd seen the way his ambitions and Richard's infant plans for Paradise would dovetail into the perfect partnership. So Harvey had asked Richard along on the illegal hunt.

Richard had never cared much for hunting, and he'd been sickened when he saw the gray wolf in the leg trap. The plan was for Mullet to release the wounded animal only minutes before the hunters, who were waiting at a cabin, arrived at the scene. With only three working legs and half-starved, the animal would be an easy kill.

Hank had been baiting the wounded animal, teasing it by shooting his .22 caliber pistol near its legs, until it lunged and snapped at the end of the trap chain, when Dub Jackson had ridden over the ridge, alone. He'd ridden straight into the group of men, pulled his revolver and shot the wolf.

When he turned to Harvey, he'd said, "I'll end your political aspirations over this, Dilson. You won't be serving the public--you're going to serve time in a federal prison. No one has the right to treat an animal that way."

Leaning against the cool door of his bedroom, Richard saw it all again. He squeezed his eyes shut and pressed his forehead into the wood, but he couldn't stop the memories.

Harvey had tried to reason with Dub. Mullet and Hank had flanked Harvey like the thugs they were.

"I'm rounding up my cows, and when I get home, I'm going to call the game warden," Dub said. Richard could still see the disgust in his clear blue eyes as he surveyed all the men.

"It won't do any good," Harvey had responded. "The game warden isn't interested in this hunt."

"Then I'll take it to the newspaper. Lots of ranchers don't want the wolves back in these hills, but this kind of crap," he'd pointed at the leg trap, "is inexcusable."

He'd turned his horse to ride away when Harvey grabbed a pistol from Hank's hip. "Don't make me hurt you," Harvey had said.

Dub had kept riding. He'd never even turned around. Harvey shot him in the back of the head.

No one had anticipated the girl, riding up from the opposite direction. No one had noticed, tucked as she was behind a rock outcropping. Once she screamed, there was no doubt she'd seen Harvey shoot her father.

Richard put his hands over his ears, trying to block the memories. The bone rattle chattered in his head, and he heard the echo of Frankie's sharp scream, then the sound of another shot, and finally the deep silence of the wilderness that fell over all of them.

Mullet had gone to check on the girl and come back saying she was beyond help. She'd been shot in the head. So they'd left her. It was just a miracle that she hadn't remembered any of it.

"Richard?" Justine's gentle voice touched him like a warm hand. "What's wrong?"

"Do you hear it?" he asked.

"Hear what?"

"The rattle. It's—" But the sound was gone. If it had ever been there at all.

"What's wrong?" Justine asked again as she grabbed the sheet from the bed, wrapped her naked body and came to him. She rubbed his back and pulled him into her arms. "Don't tell me you have nightmares?" she asked, a teasing note in her voice.

"It must have been a dream. I thought I heard someone in the house."

"Not in this fortress. I don't think James Bond could infiltrate your security system."

He let her lead him back to the bed. "I heard something."

"I'll get you something to drink." The sheet had fallen from her body, and he was mesmerized by her perfection yet again.

"Okay."

She wrapped the sheet toga style and walked across the room barefoot. At the door she turned slightly to give him a smile.

The door blasted open with such force that the edge of it caught Justine in the face. He heard her nose crunch, and bright red blood poured down her face and chest and onto the sheet.

"Uh-uh-uh." She made a strange guttural sound as she fell to the floor.

Richard had no time to think. A person dressed all in black

kicked him in the face and he fell backward onto the bed. Before he could even react, something hard slammed into the side of his head. He fought for consciousness and was aware that he was being dragged on the bedspread through the bedroom and down the hall.

At the top of the stairs, he felt a boot in his back and he began to fall, bumping on each step, turning and thudding until the blackness swallowed him.

Bud's Bar was choked with human bodies and cigarette smoke. Rachel stepped in the door then backed out, blinking her burning eyes. She inhaled and went back in, walking up to the bar.

"What'll it be?" asked Madonna, the twenty-one-year-old barmaid who sported at least two ounces of gold in her navel, lip, eyebrow, and God knew where else.

"Crown on the rocks." Rachel eased onto a barstool. Her eyes and ears were adjusting to the place.

When Madonna set her drink in front of her, Rachel smiled. She liked the young woman. They'd talked on occasion, and for all of her rebellious piercings, Madonna was a smart kid with a level head. She'd been accepted at the University of Montana at Missoula to work on her masters in creative writing. The bar, she claimed, was a hotbed of character study for her novel.

"Have you seen any of the guys Mullet or Hank used to hang around with?"

Madonna's clear green eyes went vague. "Sure. They're in and out. Been sort of scarce lately." She shrugged and occupied herself with drying glasses and putting them away.

Rachel studied the young woman. There were five years between them and an entire culture. Still, Madonna had always greeted her with a smile and a willingness to share a bit of gossip. "I didn't see them when I came in. Are they in back shooting pool?"

Four pool tables took up the back room at Bud's. During the afternoon, sociable games of eight ball helped the cold winter hours pass. On Saturday night, though, the egos came out and fistfights weren't uncommon.

"I think they left." Madonna looked at the counter and began to polish an imaginary spot.

Rachel lightly grasped her wrist. "What's going on?"

She shrugged.

That troubled Rachel more than a denial. "Madonna, you look..." It struck her. "You look scared."

The young woman's green gaze lifted and connected. "I heard Charlie and Nugent talking, Rachel. They said the sheriff's department wasn't doing anything about Mullet and Hank. They were in here 'til about an hour ago. They left, and they were looking for trouble."

"Where were they going?"

She shook her head. "They didn't say and I didn't ask. I was hoping they'd fall over drunk and sleep it off."

Rachel brought the silver boot clip out from her pocket. "You ever seen anything like this?"

Madonna shook her head. "What is it?"

"Boot ornament." She put it away. "If you see those guys would you give me a call on my cell phone?"

"Sure thing." Madonna saw a customer at the other end of the bar. "You watch your back. Those guys are fueled up and frustrated. They don't have sense enough to pour piss out of a boot, so that means they're liable to do anything."

"Thanks." Rachel headed out of the bar. It didn't take five minutes to drive to the Le Chateau Apartments. The spacious townhouses had been built to cater to the young elite of

Bisonville—a growing segment of the population. These were single residents with a good income and a desire for a luxury lifestyle.

Rachel knocked at Justine Morgan's door. By so conveniently finding the hair clamp at the mannequin scene, Frankie had made it a point to implicate Justine in WAR—yet she'd also introduced Justine to Richard Jones. Rachel was beginning to see that everything Frankie did, she did with an agenda. And Frankie had found the hairclip at the mannequin scene. Very convenient. She probably planted it there.

She rapped on Justine's door harder. It was impossible to tell if anyone was home, but the sound of her fist on wood echoed hollowly, as if the place were empty. Based on what she'd seen at the Paradise meeting, Justine was likely at Richard Jones's house.

She hesitated, longing for someone she could trust, some backup. Jones had built a palatial home on the west side of town. She'd never been there, but she'd seen the stone and glass building from the road. It was a half-hour drive. She could make it in under twenty minutes.

Derek found Justine's car parked in Richard Jones's circular drive. She'd left it in plain view for anyone to see, which told him more than he wanted to know about her relationship with Richard. She was sleeping with the guy and didn't care who knew it. She was rubbing his nose in it. The two of them were probably upstairs, in bed, laughing at him and how he'd fallen for Justine.

He walked up to the huge wrought-iron gates that worked on a pass code, or perhaps a laser beam. A ten-foot fence surrounded the entire estate. Richard didn't need a security guard. His place was protected by technology.

Derek closed his fingers around the iron bars and looked up at the palatial home. He'd always had money, the finer things, the pleasures that a trust-fund baby could afford without thought. The only thing he'd ever really wanted that eluded him was Justine. Until this very moment, he'd felt he had a chance with her. He'd thought her attraction to Richard would wane, or that the middle-aged bastard would realize a woman twenty years his junior made him look like the old dude who'd married Anna Nicole Smith.

But Jones didn't care, and Justine had always been drawn to competent, intelligent men with ambition. That was where he'd fallen short, Derek had to concede. WAR had given him his first real taste of fighting for something bigger than himself, and he was devoted to the cause, but he hadn't displayed extraordinary competence. WAR was all he had left now. And it wasn't too late to make a sensation with it.

He thought of the hair clamp that had been found at the mannequin site. Surely Justine wouldn't do such a thing to him--scare him and deliberately play him for a fool. The bitter taste of truth on the back of his tongue told him she would. She'd do whatever it took to grab the prize she wanted, whether it was the defeat of the four-lane or Richard Jones as her husband.

An idea occurred to him, one that would let both of them know he was a real man. Not to mention revenge. Justine loved her car. He got in his car and sped away. He needed a small gas container, some rags and a lighter.

CHAPTER TWENTY-TWO

Frankie used the hot shot to prod Richard Jones into the cabin. He wanted to balk and plead with her, but she gave him a jolt of the electricity that could make a seven-hundred-pound cow jump through a wooden fence. Jones was smart. It only took two jolts to convince him to walk forward and quit trying to talk.

He entered and slowed, taking in the interior, the bars on the windows. He knew. She could see it on his face. He knew this was where Mullet had spent his last days. She'd have to be careful with him. Mullet had been critically wounded, therefore less of an escape risk. For all of his tumble down the stairs, Richard could walk.

"Was Justine alive when we left her?" he asked.

Frankie felt the anger sweep into her ears with the sound of a tidal surge. "How charming that you're concerned about Justine Morgan." She smiled at the expression on his face because he realized his fatal error. "I recall a time sixteen years ago when you abandoned a bleeding twelve year-old-girl in the wilderness."

Richard was shirtless, shoeless and wearing only his boxer

shorts. Blood still seeped from gashes on his shin and back, and his thin body twitched and trembled. Pathetic.

"May I sit?" he asked.

She pointed to a chair at the table.

He moved toward it and saw a streak of blood on the seat and blanched. He sat down anyway, probably because his legs were about to collapse.

"I never intended to be part of what happened to your father or you." He spoke softly.

Frankie watched him, fascinated. He was different from Mullet and Hank. He wasn't begging. That, in and of itself, slowed her hand from what she had to do. "When I was recovering, I had these bits of memory that didn't make sense in the framework of the story that everyone told—that my father had abandoned us and that I was the unlucky victim of a target-practice or hunting accident. Everything was confused and no matter how hard I tried, I couldn't make sense of what had happened to me."

Richard looked down at the table. His thumb traced a worn groove in the oak. "I was afraid to say anything."

"I had this image in my brain. I was lying on the ground, and this man walks up to me. He stands over me. I can't look up. I can't move. All I can see are his boots. There're these fancy silver toe clips on his boots. Almost like alphabet letters, but not quite. I tried to make meaning of them. To understand that when he said to leave me, he meant for me die. I thought if I could make sense of those silver letters, everything would be right again. That silver boot ornament was the only thing I had to start to figure out who'd killed my father and shot me." She licked her lips. "It took a lot of effort to find the man with those silver toe clips. Lucky for me Hank Welford had more vanity than sense. Once I had him, I knew I could find out who else was involved. I drew the clips and had a silver smith in Montgomery make them up for me. One for each of you.."

"I'm sorry, Frankie. I tried to make it up to you." His head was bowed as he spoke.

"I almost died. I don't know how I got home. Do you know how long it took me to learn to walk?"

Richard shook his head. "Not exactly. I know some of it, because I kept up with you." His voice was little more than a whisper.

"More than two years. The bullet, when it went in, struck the part of my brain that governed motor control. When it came out, another part of my brain was damaged. And then there were the complications from the swelling." She walked around the table. "I was twelve. I saw my father murdered, and I couldn't even tell anyone because those memories were all scrambled in my head."

He closed his eyes. "You're going to kill me, aren't you?"

"Yes. But not right away."

He choked back a sob. "Please, Frankie. I tried to make amends. I sent money to your mother for your treatment. Didn't she ever tell you?"

"My mother grew to hate me, Richard. I was a succubus that drained the life from her. She had to wipe my ass, spoon food into my mouth, take my notes in school. And all along she suspected something was very wrong with me." She grinned. "She was oh, so right about that. She was the first to see me as I really am, and it terrified her to the point that she wouldn't even speak my name."

He put his elbows on the table and leaned his forehead into his hands. "I'm sorry. I'm sorry for everything. I told Harvey to be sure you got this job for the roadway. I knew I could never make up for what happened, but I did try. I put you up on that horse, Frankie. I went back and when you weren't dead, I saw that you got home. I sent money for your doctors."

"You're right, Richard. You can never make it up to me, and I'm going to give you a sample of hell. All of you think there's a difference between animals and humans. Well I'm going to put you in touch with your animal nature." She laughed. "You can bark and howl and scream all you want. The only thing left will be the basest elements of suffering. I'm going to enjoy this a lot."

"I'm not going to beg. I deserve all of this. But don't harm Justine. If she's alive, don't hurt her."

"Don't hurt Justine," she mocked him. "Oh, Justine shouldn't suffer. Where was all of this compassion when I was bleeding in the dirt?"

"I was a coward." He spoke softly. "I accept that. I deserve whatever you want to do to me."

"You're so noble, Richard." She laughed. "Aren't you afraid now? We're here all alone in a cabin where no one would ever think to look. Hank gave me the key. Is this the cabin Harvey used all those years ago, when he brought his powerful friends up for trophy kills and whores?" When he looked at her, she saw the fear in his face and felt a stab of pleasure. "I learned a lot from Hank. Before he lost his head."

He held her gaze as he spoke. "I wish I could go back in time and undo everything."

"What? All your success and wealth and dreams?"

"They aren't worth this."

"Why didn't you tell someone what happened?" She circled the table again, coming to stand in front of him. "Everyone thought my father abandoned us. He didn't. He wouldn't. What did you do with his body?"

"I told you the truth. I was afraid. Hank and Mullet were

reckless. They enjoyed hurting people, and Harvey wasn't inclined to control them. Back then, I only had ideas—no money. If I went against Harvey, no one would believe me anyway. They would have shot me on the spot and left me, too." He rubbed his eyes. "I don't know what happened to Dub's body. He was shot in the back of the head so they couldn't leave him to be found. Harvey set it up to make it look like he left."

She saw that he was too beaten to even fight back. "I'm going to leave you here, Richard, to reflect on your sins. Think about all the damage and hurt you've caused in your lifetime. There's a pen and paper on the table." She nodded toward them. "I want your confession."

RACHEL PULLED up to the gate in front of Richard Jones's estate and instantly saw the flames. A car was on fire in the driveway. Even more unsettling was the fact that no one was making any attempt to put it out.

She grabbed her fire extinguisher from behind the seat. Holding it in one hand, she began to scale the fence. Something was wrong with the alarm system she knew Richard had had installed.

She punched her cell phone as she ran across the manicured lawn. "Gladys, there's a fire at Richard Jones's place. Send a truck and backup."

"Sheriff's out at the Dilson ranch. I'll find Scott and Jake."

"Thanks." She dropped the phone in her pocket and began to spray the emergency fire extinguisher on the burning car, a 2006 Lexus. The car was a total loss, but as close as it was to the house, there was a danger the fire would spread.

Where the hell was Richard, she wondered. And how had

the car come to spontaneously combust? She glimpsed a partially burned gas can behind the car and had her answer.

When she had the blaze beaten down and there was no danger of it spreading, she dropped the extinguisher. The front door of the house was slightly open. She pressed it gently with her fingers and the door inched forward on well-oiled hinges. Silence was like a physical entity inside the house.

She was wearing civvies, but she had her gun, which she drew and held at the ready. The sense that something was seriously wrong pushed her across the threshold. "Richard! Justine!" she called as she stepped inside.

Her footsteps muffled by lush carpet, she almost stumbled over a Chinese umbrella stand that cost more than her annual salary.

"This is Deputy Redmond. Show yourselves." She crept down the foyer, vaguely aware of pen-and-ink drawings of South Dakota wildlife hanging on the walls. Before her was a massive staircase, beautifully turned, as if it hung in the air unsupported. The lights in the house were on and as she moved forward, she saw the blood trail on the blond wood. It led up the stairs.

"Richard!" She took the first two steps, pausing to listen, gun extended. She couldn't be certain, but it sounded as if someone was in the house.

"Richard Jones! Justine Morgan! This is Deputy Redmond. Show yourselves now!" She continued moving upward, her gun ready.

At the second floor, she passed an open door where a computer monitor light cast the latest equipment in pale blue light. She hesitated, but kept on. She didn't have a warrant, so any evidence she turned up would be fruit of the poisoned tree. She'd get a warrant and do it right.

Moving slowly, she heard glass crunch underfoot. More blood was in the hallway, a stain that looked as if someone had fallen against the wall and floor. She read the blood spatter, backtracking the story to a massive wooden door.

A noise came from behind the door, like something mewling. A baby? A cat? Or someone waiting in ambush.

She eased forward, her fingers lightly touching the door. A strange snuffling noise came from inside. Pushing the door open, Rachel froze. Justine was tied up on the bed, her pale body and the sheets spattered in blood. Her eyes were wide, begging for help. Her mouth, covered with silver duct tape, sucked in and out with sounds of terror and partial suffocation.

Rachel stepped inside the room, swiveling from side to side, her gun leading. The room was empty. Crossing quickly to the bed, she leaned down and pulled the tape from Justine's mouth.

Justine's eyes rolled to the right and Rachel spun, bringing the gun up. She was too late. Something hard cracked across the side of her head. She fell forward onto Justine's body, but not before she recognized Derek Baxter as he sprinted from the room.

Harvey smashed the telephone back into its base. "Where the fuck is Richard?" he demanded. "I've been calling him for an hour."

"Are you sure there's nothing you need to tell me?" the sheriff asked. He put his glass of bourbon on a coaster and leaned back in his chair. "Something frightened you, Harvey. It wasn't just someone breaking into your bedroom. Care to tell me what really happened?"

Harvey saw Jeremy standing in the doorway, listening

without even attempting to hide it. The little weasel, panicked and terrified, had called Gordon to come to the ranch. Jeremy wanted him to show the sheriff the strip of skin, but he couldn't. To Jeremy, the skin represented a threat from a psychotic serial killer. Harvey knew it was something more—a herald that the past had come a'calling. Neither the sheriff nor fifty FBI agents could protect him. He had to take care of it himself, and he had to do it in such a fashion that no one would ever know. His future depended on it, as did his fortune, Paradise, and his bid for the presidency.

"I was in the middle of an important meeting in D.C. when Frankie called me back here. Now that I'm here, I'm being targeted by whackos who want to frighten me. I want you to get busy, find some fingerprints in my bedroom, and determine who's behind this. I know it's those militant Natives. They've been too quiet. Now they're trying to frighten me." He saw Jeremy's disgust as the assistant stepped out of the room.

"I'll send someone with a print kit out tomorrow. Don't mess with the doors. If there are prints, we'll get them then." Gordon sighed. "We're short-handed and my officers are exhausted."

"I can send—" He started to offer to bring in the feds again, but he stopped himself. He'd had a bit of time to think. He didn't want this to become fodder for the FBI or Homeland Security forces. If they started really digging, they might unearth the bones of Dub Jackson.

"We don't need federal agents," Gordon said wearily. "I need—" His cell phone rang. "Excuse me." He pulled it from the holder on his belt and answered. "Got it, Gladys!" He rose as he spoke.

"What is it?" Harvey asked.

"Someone set fire to Justine Morgan's car in front of

Richard Jones's house. Justine's been seriously injured, and Rachel was knocked out."

"And Richard?"

"Gone. No trace of him so far."

Harvey tried not to show his fear, but he could tell from Gordon's expression that he'd failed.

"You sure you don't have something to tell me, Harvey?"

For the first time that Harvey could remember, Gordon's voice held a note of superiority. For all the years they'd known each other, Harvey had always been the one who gave orders. Gordon had done as he was told, with few questions.

"Not a damn thing. And don't ask again, Gordon." He stood up. "When you find Richard, tell him to call me."

"You bet." Gordon's eyes were narrowed in thought. He started to leave, but then he turned back. "What would Richard Jones have in common with Hank and Mullet?" he asked softly.

"What makes you think Richard is in danger?" Harvey had recovered his aplomb. "He's probably in St. Croix fucking some slut. For all of his weak-sister looks, he gets more than his share of the action. Women are drawn to money and power, Gordon. I told you that years ago."

"Right." Gordon put his hat on. "I'll send someone out tomorrow when we get a break."

"You do that."

As soon as Gordon was gone, Harvey sent Jeremy to the bunkhouse on an errand and dialed Richard's number. He got the answering machine for the fourth or fifth time. "Call me. I want to talk to you. Maybe we can work out a deal."

His heart was racing when he hung up. He was playing the odds that if the killer had taken Richard, he might also have Richard's phone. It was a long shot, but most of his life had been about risk and gamble. Harvey was good at it, and he was even better at doing what had to be done.

He went to the gun case and unlocked it. He studied the weapons, then selected a Glock automatic and a high-powered hunting rifle. He had no intention of sitting at home and waiting to be the killer's fourth victim.

CHAPTER TWENTY-THREE

The medics loaded Justine on a stretcher and headed to the hospital. Rachel didn't know if the girl would live or not. Her nose was badly broken and the EMTs had told Rachel they feared the shattered bone was dangerously embedded in the soft tissue near Justine's brain. On top of that she'd had her mouth taped shut—which prevented adequate oxygen from getting to her lungs and heart.

"You should come in and get a CAT scan," the medic told Rachel as he dabbed antiseptic along the gash in her temple and jaw. "And stitches. Dr. Martinez does a great job. If you don't get that sewn up, it'll probably scar."

"Thanks." The last thing on her mind was some scarring. She looked at the bed. Justine had lost a lot of blood. So much so that Rachel wondered how she could still be alive.

She stood and felt a moment of vertigo.

A strong hand grasped her elbow and steadied her. "Easy, there," Jake said.

She wanted to pull away from him but she didn't. Jake had been the first man on the scene, arriving only minutes after her attacker had fled.

"I'm okay, thanks." She eased back from his grip.

"I think the hospital is a good idea."

She shook her head and again felt her balance slip. "No hospital. I need to work the scene here." Her gaze slipped to the floor, and she forced it to stay there until her balance solidified.

"Tell me what happened," Jake said.

"Where's the sheriff?"

Jake hesitated at her tone. "He's out at Harvey Dilson's place. Someone broke in. Dilson's upset, but Gordon's on his way here."

She nodded. "Where's Scott?"

"Rachel, I can work this scene. With or without you."

She didn't want to argue. Her head was pounding, and Jake would only win anyway. He had Gordon's blessing as part of the team. "Okay."

"So what happened?"

She took a breath. "I saw the car burning outside and tried to get it under control. The door was open, and I had a bad feeling so I came in." She looked at the bed. "I saw Justine, and when I went to help her someone clobbered me on the side of the head."

Jake nodded. "Good thing you'd already called for backup." He looked around the room. "Did you see the person who struck you?"

Rachel faced the decision to tell Jake about Derek or not. "I didn't see anything except Justine struggling for air." Her own breathing was shallow enough to earn a searching look from Jake. "Was Justine able to talk? Did she see anything?"

"She wasn't coherent. Maybe tomorrow."

Rachel took a deep breath. She was holding back evidence and Richard Jones's life might well be at stake. The problem was that she no longer trusted Jake. She didn't trust anyone. She had to get out of there, away from everyone, so she could go after Derek. The little bastard knew something, and she intended to get it out of him.

She walked around the room, studying the blood on the bed and the stains on the floor that extended into the hallway. "I think I need to go home," she said.

"I'll drive you," Jake offered. "Gordon's on his way here. I can take off long enough to get you home safely."

"I'm okay to drive, just tired. Stay here and work the scene. I'll see you tomorrow."

Before Jake could object, she hurried down to her truck and put it in reverse. When she looked up at the house, Jake was backlit in the bedroom window looking down at her.

She pressed the gas to the floor and blasted out of the driveway. Guilt or regret would surely come later. By not telling Jake about Derek Baxter, she may well have condemned Richard to a terrible death. But she'd seen Derek's face. He'd been terrified. Not by her appearance, but by what had happened to Justine.

She had to find him and make him tell her exactly what he knew. She had her own theory, but she needed him to verify it and fill in some blanks. And she needed him to talk fast. This was one job where she didn't want other law enforcement officers as witnesses to her tactics.

FRANKIE SAT in the shadow of a huge boulder, her truck shut down. Across the floor of the valley, a cluster of lights sparkled in the darkness.

She closed her eyes and tried to remember, but she couldn't find her way back to the place she wanted to go. As a child, she'd traveled this road many times. It was the road into town, and her mother had spoken often, in the early days of her healing, about the many times she and Dub went into town together to buy feed or equipment. Polly had worked hard, at first, to try to reconnect Frankie with her past--until Polly realized that the young girl who'd come back from the mountains bore no resemblance to the daughter she'd once loved.

Watching the twinkle of lights that signified Harvey Dilson's ranch—the land and home he'd bought from Polly just before the auctioneer's gavel fell on a foreclosure sale—Frankie tried to squeeze even a small memory from her brain. Whatever tender moments had once resided there had been stripped clean by the bullet that ripped through her brain.

She tried again for one single image of love and tenderness from her childhood. Nothing. She smiled. It was the last test. Now she could finish.

She turned on the truck and headed away from the ranch, back to town. She'd call Harvey in the morning, see how he was doing. One of the real pleasures that came from the way she'd structured her kills was that she got to witness the fear of her victims. It was so much better than she'd ever imagined.

She'd devised the skinning and decapitating method based on the cruel lifestyle of Hank and Mullet—men who considered themselves to be such <u>courageous</u> hunters. It had seemed so appropriate, and her only regret was that no one would know what craven cowards they'd been in the end, begging and pleading for her to stop as she sliced the skin from their bodies.

Mullet had fainted before she even started, but when she slid the sharpened end of the cable—an improvement over the rope she'd used on Hank—through his tendons and set the winch to lift him, he'd come to with wild screams. And he'd screamed until he had no voice left. It had been a thing of beauty.

The death method had also brought to mind the legend of the Skin Dancer, the mythic Sioux monster. While she hadn't intended to implicate the Sioux, they'd been a handy beard, giving her additional time to complete her revenge without having to hurry. She knew Adam had been working the old legend, scaring the road crews, raising the specter of the Skin Dancer. They weren't working together, but they shared a common goal of stopping the road.

Dancing around the victims in their own shoes marked the truth that Hank and Mullet brought this death on themselves by their own actions. The owl feathers had been another stroke of inspiration. They told of death, and she could only hope that once Richard went missing, Harvey Dilson would have no doubt that he was next. She wanted him to anticipate his fate.

Logically, she accepted that she fit the definition of a serial killer--someone who killed in a series. Or perhaps she was a spree killer. That sounded a bit more fun. But those terms held no meaning for her. She'd executed four men and intended to eliminate two more. Not random killings. No, these men had been studied and targeted for years. They'd essentially chosen their deaths by the lives they led--violent, cruel, shameful, greedy.

Yuma Pete might die and that was regrettable. She should have killed him as soon as she was back in town, but she'd never imagined that one of the deputies would actually find a way to the old silversmith. She'd been wrong about that and wrong to ever allow Rachel to meet Adam. Adam had led Rachel there, and she could only hope that Rachel hadn't gotten anything essential from Pete. He'd sworn that he hadn't told her anything because he didn't remember. Even when she hurt him, he stuck to his story.

As she drove, she thought about the strange loops of destiny that had brought her back to Criss County. Much of it she'd engineered, but there had been some divine intervention. She'd been spared so that she could mete out the fate these men deserved. Before it was over, she'd find her father's body and prove that he hadn't abandoned her.

She passed through the darkened town and swung by Rachel's house. The deputy had become a problem. Rachel was smart, persistent and intuitive. Those qualities, while amusing, were also dangerous. She shared a strange kinship with the deputy, but that was beyond the point. Especially now that she'd come to the end game. Dilson was her prize, the man she meant to take in a very public way. She would expose him, strip him naked in every sense of the word.

She would have her pound of flesh.

But Rachel might be a problem. And while it would give Frankie no pleasure to kill her, she would do it if she had to. Jake hadn't proven the distraction she'd hoped. She'd have to find some other way, and if the deputy got too close, she'd do whatever was necessary.

Frankie's grip tightened on the steering wheel. Rachel's driveway was empty. The deputy never seemed to sleep. She picked up her cell phone and dialed Rachel's number.

"Hey, it's Frankie. What's happening?" she said.

"Nothing good."

Rachel's voice was guarded. Frankie was instantly on the alert. "Want to work out?"

"I'm kind of busy right now."

"Sounds intriguing." Frankie kept it light. "Anything I can help you with?"

"Maybe."

Rachel's voice crackled and Frankie gripped the phone tighter. Damn cell phone reception was iffy at best.

"Adam told me about an interesting artisan."

Rachel left the thought unfinished, and Frankie counted to seven. She couldn't afford to push Rachel. Not now. "It's a little early for Christmas shopping," Frankie said.

"No, this guy is connected to the murders."

"How would that be?" Frankie felt her body tighten.

"It's complicated, but I was wondering if you knew Yuma Pete? Ever buy any of his work?"

Frankie had several options. She choose the one closest to the truth. "He's been around. He does great work, but that's all I know."

Rachel's voice wafted in and out. "Frankie, when were you shot?"

"Why?" She cleared her throat. "I mean why are you asking about that? It's over and done."

"Just wondered."

"Hardly anyone remembers that, Rachel. And certainly not me."

"You were twelve, right?"

"Right."

"That would be 1992. Was it summer?"

"Where is this going?" Frankie slowed the truck and pulled over. She had to think. What had Rachel learned from Pete and what had she put together? The old man had lied to her. He had told Rachel something important.

"Maybe nowhere. Mr. Pete mentioned something, and I was trying to figure out if any of it fit together."

"Well, if you do, let me know, okay? So where are you? Maybe we could meet for a drink."

"I'm at my destination. Gotta go. I'll call you later."

Frankie was left listening to static. Slowly she lowered the phone. She turned the truck around and headed back to town. She had to find Rachel before the deputy ruined everything.

Derek cowered in the dense shrubbery that formed an almost impenetrable wall at the back of the house he lived in. He'd parked his vehicle several blocks away and come here on foot, scared and sick.

Justine. He put his fists into his eyes trying to rub out the image of her, broken and near death. He'd started to remove the duct tape from her mouth when the deputy had barreled into the room. He'd struck out at Rachel on instinct. She'd seen his face, though. He knew it. So now he was waiting for the sirens and the pigs to come for him.

The events of the past week had snowballed. Control over them had been an illusion. From the first moment he'd conceived of the idea of claiming a murder he didn't commit, he'd been doomed.

He pulled his cell phone from his back pocket and tried one of the other WAR members. The phone rang and rang. No one was answering his calls. It was as if they knew—he carried the disease of failure. If he kept his mouth shut, he'd do time alone. If he talked, he'd take the whole cell of WAR to prison with him. A half-million dollars worth of heavy equipment suddenly wasn't nearly as funny as it had been a week before.

Dear God, who had done that to Justine? Had Richard Jones lost his shit when he realized Justine was involved with WAR? Had he hurt her, tied her up and—-he couldn't bear to think any further. Instead of helping her, he'd panicked and run away. He stuffed his fist into his mouth to stop the cries that wanted to rise from his throat.

He was a coward and worse. He'd set fire to Justine's car in an act of petty revenge while she'd been suffocating not a hundred feet away. If she lived, she'd never forgive him. If she didn't, he'd never forgive himself.

A vehicle pulled down the shale driveway and stopped outside the back door of the big old house. He recognized Rachel Redmond. She wasn't wearing a uniform and she got out of the truck and knocked at his apartment.

Fear immobilized him. He could either step out and turn himself in or spend the rest of his days hiding.

He couldn't decide what to do. If he showed himself, it would work in his favor. Rachel didn't have her gun drawn. She might not shoot him before he had a chance to explain. Then again, if he waited, he might find some evidence that would build a legitimate alibi for the murders. The problem was that he wasn't certain when the poachers had been killed.

He banged his forehead with his fist. His mother would rag on him forever about this.

Another vehicle drove down the street and slowed. He heard the motor die and a door slam. Was someone else coming to talk to him? Maybe to finish him off?

Rachel had moved from the door to the windows. She tapped on the glass and stood on tiptoe trying to look inside.

Derek caught sight of a figure slipping along the side of the house. He couldn't tell if it was man or woman, but it moved with the grace of a panther.

The figure stopped at the corner of the house. Derek couldn't see perfectly, but he saw enough to see the baton the figure carried. He understood in a flash. The intruder meant to harm the deputy—and once again he'd get the blame for it because it was in his backyard.

"Hey!" He roared the word as he came out of the bushes. "Hey!" He waved his arms and ran toward Rachel. "Watch out! Over there!" The force of the taser hit him square in the chest. Lightning popped behind his eyeballs, and he hit the ground, unable to control the jerking and quivering of his muscles.

CHAPTER TWENTY-FOUR

He held the pen in his hand, the felt tip trembling above the page. What was there to confess? Richard understood that nothing he wrote would save him from Frankie. Were there any words that would save him from himself?

Paradise had occupied his life for so long now. More than sixteen years. In the time his dream had grown to near fruition, Frankie's father had lain in an unmarked grave somewhere. He'd assumed that Hank and Mullet had taken care of that detail, and he'd never asked. In fact, he'd learned to pretend that day never happened.

The luxury of make-believe was gone now, and he was left with the reality of what had occurred. Frankie Jackson, a girl of twelve, had been shot in the head and left to die. The bullet had gone through her brain, coring away parts of her personality. What had been left was a woman bent on a terrible revenge. The blue eyes that he'd thought so lovely when he sat at her dinner table had seemed to sparkle with life and humor. Now he'd seen them icy and dead. Frankie had learned to imitate life, but she'd died a long time ago.

He paced the cabin. He'd tried the doors and windows but

they were securely locked and barred. Mullet had sat in this same chair knowing he would die, just as Richard did.

And Justine? What would Frankie do to her if she was still alive? Though he might not be able to save himself, perhaps if he wrote what Frankie wanted to know, he could help Justine.

Picking up the pen, he willed his hand not to shake as he began to write. He confessed to witnessing the murder of Dub Jackson, and then he began to list the places Dub's body might have been placed.

Frankie had tortured the men, yet they hadn't given her that bit of information or she wouldn't need it from him.

He stopped writing. Surely, as she was peeling the skin from them, they would have told her the location of his grave. Yet they hadn't. Because they didn't know? If they didn't know where Dub was buried, Harvey Dilson did. Dilson. Sweat formed on Richard's forehead, though the evening was cool.

RACHEL SAT at her desk listening to Derek's cursing and screaming, coming from the jail. Gladys had stuffed tissue into her ears so his wailing didn't interfere with her book.

Derek's one phone call had been to his mother, who'd promptly hung up on him. Probably for the first time in his life, no one was stepping up to the plate to bail him out.

"I was trying to help you, you crazy bitch. Someone was in the shadows coming after you, I try to warn you and you pop me with a fucking taser!"

"I'm a big fan of your nobility, Derek." Rachel didn't even look up.

"Tell me about Justine!" he howled.

Rachel stood and walked back to the jail. "Settle down."

"I have to see Justine."

"Right, to explain why you torched her car?" Rachel wasn't

guessing—the smell of gasoline had been on Derek's pants and shoes. Jake had found footprints at the scene which were now being compared to Derek's. "You're facing some mighty serious charges, Derek."

"She set me up and played me for a fool." He stared down at the floor as he spoke.

"How'd she do that?" Rachel kept her voice calm, devoid of the eagerness she felt at the slight opening of a door.

"That mannequin. She encouraged me to follow Adam Standing Bear, and then she set me up. He caught me in a leg trap and knocked me out. When I came to, it was dark, and they both knew I'd head down the mountain."

"Why are you so certain Justine was involved in this?"

"Her hair clamp was found there."

"You saw it? Why didn't you pick it up?"

"I never saw it. Your dispatcher told me that you'd found it and that you could prove she'd been at that scene. That's why I burned her car."

"If it makes you feel better, I think Justine's hair clamp was planted at the scene."

His chin was trembling as if he might cry. "She never cared about WAR or about me. She set me up with that mannequin."

"Why?"

He shrugged. "She knew I'd claim the killing for WAR." His voice turned bitter. "She and that Indian were probably working together, and they knew I'd freak out and run home. They knew I'd try to grab the glory of another killing."

"Because you did that once before."

He nodded.

"You had nothing to do with Hank Welford's murder, did you?"

He shook his head. "I saw the murder as an opportunity to get some headlines for WAR. It worked, too."

"A little too well," Rachel said. "If you cooperate, I promise I'll try to help you. Derek, you could spend the rest of your life in prison, and I don't think your mother is going to rush out here to make this go away."

"I don't know anything about the murders."

"I believe you. I'll do my best to help you."

"Will you call my mom?"

"In the morning."

He slumped onto his bed. "Yeah, that would be better."

Rachel almost felt sorry for him as he leaned his elbows on his knees and dropped his head in his hands. He was a kid about to learn some hard lessons of life.

She went back to her desk. Gladys had given her yet another message to call Frankie. Instead of returning her call, she dialed Gordon's cell phone. Her pulse had increased.

The phone rang twelve times before she hung up. Gordon always answered his cell. Then again she didn't normally call him so late.

She dialed the first six digits of Jake's phone but didn't finish. Instead she dialed Kimber Long at the newspaper.

"I need your help," she said when the reporter answered the phone.

"My help?" Kimber almost purred. "Is this about the Skin Dancer?"

"Yes."

"What do you need?"

"I need to get into the newspaper files. To check some dates to see what was happening in Criss County at the time."

"I could do that for you," Kimber offered.

Rachel laughed. "I'll bet you could. But I need to do this myself. Can you let me have access to the files?"

"There's always a price for my cooperation."

"What about the promise of an exclusive?"

"The national media are just waiting for another murder. I saw reporters from Time and ABC News in town this afternoon. Aren't you tempted to go for national exposure?"

"Not when I know how much this story could mean to you, Kimber."

"Meet me at the back door in ten minutes." She hung up.

Rachel wrote a note telling Gladys where she was going and not to tell anyone. She placed it on the dispatcher's desk and left.

The Criss County Democrat occupied an old three-story stone building that had once been a brothel. Editorial was on the top floor, and a creaky elevator—the only one in town—clacked and moaned as it took Rachel and Kimber up to the newspaper morgue. Rachel had never been inside the building, but she knew the sordid history of the place.

A young woman, murdered by one of her clients, was said to haunt the place. It was a big draw for tourists who visited the area.

"Right this way." Kimber was positively perky.

Rachel followed behind her and stared in dismay at the old machine used for microfiche. "I thought you'd have a computer and..."

"From 1998 forward. The older stuff hasn't been transferred yet. It's an ongoing project."

"Point me to 1992."

Kimber worked her way around to a drawer and pulled out several spools of film. She held them a moment. "I'm not sure how my boss would feel about me doing this."

"He's been cooperating with the sheriff. I don't think he'd

mind." She felt a wave of desperation that Kimber might rethink letting her view the old papers.

"Maybe I should call him."

Rachel slowly nodded. If Alton Brooks refused her request, it would take at least a day to get a warrant. "Do what you think you should do. Just understand that Richard Jones is missing, and Justine Morgan has been severely injured by the person I'm trying to find."

Kimber handed her the spools. "Go ahead." She turned to walk away. "I'll be at my desk."

"Thanks." Rachel sat down at the machine and threaded the film. Spinning forward, she stopped in June of 1992.

Twenty minutes later, she found what she was looking for. Twelve-year-old Frankie Jackson, her head swathed in bandages, stared back at her from the front page: YOUNG GIRL SHOT IN ACCIDENT. She scanned the story quickly. It pretty much followed what Frankie had told her. The newspaper had been kind enough to bury the fact that Dub Jackson had ridden off into the wilderness never to return in the fifth paragraph.

The newspaper updated Frankie's health for several days, progress reports attributed to her doctors in Rapid City. The next issue quoted Mel Ortiz about the search for Dub. "We've found no trace of foul play. However we have found evidence that he left voluntarily and we're ending the search."

The last story detailed Frankie's move south. Polly Jackson was quoted as saying that the ranch would be sold and she and Frankie would make a new home in Montgomery, Alabama, where Frankie would work with renowned therapist Misha Woods, who was building a clinic there.

Frankie printed out copies of the stories she'd read and stood.

"Finished?" Kimber asked.

"I think so."

"Ready to spill the beans?"

"Give me until tomorrow. I have to check out a few things."

"Maybe you should get some rest. You look like you've been pulling some long hours."

Rachel suddenly felt the fatigue. She had important leads to follow, and they couldn't wait until the morning. But she also didn't want Kimber as her shadow. "Good suggestion," she said as they got on the old elevator and creaked their way to the ground floor. "That's exactly what I'm going to do."

Kimber locked the newspaper door and got in her car. She put her thumb by her ear and her little finger by her mouth. "Call me," she mouthed through the glass.

Rachel nodded and waved as Kimber drove away.

THE CLOCK in her pickup showed a few minutes after eleven. Frankie was parked on the north side of the Criss County courthouse where she had a clear view of the newspaper parking lot. She'd seen three vehicles drive by, all filled with rowdy teenagers. None of them had even noticed her.

To while away the time, she practiced inhaling and exhaling slowly. Centering. Her legs were jerky with the tedium of sitting still, but her patience would be rewarded.

Beside her on the seat was a rifle and scope. Her right hand caressed the stock where the initials DBJ had been burned in a fancy script. Her father's hunting rifle was one of the few things she'd been able to scavenge from among her mother's useless possessions. Why Polly had chosen to keep the gun, Frankie couldn't begin to guess. Polly hated weapons and noise and any honest emotion. She preferred simpering smiles and whispers and the restraint that all ladies of good breeding know how to practice. And patience. God almighty, if Polly had told her once she'd told her a million times—"You have to be patient, Frances."

She wanted to bang the steering wheel with her fist, but she didn't. Years of practicing patience had given her the discipline not to act rashly and without purpose. The plan she'd worked so hard on for so many years was about to be completed. Rachel Redmond was becoming a nuisance, but the plan wasn't in serious jeopardy. In fact, everything was in place.

Richard was in the old cabin, a place no one would ever think to look. Harvey was at the ranch barking orders and making his staff hate him even more. And Mel Ortiz. That was Frankie's masterstroke. He was at home with his wife, never suspecting that Jake would pay the tab for his sins. Mel wasn't involved in killing her father, but he certainly hadn't tried hard to find Dub. He'd let Dilson run the whole show.

When the two women came out of the newspaper office, Frankie sat up straight. She could only hazard a guess as to what the deputy was getting at the newspaper.

Rachel got in her truck and followed the reporter onto Main Street. The reporter turned right and Rachel went left. Torn between which one to follow, Frankie chose the reporter. She could make that little bird sing without much effort.

When the reporter was several blocks ahead, Frankie started her truck and followed. She didn't know this woman so she moved up a little closer. The compact car stayed ten miles over the speed limit.

The car made a right, and Frankie followed at a discreet distance. She brought the gun closer to her leg. The simplest thing to do would be to shoot the reporter in the leg or shoulder. Something to bring her down so she'd be easier to question.

The reporter turned down a narrow lane bordered by

dense shrubs. Perfect. Frankie grinned. It was almost as if God were making this easy for her. She waited until she saw the brake lights burn bright red before she turned down the lane.

The ringing of her cell phone startled her. She braked and checked the phone. Rachel was calling her.

"I got your message, but I've been swamped. I had to go to the newspaper to look up some old records." Rachel's voice was casual, friendly.

Frankie stepped on the gas and eased past the lane. She didn't want to be seen sitting there if something untoward later happened to the reporter. "Anything interesting?" Frankie asked.

"Not much. I was checking local political races."

"Why?" Frankie asked.

"Something Yuma Pete told me about Bill Clinton. Anyway, I got to looking and I found out that Mel Ortiz was working this area as a game warden several years before I moved here with his family. I didn't recall that."

Frankie tried to read between her words. "And?"

"He was one of the men sent out to search for your dad, along with Gordon. Funny, but Mel never mentioned it to me."

"Yeah. Mel led the search. Gordon was just a deputy." Frankie could hear the hot blade of anger in her own voice. She had to keep control of herself. "They said his tracks disappeared on the highway and it was like the earth swallowed him and his horse up."

"I find that peculiar. Did they ask any of the Sioux to help search?"

"No."

"Listen, I've got another call coming in. Let's get together tomorrow. How does breakfast at Lulu's sound?"

Frankie could detect nothing out of the ordinary in Rachel's voice. "Sure," she said. "Eight o'clock?"

"Great. I'll see you there." Rachel hung up.

Frankie turned the car around and made another pass by the lane that led to the reporter's house. Another murder would turn Bisonville into a media circus, which would work against her. It was best to leave Kimber Long alone, at least for the moment. She could always change her mind if she had to.

CHAPTER TWENTY-FIVE

Gladys was still reading when Rachel made it back to the sheriff's office. She never looked up and Rachel went straight to her desk and the telephone. To her amazement, Misha Woods was listed in the Montgomery directory.

It was half past eleven at night, but Rachel placed the call anyway. She was surprised when someone answered on the third ring.

"Ms. Woods, this is Deputy Rachel Redmond with the Criss County, South Dakota's Sheriff's office."

There was a moment of hesitation before a clear, female voice asked, "Why is a South Dakota deputy calling me in the dead of night?"

"It's about Frances Jackson."

Rachel counted to twenty before the therapist spoke again. "Where is Frances?"

"Here in Criss County."

"She's not hurt, is she?"

"No, Frankie is perfectly fine. But I have four dead men here. Frances is connected to each of them."

The therapist didn't say anything.

"The dead men have been skinned and decapitated. They suffered greatly. And another man is missing."

"And what do you think I can do to help you?"

"Tell me about Frankie. About her injuries and what she may or may not remember about the shooting accident."

"I can't talk to you, Deputy Redmond. You know that."

"Can you tell me how her mother died?"

"I can tell you what I heard. There was an accident. Mrs. Jackson fell down the stairs in their home. She was crippled and had to be put in a care facility while Frankie was in college. During that time I heard she passed away. I lost contact with the Jacksons."

"There are a lot of accidents involving members of the Jackson family, don't you think?"

"Polly Jackson devoted herself to Frances. We gave Frances the tools to make a living and have a productive life. Polly did the best she could, under the circumstances."

"You make Frances sound like a half-wit."

"No. She was always smart. Too smart. She can absorb anything you put in front of her. It was never her intellect that concerned us." She cleared her throat. "I can't talk to you about this. Frances was my patient."

"Was Mrs. Jackson your patient?"

"No."

"This fall. You called it an accident. Is that what you really believe?"

"How will any of this information help solve murders in South Dakota? I'm sorry, but I have to go."

"Wait!" Rachel had to ask one more thing. "Where was Mrs. Jackson institutionalized?"

"Bridgefield House. It's a full care facility."

Rachel felt the door closing, and she knew she had to stop it. "Ms. Woods, I honestly don't know what laws govern therapist and patient confidentiality. It's possible that your life is in danger. I know for a fact that Richard Jones will suffer a terrible death if we don't find him."

"Richard helped finance my clinic." Misha's voice had grown deadly quiet. "He's a kind man, a generous man."

"Frankie is after someone else. Otherwise, she would have killed Richard and fled. I have to find the person or people she intends to get. Is there anything you can tell me?"

"It's possible the nursing home kept memorabilia that Polly had. If Frances didn't claim it, they might have boxed it and stored it."

It was a long shot, but the only one Rachel had. "I'll be in touch." She felt as if glass chips were embedded in her eyes, but she called the airport and booked a flight to Montgomery the next day. The ticket, while not expensive, maxed out her credit card. She didn't want to go through the department, though. Even an innocent remark to the wrong person could push Frankie to action.

She had one more call to make. Directory assistance gave her the number for Yuma Pete. It was too late to call, but she did anyway. The phone rang and rang, but no one answered. Rachel slowly lowered the receiver. She'd told Frankie about Yuma Pete. She had a really bad feeling.

In the morning she'd check on the elderly artist. For now, though, she was going home to bed. Four hours of sleep sounded like luxury. If she didn't get a little rest, she'd start to make serious mistakes.

"Jake, I need your help." Frankie put all of the Southern belle pathos she could manage into her voice. "My truck won't start, and I'm stuck just outside the city limits headed to my place. That killer is still on the loose and I'm afraid."

"Hang on. I'll be there as quick as I can."

"Thank you, Jake. You're a true gentleman."

"My daddy taught me well. Be there in ten."

"I wonder what else your father taught you?" Frankie said to the empty air as she snapped her cell phone shut. Her truck was fine. She needed some leverage against Rachel, and that would be Jake. On her way out of town, she'd stopped by Rachel's place and left another little present for her. One that would turn her world upside down. Strange, it would be simpler to kill Rachel, but she was reluctant. She felt a kinship to the deputy. Both of them had been screwed out of happy childhoods. Both had fought their way into professions dominated by men. Rachel didn't know it, yet, but she'd been victimized in much the same way that Frankie had. They were sisters, even if Rachel didn't acknowledge it.

The cry of a small animal cut the still night. The road was empty, rather an amazing fact. Usually someone driving up to the casinos in Deadwood would pass by, but tonight no one was about. Looking in both directions, she saw only emptiness on the county road.

One of the great satisfactions of her work was that she'd make certain the four-lane never went through. By the time she finished with Harvey Dilson, his political influence would be akin to a rattlesnake bite, purely poison and unwanted. No one would touch a project he'd been involved in once she was done with him.

Headlights climbed a rise to the south, and she freshened her lipstick. Jake to the rescue. Now she had to assume the role of damsel in distress. She bent under the hood, giving him a perfect view of her taut backside as he pulled up and stopped. She heard the truck door slam.

"I think this thingy here has come loose," she said,

mumbling so that he leaned down beside her to look. She held the distributor cap wire in her hand.

"Looks like an easy fix." He flashed his penlight from the truck's motor to her face, then back down into the engine. "I wonder how it came loose. That doesn't normally happen."

"I was driving home when the truck stopped and wouldn't start. I'm lucky you were available, Jake. I might have spent the entire night out here."

"You could have called Dad or Gordon. Heck, just about any guy in town would have come."

"That's a moot issue since you rode to the rescue."

He reconnected the wires and stood. The beam of the flashlight fell on her boots. "You're good to go."

"I'm concerned that it might come loose again. I know it's a lot to ask, but would you follow me home? I'd love a nightcap and someone to talk to. I'm a little blue tonight. My crews are quitting, my job is going down the tube." She gave a pitiful, tremulous smile. "I'm feeling sorry for myself and some company would be appreciated."

"Okay, I'll follow you, but I can't stay long."

She got in her truck and took off before he had time to change his mind.

DEREK HAD COME to a full and complete understanding of the term "stew in your own juices." He'd churned and blistered. Now he wanted a lawyer and he wanted to know how Justine was getting along. No one would even speak to him, not even the old bag who ran the radio.

"Would you please call the hospital and ask how Justine Morgan is doing?" he yelled at the dispatcher's back. The door between the jail and sheriff's office was open because he was on "suicide watch." Of course, if he hung himself he'd be jerky before the old cow put her book down to check on him.

"Just check on Justine. Please!" He was frantic to get to her bedside. He wanted to explain his actions before anyone else got a chance to tell her what he'd done.

Gladys never moved. He swallowed his desire to scream vulgarities at her and fell back on the lumpy bunk. He closed his eyes, unable to stop his own thoughts as they whirled in a pattern of self-destruction. He was in big trouble. Too big for his mama's checkbook to fix. No one here would care that his father was Admiral Douglas Baxter. None of that was going to matter here, in Bisonville.

When he opened his eyes, Gladys was standing in front of his cell. He wanted to rail at her and embarrass her, to make her back away. "What is it?" he asked instead.

"Justine is still on the critical list, but the nurse said they felt she'd be able to endure reconstructive surgery on her nose either this afternoon or tomorrow."

The relief was intense. "I didn't hurt her," he said, and he couldn't stop the tears. "I couldn't. All I ever wanted was to impress her and to make this planet better for all of us, including the animals."

Gladys sighed. "You're in a world of hurt. You know that, don't you?"

He nodded. "I'll go to prison for the heavy equipment, but I didn't hurt anyone. I only said I did because I wanted WAR to get noticed."

Gladys put on hand on a bar. "Honey, your brain sure got twisted around, didn't it?"

He was too defeated even to argue. He only nodded.

"Here." She held a book through the bars. "It's about vampires and the South. Charlaine Harris is a good writer.

She'll take your mind off your troubles, at least for a little while."

He took the book, grateful for anything that would stop the horrible spinning of his thoughts. "Thank you, Mrs..."

"Folks just call me Gladys. Right before the shift change I'll make a pot of fresh coffee for the morning guys. I'll bring you a cup. Want some breakfast?"

Derek shook his head. "I want to go back in time and live the past month over again."

She smiled. "Wouldn't we all like that kind of power?"

She hadn't comforted him, but she made him feel better. "Why are you being so nice to me?" he asked.

"I told you earlier. You remind me of one of my kin. I'm just hoping someone is being nice to him, because I have a feeling he's sitting in the same place you are—big trouble. Now I've got work to do."

She left him and he opened the book, sinking into a world that contained vampires and mortals, a place far safer than his own reality.

CHAPTER TWENTY-SIX

Harvey crept from his bedroom at the first sign of the sun cresting over the hills. The ranch hands would be stirring, but none had a reason to come to the big house so early. It was safe for him to get down to business.

He opened the plantation blinds that covered the French doors of his bedroom. With the slatted wooden shutters closed, the place was like a cave. Yes, it was better for his privacy to leave them closed, but he liked the sunshine and walking out on his patio in his underwear to drink coffee and read the morning papers. It was a ritual, and one he loved. He'd sacrificed a lot for South Dakota, personally, professionally and politically.

He opened the French doors and crossed the room to open the interior door. The silver tray with hot coffee, the freshly ground beans imported from Latin America and several newspapers were waiting for him. Bettina knew the importance of the coffee and newspapers.

He picked up the tray, kicked the door closed behind him and walked out on his patio. He'd landscaped the entire ranch over the years. In this small corner he'd created shadow and light and filled it with a riot of delicate colors that bloomed all summer long. He didn't garden himself, but he'd designed the mulched beds that were filled with local and exotic blooms.

Harvey took a deep breath and put the tray on the wrought-iron patio table. This ranch was a little piece of heaven. When he'd been young, he'd thought of sharing this with a wife and family. But with age had come wisdom. He was an effective political machine because he was unencumbered. Several of his friends were either out of office or in federal jails because they'd revealed secrets during a pillow talk session. The old adage that hell had no fury like a woman scorned was especially true in the world of high-powered politics. Women were drawn to the power, the energy that sizzled on Capitol Hill. It was indeed an aphrodisiac. But it could also spell doom. If a man got a little too comfortable, a little too enamored, a little too incautious, he might find himself talking too freely.

And God forbid the things that children could ruin. He chuckled softly at the memory of fellow senator Van Cleton, whose seventeen-year-old daughter—a real stunner—decided to earn some extra cash by enlisting high school friends as call girls for Capitol Hill parties. Van had been ruined, and he'd truly been ignorant of all of it.

Harvey had made the right decision when he'd confined his lust to discreet escorts. No wife, no children, no pillow talk. He poured the rich black coffee into the bone china cup and snapped open the paper. The sun had crested the hills and the shadows on the patio were rapidly shrinking. It was his favorite time of day. For these few minutes, he would shut out all the rest of his problems.

"Harvey! Harvey! Help me. God, she knows!" The words, spoken in Hank Welford's nasal whine made Harvey jump to his feet.

The patio table overturned and china and silver crashed to the stones. Harvey whirled, but the patio was empty.

"She's going to get you, Harvey! No!" A long scream of pain was followed by begging. "Please, stop. Please. I don't know where Dub's body is. No!"

Harvey froze. He looked across at the bunk house, but no one had come out. No one had heard. Good. He stepped into the last bit of shadow near a shrub.

Hank Welford's severed head stared up at him surrounded by a puddle of water where his frozen tissue had begun to thaw.

"Oh, my, God." Harvey started to back away from it.

"Help me, Harvey! Help me!" Hank pleaded.

"What the fuck?" Harvey stepped forward. He had to stop it. No one could see or hear this. No one.

The head had been nailed onto a wooden plank in a crude imitation of how a taxidermist might mount an animal.

"Harvey! Help me!" was followed by another long scream.

Harvey knelt down beside the head. He poked his fingers into Hank's cold mouth and withdrew a digital recorder. Gagging, he stood and crushed the device under the heel of his slipper.

Hank was silenced in mid-scream.

RACHEL BIT into a hamburger that required all ten digits to hold. The lighting in Lulu's café was dim, and she noticed the place was empty, except for her. Baskets of food—all of her favorites—were spread out on the table in front of her. She took another bite, filling her mouth with the delicious meat.

Her gaze fell on a mound of onion rings, and she hesitated, holding the burger. Juice leaked from the corner of her mouth, but she was reluctant to let go of the burger long enough to find a napkin. At last, she lowered the sandwich to her plate and reached for the onion rings. They crunched in her mouth, warm and wonderful. She closed her eyes in pleasure.

When she opened them, she saw the drops of vermillion on the snowy white table cloth. Puzzled, she looked around. The emptiness of the café took on a sinister feel.

Rachel stood slowly, feeling for her gun at her hip. When she turned back to the hamburger, she saw the cold, blue fingertips of a hand poking from between the bun. The forefinger had been bitten off.

Her stomach twisted, and she felt a stab of pain.

The alarm buzzed Rachel awake and she sat up in bed, cold sweat covering her body. The dream had been so real. She could almost smell the burger and onion rings. She wiped the corners of her mouth, trying to control the nausea that came on the heels of the nightmare.

The clock showed six-thirty, and it took all of her willpower not to burrow back under the covers. Three hours of sleep wasn't enough, and her body was protesting. Her brain, foggy with fatigue, sought oblivion, but there were too many things to do. Besides, sleeping was as anxiety-provoking as working the case.

She picked up the phone and dialed Yuma Pete again. After twenty rings, she hung up, more worried than before. If the old man were able, she felt sure he'd answer.

She turned on the coffee pot, desperate for some caffeine to jolt her brain into action. While the coffee brewed, she took a shower and put on her uniform. Her pants fit loosely, an indication of the toll the past week had taken. Even though her stomach was jittery from lack of food, she didn't have the time or the desire to eat. Her dream had put her off food. She poured a go cup of black coffee and headed out.

As she passed the mirror in her hallway, she saw the writing.

"Back off or Jake dies." Beneath the words, written in bright red lipstick, was the bolo tie Jake wore every day with his uniform.

She reached out for the tie but stopped. Instead, her fingertip touched the bright lipstick. She knew who it belonged to.

Frankie.

She brought her fingertip close so she could inspect it, still trying to accept what her heart knew. "*Back off or Jake dies.*"

Frankie had taken Jake hostage.

It made perfect sense, in a sick and deadly way. Frankie had championed Jake's cause. She'd asked for Rachel's friendship. She'd been an extension of the investigation. She'd done a perfect job of laying the groundwork for a friendship with Jake. Friends were always easier to deceive.

Rachel felt the coffee rise up in her stomach. She rushed to the bathroom just in time. When she wiped her face with a cool wash cloth, she couldn't face her own reflection. This was her fault. She'd failed to see what was clearly in front of her eyes, and she'd failed to tell Jake about the skin or the figurine someone had left for her. She'd suspected Jake, in fact, and had lost her trust in him. As a result, she'd shut him out of vital information that had put his life at risk.

Still holding the washcloth to her lips she went to the telephone. She had to call Gordon and tell him. She'd tried to handle the case by herself, and now Jake had been taken by a killer who had murdered four, maybe five men. Not only murdered but cruelly tortured.

As she reached for the phone, it rang.

"Rachel." Frankie's voice was lazy, amused. "I figured by now you'd found the message I left for you."

"Is Jake alive?" Rachel countered.

"Oh, he's very much alive. He's not happy, but he's alive."

"Have you hurt him?"

"You should listen instead of asking so many questions."

"I want to talk to him." Rachel heard her heartbeat roaring in her ears.

"You don't trust me?" Frankie sounded sad.

"Let me talk to Jake."

"Jake, darling, Rachel wants to speak with you."

Rachel heard the sound of muffled cries, and she had to force herself to control her rapid breathing.

"Rachel!" Jake's voice was hoarse.

"Jake! Are you hurt?"

"Don't let her manipu-" His words were cut off by a scream.

Frankie came back on the line. "He's such a bad boy to try and act so brave. Really, he's not in a position to tell you what to do, Rachel, and I know how you hate that anyway."

"What do you want?" Rachel asked.

"Nothing. I want you to do absolutely nothing. I've spent years putting every piece of this into place, and I have a few loose ends to clip. So I want to make sure you don't do anything to muck it up."

"Is Richard Jones alive?"

"That shouldn't concern you right now." Frankie's tone had gotten harsh. "Jake is alive. That should be your focus. If you want him to stay that way you'd better back off."

Rachel knew better than to argue. "I will."

"Why is it that I don't believe you, Rachel?"

"Richard is probably dead. Jake is alive; that's where I should focus my energies."

"Very logical deduction, but you aren't a creature of logic, Rachel. That's the whole problem. Had Scott Amos been put in charge of this case, as I anticipated, I wouldn't be in this situation."

"Don't hurt Jake and I'll do whatever you want."

"Do you love him, Rachel? Do you?"

"I don't know." Frankie was too smart to be fed a lie.

"I've never loved anyone, or at least I don't remember loving anyone. I'm incapable of love. That's what the doctors told my mother. The bullet did so much damage. When there's no love or happiness or tenderness, that leaves only revenge."

"Jake never did anything to you, Frankie. Don't hurt him."

"So you think Jake is an innocent lamb. That's amusing."

Rachel almost bit, but she stopped herself. "Jake has been a good friend to me. His entire family has. I'm not sure what I feel for him, but I do know I don't want him to be hurt."

"You might change your mind about some of that."

Frankie was toying with her. "Tell me what I should do. I'm listening."

"I've already told you. Do nothing. Go to work, act normal, tell no one. In a few days, if you do what you're told, I'll let Jake go. After all, he's in this situation because of you, isn't he?"

Rachel could hear Jake's muffled protests. She put her fist to her mouth to stop the desire to threaten Frankie.

"Are you going to cooperate?" Frankie asked.

"Yes." She choked out the word. "Whatever you say."

"Good. Put the brakes on the entire investigation. Give me the time I need to finish. After that, I'll leave and Jake will be alive."

"You promise?" Rachel forced a plea into her voice. She'd never been good at acting, but she prayed for a grace note at this moment. She had to convince Frankie she was cowed and beaten.

"Even if I did promise, you wouldn't believe me, so I'll

make you this bargain. Mess with me, and I'll send Jake back to you, bit by bit."

The phone went dead in Rachel's hand.

Her fingers were gripping the receiver so tightly that they wouldn't release. She finally shook it free and flexed her hand. As the blood flow returned to her fingers, she rushed back to the toilet. Jake's life hung in the balance because of her.

CHAPTER TWENTY-SEVEN

Harvey threw the five-hundred count Egyptian cotton sheet over Hank's decaying head. He avoided any close examination. The head had obviously been frozen, and the thawing process was exceedingly unpleasant.

He bundled it up but then stopped. There was no way he could get it to his car without Jeremy or Bettina seeing him. Even the disappearance of the sheet would raise questions. He was a fucking prisoner in his own domain. The idea made him furious and he almost kicked the sheeted bundle on the ground. He couldn't even go to the bunkhouse to get a shovel. That in itself would raise questions, because he'd never done a lick of yard work in his life.

He went to the flower beds that he'd paid to have installed. Digging tentatively with his hand, he began to scoop out the mulch. The going was much easier than he'd expected because the buried sprinkler system kept the ground moist. Jimmy Hoffa had disappeared—so could Hank's head.

He dug furiously, throwing dirt and mulch in all directions, like a dog burying a bone. He had to be quick, before someone came looking for him. He had a press conference in

Bisonville at 11 a.m. to announce the first architect's rendering of Paradise. Since Richard was missing, he'd have to carry forth without him.

If Richard was dead? He pushed that question aside. Richard was the brains of the development. He had the vision to build the production plants where the workers would be employed. He had the patents on the technology that would make the whole city economically viable. Without Richard, would there be a Paradise? His hands slowed in the dirt.

For the first time, he noticed they were trembling.

He stood up and retrieved the sheet-wrapped head. He placed it in the hole he'd dug and began to replace the earth. He put the mulch back as neatly as he could, hoping that by the time the gardeners returned, they wouldn't notice. Later, when things calmed down, he'd take care of the head permanently.

Once Hank's head was buried, he felt better. As soon as the press event was over, he was going back to Washington. He was safer there.

He looked around the vista that he'd always found so restful. The four wranglers in the bunkhouse walked outside, their laughter drifting toward him on a gentle breeze. Together they headed toward the kitchen for breakfast. Life was the same, normal. Nothing had happened to change his world.

At least not yet.

The sun had climbed over the hills that ringed the ranch. Warm sunshine mingled with the scent of conifer. To his right was a field of sunflowers, a crop he approved because of the great PR opportunities. His world was intact. Any minute now, Bettina would arrive to collect his breakfast tray and draw his bath. He was unharmed.

But he couldn't convince himself that something ominous wasn't hovering on the horizon. Hank and Mullet were dead. Richard was missing. It wasn't possible that this was just a coincidence—the same four men who had killed Dub Jackson —two of them dead, one missing, and the final man, himself, the recipient of body parts. No, someone had his number, and they were working on him. Now he only had to wait to see if it was revenge or blackmail.

He thought about Frankie. She was the most logical suspect, except the bullet that he'd fired into her brain had turned her head to mush. She hadn't been able to feed herself, much less remember a murder. He'd meant to kill her, though, and he should have followed through. That moron Mullet had assured him she was all but dead.

Yet she'd lived, a twelve-year-old zombie that couldn't walk or talk. He'd kept up with her medical progress the first two or three years after she'd moved to Montgomery. The doctors and Polly had assured him that she had no memories. He'd made a lot of charitable donations to Alabama hospitals and clinics to be sure he was kept in the loop on Frankie's recovery.

Without memory, there was no motive for revenge.

But if it wasn't Frankie, who was it?

There were other possibilities. Adam Standing Bear, for one. He pondered the angles. Frankie had called him to tell him Jake Ortiz wanted to get into politics. Frankie had asked for his help for Jake. On the surface, it was an innocent enough request. But what was beneath it?

He opened the sliding glass door, checking the lock to be sure no one had tried to jimmy it, and went to get ready to go to Bisonville. He'd shower and dress. He might also pay a surprise visit to an old friend. Mel Ortiz was retired, with plenty of free time on his hands. The question was, had the devil found employment for Mel's hands in his workshop?

. . .

THE SUN finally warmed the cabin where Richard shivered in his boxer shorts. He needed to go to the bathroom in the worst kind of way, but there were no plumbing facilities. Pride, shame, something made him resist doing the necessary deed in the cabin. Pacing the old wooden floor, he thought that maybe Frankie would come and let him outside where there had to be an outhouse. The pressure in his bowels and bladder was comforting, in the sense that he could focus on this most immediate, urgent need and keep his mind off his likely fate.

He'd lain awake all night, thinking back to that long ago day when he'd reluctantly gone into the woods with Harvey Dilson and his two thugs to clench the support of several D.C. heavyweights for his concept of Paradise.

He'd been little more than a kid, a twenty-five-year-old nerd with no social skills, a master's degree in computer technology from MIT, and a desire to create a city where everyone had a well-paid job and worked in pollution free conditions.

Early on, he'd been suspicious of Harvey's interest in Paradise. At first, Harvey had pretended to care about the pollution factor and the classless society that Richard had envisioned. Practicality had been the bludgeon Harvey used to knock out parts of Paradise that Richard held dear. It was impractical to view a city where garbage men and school teachers made as much as corporate executives. It went against the American incentive of capitalism, Harvey had insisted.

Richard's entire relationship with Harvey had been one long slide into the primordial swamp of greed, corruption, and for-sale-political influence that was the U.S. Congress.

On the day when Dub Jackson had been killed, Harvey had told Richard that he'd brought several influential money men to South Dakota so they could experience firsthand the beauty and pristine glory of the Black Hills.

In the sternest tone, Harvey had warned Richard that he

had to get these men behind him, that the best bonding experience for men was a successful hunting expedition, that no one wanted to sweat to get a kill, and that he'd taken care of everything.

In that one moment, when Richard had stood with his hunting gear in hand, about to get into Harvey's Land Rover, he'd changed the course of his life. He'd entered the car and lost his soul. Now, the account was past due and Frankie had come to collect. When she finally got there, it would be a relief.

When he thought of Justine, he didn't want to live anyway. She was suffering now—was maybe even dead--because of him. Wrong time, wrong place, Harvey would say. But Richard knew differently. By some quirk of fate, Justine had begun to care for him. She'd hooked up with him to work him. He wasn't totally naïve. She was a member of that group that wanted to stop the four-lane. A bit of "progress" that Harvey had insisted on, not Richard.

Justine had deliberately met him and seduced him because she meant to use him for her own means. But something else had happened. He could see it in her eyes. She'd seen beneath his multi-million dollar existence. She was manipulative and capable, but she also had great passion for the things she believed in.

Life had become so clear to Richard. His lack of commitment to other women, his inability to fall in love with anything except his dream of Paradise—all of it had to do with the fact that he'd always expected to be punished for what had happened to Dub and Frankie Jackson. He deserved to be punished.

He quickened his steps as a twist of pain shot through his gut. If Frankie didn't come soon, he would humiliate himself. He'd never been a brave man, but he didn't want to die surrounded by the stench of his own feces.

He went to the window, checking for the thousandth time the bars that held him inside. He paced the corner that served as a dining room/den. It was a very old cabin, made back when logs were notched to fit together, which only meant that he'd never be able to find a weak spot.

Except for maybe the roof. With the coming of daylight he could clearly see the beam construction of the interior. There was no insulation, and it looked as if it was plywood covered in, he would guess, cedar shingles. If he could get up there...

A sound outside the cabin made his heart surge. The impulse to run came over him, a blind need to move, to flee.

He forced himself to freeze and listen. The distinct sound of footsteps on the front porch told him someone was there.

Frankie.

It could be no one else. Men had been hunting in the woods for days trying to find Mullet without success. As much as he wanted to believe that someone had come to save him, he accepted that his life was coming to an end.

Footsteps moved across the boards of the porch.

He sat down in the chair, his back to the door. He wasn't about to give her the pleasure of seeing his fear.

There was the rattle of a chain, then the sound of the door creaking open. Richard felt his eyes swell with tears, but he refused to turn around. He gripped the table and closed his eyes, beginning his last prayer for forgiveness.

"Rachel, have you heard from Jake?" The sheriff stood in front of her desk, a fact that hadn't even registered on her until he spoke her name.

"Not this morning?" She turned her face up to his. "Why?"

"He's not answering his cell, and I thought for sure he would've been here by now."

"He might have gotten a call or something." She tried to keep the tremor out of her voice. The one thing she believed beyond any doubt was that Frankie would kill Jake if she needed to.

"Sheriff, I know this is bad timing, but I need today off."

He looked at her as if she'd grown a third head. "Now? In the middle of all of this?" He waved a hand around the room.

She couldn't hold his gaze. "I'm really sorry, Sheriff. I just found out last night that I have a step-sister. She's dying of cancer down in Mobile, Alabama. They don't expect her to make it beyond today. I need to fly down there to at least meet her before she passes away. I might get a trace on my father from her."

Gordon rubbed the left side of his moustache, something he did only when he was agitated. "She's dying?"

Rachel nodded. "Liver cancer."

"A half-sister?"

"Apparently my dad had another family." She shrugged. "I've booked a flight out at ten. I'll be back tonight, late."

He sighed, rubbing harder at his moustache. "This couldn't come at a worse time, Rachel."

"I know." She kept her gaze on her desk. "I'll make it up to you." She couldn't afford to look at him for fear he'd see the naked truth in her eyes. She was terrified. Frankie could kill Jake on a whim, or she could make him suffer for hours and hours. Richard Jones might also still be alive, another torture victim whose last hours would be unendurable hell.

"Okay. And I'm sorry. I know you don't have much family and what a shame to find a sister only to lose her to cancer."

"Yes, sir." She had to get out of the office without drawing suspicion. "How is Justine Morgan?"

"Improving. They're doing surgery this morning to repair her nose. They're going to have to rebuild it completely, but she's mighty lucky. None of the bone shards penetrated her brain."

Justine was incredibly lucky. If she lived, Rachel had feared she'd be partially lobotomized by the bones of her own nose.

Her telephone rang, saving her from further lies. She answered it, dreading that it might be Frankie.

"Ms. Redmond, this is Adam Standing Bear."

She'd never anticipated that Adam would call her. "What can I do for you, Adam?"

"I was thinking of that silver boot clip."

Her stomach knotted. Yuma Pete still wasn't answering his phone. "And?"

"Did Yuma help you?"

She hesitated. "Yes, he did."

"He's a good man. But I was troubled by the clip. I worried about it all night long."

"Did you remember something?"

"I did."

"What?" She could hear the desperation in her voice. They'd established a certain rapport on the horse ride, and now she was acting defensive and evasive. She had to get herself under control. "What did you remember?" she encouraged.

"I've seen those clips before."

She felt the thud of her heart against her ribs. "Do you remember where?"

"I do."

She locked her jaw on the desire to snap at him. "Will you tell me?"

"If we could meet in person."

She looked around the room. The sheriff and Scott were conferring while Gladys kept trying to locate Jake. They were already treating her as if she'd stepped off the case. "Where?"

"I'm outside the courthouse."

"I'll be there in five minutes." She stood, checking to be sure her gun was in her holster. She caught sight of her reflection in the glass partition of Gordon's office. She looked like shit.

She picked up her jacket and walked out into the hall without catching anyone's attention. Good. One less lie to have to think up.

She hurried down the hallway and out into the sun where Adam sat in his red truck, waiting.

CHAPTER TWENTY-EIGHT

The county road to Yuma Pete's stretched ahead of them as the silence in the pickup thickened. Rachel could feel Adam glancing at her, reading her body language. She swallowed. In her haste to get out of the sheriff's office before she did something that cost Jake his life, she'd put herself in a moving vehicle with a man she didn't know. A friend of Frankie's.

"Last night, I remembered where I'd seen those silver toe guards. I tried to call Yuma," Adam said. "He didn't answer. Last night or this morning."

She could have told him she'd had the same experience, but she looked out the passenger window at the wispy clouds that looked like gossamer lace on the blue, blue sky. "I'm sorry, Adam."

"Has something happened to Yuma because of that toe clip?" he asked.

She wanted to close her eyes, but instead she looked at him. Worry tightened his jaw and creased his forehead, but his gaze was calm. "I hope not," she said. "You saw those toe guards at his place, didn't you?"

"It was a long time ago. They were in a box, and I opened it. Yuma closed it quickly and told me to forget I'd seen them, that they were for bad men."

Rachel wondered how much to tell Adam. She'd made the mistake of taking Frankie into her confidence—because Gordon and Jake trusted her. Now Jake was at her mercy. Because Adam had told her about Yuma, it was possible the old man was hurt. "That's essentially the same thing Yuma told me. Mullet Bellows was one of those men."

Adam pressed the gas harder as they sped down the empty road.

"How long have you known Frankie?" she asked.

"Since we were children. You know that. What is it you really want to know?"

Rachel felt the sudden pressure of tears, but she blinked them back. She wasn't a woman who cried when she found herself in a corner. She was a fighter. Mel Ortiz had recognized that in her and helped her bring it out. "Who is Frankie?"

Adam drove for half a mile before he spoke. "I'm not certain. The woman I know has nothing whatsoever to do with the girl I once knew."

She saw the square rock that marked the lane to Yuma Pete's. Adam slowed the truck. They drove the final leg in silence. When they got out of the truck, she drew her gun.

"Expecting trouble?" he asked.

"Yes." She stepped ahead of him and climbed the steps to the porch. No one answered her hard knock, heightening her fears. She nodded when Adam put his hand on the knob and turned it, pushing the door open with force.

The old man was lying on the floor, one arm outstretched toward the door as if he were trying to reach it. When she knelt beside him to feel for a pulse, she found only a weak heartbeat. "Call 911," she said. "He's alive."

Adam made the call, then knelt on Yuma's other side. "Who did this?"

"I'm not sure."

"You know. Tell me. Yuma is a gentle man. He never harmed anyone." He looked around. "This wasn't a robbery."

"No. No it wasn't." She went to the telephone and called the sheriff's office. "Gladys, I've got an attempted murder. I've called the paramedics, but we need a forensic team out at this address." She gave it.

"Who is it?" Gladys asked.

"A man by the name of Yuma Pete. Please tell Gordon or Scott to hurry out here." She hung up before the dispatcher could ask anything else. "Adam, would you stay with Mr. Pete until the paramedics arrive?"

"You're leaving?"

"I need to borrow your truck. I've got something I have to do."

He considered it for a moment. "You don't trust me enough to tell me where you're going, but you want to borrow my truck?"

"I want to catch whoever did this. I need your truck right now. Please."

He reached into his pocket and brought out the keys. "She's a little rough going into third."

"Thank you." She started toward the door, then turned back. "Don't trust Frankie. I can't tell you more than that, but whatever you do, don't trust her. Don't put yourself in a position to be alone with her."

"When you get back, will you call me?"

"This isn't something you want to get in the middle of."

"I'm already there, Rachel."

She nodded and ran out the door. She'd have to drive fast to catch her flight. If she was going up against Frankie, though, she had to be fully prepared. The only place to find the answers to her questions was buried deep in Frankie's past.

RICHARD FORCED his spine erect as the door creaked open behind him. Footsteps shuffled toward him, and he imagined Frankie with a stun gun, ropes, or chains, a glittering knife. He'd played this moment over and over again in his head.

Before he could change his mind, he turned swiftly in the chair and hurled himself at the figure that was halfway across the room. He hit her hard, bowling her over so that he fell on top of her.

"Ah-h-h-h-h-h!" He screamed like a savage animal, flailing his arms, slamming his fists into her thin body, his teeth finding purchase on her face, her beard filling his mouth.

At the taste of the beard, he lost momentum and heard a male voice yelling.

"Get the fuck off me, man!"

He slowed his fists and forced his body weight off his opponent long enough to catch a glimpse of a long-haired, disheveled man with sunken cheeks and fear in his eyes.

"Who are you?" Richard asked.

"Fuck you!" the man spat at him, pushing hard at him to get him off.

Richard eased his weight onto his arms for a better look. He'd never seen the man before. His gaze went immediately to the still open door. Escape. The word took over his brain and he scrambled to his knees and then his feet. His body, dressed only in boxer shorts, was shaking.

He stood, poised, ready to flee out the open door, but he didn't. The man on the floor was picking himself up.

"Who are you?" Richard asked again.

"Your fucking savior, asshole." He brushed at his seat and chest. "You're Richard Jones, right?"

"What if I am?"

The man rolled his eyes dramatically. "Then I expect you to give me a big reward for saving your skinny ass." He stepped toward Richard, who instinctively shrank back.

"My name is John Henry James. I heard about how you'd gone missing and were likely tied up in the Skin Dancer murders. I seen this cabin two days ago when I was trailin' a... anyway, I figured this might be the hidey hole where the Skin Dancer was keeping his victims." He grinned.

Richard tried to process what was happening. "You came to save me?"

"That's right, rich boy." A hint of amusement touched John Henry's face. "Looks like you could use some savin', too." He unbuttoned the long-sleeved flannel shirt that covered his Tee. "Take this for now. Can't do nothin' about the pants or boots. You're just gonna have to tough it out."

"You're taking me out of here?" Richard felt relief like a sweet bubble that rose from his pelvis, up his body, into his throat. He felt tears gather behind his eyes. "You're really here to help me?"

"Quit your jaw-bonin' and get on out the door." John Henry gave him the shirt. "Let's get a move on. If the Skin Dancer comes back for you, I'm not waitin' around, no matter how much reward you offer."

Richard needed no second request. He grabbed the shirt, buttoning as he hurried out the door, across the porch and into the sunshine. The ground was cold and hard on his bare feet, but he dropped in behind John Henry and started hiking at a brisk pace. His savior didn't want to linger in the area, and that suited Richard fine.

"This is a great hidey-hole," John Henry threw over his shoulder. "Hard to get here through an old mine shaft. Only way in." He looked behind him for emphasis. "Only way out. So we have to get clear of here before the Skin Dancer comes back."

Richard cast one last look at the peaceful valley nestled between steep rock cliffs. No one would ever have found him. He followed John Henry into the dark opening that was the mine shaft. He stumbled into the wall and stubbed his toe, but he kept going.

"Do you know this Skin Dancer?" Richard asked.

"Hell no. I still got skin, don't I?"

"But you don't believe it's a...ghost or demon, do you?"

John Henry spat. "What else could it be, man? Nobody in his right mind would do the things that's been done. Has to be that angry Injun spirit."

Richard felt a sharp rock pierce the bottom of his foot. There would be a blood trail. The thought worried him, but not enough to make him slow down or even look at his injury.

They cleared the mine shaft and stepped into the sunshine. The smell of the fir trees was sharp and clean. Richard closed his eyes for a second, inhaling, grateful that against all odds, he was still alive.

"Move it," John Henry said. "I don't want to be caught anywhere near here."

"I'm right behind you."

Justine's chest rose and fell with her shallow, almost nonexistent breaths. Derek held her cool hand, his forearms resting on the edge of the bed.

"Don't slip away, Justine," he whispered. "Stay here with me."

Her chest stirred slightly, the only response to his plea.

The sheriff had kicked him loose. There was nothing to show that he'd attacked Justine or the deputy. He'd confessed to the burning of the car, but that was so far down the sheriff's priority list that it hadn't even been a consideration. Besides, they were using him for bait. He knew it, which was why he had to come and talk to Justine one last time.

"Hang in here with us, Justine. I'm going to catch the killer and then I'm going to find Richard. I don't like him, but I'll do my best to save him. Then maybe you'll see the real Derek Baxter."

He leaned forward and kissed her pale cheek. The idea that she might die before he could get back to her was like a knife in his heart. The thought that his life had been an utter waste made him want to fall to his knees and beg for forgiveness, but he only brushed a strand of her auburn hair from her face. "When you wake up, I'm going to show you the man I really am."

He left the room, his legs shaking until he reached the parking lot. As he suspected, the sheriff was sitting in a cruiser outside the hospital. To Derek's amazement, the blue lights began to whirl and the siren went off full blast. The sheriff headed off somewhere in a big hurry.

Worry gnawed at Derek's gut. Had someone found Richard Jones? Was he alive? Derek climbed into his vehicle. He had to fid Rachel. She knew more about the case than anyone else. She was the first step in setting things right.

The long years of bad choices and bad decisions had created an avalanche, the force of which was pushing him to take an action that would redeem him in the sight of the only person he cared about. Justine.

He would find Richard, even if it meant that he would never claim Justine for himself. He would find the man she loved and return him to her. If she lived, he would never want anything except her total happiness. For the first time in his life, he was looking beyond his own immediate needs. Surely that would mean something to a god who was reputed to be benevolent.

CHAPTER TWENTY-NINE

Frankie lifted the field glasses once more. There was no sign of life from the ranch where Harvey Dilson would get the first taste of his fate. It was a pity she couldn't watch him discover the head of his old comrade, Hank Welford. But she knew Harvey well enough to know that every action and every thought would be centered on his own preservation.

It was what she was counting on.

She checked her watch. Richard was secured in the cabin in the woods. No one would ever find him. Rachel was effectively eliminated by her desire to save Jake. Justine was seriously injured, a necessity in that moment when she went to capture Richard.

It was odd, but Frankie found that she took no pleasure in hurting women. That's why it had been so difficult to smack Bettina's skull with the baton, while seeing the fear in Jeremy's eyes had been such a delight. He'd fallen before he could even attempt to defend himself. He'd sold his soul to the devil years before when he'd signed on as Harvey's aide.

The two of them, Bettina and Jeremy, had been in her way when she'd slipped into the house. She'd gotten Bettina to tell her what Harvey preferred for breakfast, and then Frankie had made the coffee, arranged the newspapers just so, and left them at his door. Next he would find Bettina and Jeremy tied and gagged, across from each other, like an old married couple.

Soon Harvey would have to make a move. Once he found his loyal servants, he'd have to call for help—which would then require an explanation why he had the head of Hank Welford in his possession. Or, Harvey would pretend that nothing had happened. He would continue to his Rapid City office and check the preparations for the press conference. Tomorrow he would hold it, noting that Richard Jones had been called away on business but would return in the next week.

Knowing Harvey's nature—and the capital he'd invested in Paradise—this was what Frankie had based her entire plan on.

She saw movement at the ranch. She lifted the binoculars and zeroed in on Harvey. She could kill him with one rifle shot. That was far too easy. He would suffer more than any of the others. He'd killed her father and he'd shot her in the head. She'd learned the full details of that long-ago day from Hank and Mullet, who'd been only too willing to give up Harvey in the slim hope of saving themselves. But she had a sense of honor. She'd never promised them that she'd let them go. She'd never even hinted that she wouldn't make them suffer. She'd never led them on. They'd gotten exactly what they deserved.

In the long hours of questioning them, the only thing she hadn't discovered was the location of her father's body. She sincerely believed it was because they didn't know.

Harvey was the only one who knew the location, and he would tell her before he died. She was certain of it. Then she'd see that her father's remains were unearthed and his reputation as a man who abandoned his family during hard times was cleared.

And after that? She didn't know. She hadn't completely

planned the next step, but it would involve Argentina. She had a yen for a Paso Fino.

Harvey came out the front door. He looked in all directions, as if he expected someone to leap up from the sand like a reincarnated pharaoh and attack him.

Good. She smiled. Guilt was the most effective knife in the universe. The things Harvey had done were finally coming home to cut him. In the next twenty-four hours, he would suffer more at his own hands than hers. After that, though, she would wield the knife, and he would know the true meaning of suffering. The skin, as the largest organ in the body, contained the most sensitive nerves.

She followed Harvey's actions. He was jittery, which led her to believe he'd found Bettina and Jeremy. He dropped the keys to the SUV. He wasn't used to driving himself. Jeremy had always done that job.

Harvey jumped into the vehicle and sped down the long driveway toward the main road. Frankie had done her homework. She knew where he was going. Now all she had to do was wait.

When the time was right, she'd be there with bells on.

THE PUDDLE HOPPER bounced along the runway as the props slowly lost velocity. Rachel looked out the small window at the wall of pine trees that bordered the airstrip. Heat rose in waves from the asphalt.

As soon as the plane taxied to the dock, she was on her feet and straining to get out. She ignored the frown the stewardess shot at her. The plane door opened, and she pushed past two businessmen and ran down the terminal. Luckily, the Montgomery airport was too small to get lost in. She found the rental agency and picked up the keys to the car she'd leased for the day.

She'd opted not to wear her uniform, and she wondered if she'd made a mistake. Sometimes the badge opened a lot of doors. And sometimes it closed just as many.

She took the street map she'd picked up at the car rental counter, studied the streets, then headed south to the Bridgefield nursing home where Polly Jackson had died from injuries sustained in a tumble down a stairwell.

The summer heat in Montgomery was thick and hot. Lining the street, beautiful lacy flowers of pink, fuchsia, lavender, white and cranberry flourished on trees with smooth skin instead of bark.

Rachel drove slowly, even after she located the institution, which had been built to look like a large manor house. Stepping into the building, Rachel steeled herself against the smell. It wasn't unpleasant or unclean, merely old and institutional. She didn't have a warrant or a court order, so she was going to have to convince one of the employees to give her Polly Jackson's personal effects, if such a thing existed.

Several elderly women in wheelchairs waved at her as she approached.

"Who are you here to see?" one of the women asked her.

"I'm a friend of Polly Jackson. Did you know her?"

The old woman's face fell. "I'd hoped you came to see me."

A woman in a blue robe with lively brown eyes rolled closer. "I'm Donna. Donna Vance. Polly's gone."

"Did you know her?" Rachel asked.

"Polly never had visitors," she said, sizing Rachel up. "Who are you?"

"I'm a friend of her...daughter's. I'm a friend of Frances."

The women looked at each other, nodding and communicating without words. They maneuvered their chairs to wheel away.

"Wait," Rachel said.

Rachel knelt on one knee and took Donna's hand. "I'm a deputy from South Dakota. Please help me. Mrs. Jackson may have left behind some papers that are important to a murder case."

Donna Vance stopped. The other ladies passed her by as they continued down the hall, their wheels making noises like soft sighs on the waxed tile. Donna faced Rachel. "Polly was afraid of her daughter. Frances would walk in the front door, and Polly would start screaming."

Rachel took shallow breaths. Even if she didn't find papers or documents, she might find a lead. "Did Mrs. Jackson ever talk about the past? About what happened to Frankie and her husband?"

Donna's blue-veined hand tapped lightly on the terry-cloth robe that covered her legs. "Polly said that if Frances knew the truth, she would do more than push her down the stairs. Nobody believed Polly, but I did."

Rachel's body recognized the importance of Donna's revelation with a surge of adrenaline. "What truth was she speaking about?"

Donna shrugged. "She never got a chance to say. They took her that night."

"You mean she died? Do you know what she died of?"

Donna signaled her to lean closer. "She didn't die."

Rachel searched Donna's brown eyes for a hint of madness. "She didn't die?"

"I don't think she did. I think that Frances took her someplace where she couldn't talk to anyone."

Rachel licked her dry lips. "Do you know where?"

Donna looked down the hallway at an approaching nurse. "Someplace private."

"What makes you think Mrs. Jackson is still alive?"

Donna's hands were on the wheels of her chair. "Because Frances liked to see her suffer. That's what Polly said. She said Frances would keep her alive forever to punish her." Her eyebrows rose. "Don't ask the nurses. They lie. They won't tell you the truth."

She turned the chair and wheeled down the hallway.

"May I help you?" the nurse asked as she came up to Rachel, placing her body as a block.

"I was looking for Junie Redmond. I thought she was a patient here. I'm a niece from Montana."

"We don't have a patient by that name." The nurse's sharp tone spoke of her suspicion.

"Is there another home? Or some place where a person who suffered a stroke might go to heal?" Rachel pasted a smile on her face. "There was a breach in the family and I haven't seen my aunt for a long time. I just picked the names of some care facilities out of the phone book and thought I'd try to find her."

"Come with me and I'll check for you."

Rachel could see the nurse's attention move down the hallway to the women in their wheelchairs as they huddled together.

"Thanks. I'll handle it on my own." Rachel turned to the exit. She didn't look back as she stepped into the heat.

CHAPTER THIRTY

Frankie held the telephone against her ear as she drove. The morning was almost gone, and she was hungry. She'd been up for what seemed like weeks. Sleep wasn't necessary, but food was getting to be a high priority. She could taste her body feeding on its own muscle. Ketosis. Not exactly unpleasant, but an omelet or something from Lulu's would be delicious.

When the sheriff answered, she put all of her Southern training into her voice. "Gordon, it's just me. I wondered if there was anything I could do to help. This whole thing with Richard is just awful. Is there any news?"

"No, and you need to keep Richard's disappearance under your hat, Frankie. Things are worse than you know. There's been another attack. An artist over near the Wyoming line."

She could hear the tension in his voice. He tried hard to cover it, but Gordon Gray wasn't close to being an actor. He was a relatively decent man with the ambition to have a lot of money. The two never went together. Once the serpent of greed bit, decency died of poison. In Gordon, it was a slow death.

"You think it's the same person who killed Hank and Mullet?" she asked.

"God, if there are two of them on the loose...Scott's there now, checking it out. Rachel found the man and called it in."

"Rachel? Is she still out there?"

"No. Scott's handling it."

"May I speak to Rachel?" she asked.

"She took a day off."

Frankie felt a twinge of satisfaction. For a moment she'd wondered if Rachel was behaving. But Rachel was smart enough to hold to the bargain they'd made. "Gordon, do you think Richard is still alive? Does the Skin Dancer have him?"

Gordon hesitated. "Look, reporters are crawling all over the place. Two CNN people just walked in the door with a full camera crew. I can't talk about that. We're trying to keep it under wraps for the moment."

"If something happens to Richard, the whole Paradise venture is at stake."

He didn't answer, and she smiled at how much that statement worried Gordon. Without Richard, the Paradise development would fall apart at the seams. Richard had the technology, the know-how, the vision. He was "the man" when it came to Paradise. He was also one of a gang of murderers.

"Call me if I can help," she said.

"Will do." Gordon hung up.

She swung by Rachel's. When she saw the deputy's truck was gone, she felt the first pang of uneasiness.

Derek was almost back in Criss County. He'd wasted valuable time following Rachel to the airport, hoping to talk to her but arriving too late. When the dispatcher had told him she was leaving town, he hadn't believed it. He'd assumed she'd be doing her job and hunting for Richard Jones, but instead he'd watched her board a flight to Montgomery. He had no idea why the lead investigator on a murder case that had almost included his girlfriend was leaving town, but she had. He'd seen it with his own eyes. She was going on vacation in the middle of a murder spree.

Instead of going into town, he took the road that went to Richard Jones's estate. The cops were so over-worked that they'd left yellow crime scene tape over the door and around the charred remains of Justine's car, but there was no one guarding the premises.

If all the cops were leaving town, he'd find Richard without Rachel's help.

He drove past the house then parked down a dirt road. It was a long trek back, but he jogged it in under fifteen minutes. Climbing the fence, he vaulted to the ground and headed to the house. If there was any evidence of where Richard had been taken, he'd find it.

The house was unlocked, and he eased inside, his heart thudding. He had no idea what he hoped to find, but he was smarter than the sheriff and his deputies. And he was more motivated. Justine might have been in bed with Richard, but once Derek proved what kind of man he really was, she'd come back to him.

He went up the staircase slowly. Though it curved with grace and elegance, it was sturdily built. Not a single step creaked. At the second floor landing, he hesitated. The idea of walking into that bedroom where he'd found Justine, bleeding, was almost more than he could take.

He forced his feet forward. When he pushed open the door, he inhaled sharply several times. Blood had soaked the mattress and stained the carpet. A lot of blood. Certainly not all of it could be Justine's.

He inched slowly into the room. There was something here. Something that would tell him what he needed to know. He got on his hands and knees and began to pat the carpet inch by inch.

Caught up in his work, he didn't notice the slender figure that moved through the doorway like a wraith.

"Hey, what are you doing?"

He almost screamed, wheeling so fast that he felt the bones in his neck grind. "What the fuck!" He was on his feet, facing the woman he recognized as the road crew foreman, Frankie Jackson. "What are you doing here?"

"That's exactly the question I asked you."

"I'm looking for evidence. So what are you doing here?"

Frankie leaned against the doorframe. "The same. Richard is a friend of mine. I guess neither of us trusts the competence of the local law enforcement."

"Bunch of dorks." Derek's gaze slipped back to the floor. He didn't have time to waste talking to Frankie. From what he could tell, she was up the sheriff's butt. She was the one who introduced Justine to Richard, and she was also the person pushing the four-lane through the wilderness. He turned away from her. "I got things to do."

"I can't believe they left this place wide open. It's a crime scene. A serious crime. Kidnapping and assault. They should've left someone here to guard it." Frankie stepped into the room.

"Right." Derek sank to the carpet and began his search. "Half the sheriff's department just went on vacation today."

"Oh, really? That's insane. Gordon wouldn't give Scott time off in the middle of this case, not even to be with his wife and new baby."

Derek's hands moved over the complex pattern woven into the carpet. Frankie was getting on his last nerve. "Scott didn't leave. Rachel Redmond did. She went to freaking Montgomery, Alabama. Get that. Just goes to show she has bad taste in destinations as well as career choices."

He searched the carpet for a few seconds, waiting for Frankie to respond. When she didn't, he looked up. The doorway was empty. There was no sign that she'd ever been there.

FRANKIE PUNCHED in Harvey's cell phone number as she sped down the road toward the airport. As soon as he answered, she got straight to the point.

"I need a jet. Now. I have to get home to Montgomery."

"What's this about, Frankie? I don't have time. I've got—"

"Harvey, I need this. You've never failed me. I have to get home. Now. I can't wait to explain."

There was silence and Frankie thought of where, exactly, she would start to strip his skin. Inner thigh. The underside of his arm.

"Okay. One of the Halliblast corporate jets is at the airstrip outside of Bisonville. I'll call and make the arrangements. You have to be back by tomorrow morning, though. Once the press conference is over, I'm heading to Washington."

"Oh, I'll be here. I wouldn't miss the press conference for all the tea in China." She was relaxed now. The crisis was over. She'd get to Montgomery and take care of Rachel, and then she'd come back and finish what she had to do with Jake.

In a way, Rachel had disappointed her. But in another, she'd made Frankie proud. Rachel hadn't rolled over like a whipped dog. She hadn't begged and pleaded. She'd done the unexpected—she'd taken action. And a smart step, at that.

"What's going on in Montgomery that's so urgent?" Harvey asked.

"I'll tell you when I get back. It's a surprise. But you sound a little strained, Harvey. You haven't been carousing with the young ladies, have you?"

The pause told her a lot. "Of course not. I've had a cold."

"Take care of yourself, Harvey. Criss County is depending on you."

"Have the jet back here."

"Roger. Over and out." She hung up. She was almost at the airport. She'd had fun stalking the men here in South Dakota, but she was looking forward to tracking Rachel on home turf.

By the time she parked and was cleared through security, the four-passenger jet was ready to go. She climbed on board and sat back. She was still hungry, and there was nothing she could do about that. But she could catch a two-hour nap. She needed to be refreshed and alert when she got to Alabama.

STARING at the sole of his dirty foot, Richard could see the delicate bones. He'd stepped on something sharp, and though he'd tried to continue walking behind John Henry James, he couldn't go any farther. The wound was bleeding more freely, leaving a trail that a blind tracker could follow.

"You got to get up and move," John Henry said, rubbing his scraggly beard. "Somebody wants you dead, and if you sit here waitin' for 'em to come, they will."

"I can't keep going." Richard's voice was level, calm. "You go on. Leave me here. I don't want you caught up in this."

John Henry walked back to stand in front of him. "Man, whoever is after you is gonna hang you upside down, strip the skin off you and chop off your head. You might wanna rethink this quittin' business."

Richard held up the bottom of his foot. He saw concern touch John Henry's face. "It's not that I don't want to. I can't."

John Henry knelt down and examined the wound more closely. "Looks like you stepped on a sharp stick. We need to clean this up, get the bark and dirt out of the wound, else you're gonna have a real mess on your hands."

Richard almost laughed. He'd been kidnapped by a serial killer who meant to skin him—and he'd escaped. It would be ironic if he died of an infected foot. "You go on. Maybe you can find a phone and call for help."

John Henry rocked back on his heels and thought about it. "It's a trek to anywhere there might be a phone. I was hopin' to get you to my place to rest, but it's still a good four miles to go."

"I can't make it. But if you do call and get someone to come..." He felt hope surge. Funny how hope never truly died. Not even when the situation was impossible. A deputy on an ATV could whisk him to safety.

"Why does the killer want you?" John Henry asked.

Richard almost brushed him off, but he changed his mind. "A while back I was involved in something really bad. A man was killed and a young girl shot in the head."

"You killed a dude?" John Henry drew back. "Shit man, that's heavy."

"I didn't kill anyone. But I didn't stop it. I should have stopped it, and barring that, I should have turned the people who did it over to the authorities." He felt the shame he'd suppressed for years. "But I did neither of those things. What I did was pretend none of it had ever happened. I just went on with my life and my dream, and I did nothing."

John Henry stood up. "Hindsight's a thing of beauty, Mr. Jones. For the past eight years I laid up in a jail cell remembering the night my wife died. We were drunk and arguing. We did it ever' night. But this time she threw a can of beer at me and hit me in the lip. It hurt like hell and I grabbed her wrist. I meant to slap her, just get her to snap out of it. She was crazy wild. She snatched her arm free and fell backward." He took off the T-shirt he was wearing and began to tear it into strips. "I knew when her head hit the corner of the table that she was dead. It made a sound like thumpin' a ripe melon. She was dead before she hit the floor, and there was nothin' I could do to change a thing."

John Henry took the strips of cloth and began to bind Richard's foot. "You got to keep goin'. I leave you here, you won't be found by the time I get back."

"If you stay, she'll kill you, too."

"She?" John Henry's eyes held surprise and interest. "The Skin Dancer is a woman?"

"Yes."

"Then we better hurry quicker. I'd rather face a hungry bear than a mad woman. Let's get shaking." He pulled the bandage tight around Richard's foot.

Pain shot up his leg, but Richard gritted his teeth and made no sound. "If we get out of this, you're going to be a wealthy man, Mr. Henry."

"Now those are words to live by." He pulled another strip of cloth tight around the foot. "I don't aim to let you disappoint me on that count."

The sound of leaves crackling made them both go silent. John Henry stood up, his gaze raking the woods in all directions as he turned. "Someone is out there," he said softly.

Richard hobbled up on one foot. "Is it her?"

John Henry shook his head. "I don't know, but we can't stay here any longer. Let's move." He offered Richard his arm to lean on.

Putting weight on the foot was like jamming a hot poker up the bone of his leg, but Richard started to walk. He could feel someone's gaze digging into his back. Had Frankie returned to finish him off? He stepped faster at the idea.

"Don't think about anything but the next step," John Henry whispered to him. "Step, step, step..." Branches whispered behind them.

"Run for it," Richard said, pulling his arm free. "Go. I don't want you to die. She isn't after you. It's me she wants. It's me."

As John Henry sprinted forward, Richard turned to meet his fate.

CHAPTER THIRTY-ONE

Sweat trickled down the small of Rachel's back, catching in the waistband of her jeans. The air was heavy, and even though she was parked in the shade of a magnificent oak, she was dying. Where the hell was Misha Woods? When she'd called a minute ago, the receptionist had said she was leaving for the day.

The front door of the therapy clinic opened, and a tall, dark-haired woman stepped into the sun. She carried a sheaf of folders under one arm.

Rachel got out of the car and walked to meet her. "Ms. Woods?" she asked.

"Yes?" Her brown eyes were curious.

"I'm Deputy Redmond. We spoke—"

The therapist's expression changed to one of agitation. "I can't help you. I've told you everything I know." She started to brush past Rachel.

"Polly Jackson is alive."

That stopped her. She faced Rachel. "No, that's not possible."

"It is. I believe she's at another full care facility, Frankie moved her away from her friends and I can't find the name she's using. Do you have any idea where she might have gone?"

"I work at four of the other five facilities. If Polly were there, I would certainly know it."

"And the fifth?" Rachel felt as if the heavy air was slowing everything, like being underwater.

"Heritage Manor." Misha rubbed her neck in thought. "I don't have any patients there. I'm sorry."

"Could you make some calls?" Rachel had to find Polly. "Frankie is holding Richard Jones and another man hostage, and I have no doubt she'll kill them. There's no one else who can help me."

Misha clutched the folders to her chest. "Frances scares me. She doesn't have a moral compass. The doctors said it was possible that the bullet, or the resulting swelling of tissue, damaged the part of her brain that delineates right from wrong. She's a dangerous woman."

"I know what I'm asking. You're my only hope."

Misha turned back to the clinic. "I know someone who works at Heritage Manor. I'll call her and see if there's a patient there who has the same injuries that Polly Jackson had."

"Thank you." Rachel wiped the sweat from her forehead as she followed the therapist into the air-conditioned cool of the building.

Frankie ate a burger and sipped on a chocolate shake as she waited in the rental car parked half a block down the street from Rachel's vehicle. The deputy had found Misha Woods and was no doubt getting an earful. Because she'd never expected anyone to come to Montgomery to check, Frankie hadn't worked all that hard to cover her tracks. Rachel would find Polly Jackson. Rachel had brains and determination. And she'd become an unnecessary complication.

Once Rachel was dead, Frankie intended to drive back to the airport and jump her flight home.

She settled back against the seat. It was only June but it was humid. When she and her mother had first moved to Montgomery, Frankie had been unable to move or talk. Her mother had pushed her along the sidewalk every evening.

Frankie remembered how the air had felt almost solid, as if she were cutting through damp layers of meringue. Today, the feeling was almost the same. She closed her eyes and leaned her head against the car seat. She'd missed the South. As much as she loved South Dakota, she could never rid herself of the anxiety and dread that came each winter. Alabama, at first, had been one long slow drawl of pain, but it had also been days and weeks of hard-fought accomplishment. South Dakota, so beautiful and lush in the summer, was terrifying when the winter set in.

Sometimes she'd dream about the snow, high up to her chest, trapping her so that she couldn't move. It always reminded her of the winter the cows had starved and frozen in the fields. That was the winter she'd watched her daddy suffer, and she'd been helpless to do a thing for him.

After the thaw, her dad and some of the hands had gone out. He'd told her to stay behind with her mother, but she'd managed to get in the back of a truck. By the time Dub found her, it was too late to send her home.

The carnage was horrible. Pits had to be dug and the dead cows pushed into them. Sanitary precautions. Her father had come in from the range that day bent, like something vital had broken. He never recovered. He did the work. He tended the ranch. But he'd lost the swagger in his walk and the quick smile that teased the corners of his mouth.

She'd stayed by his side every day that spring and summer, and she'd thought she'd seen the shadows retreating, bit by bit. But he hadn't lived long enough. His life was stolen from him and he'd been labeled a coward and yellowbelly, a man who left his family to starve.

She was pulled from her memories when she saw Rachel exiting the clinic. The deputy was running toward her car. Frankie drained the last of the milkshake and tossed the paper cup on the floorboard. No hurry. She knew where Rachel was headed.

One of Richard's automatics and her baton were on the seat beside her. Rachel had become a loose end. Too bad, but she couldn't afford loose ends.

Sitting in the hot car, she took her time. So many years, when she'd been a prisoner of her unresponsive body, she'd tried to fit the pieces together. Visitors to her hospital room had talked, thinking she couldn't understand. She'd gleaned the first bits of information that told her what had really happened. Helpless, unable to talk, she'd listened, remembering the strange silver boot ornament worn by the man who'd left her to die. Now the puzzle was complete. Everything was in order. The confessions of Hank and Mullet had been icing on the cake. She knew the exact details now. Dub had ridden up and caught Harvey and his cohorts in the middle of one of their canned hunts. Dub hated poachers and people who abused animals in that manner. He'd threatened to turn Harvey over to the authorities. Harvey shot him as he rode away. When she'd ridden up, he'd shot her too. It was that simple.

Harvey was never one to believe he deserved punishment. The ends justified the means—his motto. Because he delivered for his constituents in South Dakota, most of them felt they same way. They'd returned him to office twice already; he brought home the bacon in federal funds.

She started her car and drove slowly down the familiar tree-lined streets. She could only imagine her mother's face when she saw her. She had to be careful, though. She didn't want to end up arrested in Montgomery. Her escape route was planned through South Dakota. She had to be in Criss County by nightfall to bring everything to fruition.

HERITAGE MANOR WAS a French Provincial building at the end of a long, curved drive lined with live oaks and hydrangeas. Rachel took in the scene as she drove. Whatever Frankie had done to her mother, she'd also provided her with the best care money could buy.

Polly Jackson was registered under the name Sarah Powell. She was in room 234. Misha Woods's friend had been more than helpful.

Rachel slipped into the lobby, walking as if she knew exactly where she was going. It wasn't a large facility, and she located the room without trouble.

When she opened the door, she found Polly Jackson sitting up in bed. Her tired hazel eyes noted Rachel's presence, but she didn't seem enthused over a visitor.

"Mrs. Jackson, I need to ask some questions."

The first hint of alarm sharpened the focus of her gaze. "My name is Sarah Powell."

"I don't have time for games." Rachel closed the door. "I'm here about Frances."

Polly turned her face away toward the wall.

"Mrs. Jackson, peoples' lives are in danger. I have to know about Frances."

She turned bruised eyes toward Rachel. "There's nothing I

can tell you. I don't know this person who has my daughter's body. I don't want to know her."

"What really happened to your husband, Mrs. Jackson? Mullet Bellows and Hank Welford are dead. Two other men are missing. If Frankie is killing the people she thinks are responsible for Dub's death, who else will she go after?"

The intensity in Polly's eyes faded, as if she looked upon another time and place. "Frances killed those men in the Black Hills?"

"Yes." Rachel had no time for qualifiers. "Who else was involved in your husband's death? You have to know. Frankie thinks you know. Why else would she treat you like this?"

"He said it was a mistake." Her voice faded and then came back, stronger. "I didn't know for a long time. I never suspected. They made me believe Dub had left and Frances was shot in an accident. They had evidence that Dub left us, alone out there with the cattle hungry and no way to feed them. I couldn't believe that Dub had done that, but they said there were tracks, that people had seen him in Texas..."

"WHO? WHO SAID THOSE THINGS?" Rachel wanted to grasp the older woman's hands to convey the urgency, but she forced herself to stand calmly.

"You have to understand. Dub and Frances were closer than they should have been. I couldn't have another child, so she became my daughter and Dub's son. He taught her to ride when she was so little her legs barely straddled the pony. She started going to work with him on the ranch when she was five. She adored him."

Rachel pulled up a chair beside the bed. Not even the screech of the metal legs on linoleum could dislodge Polly from the past where she now lingered.

"It was summer the day Dub disappeared. School was out. Frances had finished the sixth grade, and I'd asked her to go into town with me to get fitted for a bra and some dresses. It was time for her to give up her britches. She didn't want to go, so the minute my back was turned she slipped out her bedroom window, saddled her horse and took off after her dad.

"Dub had a good head start up into the hills, but he'd taught Frances to track. Dub was hunting twenty cows that had strayed. Those were valuable cows since so much of our herd died the winter before."

She cleared her throat as if it had gone dry, and Rachel handed her a plastic glass of water with a straw. Her old hands wrapped around Rachel's as she gripped the glass.

"Dub never came back. When Frances rode home that day, barely hanging on to the saddle horn, blood covering her hair and body, dripping down onto the horse and leaving a trail in the sand, I looked into her eyes and I knew she was gone." Her grip on the glass tightened and water gushed over the top.

Rachel got a towel from the bathroom and mopped the floor. "What did Frankie say?" she asked.

Polly shook her head. "She couldn't talk, but the fear... She was like a wild animal in a trap. We took her by car to Rapid City because we couldn't wait on the ambulance. They told me the bullet had done extensive damage to her brain. They wanted to institutionalize her after she was released from the hospital, but I couldn't."

"And Dub was gone?"

"I thought so. It almost killed me. Gordon Gray—he's a good and decent man--he searched those woods day after day after day. Frances couldn't remember anything, but he and the volunteers followed Frankie's blood trail back to the hills. They found where she'd been shot, but no evidence that Dub had ever been there. The only sign they ever found was Dub's horse's tracks and then the tire prints from a horse trailer. They said he'd loaded up his horse and took off long before Frances was shot. Dub would never have left her hurt."

"How did Frankie get up on her horse?"

"No one could ever figure that out."

"And no one was questioned about the shooting?"

"It was a .22. Not something a person would hunt with. They found a target and figured kids had been up there practice shooting. It was written off as an accident. Kids never thinking where a bullet might end up. Mel told me that there wasn't a point in making a criminal out of a kid, that it would be best to let it go."

"And Dub?"

"I waited until September, when Frances was released from the hospital. Then I put the ranch up for sale. We were so far behind, I was hoping to cover the debt and be done with it. Before I could even put the sign up, Harvey Dilson bought it and with a handsome profit for me. Enough to bring Frances here and hire a private therapist to work with us."

"I knew Dilson owned a ranch, but I never knew it was the Jackson ranch."

She nodded. "I thought he was so kind, so generous. For the first few years, someone would leave money on the front step of the house every six months. It was more than enough to pay for the therapy and the things Frances needed, with some left over for me to invest. I thought that was Harvey because..." She looked out the window.

"Dilson left the money?"

When she turned back her face was haggard. "No one ever owned up to it, but I thought it was Harvey. He wrote letters for Frances and got her accepted into MIT for the engineering degree. He got her the job on the road project in South Dakota."

"Did you ever ask yourself why?"

Polly's gray eyes came into focus. Her right hand twisted the wedding band that was now loose on her finger.

Rachel almost gasped. She leaned forward. "Mrs. Jackson, were you involved with Harvey Dilson?"

Tears moved slowly down the wrinkles of Polly's face. "Dub and Frances never needed me. They were all each other needed. I was left out, and I needed someone."

"Does Frankie know about this? Is that why she hurt you?"

Polly shrugged one shoulder. "She can smell guilt. She's like an animal, sniffing out the guilt and the sorrow. That's what she feeds on."

Rachel mentally flipped through the conversation she'd had with Frankie. "I believe Frankie is looking for her father's body. I think she has to prove that he died, that he didn't abandon his family. That's why she's been torturing the men before she kills them. She has to find his body. Do you know where Dub is buried?"

Polly let her head fall back against her pillow. "There's an old mine shaft. If you walk all the way through it, there's a cabin that Harvey used on occasion. Dub's body is in the mine shaft, down a tunnel."

"Dilson told you?"

She nodded. "Not for a long time. Not until Frances was grown and in college and I'd taken so many things from him."

"Why did he tell you?" Rachel couldn't fathom his motivation.

"Harvey had never married. I was so alone. I'd spent years helping Frances recover from her injuries, and she'd finally left home. I wanted something, someone to care about. Someone to care about me. Harvey and I...once it had been so good. I thought maybe we could be together. So he told me, because he didn't want to me ever believe I could be anything to him. He destroyed any dream I might ever have had."

"You could have turned him in? You could have gotten—"

"Justice?" She shook her head. "Frances would have done something terrible. I knew she was capable of anything. But she's the only thing I have left, Deputy. If I'd made Dilson's actions public, Frances would have gone after him. So I kept quiet. It was all I could do to try to protect my daughter."

Rachel had what she needed. Dilson was the ultimate target. That's who Frankie was after. Jake and all the others were just window dressing for the big kill.

"You should understand that Frankie is—"

"Dangerous?" Polly laughed softly, a sound like the wind in dry leaves. "I know that better than anyone. It would be a relief if she came here and killed me, put an end to this—" she waved a hand around the room "living hell. You tell her that I'm ready for her."

Rachel had no time to argue. She had to get back to South Dakota.

WHEN THE DOOR to her mother's room started to open,

Frankie slipped into room 233. She smiled and put a finger to her lips when the old gentleman started to speak. Charmed, he smiled and settled back onto his pillows.

Frankie watched the hallway through the cracked door. As soon as Rachel had left, she eased across the hall into her mother's room.

Polly Jackson stared out the window. She didn't stir, even when Frankie walked to the foot of the bed.

"Hello, Mother," Frankie said.

Polly looked at her. "Frances, so you've come at last."

"All along, you knew." Frankie felt strangely detached. "I've gone to a lot of trouble to get that information, and you knew it all along."

"Yes," Polly said. "I knew. Not at first, but eventually."

Frankie shook her head. "I'll be back, Mother. You can count on it." She left the room. She had to head Rachel off at the airport before she screwed everything up.

CHAPTER THIRTY-TWO

Richard balanced himself on his bad foot. John Henry didn't want to dig in and fight, but Richard knew it was his only option. He couldn't run. Hell, he could barely hobble. He wasn't a medical doctor, but he had to wonder if they'd have to amputate his foot if he lived long enough to get to a hospital for help.

Something moved again deep in the trees, and he stopped, standing as tall as he could. It didn't matter that he was in his underwear and another man's shirt. The events of the past twenty-four hours had reduced him to sheer survival impulse.

"Whoever's there, come on!" he shouted.

"Have you lost your friggin' mind?" John Henry whirled around, snatched his arm, and started to drag him. "Let's get the fuck out of Dodge."

The brief image of a man—or a large hairy creature walking upright--slipped among the trees.

"It's not her." Richard pointed to the woods. Someone moved through the trunks so quickly that Richard couldn't be certain who it was, but it wasn't Frankie. This figure was taller, thicker.

"What the fuck?" John Henry saw it, too. "It ain't no bear, but it's covered in fur!"

"Hey!" Richard raised his voice. "Hey, you! Help us!"

"Stop it!" John Henry hissed in his ear. "Let's just keep going. Don't bring it over here."

Richard shook him off. "Help!" He hollered again.

The creature stopped, more phantom than real in the dimness of the woods. A chill passed down Richard's spine, but he brushed it away. Nothing could be scarier than Frankie Jackson.

"Whoever you are, we need help!" Richard felt giddy. There was a chance, a slim chance that he might make it. He could get back to town, check on Justine, make sure she was going to be okay. He stumbled toward the dim figure. "Help us! Please!"

John Henry tugged the back of his shirt. "Let's go." There was fear in his voice. "I don't know what that is, but I don't like the looks of it."

"You can't see anything," Richard said. "Whoever it is, he may have a four-wheeler."

"I don't think so." John Henry backed up. "That don't look like nobody with a four-wheeler. That don't look like no body at all. Look, I been livin' out here for months now, and I've seen some things. Scary things. In the woods at night. Folks think that Skin Dancer is a legend, but maybe it ain't."

Richard could smell the fear on John Henry. The man was terrified. "What have you seen?"

"I've heard children cryin' and the sound of buffalo stampedin'." He held up a hand. "I know there are buffalo, but the closest herd is down on Pine Ridge Reservation. That's a'ways. I heard 'em, though, runnin' like the devil was on their tail. And I heard an Indian cryin' out like a huntin' call, but when I looked out, there was nothin' there. Not even a tree branch swayin' in the breeze."

"You've spooked yourself. That person may be our ticket back to civilization."

John Henry clutched Richard's arm. "These hills are a special place. If you forget that, you'll pay a price. This is sacred land for the Sioux. It has powers that you don't know about or can't begin to understand. I'm tellin' you, man, you need to respect this. Don't be messin' with something you don't understand. Now let's start walkin'."

Richard saw it again. The creature moved through the trees too fast. It seemed to glide, more shadow than substance. "Who is that?"

"More like 'what is that?'" John Henry said. "Let's go!"

Richard let John pull him back to the path. He tried to keep his gaze on the distant figure, but it was hard to do while he hobbled. The pain seemed to blind him at times. When he chanced a look, the shape seemed to stay parallel with them, using the thick wilderness as a screen.

"We need—"

"We need to keep movin'." John Henry put Richard's arm around his shoulders, supporting him.

"Frankie killed those men. There's no such thing as the Skin Dancer." Richard said it aloud, but his voice lacked conviction, even to himself.

John Henry kept walking, forcing Richard to go along. "You think what you want, but I know what I know."

In the silence, Richard heard a sound that pierced him to his soul. The whisper of a bone rattle carried on the breeze. "Is that—"

"I been hearin' that, and the other things I mentioned. I know what it is. And I know who uses such things. Not any of the flesh and blood Sioux. That's somethin' from way in the past. Somethin' that don't bode good for any of us. Now keep walkin'."

Richard focused on the path, trying to block out the sound of the rattle that seemed to come from all directions. He'd heard that noise just before he and Justine were attacked. Though it was a Sioux ritual tool, anyone could get his hands on one. It wasn't supernatural. It was all too real, and he had to keep moving.

0Each step was a victory. If he had to walk all the way to Bisonville, he would do it. He wasn't going to quit.

The noise stopped. He and John Henry both paused, looking through the trees where they'd last seen the phantom. There was nothing, only the call of a songbird hidden somewhere in the woods.

RACHEL FLIPPED through the magazines in the airport concession stand for the eighth time, aware that the clerk now viewed her with disapproval. She was killing time, but she had only ten minutes before her flight boarded. The terminal was almost empty. With any luck, she'd be home by dark. She'd pulled out her cell phone a dozen times to call Gordon or even Harvey Dilson, but she'd always put it back. Frankie had Jake. Jake was innocent. Dilson was a murderer.

She pulled the phone from her pocket again, hesitating. There was someone she might call. Someone who would never endanger Jake. Someone who would begin the search for him with the utmost discretion and love.

The bustle of an incoming flight distracted her. A half dozen children ran by, screaming and bumping into passengers headed in the opposite direction. When the in-bound passengers were gone, the terminal was empty once again. Rachel stepped into the ladies room, praying for a moment of serenity.

She dialed Mel Ortiz's number. It rang three times before he answered.

"Mel, it's Rachel. Listen, I don't have much time and this is going to be hard to process. Jake's been taken hostage—"

The restroom door slammed into the wall. Frankie came through in one stride, raising her right foot for a kick that caught Rachel in the jaw. Her head snapped back and the cell phone flew from her hand, shattering on the floor.

Frankie lodged another kick at her head, but Rachel managed to duck and roll. She came up fast, grabbing for Frankie's ankle while it was still in the air. She almost got it, but Frankie twisted. She was fast, fluid, and deadly accurate with her kicks.

The two women circled each other in the small space of the bathroom. The door started to open and Frankie slammed it hard with a kick. She pushed her baton through the handles, effectively locking the door.

Rachel rushed her, hoping for that split second of inattention that would give her the advantage. Frankie countered with an elbow in the back of her neck.

Rachel hit the ground hard. She felt the shock in her jaw and the cracking of a tooth. Before she could get up, Frankie was on her, kneeling on her back, pressing her into the cold, gritty tile.

"I don't want to kill you here, but I will."

"You have to stop." Rachel puffed the words, unable to get enough air to talk properly.

"I don't have to do anything. But you do. You're going to clean yourself up and walk out of here with me. We're going to get on Harvey's jet. Then we're going to fly to South Dakota, and then I'm going to kill Harvey."

Rachel's lungs were on fire. She felt as if her head might explode from the pressure.

"Once Harvey is dead, I'll decide about Richard and Jake."

Frankie eased the pressure on her back, and Rachel dragged in a lung full of oxygen. The pounding in her head lessened, then stopped.

"If you do a single thing to call attention to us, I'll kill whoever sees." Frankie pulled her to her feet. She lifted her shirt to show the gun. "I'll use it. You know I will."

Rachel didn't say anything. She found the piece of her tooth with her tongue and spit it into the trash can.

"You did me a service, Rachel. You got my mother to say where my father is buried. Now I know. Now I can prove he didn't leave us."

Rachel watched her in the mirror. She was beautiful, a woman graced with physical perfection. Except for her blue eyes. They were clear and the color of an October sky, but there was a glassiness that reminded Rachel of a porcelain doll. How was it possible that she hadn't seen the vacantness before now?

"You have what you need, Frankie. You don't have to kill anyone else."

Frankie's smile was angelic. "Oh, I don't kill because I have to. I kill because I like it." She dug her fingers into Rachel's arm. "Now walk out with me and don't do anything stupid. We'll be home before you know it."

THE GRIT from a passing truck stung Derek's face as he raced the four-wheeler along the roadway. He was headed for Dixon Point. He'd found nothing in Richard Jones's house. Nothing. And no matter how much he'd talked to Justine, she hadn't acknowledged him. The doctor said she was resting comfortably and that it was up to her. If she wanted to wake up, she would. It was more than Derek could bear. He'd already contacted the other members of WAR. Most had dispersed, abandoning of the South Dakota area, in search of new causes.

But he wasn't giving up.

He opened the throttle on the ATV and roared along the road until he found the path that led up to Dixon's Point. He turned off onto it. There had to be something he could do other than sit around and wait.

As he took a sharp curve, he saw the figure of a man moving swiftly through the trees. Derek braked and turned, sending the machine into a dangerous slide. He recovered and went back. Disappearing deeper into the woods was the Indian.

Derek remembered the day he'd pursued Adam and had been set up to play the fool who found the mannequin.

"Hey!" He throttled up and gave chase. The Indian was fast, but he was no match for the ATV. Derek caught up with him. "Hey, you!"

Adam Standing Bear faced Derek. "What do you want?"

"I'm looking for Richard Jones. Have you seen him?"

Adam appeared to consider the question. "Why do you ask?"

"My girlfriend was attacked last night. She was with Richard. Seems like someone kidnapped him."

"As you can see, I don't have him." Adam started to turn away.

"Did you set up that mannequin?" Derek swallowed, his throat dry. His question halted Adam. The Indian studied him, reading whatever he could from Derek's expression before he answered.

Adam nodded. "I did."

"Why did you do that?"

"To frighten you."

Derek wanted to smack him. He stood and swung his leg over the ATV. "You're a bastard."

"This land belongs to the Sioux." Adam held his ground. "The only weapon we have left is our superstitions. I used you."

"Why couldn't you ask me to help? I tried to talk to you."

Adam stepped forward. "You never asked to help, Derek Baxter. You had your plan, and there was no stopping you. You burned the machines. It was highly probable that my people would be blamed for that. I had to stop you the only way I knew how."

"Which was to discredit me?"

"That or frighten you away. It didn't matter how you left, as long as you left. The Lakota people hope to stop the four-lane, but not by destroying property or lives. We have cases in the court system, and with time, we'll have the legal standing to protect the land we love. Until then, superstition is the tool I use. Fear of the Skin Dancer will slow the destruction."

Derek felt the loss of his anger like the bleeding of a wound. "Do you know where Richard Jones might be?"

Adam nodded slowly. "I do. He's headed toward Dixon Point. I think he'd greatly appreciate a ride. But don't tell him you saw me in the woods. If you want to save the wilderness, let that be our secret."

The hint of a smile hovered at the corner of Adam's mouth. Derek felt his own lips twist up. Adam intended to stop the four-lane. Derek didn't know what the man had done to move toward that goal, but it was something that required his collaboration.

"You got it." He climbed back on the ATV and gunned it up the steep trail toward Dixon Point.

THE FOUR-SEATER JET zeroed in on Bisonville. Rachel sat back, her body as relaxed as she could make it. Beside her,

Frankie kept the gun alternately pointed at her ribs and the back of the pilot's head. One of the great things about flying in a private plane was the lack of security check. It did make things easier when a gun was involved.

"Are you wondering if I lied about being able to fly this plane?" Frankie asked.

"No." Rachel believed Frankie. The woman had spent her life building this plan, creating this moment, acquiring the skills necessary to make it happen. If she said she could fly a plane, she could. It was likely part of her escape scenario.

"I've got it almost straight," Rachel said, "but there's one thing. How did you know you'd be hired to work on the four-lane this year?"

Frankie arched an eyebrow. "The plans for Paradise were in the works when my father was alive. Richard was much younger, but he had the dream. He'd spent the summer interning with Bill Gates. He idolized Gates and what he'd created. Then he had the idea for using technology in DNA studies, and he made his fortune. Paradise was just an extension of his success. And Richard, for all of his narrowness, loves South Dakota. I knew he'd build Paradise in Criss County because he honestly wants to help the economy."

"You got a college degree in engineering on the slim chance you'd be offered this particular job?"

"Not slim. I'm not that much of a gambler. I kept up my contacts with the Lakota people. I did my civic duties by guiding Harvey's re-election campaigns and helping him side-step tough voter issues. Want to hear something funny? Richard doesn't want or need the four-lane to Paradise. This is all for Harvey. He stands to make millions on land right-of-ways in the northern part of the county. I told Harvey I'd make sure the road happened if he'd guarantee to hire me to act as liaison with the Sioux and project manager."

"You've been so helpful to him. Without you, he might have been defeated in an election."

Frankie laughed softly. "You are naïve, Rachel. Harvey is a hometown hero. He presents himself as a concerned rancher, a resident of South Dakota, a man who loves the wilderness, which, by the way, he's sold out in every vote in Congress over the past twelve years. Logging, mining, slapping back alternative energy research. Harvey couldn't be deeper in big oil and big corporation pockets."

Rachel said nothing. She was naïve. Her focus on politics had been local. She never saw the bigger picture.

"How did you put it all together? These men covered their tracks."

"Those damn boot clips led me to Hank. After I was shot, he stood beside me. I couldn't lift my head, but I could hear them talking. I knew there were several of them. I opened my eyes and that boot clip was right in my face and I memorized it, every whorl and curve. It was branded in my mind.

"When I couldn't talk, I'd lay in bed, remembering it and trying to figure out if it meant anything. Once I could get around, I started searching. I'll admit, it took a while. I checked boot companies, silversmiths, western organizations, everywhere I could think. Then one day in the Bisonville paper, which I subscribed to, there's Hank, standing beside a dead elk, grinning like a possum. To get the big elk in the photo, it was a full body shot of Hank. He was wearing fancy cowboy boots with silver ornamentation on the toes. The design wasn't distinct, but it was worth some effort to find out for sure, so I got a copy of the photo from the newspaper and did some digital enlarging. I had the first of the men who'd killed my father and left me to die. Once I had Hank, he gave me the others."

"Dilson will be impossible to get to. Why don't you tell the pilot to turn around? You could fly to Mexico or South America. Refuel. Move on. Change your name and get a new identity. You don't have to kill Jake or Richard Jones."

"No, I don't have to. But I want to." Her smile revealed perfect teeth. "I like killing them. I like cutting the skin then pulling it free of the fat and fascia. Most of all, I like hearing them scream."

Rachel looked out the window. She'd lost her sense of time and place. She was caught in a nightmare. "I'm sorry about your father, Frankie. The betrayal must be difficult."

"Yes, it is. I suspected there was something between Harvey and my mother, but I couldn't be certain." She patted Rachel's leg. "You got it out of her, didn't you? She would never have told me. She would have died screaming rather than tell me."

"She's suffered enough."

"Oh, I disagree." She stood up. "That kind of betrayal is the worst. But you're going to find that out for yourself. When you do, you can tell me if physical suffering is enough. I'm getting a soda, would you care for one?"

"No—Yes, I would." Rachel wasn't thirsty, but she had no weapon at all. Perhaps, if the moment presented itself, she could use the soda to momentarily blind Frankie.

Frankie poured the drinks in plastic cups and handed one to Rachel. "If I decide to let both you and Jake live, you should rethink your feelings for him."

"Thanks for the recommendation." Rachel sipped her cola, looking for her moment. "It's interesting to me how you manipulate people with guilt and shame, yet you never feel it yourself."

Frankie crunched a piece of ice. "That's the one advantage of my condition. I'm not limited by certain feelings." She leaned closer. "We're headed to the landing strip in Bisonville now. Be good another ten minutes, and our pilot lives to fly another day. Be naughty and I'll shoot him in the head."

If she was exaggerating, Rachel didn't want to test it. Yuma Pete was hurt. Frankie could have spared him, but she didn't. She had no remorse about harming innocent people, and at this stage in her madness, she viewed any excuse as good enough.

Rachel forced herself to relax back in her seat. Once they were out of the plane, on the ground, she'd find the opportunity to take Frankie down.

CHAPTER THIRTY-THREE

Harvey hefted the hunting rifle, feeling the weight, the balance. He sighted through the scope, a powerful one that brought images a quarter mile away up close and personal. It was perfect. Almost as good as his own weapons, which he'd left with Bettina and Jeremy in case Frankie returned. He'd untied them and ordered them to remain at the ranch and not to call the law.

"I'll take it. And the pistol with the ankle holster, too."

"Sir, there're laws—"

"I'm a U.S. Senator." He brought out his wallet with his congressional identification. "This is an emergency."

The clerk looked confused. "Maybe I should call—"

"Don't call anyone. This is top secret."

The clerk, who was tall and thin, looked alarmed. "Terrorists?"

"Exactly," Harvey said softly. "Law enforcement officers have been informed, but we can't start a panic. Now work with me, and I'll see that you're mentioned in the media as a special volunteer."

"You betcha," the clerk answered. He brought a box of shells out from under the counter. "You'll need these."

"Thanks." Harvey whipped out a roll of cash.

While the clerk rang up the transaction, Harvey thought of his next move. So much depended on what Frankie had learned. Dub's death was such a long time ago, he'd forgotten the details. Polly had been a pliant bed partner, a woman who bloomed with the slightest attention.

Unlike most of the women he slept with—the prostitutes and women on the climb for personal favors—Polly had been eager to please him, not for personal gain, but merely for an evening of his time. At first, he'd been completely deluded by the fantasy of her.

Had he hinted that he wanted to marry her? He didn't think so. Somewhere, though, she'd gotten the idea that she was going to tell Dub about them, confess, make a clean break, divorce. That had been impossible.

After he'd killed Dub, he accepted that he'd wanted him dead, wanted him out of the way. Dub was the kind of man who'd make it a point to ruin Harvey's future. The kid. Shit, he'd acted in desperation. He'd shot her without even meaning to. He saw her, the rifle went up, bam! She was hit in the head. And she should have died.

A second gunshot would have looked deliberate. As would bashing in her head with a rock or smothering her. Forensics were too good. So he'd opted to let her die on her own, just another terrible shooting accident in the wilderness. Some fool out with his .22 target shooting.

It should have worked, too. Frankie wasn't capable of getting up on her horse. So how had she done it? He must have asked himself that question a million times. He thought he had the answer, and if he could kill Richard Jones personally, he would. The bastard must have gone back and lifted Frankie onto her horse. That was the only explanation.

Now Harvey had some serious questions for the doctors

who'd explained to him that Frankie would be a vegetable, and then the doctors who'd told him she'd never remember a thing, and then the doctors who'd assured him that the past was a complete blank for her.

Wrong! Wrong! Wrong! They'd been wrong on all counts. Not only could Frankie remember, she was mad as hell, and she meant to kill him. If she hadn't remembered every detail, she'd tortured it out of Hank and Mullet. She knew. And she was out for vengeance.

So he'd have to take care of it himself.

"Senator Dilson. Senator Dilson!"

The clerk was waving the receipt in his face. He took it and picked up his weapons. He had to kill her and get it over with.

FRANKIE WALKED behind Rachel to her truck. The deputy was being careful not to do anything to draw attention to herself, which was good, because Frankie would shoot her in the back. Not that she wanted to. She respected Rachel, who'd risked so much and figured out so many things. Rachel had ferreted out the place Dub's body was buried. They were, indeed, like sisters. "You drive," she told her.

"Where are we going?" Rachel asked.

"To the place where everything is going to end."

"Will Dilson be there?"

Frankie was amused at Rachel's question. The deputy hadn't given up. She still thought she could affect the outcome. "Yes. I'll make sure of it."

She pulled her cell phone out and dialed. When Harvey answered, his voice was terse as he said her name.

"You've been expecting me, haven't you?" she asked.

"We can strike a bargain, Frankie. I can make you a rich woman."

"My mother gave up her child and her husband for you, Harvey. How many times did you visit her in Alabama? Once, I think, but that wasn't about her, was it? That was to make sure I didn't react when I saw you."

"What do you want?"

"You remember the old hunting cabin? I fixed it up. Meet me there," she said. "Richard is waiting for us. I want to finish this."

"You think I'm stupid enough to go to a hunting cabin with you?" Harvey asked.

"If you don't, I have the evidence I need to prove you're a murderer and a thief. Your career will be over, and you'll spend your last days in jail."

"And that's worth my life?" Harvey asked.

"Of course it is. We both know that. Besides, I have Richard. Without him, you have no future. He is Paradise." She hung up. Rachel was watching her, trying to read the outcome of the conversation in her face. "Harvey won't be at the cabin, but I know where he'll be," she told Rachel. "Harvey has the heart of a hunter, and he views me as the prey. He thinks I'll go to ground."

The sun had begun to set. She got in the passenger seat with Rachel behind the wheel. "Mother told you about the hunting cabin. You enter through a mine shaft. Imagine, I've been there dozens of times in the past week, but I never thought my father was so close. They put him in a mine shaft. He would hate that. I'll bury him on the range, a place he loves."

"Are we going to the mountains?" Rachel asked.

"No." Frankie checked her gun. "We're going to my place. Drive."

Rachel put the truck in gear and took off. "Is Jake at your place?"

"Maybe." Frankie checked the clip in her gun. It was fully loaded.

"Frankie, is Jake still alive?"

She was surprised by the question. "Of course."

"Is there anyone else involved in this? Hank and Mullet are dead. Richard is your captive. Dilson knows he's a target. Is that the end of it?"

"Oh, I think there's one more twist you're really going to appreciate."

"Not Jake."

Frankie smiled. "Jake's life is in your hands. I have nothing against Jake."

Rachel inhaled long and slow.

"One thing you have to remember, Rachel. These men have earned their fates. All you have to do is let this play out. I don't want to kill you. I don't want to kill Jake. I don't even want to kill Richard. He's a coward, but he tried to do what was right. Anyway, you do what I say and maybe the three of you will get out of this alive."

"Frankie, I can put Dilson behind bars for the rest of his life. I can recover your father's body and clear his name of all the taint that Dilson stained it with. I can—"

"Not good enough." She put the gun in the holster under her arm. The knife was sheathed between her shoulder blades. She reached behind her back and brought it out, the wicked blade glinting in the slant of the late afternoon light. "I'm going to hurt him. I'm going to make him suffer in ways he never imagined."

"I understand how you must feel, Frankie. I do. Revenge is a very human emotion."

"Oh, I think you'll understand a lot better before this is over."

"Look, you can tie me up and leave now. Dilson won't call

the law. He's going to try to get out of this and keep everything hush-hush. He still thinks he can rise above all this."

"I know." Frankie stroked the blade. "That's exactly what I'm counting on." She replaced the knife and pulled her keys from her pocket. "My plan was to take Harvey at his press conference in the morning. To publicly take him and make him beg, make him confess in front of the media. I wanted to humiliate him and for him to know his career is over. This is going to be better. Something private, where I can take my time."

They arrived at the gate to Frankie's house. "Drive to the back. If we make it too easy, he'll smell a trap."

HARVEY PERCHED in the large elm three hundred yards from the back of Frankie's property. He held the rifle across his lap as he looked through his field glasses. She was pulling into the drive. Another woman drove. It took him a moment to recognize the deputy, Rachel Redmond, behind the wheel. Wrong place, wrong time.

The women got out of the truck. Frankie held a handgun. So the deputy was a hostage. Good. More fodder for the PR machine once he got it cranked up.

He lifted the rifle and sighted. Rachel's head came into his crosshairs. His finger teased the trigger as he followed them up to the steps. At the door, when Frankie paused to open it, he'd take the shot and eliminate Rachel. Too bad, she was a pretty girl. Like her mother. But he couldn't risk what she'd learned. She would die, then it would be between him and Frankie.

His finger registered the tension on the trigger. One more iota of pressure, and the bullet would go singing into Rachel's head. This was no .22. He'd bought a rifle that could bring down a moose.

The women climbed the back steps. Frankie fumbled with the keys to the back door.

He pulled the trigger.

CHIPS OF BRICK and mortar stung her face, and Rachel felt herself flying through the air. First her shoulder struck the tile near the steps, then her head. Consciousness started to slip from her, but she fought against the darkness.

Beside her, Frankie was laughing. "I'm impressed with Harvey. He's thinking ahead. He meant to take you out, Rachel, because he figures you know too much. Then it would be just me and him, mano-a-mano, so to speak. Killing all of those drugged and injured animals has given him delusions of grandeur. He thinks he's a crack shot."

The truck blocked them from further fire, and Rachel eased herself into a sitting position beside Frankie. "You saved my life."

"I'll kill you if I have to, but I don't necessarily want to do that."

"You knew Harvey would take a shot here."

She nodded. "It was a safe assumption. It's what I would do. He could hit you, claiming a mistake, then take me out. He doesn't know if Richard is alive or dead, so he's assuming that all of the witnesses to his past will be gone."

Rachel digested the events. Dilson was a righteous bastard. If she had a gun and a clean shot, she'd be tempted to take him out herself.

"You want to kill him yourself." Frankie nudged her shoulder. "I see it in your face. See how easy it is to step across that line. Imagine me, a prisoner in a wheelchair, unable to walk or talk for several years. All I had was the fantasy of my revenge."

"Is Jake here?" Rachel didn't want to encourage Frankie by talking about killing Dilson.

"Let's go inside and see."

"Dilson will kill us if we move."

"No, he won't. He's gone."

Frankie spoke with such assurance. "How can you be sure?" Rachel asked.

"He's moved to a new location. He's afraid I'll target him because I can figure out the angle of the shot. I'm an engineer, and he won't forget that." She handed Rachel the keys to the door. "Open it and go inside."

Rachel held the keys. "What if you're wrong? What if he's still there, waiting for us to show ourselves."

"One of us has to open the door. In my opinion, you're more expendable than I am."

Rachel's fingers clutched the keys. She rose slowly. If she made it, she could bolt the door, maybe find a weapon, search for Jake. It was a chance.

She dashed up the steps and thrust the key home. The door opened but the key refused to come out of the lock. She left it. She was inside. Frankie was two seconds behind her, but it was two seconds too late. She slammed the door hard, driving the deadbolt home, leaving Frankie standing on the steps.

"Rachel! Open the door!" Frankie yelled.

Rachel found herself in a mud room. Coats and boots neatly lined one wall. Gardening tools hung next to the coats. She grasped a hand rake with tines as sharp as stilettos.

Frankie's body slammed into the door. Then silence.

Rachel moved swiftly, going to the east side to check the French doors. She could only pray that with Frankie's exquisite taste, the glass was shatter proof and the door strong enough to withstand an assault. She moved on to the front door. It was locked tight. She made her way to the west side of the house, checking doors and windows, her breath coming short and shallow in her fear.

When she'd made a circuit of the main floor, she stopped and listened.

Silence.

Frankie was out there, somewhere. And so was Harvey Dilson. Either one of them would kill her.

Frankie would have an arsenal in the house, but Rachel didn't know where. She clung to the rake, listening. Which direction would the assault come from? She had to second guess Frankie. It was her only chance to stay alive.

A cordless telephone was on a table in the hallway, and she picked it up. She wasn't surprised to discover the line was dead. Frankie had beaten her to it, cutting the line at the box on the side of the house.

All the downstairs rooms were empty, and Rachel moved upstairs. That would be the best defense point. She could set some booby traps, hold her position at the top. First she had to find Jake.

She moved along the spacious hallway, her footsteps falling softly into the thick, beige carpet. The bedrooms circled an atrium. All of the doors were closed, and if Jake was a prisoner, he could be anywhere. Rachel felt time ticking away. Frankie would come, and soon.

She opened the first door. The empty bedroom looked as if it had been designed for a fashion shoot.

The same with the second, third, and fourth. When she got to the master suite, Frankie's room, Rachel stopped. As soon as the door opened, the whiff of blood seeped out to her.

"Jake?"

She crept into the room. It was almost too late when she heard the growl of the dog. The huge Rottweiler charged at her, jaws open and saliva dripping. Armed only with the rake,

Rachel stumbled backwards out of the room. She hit the railing and flipped.

At the last moment, one hand caught a banister. She gripped it for her life, her body swinging over the open void of the atrium.

She had to drop the rake to hold on. It clattered to the tile floor below. As she found a purchase with her second hand and began to pull herself up, she came face to face with the jaws of the dog.

He lunged at her, going for her fingers that gripped the banister spindles. With one powerful arc of her body, she swung her leg over the railing.

The dog was on her in a flash. He sank his canines into her calf. The pain was electric, and she had no weapon to beat him off. She could feel his teeth sinking deeper into her muscle, chewing and tearing.

Focus. She mentally grasped the training she'd struggled so hard to attain. Focus. She brought her free leg over the railing and planted the kick at the dog's nose.

Blinded by pain, the dog let loose. Rachel ran. Her leg gave with each step, but she didn't stop. She hurled herself into the master bedroom, slammed the door, and turned the lock.

She looked at her leg and felt nausea rise in her throat. No time now. No time. She had to find a weapon and she had to find Jake. Frankie was out there. She wouldn't wait forever to attack.

Blood trailing behind her, she hobbled into the bedroom. She saw Jake instantly, tied to the bed.

Her breath caught in her throat. It looked as if the dog had bitten his hands and feet.

"Jake!" She didn't care that her voice broke and the sob she'd tried to hold back finally escaped. "Jake!"

His head turned slowly. "Get out of here, Rachel," he managed. "Every time I move, the dog is on me."

She went to the bed. He'd been bitten, but she didn't see any abdominal wounds. Jake's hands were tied with scarves, and she worked to unknot his right one.

"Get out." His voice was weak. "There's a dog."

"I know about him. It's okay."

"Where's Frankie?"

"Outside the house. She'll be here any minute."

"She's the killer. She's got Richard Jones."

"I know." His right hand was free. She set to work on his leg. "She's outside and so is Dilson."

"The senator?" Jake sounded groggy.

"Yeah. Dilson murdered her father. He hid the body in a mine shaft. He was screwing her mother. Look, I'll explain it all later, but we have to get out of here. Dilson tried to kill me, and he'll kill us both if Frankie doesn't."

"Rachel, leave me. I—"

She put a hand on his lips. "Stop it. I'm going to get you some water. Untie your left arm and leg. If she gets in here, you're going to have to move and fast."

"The dog?"

"Outside." She hurried into the master bath and brought a cup of water which Jake drank greedily. He gingerly moved his arms and legs.

"Can you walk?" she asked. Her gaze went to the window. From this angle she had a clear view of the backyard, her truck, the tree at the far back edge of the estate where Dilson had obviously hidden in his ambush.

"I'm not sure. She gave me something."

"Are there any guns up here?"

He shook his head. "I don't know."

She went to the dresser, pulling out drawers and dumping

the contents. Silky underpants frothed to the floor. Hose, nighties, bras followed. She moved to the closet, dumping boxes of shoes from the shelves and tossing them into the center of the room.

"Try to stand," she ordered as she worked. As soon as Jake was off the bed and standing, she flipped the mattress. Her calf burned, and she could only imagine what Jake felt like, but he was walking, searching for a weapon.

"Is your cell phone here?" Rachel asked.

"She took it."

"Radio?"

He shook his head. "She took everything."

"There have to be guns in this house."

"If there are, you're going to have to go through Brutus to get them."

At the sound of a low whistle that came from somewhere in the house, Rachel turned to Jake. "Maybe not," she said. "Frankie's home."

CHAPTER THIRTY-FOUR

Harvey left the tree as soon as he fired. It was impossible that he'd missed Rachel. Frankie had pushed the deputy out of the way as if some sixth sense had warned her. Damn it. Now they were in the house. It was going to be a lot harder to kill them.

Circling the property, he stopped to scan each window on the west side of the house, hoping for telltale movement that would indicate where they were located.

The house was still. It looked empty, but he knew better.

He went to the front and maneuvered down the driveway. Frankie didn't have gates and alarms. She probably thought she didn't need such things.

As he got closer, he saw that the front door was open. An invitation to a trap? Moving from bush to shrub, he drew closer. This was the hunt, the real thing. As annoyed as he was at the disruption of his carefully laid plans, he couldn't help but feel the rush of blood. He'd hunted many things, but never anything that could hunt him back.

As he slipped to the front door, he hesitated. Frankie was likely waiting on the other side, but he had to go inside if he was going to kill her.

Careful not to make noise, he stepped onto the marble of the foyer. It was as if the house held its breath. Not a single sound came to him.

He moved forward, the rifle pointed down but his finger on the trigger. Edging into the parlor, he was startled by the dark shape of the sofa. For a moment it had looked like a rhino he'd killed when he was entertaining a group of Russian businessmen. They'd never known the old beast was bought from a zoo and drugged. Turning back to the hallway, he felt the cold barrel of the gun right behind his ear.

"Hello, Harvey," Frankie drawled. "So nice of you to stop by for a visit."

"Frances." He used her formal name, the name Dub had always called her. "You had us all fooled, didn't you?"

She never answered. She drew back the gun and whacked him with the butt. He sank to his knees and fell face-forward into the carpet.

"Now," Rachel ordered.

Jake opened the door. When the dog burst into the room, Rachel jammed the chair from Frankie's vanity at him. As Brutus hit the chair legs, Rachel rolled backwards, using the momentum of the dog to push it over her head on the chair. Brutus landed across the room with a thud.

"Run!" she ordered Jake. As he hobbled from the bedroom, she was right on his heels. She managed to slam the bedroom door before Brutus could reorganize and charge them.

The wham of the dog's body on the wooden door made the frame shake.

"Come on," she whispered to Jake as she put his arm around her shoulders. "We have to try to get out."

They were halfway down the stairs when Rachel heard footsteps in the foyer. She pressed Jake against the wall. "Stay here."

"No." He tried to hold her.

"Stay here!" She eased away from him. She'd tied her dog bite with strips of Frankie's clothes. The pressure helped, but each step was painful. When she got to the bottom of the stairs, she looked for the hand rake, but it was gone.

She slipped past the dining room and the kitchen. At the foyer, where she had a clear view of the parlor, she stopped. Dilson was tied in a straight-backed chair. Frankie sat on the edge of the sofa, watching him. She held a tape recorder and the rake.

"Tell the truth, Harvey. I want to record it in your own words."

"Fuck you."

"That's not a nice way to speak to me." She swung the rake and dug it into his knee.

Harvey's scream echoed in the house. Rachel pressed herself against the wall. She had to find a weapon. She couldn't take Frankie alone. Jake was in no position to help her. She had to have something.

She moved silently past the parlor and into the kitchen. From a rack she took a meat cleaver, and from a butcher's block she picked up a carving knife. A gun would have been much better, but she didn't have time to look for one.

Dilson's scream echoed through the house. "Okay, okay. I killed your father and hid his body in the old Minola mine shaft." Dilson was gasping as he talked. Rachel didn't want to imagine what Frankie was doing to him.

She went back toward the parlor. Dilson's voice continued the litany of his sins. Whatever Frankie had done, she'd loosened his tongue. Once he'd confessed, Frankie would kill him.

At the doorway of the parlor, Rachel stopped. Frankie was speaking soft and low, and Dilson's voice was filled with pain and fear. He spoke with urgency.

Rachel sank to the floor. Frankie and the senator sat knee to knee. She held a pistol pointed at Dilson's crotch and the tape recorded spinning in her lap.

"Is that everything?" Frankie asked.

"It was an accident. Once it was done, I had to hide it. My career would have been ruined."

"Yes, an accident." Frankie stood up. "I understand." She turned and pointed the gun at Dilson's forehead. "I understand so well, Harvey. And I'm sure you understand why I'm going to kill you. I'd hoped to make it last a long, long time, but my agenda has changed."

Rachel had to act. She launched herself from a crouched position, hitting Frankie hard at the hips. They tumbled to the floor, the gun skidding away on the hardwood.

Rachel rolled, and just in time. The tines of the hand rake dug into the floor only inches from her face. Frankie knocked the knife and cleaver from her hand, sending them sliding across the room.

Rachel looked up into Frankie's cold blue eyes. "I told you not to interfere," Frankie said. "You should have stayed upstairs with Jake."

"I can't let you kill him." Rachel chanced a look at Dilson. He was working frantically at his bonds, leaning forward, reaching toward his ankles with his hands.

"He's a dead man, Rachel. Let him die. It'll be a kindness."

"I can't!" Rachel rolled to her stomach and sprang up, her leg on fire with pain. She balanced and swung a kick that caught Frankie in the shoulder.

Instead of falling, Frankie spun. "Good move," she said. "Now get out of my way and let me finish Harvey."

"Stop her! Stop her!" Dilson was trying to walk the chair out of the room.

The old bastard had tried to kill her, but Rachel had taken a vow. As Frankie lunged at him again, the rake held high, Rachel stepped in her path. They struggled, hand to hand, bodies straining. They were equally matched, but Frankie wasn't injured. She jammed her leg behind Rachel's knee and brought the deputy down. Rachel hit hard, the wind knocked from her lungs.

"I think this has gone far enough." Frankie retrieved the gun from the floor. "I'm sorry, Rachel. I can't let you interfere any more. Harvey and I have to finish our conversation." She pointed it at the deputy.

Rachel caught her breath and eased into a sitting position. Now that the moment of death was upon her, she felt a strange calm. Out of the corner of her eye she saw Dilson finally reach his feet. His fingers clamped around something and he brought it up in one smooth motion. The barrel of the gun was short and black.

"Frankie!" She threw herself forward, knocking Frankie out of the way of the bullet just in time. They tumbled on the floor as the gunshot echoed in the huge house.

"You goddamn fool!" Dilson cursed. "I had her."

Frankie vaulted to her feet. She swung the gun directly at Rachel. In a split second, she shifted it at Dilson. The shot exploded in the house. A red hole appeared at Dilson's hairline.

Rachel shifted to her feet. She started forward, but Frankie turned the gun on her. "Don't," she said. "Don't even think about it." She went to the senator.

"Harvey?"

He tried to talk but couldn't.

"Harvey, can you hear me?"

Blood seeped down Dilson's forehead, a single line moving

along the furrows in his skin.

Frankie kept the gun pointed at Rachel. "Can you see the irony of this?" She laughed. "It's too good. He's alive. Sort of."

In the distance the sound of sirens came thin and weak. "They'll kill you," Rachel said.

Frankie shrugged. "Maybe."

"Give yourself up!"

Frankie shook her head. "It's not in my nature."

They both looked up when Jake stumbled into the room. He carried a chair leg as a weapon, but he was barely able to hold it. He looked from Dilson to Rachel and then fell.

"So much for the rescue," Frankie said. She walked toward the hallway.

Rachel followed her. "I can't let you leave."

"You can't stop me, Rachel. Take care of Brutus, he's really very gentle. And when you see Mel Ortiz, tell him I'll be back."

"Mel?"

"He knew. He didn't pursue the investigation because he knew it was Dilson. Dilson who gave him his plum job here in Criss County. He also knows more about your mother's death. He took Junie to the hunting camp where she overdosed. That's why he took you in."

Rachel felt the stab of betrayal.

"Not a good feeling, eh?" Frankie asked. The sound of the sirens grew louder. "I have to go, but I'll be in touch."

"Stop!" Rachel started after her.

Frankie turned back. "Dammit, I don't want to hurt you, Rachel, but you just won't quit." She aimed the gun and fired once. Rachel felt the pain tear through her shoulder. Frankie fired a second time.

Dilson slumped in the chair.

Frankie disappeared around the corner. There was the sound of the back door slamming and a vehicle starting.

EPILOGUE

Rachel, her arm in a sling, opened her apartment door and stepped inside. Brutus met her with a big sloppy kiss.

She picked up the mail from the floor where the mailman had shoved it through the slot. She needed something to eat and a drink. It had been another long day at the office with a stolen automobile and a high school bomb threat that ended up as a practical joke.

The telephone rang, and she answered it on the way to the kitchen to rummage through the refrigerator.

"Jake," she said, glad to hear his voice. "I've missed you. How are things going in the big city?"

He'd transferred to the State Game and Fish offices in Rapid City while his injuries healed. Rachel believed he'd stay there. Though she'd never mentioned what Frankie had said about Mel, Jake had heard it. He'd severed his ties to his father, and so had she. Junie Redmond had died of her addiction, and while Mel wasn't responsible, he had been involved.

"I wanted to let you know I'm changing jobs," Jake said. "I'm consulting on a statehouse committee on environmental issues. I'll be helping to write legislation to preserve the wilderness in Criss County."

"I'm glad for you." She meant it, too. "Will you be over this way any time soon?"

"No, I don't think so, Rachel. Not yet." He inhaled. "The reason I called is to tell you that Richard Jones publicly testified today that the four-lane isn't necessary. The road has been cancelled. The Sioux sacred grounds won't be disturbed. Adam was here, and he's very pleased."

"That's wonderful news. I'm sure you'll be celebrating this evening. I wish I could be there." She was reaching out to Jake as he'd held out a hand to her for so many years.

"I wish that, too. Maybe soon." He cleared his throat. "Derek was here. He's on Richard's payroll, and Richard has offered to pay for the heavy equipment Derek and WAR destroyed. Richard's intervention will go a long way when Derek is sentenced."

"And Justine?"

"I think she and Richard will be announcing an engagement soon. They show all the symptoms of being in love."

"Poor Derek, I think he truly loved Justine. I guess not everybody gets a happy ending." Rachel hadn't meant to sound so bleak but the words had slipped out before she could stop them. "Hey, I sound like a sad sack." She rifled through her mail. It was hard to make small talk with Jake, but now wasn't the time to talk about the issue that stood between them. That could wait until they'd both healed a bit more. "When you're back in Criss County, let's grab a burger at Lulu's. I'd like to see you."

"Maybe when you get back from your training tour at the FBI academy. Congratulations, Rachel. You're one hell of a detective."

"You've got a date," she said.

She replaced the phone and turned the coffeepot on as she continued through the mail. She stopped at the envelope that bore a Buenos Aires postmark. She didn't know anyone in Argentina.

She tore open the envelope and a picture fell on the table. Picking it up, her heart started to beat faster.

Frankie sat on a beautiful black stallion, a Paso Fino. The horse's long, flowing mane matched Frankie's hair. She waved, and in the background cattle grazed peacefully on hills that sloped in sunshine. The landscape looked a lot like South Dakota, but Rachel knew better.

She flipped the picture over and read the back. "There are many local legends here. And much injustice. I'll be busy for a while, but then I'll be home for a visit. Love, Frankie."

ACKNOWLEDGMENTS

With each book, I meet the most incredibly generous people who willingly give their time, talents and resources to help me tell my stories. This book is no exception.

First I want to thank Patsy Kringel, research associate, and Colleen Kirby, assistant state librarian, at the South Dakota State Library in Pierre. These two professionals helped me with details of a region I've always loved—but never lived in. They went way above the call of duty with insight and suggestions. Any mistakes are mine alone.

Thanks to Ron O'Gorman for his fine editing eye and surgical skill at cutting out dead wood.

Marian Young, my agent, is the best. No writer could ask for better representation.

I hope all who read this will let me know your thoughts. It's hard to get a writer out of the South, but if I could spend a summer anywhere, it would be in South Dakota. The land there simply speaks to me.

ABOUT THE AUTHOR

Carolyn Haines is the *USA Today* bestselling author of over eighty novels in a number of genres, including the acclaimed Sarah Booth Delaney mystery series and the Pluto's Snitch mystery series.

She has been awarded a lifetime achievement award by the Alabama Public Library Association and the Mississippi Writer's Guild and in 2020 she was inducted into the Alabama Writers Hall of Fame.

Born and raised in Mississippi, she now lives in Alabama on a farm with more dogs, cats, and horses than she can possibly keep track of! She has been an animal advocate and activist her whole life and urges all pet owners to please spay and neuter.

www.carolynhaines.com

facebook.com/AuthorCarolynHaines
twitter.com/DeltaGalCarolyn
instagram.com/carolynhaines
goodreads.com/CarolynHaines
amazon.com/author/carolynhaines
bookbub.com/authors/carolyn-haines

KEEP IN TOUCH

Join my Mailing List!

www.carolynhaines.com/subscribe

carolyn@carolynhaines.com

facebook.com/AuthorCarolynHaines
twitter.com/DeltaGalCarolyn
instagram.com/carolynhaines
amazon.com/author/carolynhaines
goodreads.com/CarolynHaines
bookbub.com/profile/carolyn-haines

ALSO BY CAROLYN HAINES

PLUTO'S SNITCH

The Book of Beloved

The House of Memory

The Specter of Seduction

A Visitation of Angels

THE JEXVILLE CHRONICLES

Summer of the Redeemers

Touched

Judas Burning

NOVELS

The Darkling

The Seeker

Revenant

Fever Moon

Penumbra

Skin Dancer

Deception (originally published as Summer of Fear)

FEAR FAMILIAR

Familiar Tale

Bewitching Familiar

Fear Familiar

Too Familiar

Thrice Familiar

TROUBLE CAT MYSTERIES

Bone-a-fied Trouble

Familiar Trouble

The Trouble with Cupid

SARAH BOOTH DELANEY MYSTERIES

Them Bones

Buried Bones

Splintered Bones

Crossed Bones

Hallowed Bones

Bones to Pick

Ham Bones

Wishbones

Greedy Bones

Bone Appétit

Bones of a Feather

Bonefire of the Vanities

Smarty Bones

Booty Bones

Bone to be Wild

Rock-a-Bye Bones

Sticks and Bones

Charmed Bones

A Gift of Bones

Game of Bones

The Devil's Bones

A Garland of Bones

Independent Bones

Lady of Bones

Bones of Holly

Tell-Tale Bones

SARAH BOOTH DELANEY SHORT MYSTERIES

Shorty Bones

Bones on the Bayou

Guru Bones

Jingle Bones

Bones and Arrows

Clacking Bones

Enchanted Bones

www.ingramcontent.com/pod-product-compliance
Lightning Source LLC
Chambersburg PA
CBHW030604310726
48979CB00003B/561

* 9 7 8 1 7 3 3 0 1 6 9 9 5 *